THE
DEFIANT

THE
DEFIANT

A VALIANT NOVEL

LESLEY LIVINGSTON

RAZORBILL®

RAZORBILL®

An Imprint of Penguin Random House LLC
Penguin.com

RAZORBILL & colophon is a registered trademark
of Penguin Random House LLC.

First published in the United States of America by Razorbill,
an imprint of Penguin Random House LLC, 2018

Copyright © 2018 Lesley Livingston

LIBRARY OF CONGRESS CATALOGING-IN-PUBLICATION DATA IS AVAILABLE.

ISBN 9780448494722

Printed in the United States of America

1 3 5 7 9 10 8 6 4 2

Interior design: Eric Ford

For Carol Ann Gallagher

I

CLEOPATRA, QUEEN OF Aegypt, was bored.

And so I found myself hanging from the deck rail of a galley, cursing loudly in the moments before my vessel was rammed again by an enemy ship and I was thrown into the waves, sparkling with sunlight, far below. This, I thought, was *not* how the campaign was supposed to go. My shipmates and I—all students of the Ludus Achillea, foremost academy dedicated to the training of female gladiators in all of the Republic of Rome—were *supposed* to be victorious in this, our very first nautical outing.

Instead, we were getting kicked all over the waves of Lake Sabatinus by the girls of our rival academy, the Ludus Amazona.

"Fallon!"

I struggled to look up to see who was calling me.

It was Elka—usually the first to notice whenever I got myself into trouble. I would have hailed her back, but I was too busy not letting go of either the railing *or* the hand of Leander, the ludus kitchen slave, whose life I was preoccupied with trying to save.

Leander couldn't swim. He'd made that abundantly clear, even over the din of battle. So it was a bit of a mystery as to how he'd even wound up flailing around in the water in the middle of our mock sea battle, a spectacle staged at the behest of the queen of Aegypt.

The spectacle, itself, was less mysterious.

Gaius Julius Caesar, Consul of Rome, legendary general, owner of the Ludus Achillea, and Cleopatra's paramour, had been gone from Rome for the better part of a year on another military campaign. Cleopatra, ensconced in his estate on the western bank of the River Tiber—but expressly unwelcome within the walls of Rome itself—had been driven to her wits' end with restlessness.

So she'd packed up her entourage and headed north up the Via Clodia, to a private villa nestled on the banks of Lake Sabatinus, where her restlessness could, at the very least, enjoy a change of scenery. And the company of her dear friend, my sister Sorcha. Or, as she was known in Rome, the Lady Achillea, former champion gladiatrix and current *Lanista* of the Ludus Achillea.

One morning, not long after Cleopatra had arrived with a full entourage in the lake region, Sorcha dragged me along with her to an audience at the queen's behest.

"I'm positively *languishing* with tedium!" Cleopatra had exclaimed that day, over roast peacock and raw oysters, served on the deck of her pleasure barge. "I want to have a celebration. A triumph of our very own to commemorate the new ownership of your ludus . . ."

For my part, I'd turned a surreptitious glance on Sorcha to see how she was reacting to Cleopatra's suggestion, but my sister just nodded and calmly sipped at her goblet.

"*Impending* new ownership, Your Highness," she said. "Once I receive the papers from Caesar—"

"Pssh." Cleopatra silenced her with a wave. "They're on their way, I'm sure. And then you too will be the queen of your own domain, my dear." She paused to choose a honey cake from a tray. They were sprinkled with gold dust and sparkled in the sunlight. "Men shouldn't be the only ones in this wretched Republic who can stage a spectacle to flaunt their accomplishments," Cleopatra continued. "And you, my darling Sorcha, are definitely accomplished. As is your extraordinary sister."

She turned one of her beguiling smiles on me then, and waved for my wine cup to be refilled. "The Optimates fight the Populares because they are afraid," she said. "Afraid of change, of innovation. They are afraid of Caesar, and they are afraid of *me*. Caesar is a god among men, and I'm not shy about reminding him of that. They fear his power. And so they lure him into wars far away from my bed and company. It makes me waspish. Forgive me."

"Nothing to forgive, Majesty," I said.

"Of course." She chuckled, licking honey and gold dust from her fingers. "You, Fallon, understand my restlessness. It was unkind of my lord to drag your handsome young decurion with him all the way to Hispania."

I felt my cheeks reddening at the mention of Caius Antonius Varro. But, in truth, I'd been feeling a bit waspish myself about *his* protracted absence. I steadfastly ignored the eyebrow my sister raised in my direction.

"Never mind." The queen grinned her sly grin at us. "While our boys are away . . . let's throw a party."

Cleopatra's idea of a "party" had been to commission her very own scaled-down version of one of the more preposterous spectacles of Caesar's Quadruple Triumph—a celebratory extravaganza of performances and processions wherein Rome had run riot with feasting and games, beast hunts and contests, for an entire month. Caesar had masterminded a closing spectacle he'd dubbed the *naumachia*: an actual sea battle, staged in a man-made basin dug into the banks of the River Tiber, with thousands of men—captives taken in Caesar's many campaigns—sailing real warships. The fighting had been fierce. Deadly. And the river had run red for a day and a night afterward with blood.

Thankfully, Cleopatra wasn't *that* bored.

She'd settled for a nonlethal game of capture the flag, a competition staged between our ludus and the gladiatrices of our rival, the Ludus Amazona—"I'll invite that odious Tribune of the Plebs to lend us his girls for you to fight against," the queen had decided with a wicked grin— and only two boats. The large, lumbering pleasure craft had been provided by one of her wealthier neighbors who owned a villa on the opposite side of the lake from the Ludus Achillea. The queen's slaves had dressed the boats to look like miniature versions of the warships of Rome

and Carthage. And we were to perform a spirited reenact-
ment of the historic Battle of Mylea. Wherever that was.
Whatever that was.

"Fallon!" Elka hollered at me again. "Stop messing around!
We're supposed to *win* this fight—"

I opened my mouth to yell back that I wasn't exactly
taking my leisure, but Leander shrieked again and lost his
grip, tumbling back down into the sapphire water below.

I glanced skyward and sighed.

"Be right back!" I shouted to Elka.

Then I let go of the railing, plunging through the emp-
tiness into the shock of the chill waves below. The armor I
wore that day was thankfully light and flexible—leather,
not bronze and iron—but it still dragged in the water, and
for a few panicked moments I thrashed and kicked my
legs, trying not to sink too deep. When I surfaced, gasping, and shook my hair out of my eyes, I could see Leander
clutching helplessly at the air, only a few arm's lengths
away. I hadn't been swimming in a long time—not since
I'd become first a slave, then a gladiatrix—but I'd grown
up on the banks of the River Dwr back home on the Island
of the Mighty, and I had been swimming like a fish since I
was a little girl, almost before I'd learned to fight.

"Stop struggling!" I sputtered as I wrapped an arm
around Leander's torso. "Relax—I've got you!"

He went limp, more from relief, I think, than any conscious effort to follow my command, but it made things
easier. In fairly short order, I'd managed to drag him back

to shipside. I hallooed my fellow gladiatrices and, after a moment, Damya appeared at the railing, blinking down at me.

"This is no time for a swim!" she shouted.

"Tell *him* that," I said through gritted teeth as a wave washed over my head, making my eyes sting. There was a tang to the lake water, and I glanced over at the remains of the skiff Leander had been rowing. The fragile little craft had been impaled on our boat's elaborately carved prow when we'd run him over. He'd been ferrying over a fresh supply of libations from the ludus stores to Cleopatra's barge and decided to row a path straight through the middle of the battle. Shattered clay amphorae leaked wine that stained the water red—as if in merry parody of Caesar's spectacle—and a few escaped beer barrels floated serenely back toward the shore. Over on the queen's barge, cries of outrage mingled with gales of laughter at the mishap. Truthfully, I thought, it sounded as if the revelers had already imbibed quite enough that afternoon as it was.

"Throw me a rope!" I shouted.

I looped the line around Leander's torso under his arms and waited, treading water, until Damya got him up on deck. Then she tossed the rope back down and hauled me aboard, the muscles of her arms bulging beneath the bronze bands she wore. As I threw a leg over the rail and flopped onto the deck like a landed trout, a ragged cheer went up from the barge across the water for my heroic rescue. I lay there gasping, feeling rather less heroic than ridiculous.

Up in the rigging, perched high above my head, Tanis was calling out the positioning of the other ship's flag, which they kept moving around the deck to keep it safe from our attempts to board their vessel and capture it. Tanis was a promising young archer—she'd sworn her oath the same night Elka and I had—but she'd proved herself fairly useless in close combat. So we'd sent her up to the high vantage point where we could put her keen eyes to use.

Every time the ships drew abreast of each other, we exchanged fighters, with some of our girls leaping to their ship and the reverse. Even though the blades we fought with that day were wooden practice swords, accidents happened. Not just accidents. There was still a good deal of bad blood between the Achillea and Amazona ludi. During Caesar's Triumphs, our two schools of warriors had been pitted against each other in a huge pitched battle meant to commemorate Caesar's conquest of Britannia, and there had been bloodshed. Even death. We'd all made enemies that day.

The worst one I'd made had been originally from my own ludus.

A gladiatrix named Nyx.

Nyx had never been a friend. But she'd been sold to Pontius Aquila, the owner of the Ludus Amazona, after Caesar had chosen me over her to perform in the lead role of his Spirit of Victory. It wasn't something Nyx had taken lightly or well. Neither was the fact that, in the midst of the spectacle, I'd bested her—with a little help from Elka and her trusty spear—in a chariot duel.

All of that was more than enough cause for Nyx to hate me.

But I'd taken it one step further.

When Caesar had conferred the ceremonial sword of freedom on me for my performance, I'd asked instead for him to grant that freedom to *her*. In doing so, I'd effectively had Nyx barred from ever again taking up arms as a gladiatrix in the arena. It was the worst thing I could have done to her, in her mind. The fact that I'd done it for her own good was something that I'd never been able to tell her. She wouldn't have listened anyway.

I hadn't seen her since that day.

Which was probably one of the reasons I still had all my limbs in good working order. Nyx left behind a band of cronies, but, without her driving malevolence, they were about as bothersome as horseflies. In the dining hall or the bathhouse, that is. In the arena, we were all capable—if we weren't careful, and sometimes if we were—of inflicting a great deal of damage. But that, of course, was rather the point. For our spectators and patrons, at least.

I'd long since realized that Roman civilization was a thin veneer. The spectacle of our "sea battle" with the excitement of the flag-capture challenge was entertaining for Cleopatra's party guests, certainly, and we put on a good show. But it was the thrill of *real* danger that set Roman hearts racing. The idea that we were willing—and able—to maim and kill for the amusement of the mob. Even draped in silks and jewels, sipping wine and slurping oysters, that's what the men and women on that gilded barge really were. A bloodthirsty mob.

To that end, I thought, *I'd best get back in the fray and stop wasting time rescuing kitchen boys instead of satisfying that thirst.*

I pushed myself to hands and knees to find Leander still lying on the deck, propped up on one elbow and grinning at me. "Thank you, *domina,*" he said, flashing a mouthful of teeth at me. "Thank you for my life."

I rolled my eyes and hauled myself to standing. As kitchen boys went, Leander was more than just a drudge. He was a sly charmer, always chatting up one gladiatrix or another. It had gotten him in trouble—and cost him ten lashes—when Nyx had capitalized on his flirtatious ways to escape the ludus townhouse in Rome one night. All in the service of trying to end *my* gladiatrix career, and maybe even my life. But Nyx had failed, and I bore no ill will toward Leander.

Just a growing irritation in that moment that he was so very in the way.

The ship heeled over in a tight turn as he clambered to his feet, knocking him off balance and into me—almost sending me tumbling back over the railing.

"Sit!" I barked at him, taking him by the shoulders and plunking him down firmly on a coil of rope. "We're coming around for another attack . . ."

"I'm not afraid." His grin never wavered.

For an instant, I contemplated running him through.

"Stay there and stay *down*," I snapped. "Or you're going to get someone—probably *me*—killed."

"Fallon!" Ajani shouted at me from the bow. "Leave that pot-scrubber alone! We're closing on the other ship again. *Fast.*"

I turned and loped across the damp-slick deck. Ajani met me halfway and fell into step alongside me. Normally, Ajani would have been carrying her bow and have a quiver full of arrows strapped across her back. But in this case, she carried a short wooden sword—like the rest of us— in one hand, and an Aegyptian-style flail in the other. It seemed she'd gotten used to the new weapon with its knotted leather lashes nicely. I was fairly certain that more than one or two of the Amazona girls would walk away from that battle with deep red welts on arms and legs.

"We're trying to get close enough this time to attempt a proper boarding," Ajani informed me.

High above us, Tanis was calling out the other ship's every move and the placement of their fighters. In that, we had an advantage—up until the moment one of the Amazona girls decided to put a stop to it and threw a dagger at our lookout. I saw the blade spinning through the air and gasped in anger. The sun glinting off the blade meant that it was real—not wooden—and therefore expressly against the rules of engagement.

Fortunately, Tanis saw it coming.

*Un*fortunately, she ducked out of the way as if she wasn't perched almost thirty feet above the deck. I heard her scream as she pitched backward and into thin air.

"Tanis!" I shouted. She screamed again as one of the rigging ropes tangled around her leg tightened in a loop around her ankle and jerked her to an abrupt halt about ten feet above the deck. She hung there upside down like a carcass in a butcher's shop, howling in pain.

A roar of excitement went up from the queen's barge. Our ship had closed broadside with the Amazona vessel and run out the boarding planks.

"Ajani, go!" I barked. "Help Elka and the others—I'll get Tanis."

"Get her how? She's too far up!"

"I'm going to have to cut her down," I said. "Before that rope cuts off her foot. Go!"

I ran back to the ship's single mast rising up from the center of the deck. The throwing knife lay only a few feet away, and I picked it up. The blade was sharp, and I snarled at the thought of whoever had thrown it. But at least I could use it to my advantage now. The only other weapons I carried were wooden. Shoving the knife into my belt, I reached for the rope ladder that led up to the yard-arm and started to climb.

Just below the yardarm, in the lee of the billowing sail, I stopped to catch my breath and looked down to see that our boarding attempt had been successful this time. The Amazona ship deck was filled, shoulder to shoulder, with pairs of combatants. The two vessels were grappled together with hooks, and even the skeleton crew of galley slaves who sailed the boat for us had abandoned their posts, joining with the gladiatrices in gleefully bashing away at their counterparts as part of the whole ridiculous pantomime.

The deck of the Achillea ship beneath me was deserted.

Except for Leander, who had an axe and was busily hewing away at the ship mast as if it was a mighty oak tree in the forests of home that needed felling for the great fire.

"What in Hades are you doing, you lunatic?" I shouted from where I was perched on top of that very same mast.

A silly question. It was obvious what he was doing. But for a moment, I couldn't believe my eyes. Kitchen slave that he was, I'd seen Leander day after day in the little yard by the stables, chopping firewood for the cooks to feed the small army of gladiatrices that lived at the Ludus. His sun-browned arms were taut with long muscles, and he was very good at chopping.

I just didn't know why he was chopping down our *mast*.

The mast shuddered with each bite of the blade, and the deck was littered with splintered chunks of wood. All ships, I knew, carried axes on deck in case a mast was damaged in a storm and had to be cut loose—so I knew how Leander had come by the thing—but that certainly wasn't the case here.

Another roar went up from Cleopatra's barge and gave me my answer. A group of partygoers stood at the rail, madly urging Leander on with each stroke of the axe, frantically trading wagers. Someone, I suspected, had paid Leander to even the odds in favor of the Amazona side.

I could hardly believe he thought a few coins were worth the hell I would unleash when I got my hands on him. But in that moment, there was nothing for me to do but hope the mast would withstand Leander's woodsmanship long enough for me to rescue Tanis.

I edged out over the yardarm, placing my feet in the sailors' footropes as carefully as haste would allow. Below me, I could see Tanis's face had turned almost purple. So had her left foot, where the rope bit into her flesh. After what seemed an eternity, I reached the rope where the line was caught in the rigging and frantically sawed through the tough hairy fibers. Sweat ran in streams down my face and back, into my eyes, and between my fingers, making the knife hilt slick.

The mast was beginning to sway perilously.

I paused for a moment to draw my wooden blades from their scabbards and lob them at Leander's head. The second one glanced off his ear, and he yelped and dropped the axe. It spun across the deck and he scrambled after it, yelling curses at me. Another chorus of shouts—half cheering, half jeers—sounded from the barge crowd as I turned back to working feverishly on the rope.

"Tanis!" I shouted. "Be ready!"

She twisted and writhed, staring up at me with fear in her eyes. The distance she would fall wouldn't kill her. Unless she landed on her head or broke her neck . . . I shoved the thought from my mind. If I didn't cut her loose—and soon—the falling mast would probably kill her anyway.

The last rope strand finally parted, and I watched her throw her arms up around her head, curling inward as she fell. I winced as she hit the planking with a hard thud, but she rolled and was up on her hands and knees a moment later. She'd be fine.

Now *I* was the one in trouble. Down below, I could see some of the fighting had spilled back over onto our ship. But in the din of battle, all of my friends were far too occupied to notice my predicament.

The entire rigging was becoming dangerously unstable with each hewing stroke. Leander was nothing if not industrious, but thankfully the axe he wielded was a dull old thing, and that alone gave me the opportunity to do something incredibly stupid. The sail beneath me shivered, and the yardarm tipped drunkenly. I didn't have time to shimmy back to the ladder and climb down, and if I fell when the mast toppled, I would most likely hit the deck and break every bone in my body. My options were limited.

The yardarm wobbled and one end swung out over the open water . . .

As fast as I could, I unbuckled one side of my breastplate and threw it to the deck, narrowly missing Leander again and making him back off. Then I heaved myself up into a crouch on top of the yardarm. The wood beam was straight and about as wide as the yoke pole on a chariot, if a little longer . . .

The single act that had made me famous in the ring was a chariot maneuver called the Morrigan's Flight—running the length of the yoke pole between two racing ponies, balancing, and running back . . .

I could do this.

The rigging shuddered and began to drift-fall toward the other ship.

I heard the panicked screams of the girls below as they watched it go.

And I ran.

Like an acrobat, arms wide, feet curving around the pole to grip with each fleeting step, I held my breath and ran the length of the spar and—as the mast finally toppled—I leaped out over the water in a swan dive, just like I used to do back home from the cliffs above the River Dwr. The world went from bright sunlight to chill darkness in a moment as I hit the water with a splash.

When I surfaced again, sputtering, it was to see the rail lined with Achillea fighters, all peering down at me in astonishment.

"What in Hel's name was that lunatic trying to prove?" Elka shouted over the roaring of the spectators, gesticulating at the chaos caused by the fallen mast.

"Never mind!" I shouted back. "Grab their flag!"

I could see where the Amazona flag had been left unattended at the bow of the other ship when the gladiatrices scattered.

"The *flag*!"

Maybe I was a bit single-minded in my desire to win, but I was suddenly feeling awfully motivated to thwart the ambitions of whoever had given Leander his purse of coins. Elka looked at me like I was crazy, but she spun and was already running for the banner before the Amazona team knew what she was doing. She hurdled the space between the boats, hailed Meriel as she swept up the flag on its pole and threw it like it was her spear, back over to our side for Meriel to catch. Shouts of outrage and cries of victory burst forth from the Queen of Aegypt's barge as I scaled the rope ladder thrown down to me and staggered over to where Tanis still lay sprawled on the deck.

"Come on," I said, and held out a hand to help her stand.

She hobbled with me to the bow of our ship, and, in full view of the elite entourage across the waves, together we threw up our fists in triumph. A cacophony of cheers rolled like thunder across the water, and I felt a bit ridiculous, even as my chest was heaving with exertion and I felt myself grinning madly. We'd been play-acting. Not fighting. This was not what being a gladiatrix was about. Not what I had traded my freedom to achieve.

And yet, it was . . . something. Something just a little bit extraordinary.

It was fun.

II

THE MERRIMENT WAS contagious. Well, among the Achillea crew, at any rate. The Amazona girls were uniformly sullen. It seemed they took things very seriously in their ludus. Of course, when I thought about who owned the Ludus Amazona, that wasn't at all surprising. Defeat, I didn't doubt, bore consequences in Pontius Aquila's academy.

I might have felt a twinge of sympathy for them but, to be honest, in that moment, I couldn't have cared less. My friends and I were victorious, and that was all that mattered.

Over on the queen's barge, the spectators lobbed sheaves of flowers out over the water. Out of the corner of my eye, I noticed Elka grinning past me at Ajani. Then suddenly—and for the third time that afternoon—I found myself plunging over the side of the boat and into the water below.

I surfaced in time to see Damya, our fearsome Phoenician fighter, pick Elka up and heave *her* over the side. Then Meriel. Then Damya leaped over the side herself, warbling a joyful war cry and sending up an enormous splash. Others followed until the waters of Lake Sabatinus began to resemble the mosaics on the bathhouse wall of the ludus, replete with frolicking nymphs.

"Victrix!" One young patrician shouted at me from the deck of the barge, leaning far out over the water with a jewel-set goblet sloshing over with drink. "A cup for your bravery!"

I swam beneath his outstretched arm and reached for the cup, but he yanked it out of my grasp and leaned further out over me, a lascivious grin on his face.

"Uh!" he said, licking his lips. "*After* a kiss for your beauty!"

"Beauty doesn't win battles, sir." I smiled up at him sweetly. "But strong legs and a fearless heart can overcome a wobbling mast-pole." With that, I snatched the cup from his hands and drank the wine in one gulp.

His grin froze on his face, and his friends howled with drunken laughter.

I swam back toward the rest of the girls, and the expression on Elka's face told me she'd heard the exchange. My *actual* stunt with the wobbling mast-pole, she apparently found far less amusing.

"You know, you could have been killed when that sail fell," she said.

I shook the wet hair back off my face and nodded. "I know," I said. "But Tanis probably *would* have been, if I hadn't helped her."

Ajani swam up to tread water in front of us. "That's the kind of help that gets you hauled out of the arena face-down by hooks," she said. "Elka's right. You could have let her fend for herself."

"I could have. But I decided not to." I grinned, unwilling to let their scolding mute my good mood. "And that's what this is all about, isn't it?"

"What?" Elka asked.

"The right to decide for ourselves!" I splashed a handful of water at her. "As soon as Achillea receives the deed to the ludus from Caesar, we're *free!*"

"*You're* not, little fox," Elka reminded me. "That was the idiotic deal you made."

"Shush. Be kind," Ajani admonished. "I for one am glad of her idiocy."

"See?" I said. "And at least I'm *more* free than I was. More free than *they* are." I nodded at the Amazona boat deck, where our adversaries still stood, sulky and defeated. "And I intend to make the most of that."

We paddled languidly back and forth in front of the pleasure barge for a while longer. The revelers poured down wine and tossed sweets to us, and Sorcha indulged the revelry for longer than I thought she would. Finally, with a signal blast from a conch shell, we made our way back to the ludus shore. The naumachia certainly hadn't gone as planned, but it *had* managed to fulfill its purpose of entertaining a barge-load of high-society butterflies.

The sun was westering as we neared the shore where the ludus gates stood open. The girls from the Ludus Amazona had already been herded like goats through the gates and out of sight by their guards—an ever-present contingent of grim, glowering brutes in black armor and helmets. The Amazona girls were to remain quartered in a newly built barracks wing as our "guests" for the next several days, and there would be a series of "friendly, collegial" competitions. The prospect had prompted equal amounts of groaning and glee from the Achillea girls. In the meantime, we were allowed the rare treat of a cookout on the beach that night—food, drink, and just that little extra bit of freedom that was a taste of things to come for the ludus.

As we set out rugs and cushions on the sand, I looked back over the water to see the shadow-black silhouetted figure of Thalestris—the academy's *primus pilus*, the Lanista's right hand—far in the distance. She stood balanced on a reed skiff holding a fishing spear poised above her head, ready to strike. In the days leading up to Cleopatra's naumachia, the fight mistress, who boasted of being a *real* Amazon, had made no secret of her disdain for the spectacle—something she regarded as useless frivolity and an insulting waste of the carefully honed and nurtured gladiatorial talents of her charges.

Sorcha had known full well Thalestris wouldn't be able to keep her sharp tongue sheathed in the presence of a bunch of lolling elites, and so she'd been given leave to spend the day fishing. As far away from the spectacle as she could paddle. I watched her spear pierce the surface of the water with the swiftness of a striking serpent.

Thalestris was not someone I would ever want to rouse to anger.

Night fell and we sat on the beach, warming away the lake chill with the flames of crackling bonfires and mugs of beer out of barrels rescued from the disaster of Leander's supply skiff, brought ashore as rightful booty from our "conquest." It was better stuff than any of us had ever tasted—better even than the foamy dark brew I used to drink in my kingly father's feast hall back home in Durovernum—and we relished it.

Leander, himself, did not receive the same outpouring of good cheer.

"It's a peace offering!" he squeaked, hiding behind the wicker basket he carried as if it were a legionnaire's shield. He probably should have announced his presence before stepping out of the shadows beyond the circle of firelight. For a moment, I almost felt sorry for the poor lad.

"Peace offering?" Ajani purred at him like a cat with a cornered mouse. She considered Tanis her archery protégé and was less than impressed that she'd been imperiled by Leander's stunt.

"Ajani . . . pretty—no, no . . . beautiful—*beautiful* Ajani," Leander stammered, dark eyes huge and liquid, like a puppy begging for scraps. "I was only trying to help you win glory!"

I laughed out loud and almost choked on my mouthful of beer. *"Help?"*

He glanced over at me, and his stance shifted back to the cocksure attitude I was used to from him. "Yes, domina!" he said, grinning. "Without me, you wouldn't have had the opportunity for such a spectacular leap—such heroism! I was so happy to help."

I marveled at his brashness.

Meriel rolled her eyes. "You're an idiot," she said.

"A *beneficial* idiot." He nodded and held out the basket again, lifting the lid. Inside, there were six plump lake trout, gleaming and gutted, ready for the fire. Also several loaves of bread, and a wheel of cheese wrapped in cloth.

My mouth watered at the sight.

Elka glared at him. "Where did you get all this?" she asked. "And how much trouble are you going to get us in by bringing it here?"

"No trouble at all!" Leander's grin widened. "The trout are from Thalestris—the noise from the naumachia drove all the fishes to her end of the lake, and she caught more than we can use in the kitchen. I offered to take them off Cook's hands."

Damya snorted. "You pilfered them."

"No! Cook gave them to me fairly," he protested. Then he shrugged and smiled slyly. "Now, the bread and cheese . . ."

Ajani cuffed him across the top of his head, ruffling his dark hair, and let the matter drop. It was hard to stay mad at Leander for any length of time. Meriel plucked the basket from his hands and went to work setting the fish on the fire to cook. The night settled down around us, stars winking and waves whispering in the darkness, and the mood was as light as the breeze off the lake. I felt almost like I was home, back in Durovernum. With my friends . . .

"Hey, Fallon!" Elka hailed me from behind the mound of food piled on her platter. "Come eat. You have to build up your strength if you're going to keep leaping about like a Minoan acrobat."

Damya grinned. "Maybe we should find her a bull to vault in the arena."

"At least until that decurion of hers gets back from the wars!" Lydia said.

"I'll stick with chariot horses, thanks," I said, ignoring her lewd cackle.

I took the platter Antonia offered me, balanced deftly on the bronze-and-leather sheath that encased the stump of her left forearm. It had taken us all a bit of getting used to—the fact that she was missing her hand, severed at the wrist in a practice bout accident—but Antonia had decided early on that it wasn't going to impede her. That had gone a long way toward the rest of us accepting it. Indeed, since the mishap, once it had become apparent that Antonia was no longer in danger of dying from her injury, she seemed to have grown beyond the bounds of what had once been a pronounced shyness.

With Neferet—the girl who'd not only been the one responsible for the amputation but who'd dedicated herself wholly, fiercely, to nursing her back to health—Antonia had made impressive progress. I saw Neferet smile at her and suspected that her heart might have been just as instrumental as her healing hands during Antonia's convalescence.

"Where did Thalestris learn to fish like that?" Meriel wondered through a mouthful of trout.

"She grew up on an island," Leander said.

"An island?"

He nodded, pouring more beer. "Mm-hm . . . that's what I heard her say."

I frowned. Even after more than a year spent living near the very heart of the Roman Republic, I was still a bit hazy on the concept of geography. But I'd seen maps, been told how to read them, and had a basic understanding of who came from where. And I knew enough to know that Scythia—the place where the so-called Amazons came from—wasn't an island.

When I said so, Leander shrugged but stuck to his tale.

"He's right," Gratia grumbled into her cup of wine as she washed down a mouthful of fish. "Thalestris is as Amazon as my arse."

We turned as one to blink at her in the gathering darkness. She raised her head and blinked back. A bit blearily.

"Amazon," Gratia said again, loud enough so that the rest of us could all hear her above the crackling of the logs and drawing out the word with a sneer. "My *arse*."

Elka snorted in amusement. "It *will* be," she agreed. "On latrine duty for all eternity, if she hears you talk like that."

"What?" Lydia asked, clearly not understanding. "She is. An Amazon, I mean. So was her sister. Right?"

That had always been my understanding. *My* sister's very first fight—the first ever female gladiatorial bout—had been fought between her and a warrior named Orithyia. Thalestris's sister. Sorcha had triumphed in the arena. And Orithyia . . . had died. I'd secretly marveled at how Thalestris had been able to overcome that loss to serve as Sorcha's primus pilus, but I supposed the code of the Amazon sisterhood transcended bonds of blood. And that first fight had been immortalized in the names of the two original gladiatrix academies: Achillea and Amazona.

Gratia didn't seem to think the reputation was warranted, though, and her scorn was almost hotter than the bonfire's flames. Thalestris always rode her hard on technique, and Gratia, clearly, was fed to the teeth with it—along with the trout Thalestris had caught that afternoon. "In their mead-addled dreams they are," she scoffed. "Where I come from, we know these things. The Amazons—if they ever even truly existed—died out hundreds of years ago. They're just a myth now."

"Well, she seems pretty Amazon to me," Lydia said, sloshing more wine into her cup. "Why are we arguing about this again?"

"Because we're all a bit drunk," Damya offered philosophically.

Gratia nodded. "And Thalestris is a bitch."

"And," I said, "we all wish we were able to fight just like her."

The grumbling and muttering ground to a silent halt. Elka raised her cup.

"*Ave*, Thalestris," she said with a wry grin.

"Ave, Thalestris," Meriel echoed, punctuating the sentiment with a snort before downing the contents of her cup.

And then, one by one, the other girls raised their cups in salute.

"Ave!"

"Ave to that hard-arsed, cold-eyed, wicked, brilliant, hobnailed gorgon," Damya agreed enthusiastically.

"Who, if the gods are kind," murmured Ajani, "is fast asleep in her bed and has heard none of this."

"Here's to many more blissful years toiling—*of our own free will*—under her merciless lash!" Elka said, elbowing me. "Right, little fox?"

We all laughed at that. At the joke, but also at the giddy prospect of soon—very soon—becoming rulers of our own destinies. Free to leave the ludus if we chose, but staying to fight because we wanted to. Outwardly, it wouldn't even look like much of a change. But inwardly . . . my Cantii soul burst with happiness at the very idea—

"What . . . what happens if we don't want to stay?"

The laughter died to mute silence. One by one, we all turned to look in the direction of the voice that had asked that question. Tanis. Ajani's archer protégé. The girl I'd cut down from the rigging on the ship that afternoon. Even in the flickering firelight, I could still see the angry red welts from the rope on her ankle.

"I mean . . ." Tanis shrugged, looking from face to face, and shut her mouth.

"You mean *what*?" Meriel leaned forward, tilting her head as if trying to understand words spoken in an unknown tongue. "Leave here? Where in the great world would *you* go? You don't even know where you're from, Tanis. Your tribe was a bunch of wanderers. At least here you belong."

"That's what you think."

"And you don't? Last time I watch your back in a fight."

"That's not what I meant, Meriel. Don't be such a bitch."

"What exactly *did* you mean then, *gladiolus*?" Meriel sneered, calling Tanis by the nasty little nickname we'd all suffered under when we'd first arrived at the ludus. Gladiolus: a play on the word for the spear-shaped blooms that grew tall in the ludus gardens, pretty but so easily cut down. It was how Nyx, the top dog at the academy at the time, would remind a raw recruit of her lowly status in the ranks of the students—not fighters, but flowers.

"Hey!" I snapped, silencing them both before things got out of hand. "Both of you, back away. Nyx is long gone, and we don't play those kinds of games anymore. We're equals, like Achillea said—"

"Achillea?" Tanis scoffed. "You mean your sister, Sorcha? I'm *sure* she sees you as exactly equal to the rest of us."

I blinked at her in surprise. When the girls of the ludus had discovered, in the wake of the Triumphs, that the Lady Achillea was actually my sister, I'd worried what their reactions would be. If they would think that I'd be shown some kind of favoritism because of it. But when that hadn't happened and Sorcha had continued to work me just as hard as—and sometimes harder than—the rest of the girls, they'd all come to accept it without any resentment. At least, I'd thought so . . .

"Tanis, I was defending you—"

"I don't need you to defend me, Fallon! I can defend myself."

"Not really." Elka shrugged. "I mean—good with a bow, but you're terrible in hand-to-hand."

Ajani winced. "Elka—"

"Shut up!" Tanis screeched. "You're *all* horrible!"

"Then leave, why don't you!" Gratia leaned forward, thrusting out her jaw.

"Stop it." I stood, all that Cantii-souled happiness flaring to equally potent anger. "Stop it! No one's going anywhere. Not even you, Tanis."

"You're not my owner, Fallon." She shot to her feet, stumbling on her injured ankle. "Neither is your sister. That's the whole point, isn't it? Don't any of you understand that? No one *owns* us anymore. We're all *alone* again. Just like we were before we came here. Only nothing about the prison has changed except the bars!" She turned and hobbled up the beach, disappearing into the darkness.

"Let her go," Meriel said, rolling her eyes. "Where's my mug?"

I stayed where I was, on my feet, and exchanged a look with Elka. After a moment, she shrugged and waved me in the direction Tanis had gone. I sighed and went after her.

She hadn't gone far. Just far enough to still hear the others' laughter drifting on the night breeze.

I sat down beside her on the flat rock that looked out over the black glass mirror of Lake Sabatinus. A young crescent moon rode low in the cloudless starlit sky, as if gazing down at her luminous profile reflected in the water. The night was just bright enough for me to see the tracks of tears on Tanis's cheeks. I sat there beside her, silent for a long moment.

"Are you really from a tribe of wanderers?" I asked quietly, when it became clear that she wasn't going to start a conversation.

"Desert herders," she sniffed, not looking at me. "What's it to you?"

"Nothing." I shrugged. "I just didn't know that. How will you find them again if you leave us?"

I could see the prospect of that terrified her. Just as much as the prospect of staying. But if there was one thing all of us had learned in our time at the ludus, it was that you never admitted fear. Not if you could absolutely help it.

"I don't know," she admitted, finally.

I nodded and said nothing.

"Must be nice not to have to worry about such a thing," Tanis continued. "For you, I mean."

"How so?" I asked.

"You can just go back to your life as a pampered princess in Britannia once you win back your freedom," she said. "But then, you'd probably miss all of those crowds yelling your name every time you so much as stepped onto the sand."

"Is that what you think I care about?"

"Why wouldn't you?" she asked, and I could tell she meant it. "The only time anyone yells *my* name in the arena is if they want me to get out of the way."

"Ajani thinks very highly of you," I said.

"That's just because I can shoot."

"That's not a small thing, Tanis. You're very good and—"

"I'm a *coward*, Fallon!" she spat vehemently. "Don't you understand? I'm really good at fighting from a distance because I'm terrified of having to do it up close! All of the rest of you—you and Damya and Meriel and even Ajani, once she's used up all her arrows—you all seem to think nothing whatsoever of charging headlong at a wall of swords! *How?* How do you do it? Every muscle in my body tries to run the other way."

"But you don't," I said. "You haven't. I mean—I've seen you stand your ground and fight. You—"

"*Defend* myself," she sneered. "Badly. Elka was right. And I only ever did it because running would have just meant flogging once they caught up with me. Flogging if I was lucky."

She glowered at me, as if daring me to contradict her. But I couldn't. For the first time, I thought about what it must have been like for the girls at the ludus who hadn't grown up wanting to do nothing more than swing a sword. I'd never seen that in Tanis before, but now that she'd said it, I tried to put myself in her place. When she'd been nothing but a slave—when she'd had no *choice* but to fight as a gladiatrix for the ludus—Tanis had fought alongside the rest of us, day in and day out. Fight or suffer punishment.

Now—in spite of Elka's jest about us freely toiling under her lash—the *actual* threat of Thalestris's whip was about to disappear with the advent of the Nova Ludus Achillea. And Tanis was afraid that, without that kind of external motivation, she would no longer be able to find it within herself to fight. To go into the arena and—spurred on by nothing but her own free will—risk defeat or injury. Or death.

I could see the muscles in her jaw working as I sat there looking at her. It had taken a good deal of courage to admit it. But I wasn't sure I could make her see it that way.

Instead, I asked, "How's the ankle?"

She stuck out her leg and flexed her foot. "Hurts. But it'll heal." She fell silent for a long moment and I thought maybe that was the end of our conversation. But then she said, "Thank you."

"For what?"

"For saving me back on the ship." She shrugged. "And for not trying to tell me I'm wrong now. We both know I'm no fighter, Fallon. If I have a destiny, I don't think it's here."

"I wouldn't jump to that conclusion if I were you, Tanis." I put a hand on her shoulder. "Wait and see. You might find that, once you no longer *have* to fight . . . you might *want* to. And you might just do it better."

She frowned, unconvinced, but at least I was able to talk her into coming back and joining the others. By the time we returned to the fire, it was as if the sniping between the girls had never happened. Meriel pressed a mug into Tanis's hand and made room for her in the circle of bodies. I sat there, silent, looking from face to firelit face and thinking about just how much that circle of girls had come to mean to me in such a relatively short time. I didn't want any of them to leave the ludus. Not Tanis, not even Meriel or Lydia. They were my sisters, and I wanted them to stay and fight with me—as much as I wanted to fight for them.

Elka threw another log on the fire, and the flames belched clouds of sparks into the night. The general merriment continued undiminished all around me, highlighted by Leander's outrageous flirtations with each and every one of us.

"My heart belongs only to you, sweet Ajani!" he was saying, looking every bit the cheerful, leering satyr through the shower of sparks. "But also you, fair Damya."

"Ha." She grinned back at him, and I thought she might actually be enjoying his advances. Except her idea of flirting back was "It would, if I ripped it out of your chest and kept it in a jar."

Leander swallowed his next retort, and Damya threw back her head and laughed, slapping him so heartily on the back that she almost knocked him into the fire. I tried to laugh along at the banter, but my own thoughts started to careen away from me. My *own* heart, I suddenly remembered, had been missing for months. Stolen and carried away into battle in far-off lands. By Caius Antonius Varro, decurion in Caesar's legions . . .

I sighed.

Clearly, I thought, *I've drunk far too much of the kitchen boy's beer tonight.* Still, the warmth of the fire on my face made me close my eyes and imagine it was Cai's breath on my skin as he leaned close to kiss me.

"You sigh any louder and somebody's going to tattle to Heron that you've got a case of evil humors," Elka's voice murmured in my ear as she sat down beside me and handed me another cup of beer.

I opened one eye and squinted at her.

"*I* know it's just love-pining," she said, "but he'll march you to the infirmary to have you stuck with bloodletting skewers and wrapped in one of his stinking poultices."

I opened my other eye and grumbled something unpleasant under my breath before gulping my drink. Elka nodded and drank from her own cup.

"How long since you've heard from him?"

"Weeks," I said sourly. "Four of them less a day, to be exact. Plus however many hours it's been since I woke up this morning."

"At least you're getting the knack of the Roman calendar."

"Barely."

"And you're learning to read their letters."

"*Less* than barely."

The Cantii had no written language. All our stories were told face-to-face, passed down through the songs and poems of our bards. We had no need for scribbled marks on tablets and scrolls to convey our hearts and minds to others.

Rome, and Romans, were different. And so I'd resolved to learn their written words as best I could. Sorcha had made a tutor available to any of the girls at the ludus who wished to avail themselves, though few of them did. Ajani, with her quiet thirst for knowledge, was one. I was another. Admittedly, I had a very *specific* reason for doing so. An armor-wearing reason with laughing hazel eyes and an infuriatingly kissable mouth who was, at present, a whole wide world away from me, smiting the enemies of the great and mighty Caesar.

Before he left, I'd promised Cai that I would try to write. Or rather, that I would try to dictate letters to Heron, the ludus physician, and perhaps the only man I would trust with such words. And Cai had promised me, in turn, that he would send me letters back whenever he could. Letters written in basic—*very* basic—Latin. Usually the missives were no more than two or three lines of neat black script on a square of papyrus or vellum. But beyond the words and phrases I could recognize, like "smile" and "miss you"— or, depending on how Caesar's campaign fared, "fight" and "enemy" and "seige"—Cai always sent me something else. He sent me *pictures*. They made my chest ache for him.

Because they were magic. And they were just for me.

Like the murals painted on the walls of the Ludus Achillea—scenes from the arena captured and frozen into single unending moments—Cai's charcoal drawings of people and places, birds and animals and flowers struck me speechless when I gazed at them.

Every few weeks, a scroll sealed in a copper tube would arrive at the ludus, delivered by courier along with whatever other correspondence there was for the Lanista or the other girls. There wasn't much of the latter—most of us didn't have anyone to correspond with outside of the walls of the academy—and so I always felt a little guilty when the courier would ride through the gates and the other gladiatrices would sigh or snicker or, some, gaze longingly at the letters I received. In the privacy of my cell, though, that guilty twinge would vanish the instant I twisted open the seal.

Inside were scenes of the countrysides Cai and the legions marched through: rolling hills dotted with strands of trees, craggy ravines seamed with creeks, soaring forests, and endless plains. Sometimes, he drew the creatures that inhabited those places: a herd of deer grazing, an eagle perched on the high, bare branch of a lonely pine, a crow sitting on the peak of an army camp tent, wings hunched against the wind and black eyes gleaming bright. And always, beneath the sketch, Cai would write the name of the thing in neat black letters to help me learn their names in his language.

Cervos. Aquilam. Corvo.

My favorite of all the drawings he'd sent me, though, wasn't a pretty landscape or an animal. It was a picture of his hand. When I'd first unrolled the vellum scroll, my breath had caught in my throat because I could recognize it plainly. That familiar, calloused palm lay open and upturned as if Cai held it out for me to take. The scroll lay on top of all the others in the trunk at the foot of my pallet in my cell. I'd taken it out to look at it almost every day since he'd sent it. But what I'd told Elka had been truth. I hadn't received anything from him in almost a month. And I was beginning to worry that something was wrong.

The spirit of the beer I'd drunk that night began to work its maudlin magic on me, and I felt a proper sulk coming on. But before it had a chance to take hold, I noticed that the ludus guards had wandered close. I stood and stretched and announced somewhat unneccesarily that I was going to turn in for the night, as we were once more rounded up and herded back through the gates. It was an ungentle reminder that, until those papers arrived from Caesar, we weren't free.

Still, as we passed the new-built barracks where the Amazona girls were quartered that night, and I saw the black-clad brutes who guarded *their* cells, I counted myself infinitely fortunate that, over a year earlier, in the Forum of Rome, a certain slave trader had been canny enough to sell me to my very own sister. I shuddered to think what would have happened to me if Pontius Aquila's bid had won out that day.

III

THE NEXT MORNING I awoke with a head full of sheep's wool and bootnails. My dreams had been full of drowning—dark figures in black cloaks lurking beneath the waves like statues on the seabed, waiting to drag me down and away from the sun and my sisters, away from the ludus forever . . .

I blamed a certain kitchen slave's barrels of beer and doused my face with cold water from my washstand until I could open my eyes without wincing.

"Are you still mooning over your decurion?" Elka asked, peering at me as we stretched out our muscles in the lee of the equipment shed wall before practice.

"No," I snapped.

"Ah. I thought so." She nodded. "That would explain your mood, then."

"I said *no*—"

"Maybe his father can give you some insight into your true love's whereabouts these days," she said with a casual shrug, turning away to pluck a practice javelin from the weapons rack.

"What?" I blinked at her.

"The good Senator Varro?" She turned a guileless expression on me. "I heard he's in the main yard with a big old oxcart. Some sort of gift for the Lanista, according to Kronos. I think they're waiting for you—"

"What—why didn't you *say* so?" I sputtered and spun in a circle, checking my tunic for obvious stains or creases and patting down my hastily plaited hair.

Senator Decimus Fulvius Varro was one of the wealthiest, most influential men in Rome. He was a war hero, having served with distinction under Pompey the Great, and now, in his retirement, was an esteemed senior member of the senate and a successful businessman.

More to the point, he was Cai's father. And he liked me.

At least, that was the impression he'd given. My mind flashed back to the very first time I'd met him. It was in the heady moments after my victory in the Triumphs—and in the wake of a very public display of affection from the senator's son. Cai had vaulted the spectator barrier of the Circus Maximus to, quite literally, sweep me off my feet in an embrace. Our kiss had sent the crowd in attendance into a frenzy of cheering and swooning.

I'd been half-convinced it would be the end of us when, afterward, I saw a man pushing through the celebratory crowd with focused purpose. A man who looked like Cai.

Tall and handsome, an elegant figure with a soldier's bearing, draped in a purple-striped toga with dark hair just beginning to shade to silver.

"Victrix," he'd greeted me with a serious look on his face. "I salute your victory. But I couldn't help noticing that not only have you defeated your adversaries, you seem to have ensnared the affections of my one and only son whilst doing so."

Cai had been pulled away from me by a group of young men, friends of his from the stands who were heartily back-slapping and cheering him over his impulsive, romantic declaration. I was on my own.

"Senator Varro." I bowed, my mouth going dry. "I . . ."

"We shall have to have you to the house to dine."

"I . . . I beg your pardon?" I blinked at him, thinking I'd misheard.

His expression, with the twitch of his lip, softened into an amused grin. "So that I might come to know you better, my dear," he explained. "I can already see from your performance today why his warrior's heart is drawn to yours. In time, perhaps, I may come to know better the woman who appeals to his soul."

I'm certain I blushed a fiery shade of crimson, but he was kind enough to pretend not to notice.

As a gladiatrix—even one who'd just won the crowd in spectacular fashion—I was still *infamia*. A social pariah where the houses of the Roman elite were concerned. But not, it seemed, to the senator. In the few brief moments we'd shared at the Triumphs, he was kind. Gracious. Effusive in his praise of my martial prowess, and clearly bursting with pride over his son's accomplishments. And in the months since that time, he hadn't actively discouraged a relationship between Cai and me, although I hadn't yet received that invitation to dine at his house in Rome. Mostly because Cai had been called away soon after to Caesar's campaign in Hispania, and the opportunity hadn't presented itself.

Now, though, Senator Varro was in the courtyard of the Ludus Achillea, and I wondered what in the wide world had brought him there.

"Well, Fallon?" the senator asked me for the second time. He gestured toward the heavy-axled cart before him. "What do you think?"

I stood there, staring. Lost in a moment frozen in time.

"Do you like it?"

An exquisitely sculpted marble frieze lay on the cart. It looked as though it weighed more than the team of oxen that had transported it there. It was a gift—commissioned for the ludus, to be placed above the main entranceway of the academy: longer than two tall men stretched out end to end on the ground, it was a breathtaking, lifelike depiction of a band of warrior women engaged in fierce battle, facing off against an opposing army of men, weapons brandished, mouths open in battle cries.

Senator Varro had generously funded the piece from his own overflowing coffers to commemorate the occasion of my victory in the Triumphs and the imminent passing of the Ludus Achillea into my sister Sorcha's hands.

"Such things—such extraordinary occasions, and such extraordinary women—should be celebrated," Varro had said when I'd first arrived, out of breath and trying not to look it, in the yard where he and my sister stood waiting for me.

Then he'd thrown back the canvas sheet covering his gift so that Sorcha and I could see.

"Sisters in arms," he said, with a sweeping gesture. "For sisters in arms."

In the wake of the Triumphs, it had become general knowledge that the Lanista of the Ludus Achillea was my sister, so I'd known Cai's father was aware of our connection. But, as a Roman statesman, I wouldn't have necessarily thought he'd consider it important. I wouldn't have thought he'd consider it at all. But he clearly did. He *had*. And it made my heart beat a little faster, thinking that the father of the boy I loved could appreciate the kind of bond that Sorcha and I shared. It gave me small, secret stirrings of hope for another bond—the one between me and Cai . . .

I shook my head and dragged my attention back to the marble lintel.

The stonemason artisan who'd created the masterpiece was flapping about underneath the archway, directing his apprentices to erect the wooden scaffolds they would use to maneuver the heavy slab into place above the main gate. Along with ropes and, I suspected, a generous amount of swearing.

"It's beautiful. That one looks like you, Sorcha," I said, pointing to the main figure on the frieze.

My sister glanced at me sideways. "That was *not* the intent," she said, deferring to the senator, "I'm sure."

Senator Varro grinned. "A happy coincidence, perhaps," he said.

I noticed the hint of a blush creeping up Sorcha's cheeks as the senator pointed to the two main figures, facing off against each other at the center of the carving.

"It's a representation of the legendary battle," he continued, "between the Amazon queen Penthesilea and the hero Achilles at the Fall of Troy."

"Like the tapestry in your room," I said to Sorcha.

"A gift from Caesar," she explained to the senator. "From when he and I first founded this ludus, together."

"But this is different," I said. "On the tapestry, the queen is dying."

"She is," Sorcha said. "That scene shows the moment of the Amazons' defeat by Achilles and his men."

"Like your first fight as a gladiatrix against Thalestris's sister," I said. "That's why they called you Achillea and Amazona."

Sorcha nodded, gazing at the marble frieze as if mesmerized. "Here, though, she's barely even begun to fight. An interesting choice, Senator."

"Caesar is, of course, entitled to his idea of the story's key moment," Senator Varro said pointedly. "I only hope you can enjoy my own humble interpretation as well."

I glanced at the senator, surprised. There were not many men in Rome who publicly disagreed with Caesar, even when he wasn't there to hear it. The only other man I'd seen do such a thing was Pontius Aquila. And Caesar still took every opportunity to remind him of that particular folly. Coming from the senator, such a thing was an impressive display of either confidence or recklessness. I wasn't sure which. But if Sorcha, as Caesar's own Lanista, was taken aback by Varro's comment, she didn't let on.

"Of course," she said, gracing him instead with one of her rare, full smiles. "It is a generous and thoughtful gift. The ludus will treasure it. As will I." She linked an arm through his. "You will stay and dine with us tonight?"

"I would love to, Lady Achillea," he said, patting her hand, "but my business calls me home to prepare for a trade expedition. I only wanted to deliver this before I go."

"A cup of wine, then," she said. "At least."

"If your delightful sister will join us," he said, turning to me.

Sorcha led him toward the main house, saying, "Indeed. She can pour the wine."

"It seems you made quite an impression," Sorcha said later, after we'd walked the senator back to his horse and seen him on his way.

The dryness of her tone made me glance at her sideways. "I barely said a word!" I protested. "I was trying to behave myself. Like you—a proper Roman lady."

It was true. I *had* tried. Although to what degree of success, I wasn't sure. Sorcha, in her time living among Romans, had managed to figure out how to fit into their society. How to dress like them, eat like them, and navigate her way through their baffling customs and social niceties. Me? I'd sat there, a cup of wine in my hand, listening to endless small talk about politics and Caesar's wars and senate squabbles, and the state of the Republic, and on and on . . .

When all I'd wanted to do was ask Senator Varro if he'd heard from Cai. How was he? When was he coming home? Did he ever mention me in his letters?

My raging curiosity was to remain unsatisfied.

"I didn't mean just now," Sorcha said, turning back from watching the senator depart. "I meant in general."

"I don't understand."

Together we walked back toward where the marble slab still lay gleaming in the sunlight upon the cart.

"This frieze is meant to be seen by everyone who passes through that gate," she said. "And everyone will know that it was Senator Varro who gifted it to the ludus. A man of power and prestige. Your win at the Triumphs has helped legitimize what we do here, little sister. I'm proud of you."

I half wanted to roll my eyes at her, and half wanted to bask in that praise. It was something I'd never thought I'd hear from Sorcha, even though I'd lived my whole life wanting to. I glanced over at her, but her attention had drifted and she seemed lost in thought, gazing down at the carved figures. Her lips moved and she murmured something in Greek. I could recognize the language, but I couldn't understand the words.

When she noticed me looking at her, she smiled and repeated herself, not in Latin but in our own tongue. "'Not in strength are we inferior to men,'" she said, "'the same our eyes, our limbs the same; one common light we see, one air we breathe. What then denied to us have the gods on man bestowed?'"

"What's that from?" I asked. "Some bard's tale?"

"Penthesilea was said to have uttered those words at the battle of Troy."

"That women are equal to men . . ."

She nodded. "Not better, not different, not lesser. The same. She was a wise woman."

I ran my fingertip over the wheel of the stone chariot the Amazon queen rode in. "I think the legends got it wrong," I said. "I think Penthesilea's side won this battle."

"Why do you say that?" Sorcha asked, one eyebrow raised. "Because she looks like me?"

"No . . ." I pointed to the figure with swords raised, running toward the fight directly behind the queen's chariot. "Because *that* one looks like *me*. How could she possibly lose?"

Sorcha laughed and swatted at my ear. In the distance, the faint sounds of combat practice echoed through the ludus yards. I looked at my sister and saw that, as ever, a corner of her mind was attuned to those noises. The sharp ring of metal, the shouts of the fight masters and cries of the girls as they challenged each other. I imagined Sorcha could see in her mind everything that was happening just by the sounds she heard. Every blow that hit its mark, every swing that went wide . . .

"Do you miss it?" I asked.

"What?"

"Fighting. The excitement . . . the glory."

Her hesitation was so slight, it could almost have been my imagination. But it wasn't. "No." She shrugged. "Of course not. And with my limitations I'd only be a liability in the arena now, anyway." Her left hand clenched once, convulsively.

"I think you're wrong."

She lifted an eyebrow at me. The gesture gave subtle emphasis to the scar that ran from her hairline down her forehead, stopping just above her eye. "Really."

"I think, in your case, your 'limitations' are actually assets."

She frowned, but I put up a hand.

"I'm serious!" I said. "I've *seen* you fight, Sorcha— and I don't mean just when we were girls growing up in Durovernum. That night I saw you sparring with Thalestris? The way you compensated and improvised . . . it makes you unpredictable. And *that* makes you dangerous. I mean, even more dangerous."

She hesitated again, but then shook her head, smiling. "I'll leave the arena to you and your friends, little sister," she said. "And the glory. My warrior days are done and I'm content."

Maybe that was true, but the strange thing was . . . I wasn't sure contentment actually suited her. Like an exquisite Roman stola, she wore it well. Maybe just not quite as well as she used to wear war paint and leathers. I tried to think if I'd ever seen her relaxed, even when we were girls, and I didn't think I had. I'd seen her fiercely happy, determined, focused, busy, but never just . . . present. Never soaking in a moment. There had always been a kind of tension in the air around Sorcha, even in stillness. She carried it with her, like she was her own little cloudburst just waiting to explode into a full-blown tempest.

A restless heart, our father had said of her. Of me? A *reckless* one.

"Virico would be proud of you," Sorcha said quietly, as if she could sense I was thinking of him in that moment.

I shrugged. "I'm not so sure. I wear Roman armor and fight at the pleasure of his greatest enemy."

"You've done what you had to to survive. And you've thrived."

"We both have."

She nodded, her gaze thoughtful and fixed on a faraway vision in her mind. She missed home, I knew. We both did. When Sorcha had made a deal with Caesar, she'd done it to save our father's life, pure and simple. My deal had been a bit more complicated. But both had meant neither of us would return home any time soon.

"We could send word . . ." It wasn't the first time I'd suggested it.

"To what end, little sister?" She sighed. "No. Far better for Virico to think of his daughters happy in the Lands of the Blessed Dead with our mother, rather than living in the marble halls of his worst enemy halfway across the world."

She hugged me—a brief, hard hug—and sent me back to my practice. I made my way to the equipment shed, thinking about what she'd said. She was right. And there was no way Father would ever know the difference anyway, I reasoned to myself. Aeddan was the only one who even knew that Sorcha and I still lived, let alone where and how, and Aeddan was an outcast and a murderer. He would no sooner return home than I would.

The last time either of us had seen the shores of Prydain had been shortly after the night of my seventeenth birthday and the feast in my father's great hall that had ended in heartbreak. And bloodshed. The night I'd asked Maelgwyn Ironhand, the boy I'd loved, to wait for me to be made a member of my father's royal war band before pleading for my hand in marriage.

Warrior then wife—*that* was what I had decided.

And then the door slammed in the face of both those dreams. My father had not made me a warrior but he had tried to make me a wife, in the worst possible way. By giving me, instead, to Mael's brother Aeddan. They'd fought . . . and Mael had died. And I'd run away from the whole sorry mess, only to find myself a slave. And then a gladiator.

Sorcha was right, Virico was better off never knowing. If he ever found out the truth of that night—how, in trying to protect me from a life of danger, he'd instead set me on a path headed straight to the arenas of Rome—he would never forgive himself. I still wasn't even sure I'd forgiven him. But there was also a part of me that wondered if my father's decision hadn't been a part of the goddess Morrigan's plan for me all along. It had set my feet on the path that had led, ultimately, to the Ludus Achillea. To Sorcha. To the one place where I truly seemed to belong.

I thought about that as I chose the blades I would practice with that afternoon. I was what I was. A gladiatrix. More than that—I was Victrix.

And that was the way I wanted it.

Life at the Ludus Achillea carried on, and almost a week after the senator's visit we were still hosting an utterly joyless pack of Amazona gladiatrices. My patience with them was wearing extremely thin. They were a sullen and humorless lot and cast a pall over the practice pitch— made worse by the gloomy presence of their black-garbed "escorts"—and, on top of that, I was beginning to give up hope I'd ever get another letter from Cai.

Even Elka had begun to take pity on me.

"I'm sure everything is fine," she said that morning, putting a hand on my shoulder after I'd let loose with a particularly exuberant stream of cursing, having absent-mindedly bashed my shin in practice right in front of a contingent of smirking Amazona girls. Elka must have noticed—as had I—that there'd been no mail courier at the gates that morning. Again. "He's probably just too busy hacking Caesar's enemies to bits to pick up a quill."

I stood there, unwilling to be mollified, glaring bleakly at Elka as her gaze slid away and drifted over my head.

"On the other hand," she continued after a moment, "I suppose it's possible that he's forgotten about you entirely."

My glare, I'm sure, went from bleak to baleful.

"I mean . . . *probably* not." She rolled an eye at me. "But you never know. Soldiering is a lonely life. Tedious. All that marching through foreign towns filled with strange women. Those Hispanian girls . . . I've heard they can beguile a man with a dance."

"A dance . . . ?"

She nodded. "They do it *barefoot* and—"

"The only dancer *I'm* interested in wears sandals and carries two swords."

I spun around at the sound of a familiar voice just beside my ear.

"Cai!"

Decurion Caius Antonius Varro—real as life and standing not two paces away—grinned down at me, his clear hazel eyes sparkling with light. I felt a huge smile split my face, ear to ear. A laughing Elka slapped me on the shoulder and wandered off. It took every last infinitesimal amount of self-control I could muster not to throw myself into Cai's arms and devour him with kisses, right there in front of the whole academy and those of the Ludus Amazona who cared to watch.

"Would you honor me with a dance, Victrix?" he asked.

I stood there, speechless, drinking in the unexpected sight of him. Every line and angle, the planes of his face beneath the brim of his helmet, and the contours of his body beneath his armor. He was sun-browned and leaner than I remembered, with a week's worth of stubble on his jaw and dust on his arms and legs. He was glorious.

Cai handed his horse's reins to a fellow legionnaire, who nodded sharply and led his horse, and that of another soldier who accompanied him, toward the stables. The other soldier walked up beside Cai and stood, fists on his hips, gazing after Elka as she walked away, tossing her long pale braids over her shoulder. For a moment, I thought the young man's head might actually twist off its stalk as he craned his neck to keep her in view.

"This is Quintus," Cai said. "My second."

When Quintus the second didn't seem to have heard his introduction, Cai rapped on the young man's helmet with his knuckles.

"Hm?" Quintus turned around, his expression a bit dazzled.

"Quint?" Cai regarded him from under a raised eyebrow.

"I am. Yes." He turned and offered me a perfunctory nod. "But more to the point . . . *who* was that divine nymph?"

I almost choked on the laugh that burst out of my mouth. Quintus the second was lucky Elka was far enough away not to have heard him, I thought. *Nymph?* If there was any mythological creature Elka saw herself as, I was fairly certain that "nymph" was as far away from it as one could get and not fall off the edge of the world.

Cai cleared his throat, and Quintus seemed to realize he was slack-jawed and gawking. He straightened up and snapped to semi-attention. "Sir," he appended belatedly.

Cai shook his head and grinned. "Quint, this is Fallon."

"Oh, I knew that." He nodded at me. "I could have picked you out of a crowd at fifty paces, what with the way Cai here's gone on about y—" Cai elbowed him in the ribs, sharply enough that Quintus must have felt it through the shirt of ring mail he wore, and his jaw snapped shut. "What I mean is," he continued after a moment, "I'm pleased to make your acquaintance. Your reputation in the arena precedes you, Victrix."

I would have responded, but his attention had drifted right back after Elka, so I turned to Cai instead. "Your father was here visiting only a week ago," I said. "He never mentioned you were coming home."

Cai shook his head. "He didn't know at the time. It's not exactly a scheduled return." I frowned at him in confusion, but he handily shifted the subject, saying, "How about that dance? I'm saddle-weary and could use the exercise to loosen up my muscles."

He gestured me over to the practice pitch and reached up to unfasten the crimson cloak that hung from his shoulders. It was then that I noticed Cai wore not one gladius but two. His sword belt bore a sheath on *both* hips. *Dimachaerus*—fighting with two swords at the same time, one in each hand—was definitely not standard fighting procedure in the legions. But it was the way *I* had chosen to fight in the arena.

I raised an eyebrow at Cai, but he just grinned.

The very first time he and I had sparred it had been with single blades—wooden ones—and he'd offered me the use of a shield. I'd foolishly declined, given him the advantage, and he'd trounced my sorry carcass soundly all over the pitch . . . right up until the moment when a last, lucky blow had given me the win. And him, a broken rib. This time, I would be the one starting out with the advantage—double swords were, after all, my chosen weapons—but I had no illusions that would necessarily mean I'd win again.

Just as Cai—with *his* advantage—hadn't, that first time.

At the first moment of engagement, I could tell Cai wasn't about to pull any of his blows or go easy on me.

Good.

Because neither would I.

He was a seasoned soldier, trained and hardened in actual battle. And he was very skilled. As the sun climbed higher into the sky, the sweat was running into my eyes, blurring my vision as we chased each other back and forth across the practice pitch. The scarlet plume of Cai's helmet crest tossed like the mane of a stallion as he came toward me, aiming alternating blows at my head and hips, side to side in a familiar sequence that I suspected he must have learned from watching me practice. Which meant I could counter his moves almost without thinking . . .

Until I couldn't.

I heard myself shout in surprise as Cai suddenly broke the pattern and ducked low, bringing both his blades up in a sweeping right-side attack that screeched along the length of my frantically blocking blades. He let the momentum of that carry him around in a full circle and came at me again, slashing straight across with a single blade from the left. I felt the wind of the weapon's passage on my skin at the near miss and backed off a step, tracking the angle of his shoulders to anticipate the next blow. Both swords again this time—circling overhead. I crossed my blades high in front of me and braced for the blow. When it came, I felt it all the way down into the soles of my feet, and sparks flew from the edges of our clashing weapons.

Every muscle in my body strained to keep those swords at bay.

I blinked rapidly, trying to clear the sting of sweat from my eyes, and looked up into Cai's smiling face.

"I've been practicing," he said.

"I noticed." I grinned back at him through clenched teeth.

"How's my form?"

"Very nice," I said.

Then I shifted forward and tipped my top guard on a sharp angle—a dimachaerus-specific move I'd worked hard on perfecting. Cai's blades slid past my shoulder as he lost his balance, falling toward me. He caught himself a moment too late and found the tips of my blades resting in the hollow at the base of his throat.

I leaned in close and whispered, "But your *technique* needs work."

Cai laughed and said, "Then I've come to the right place."

He held his blades out to the side, dangling from his fingertips, in a gesture of surrender. I stepped back and crossed my swords in front to me in salute, smiling, sweaty, ridiculously happy. Cai sheathed his blades in the double-scabbard belt he wore around his waist and reached up to lift his helmet off his head. I looked around to see that we were alone in the courtyard. The sun was high overhead, and it seemed everyone else had wandered indoors, out of the heat, and left us to our sparring. Cai scrubbed a palm over his sweat-damp legion-short hair.

"The dimachaerus style is a challenge, I admit," he said. "But I wanted to be able to spar with you the way you like to fight, Fallon. As you say, I need work. But I was hoping you might find the time—"

That was as far as he got before I lunged at him, reaching up to pull his head down toward me, and silencing him with the kiss I'd been waiting on for months. And *months . . .*

From his reaction, it seemed he'd been waiting on it too. I felt a rumbling in his chest that was almost a growl, and his mouth opened hungrily on mine. His arms wrapped around me and he lifted me off the ground. He smelled of horse and iron and leather and he tasted of salt and sunshine.

"Never seen anyone fight with their lips like that," Elka called out as she passed through one archway and out another, in a perfect example of terrible timing.

I groaned. It seemed we'd have to wait a bit longer to make up for all those months apart. Cai put me back down on my feet, and I reluctantly disentangled myself from his embrace. As I turned to glare daggers in Elka's direction, I saw Cai's friend, Quintus, following in her wake, just far enough behind that Elka hadn't yet noticed him.

I shook my head in amusement.

"He's an ass." Cai sighed, watching him go. "But he's a loyal ass. And a good soldier."

"Elka will take him apart, you know," I said.

Cai grinned wickedly. "Piece by piece. That should keep the two of them occupied for a while and give us some time alone." Then he looked at me wordlessly, his mouth opening and closing, as if he was suddenly uncertain what to say. "I've missed you, Fallon . . ."

I started to tell him I'd missed him too—so very much—but then Kronos, the fight master, appeared at the far end of the pitch to shout my name. I'd forgotten that I was on weapons-check duty that day. In truth, I'd forgotten everything except for Cai standing in front of me. But there was an entire shed full of swords and shields that needed inspection, checking for loosened tangs and dulled edges and fraying leather strapping. It would take me the better part of the afternoon.

"Go," Cai said with a rueful smile. "I need to deliver Caesar's deed to the Lanista, anyway."

"You mean—"

"That's the official reason I'm here," he said. "And one of the most pleasant duties I've been privileged to perform as Caesar's errand boy."

"Cai, that's . . . that's *wonderful!*"

I held myself back from hugging him again, because there were others now drifting back onto the pitch from the dining hall. I could sense one of the Ludus Amazona guards staring at us from behind his helmet grate, and the last thing I needed was to cause a scene and start rumors about lax discipline and loose morals at the Achillea school. Sorcha would have my hide—especially now that the ludus was about to become finally, fully hers. And hers alone.

I stepped back, politely inclining my head and letting my hair fall forward so I could smile at Cai without anyone else taking note. "I'll see you at the evening meal then, decurion?"

"And after," Cai murmured. "I hope."

IV

IT'S POSSIBLE I might have taken a bit longer than usual dressing for dinner that evening. Normally, I wouldn't trouble myself much beyond washing my face and hands and making sure whatever tunic I was wearing wasn't torn or stained too badly. Which was probably why Ajani glanced at me sideways when I arrived at the mess hall with my hair combed out and wearing a fresh, fine wool tunic bordered in a blue wave pattern and belted with my good leather cincher.

"I wouldn't have thought the Amazona girls warranted such finery," she said as I sat down beside her with a platter of cheese and meat.

"They don't," Elka chimed in, reaching across the table to pilfer a bunch of grapes off Ajani's plate. "*He* does."

She nodded in the direction of Cai and his soldier companions, who'd just stepped through the door at the other

end of the hall. It was with a degree of extravagant casual-
ness that Cai threaded his way through the rows of long
tables with his platter and mug, Quint and the legionnaire
whose name, I'd learned, was Tullius following him.

"May we join you, ladies?" Cai asked the table at large.

I murmured assent with my eyes on my plate as the
others nodded and laughed, shifting down the bench to
make room for them. Cai sat across from me, beside Elka,
and I had to force myself to concentrate on eating and not
distractedly stabbing my hand instead of my food, as I felt
his gaze warming my skin. The girls crowded in, eagerly
asking Cai and his companions all sorts of questions about
the campaign and Hispania.

"I hear the girls there are beautiful," Elka said, nudging
my shin under the table and smirking.

"They are as nothing compared to *you* divine nymphs,"
Quint enthused and then went on to wax poetic until Gratia
lobbed a hard roll at his head and informed him that *she*
was from Hispania.

As the girls hooted with laughter, I leaned in toward
Cai. "In all seriousness," I said, "what in the world are *you*
doing here if Caesar's legions are still on campaign? And
before you say 'Caesar's errand boy' again, don't. I'm sure
he has couriers aplenty."

Cai hesitated, but Quint joined in our conversation,
adding, "And it *wasn't* as if you were in the consul's tent
for the whole of a dinner hour begging on bended knee for
the job, after all."

I regarded him warily. "You didn't beg."

Cai rolled an eye at his friend. "Pleaded a little," he said. "Maybe. But I stayed standing the whole time, I assure you."

Quint laughed and reached for a slab of thick bread and slathered it with honey, saying, "And then, when Caesar agreed—just to spare his dignity, I'm sure—my good friend Caius did *me* the unkindness of dragging me along for the ride."

"Unkindness?" I asked.

"Tall, blonde, leggy unkindness," he sighed and stuffed the bread into his mouth, gazing off where Elka had gone to fill her plate for the second time. "She won't even look my way," he complained through his chewing.

"Try throwing something heavy at her head," I suggested. "That usually gets her attention."

Quint considered that a for moment. Then he tossed the rest of the bread onto his platter and stood, picking up a stout clay mug half-full of beer. "Worth a go," he muttered as he downed the rest of the beer, hitched up his sword belt, and strode determinedly in her direction.

I blinked and turned my attention back to Cai.

"It's getting late in the day for traveling," I said, trying not to sound too hopeful.

"And accommodations around here are scarce, I know. Quint and Tully and I are lodging in the stables tonight." He grinned ruefully. "I almost suggested we could double up in a select few of the gladiatrix barracks, but it seems your Lanista is still a strict arbiter of your virtue and—"

It was a particularly opportune moment for Sorcha to pass by. Cai cleared his throat loudly as she shot him a death glare.

"—*and* rightly so," he continued with a stern frown.

She rolled her eyes, gave me a pointed glance, and continued on her way.

"Will you be staying here for a few days, at least?" I asked.

He shook his head. "We leave with first light in the morning."

I felt my heart sink.

"My father is anxious to have me back," Cai explained, shrugging helplessly. "Once he found out I was headed here, he sent word to me on the road. And, well, he can be quite . . . insistent."

"Of course," I said, biting down on my disappointment.

"He's due to leave for Brundisium on the eastern coast in a week," Cai said. "From there, he takes a ship to Greece as part of a key trade delegation. It's why he's so adamant about seeing me. He'll be gone for several months. Otherwise, I would—"

"It's all right," I said, shaking my head. "You don't have to explain. I know how much he's missed you . . ."

"He's not the only one, I hope."

The look on Cai's face in that moment made me want to crawl over the table to get to him. The noise of the dining hall drifted into a muffled background murmur, and I let myself drown for a moment in the warmth of his gaze. I didn't even notice that our hands had reached across the table, fingertips touching, until I sensed we were being stared at.

I'm not even sure what it was that made me look away from Cai, but in the constant motion of the crowded hall, there was a dark stillness that drew my attention. I glanced up to see one of the Amazona guards standing near a pillar, the blackness of his armor and uniform like an ink stain on white wool, and his eyes focused on me and Cai—on our reaching hands—like a falcon spying a field mouse.

I pulled my hand away, simmering with frustration. Cai would be gone in the morning, and there was nothing I could do about it in the meantime. Even the sound of crockery shattering and Elka's voice rising above all the others as she let lose a string of invective in her native tongue from somewhere on the other side of the hall couldn't distract me from the ache in my chest as Cai and Tully rose to go collect their companion and rescue him from a gladiatrix's ire.

Later that night, there was a knock on my door. So quiet I almost didn't hear it.

Then it came again. And the soft whisper of my name.

I opened the door to see Cai standing there, grinning. He put a finger to my lips and, plucking my cloak from the peg on the back of my door, whispered, "Bring the light."

The glow from my oath lamp carved Cai's face into stark planes and sleek curves, and the flame danced, reflected in his eyes, sparking off the flecks of gold suspended in his clear hazel gaze. He led me by the hand out into the formal gardens of the ludus, down a winding path that led to a grove surrounding a little hidden clearing with a stone bench. There was a small clay amphora of wine and two glass goblets waiting for us on the bench, along with a platter of cheese and grapes.

"What about the ludus guards?" I said, glancing around as if they were lurking in the shadows beneath the trees at that very moment. "We still have rules, you know."

"Oh, aye . . ." Cai tugged me forward. "But what the guards don't know won't hurt them."

A thrill of excitement shivered up my spine. It occurred to me that I really wasn't used to having fun. Swinging swords day after day held its own kind of satisfaction, but it wasn't exactly what I would have called a good time.

"What if they come this way?" I asked, feeling a flush in my cheeks.

"They won't," he said. "They're a bit busy at the moment."

"Doing what?"

"Losing their week's wages to Quint at dice." Cai laughed at my expression. "Never gamble with a Corsican. Especially one as devious as him."

"I have a feeling *he's* not the truly devious one. You put him up to this?"

"I asked a favor. Now come here. Let's not waste it."

I felt myself smiling as Cai plucked the lamp from my fingers and placed it on the bench to illuminate our midnight repast. This was the place where we'd come a fingerbreadth away from sharing our first kiss on the night of my oath swearing. This time, there was no near miss.

The shadows beneath the tall cedar trees circled us like a dance of phantoms as Cai lowered his face to mine and kissed me on the mouth. I felt myself melting into his embrace as my arms circled around his neck. The night was warm and fragrant and wrapped around us as we wrapped around each other and sank slowly to the soft grass, the call of a nightingale soaring high over our heads in the darkness.

My hand slipped beneath the short sleeves of Cai's tunic and up over his shoulder. His, traveling the outside length of my thigh, traced the curve of my hip up past the hem of my tunic skirt. We both broke out into gooseflesh, shivering at one another's touch . . . and then his hand stopped moving at almost the exact same moment mine did.

Cai's lips pulled away from my mouth, and he opened his eyes.

"What's this?" he asked, tapping a finger against my skin.

"I was about to ask you the same thing," I answered.

My fingers rested on a raised ridge of flesh that crested the curve of his shoulder and felt puckered at the edges. *His* hand rested likewise on the scar of a recently healed wound I'd received in a bout with a gladiatrix from a new ludus that had recently begun operations on the outskirts of a coastal town north of us called Tarquinii. They'd held a day of games to celebrate the opening of the fledgling academy, and I'd sparred with a girl who'd fought *retiarius*. A less experienced fighter than I was, maybe, but I suspected that she'd grown up spearfishing; she tagged me soundly with her trident. One of the weapon's three tines had sliced up under the leather straps of my battle kilt and left a gash that had thankfully been longer than it was deep. Heron had used the opportunity to teach Neferet how to sew a wound closed using sinew thread. I had passed out only once while she practiced her handiwork—more from the sensation of the needle tugging thread through my flesh than any actual pain, because Heron's potions had already ensured I would feel none of that.

I'd almost forgotten about the incident. It was nothing—a day in the life of a gladiatrix—but I knew Cai wouldn't see it that way. He reached past me for the lamp and brought it down so he could get a closer look at my hip, hissing through his teeth when he saw the scar. When he looked back up at me, his expression had clouded over.

"It's *just* a flesh wound," I said, tugging down my hem. "No damage to the muscle, and no infection. I limped for a week or two—that's *all*. And I *won* that bout!"

"I don't like the thought of you getting hurt in the arena," he said.

I snorted. "We have that in common, believe me."

Cai opened his mouth and the look in his eyes told me I was in for a stern lecture—which I forestalled immediately. "Unh!" I exclaimed and tapped his shoulder. "I showed you mine. Now let me see yours."

He seemed rather more reluctant to share, and when he finally tugged aside his sleeve, I understood why.

"Lugh's teeth, Cai!" I gasped. "You look like you were attacked by a bear!"

I was more than a little surprised when he started to laugh. "I was."

"*What?*"

He nodded ruefully.

"We were on a march through a thick forest," he explained. "The troops were strung out in a narrow, tree-choked pass. I was mounted and checking the rear for any stragglers when I had the misfortune of coming between a mother bear and her cub. I've been convalescing for the past month. You might have won *your* bout, but I wasn't quite so lucky with *mine*. Then again, the old sow wasn't really fighting fair, but she definitely walked away from that bout the champion. I was just lucky that Quintus circled back to find me when my horse suddenly bolted past him, riderless."

"Oh, *Cai* . . ."

The scars—three long parallel gashes—were still a bit livid, with ragged edges, and I could see the suture holes from where they'd sewn him up. Neferet had done a far neater job on me, I thought, than the army doctors had on Cai. Mind, I hadn't been mauled by *claws*.

"Does it still hurt?"

He shrugged the material back down over his shoulder, stifling a wince. "It's made it . . . challenging." He frowned a bit. "I can still ride and swing a sword. But in a standing fight I'm useless in formation unless I can hold a shield. And I'm not quite up to that yet."

That didn't surprise me. A *scutum*—the standard-issue legion shield—was a great heavy rectangular thing that covered a man from shins to shoulders. In a fight against a tribe of angry Gauls hurling javelins and fireballs, I would have cheerfully hidden behind one, but it took a deal of brute strength to use one properly. Gratia and Damya were fine with scuta, but I found the things awkward and near impossible to use.

I moved to pull my hand away, but Cai reached up and held it there, pressing my palm against the scar through the material of his tunic.

"The strength returns," he continued. "Only slowly, and I'm a little less limber on that side. I decided I would try to make myself useful in other ways and requested this courier duty. Caesar agreed that his legions would somehow muster up the strength to soldier on without me and gave me the assignment to carry his papers to the Lanista. On the journey, I started practicing some basic dimachaerus sequences."

"So that's it."

"To help build my strength back up . . . and in case I can't return to regular soldiering." A shadow passed over his face. I thought about what that prospect might be like. It would be like my not being able to return to the arena.

"You'll be fine," I said. "It's just a scar."

He ran his fingertip over my hip again. "Like this one?"

I nodded. "Or . . ."—I reached up to pull aside the shoulder of my tunic and swung my hair out of the way so he could see my shoulder—". . . this one."

I heard Cai make a small noise in the back of his throat as he traced the line of another scar. One of a pair of faded white lines, all that was left of some particularly nasty welts acquired during an encounter with Nyx's whip. No permanent damage, but the marks had refused to fade, as if to perpetually remind me of my rival, even long after she'd gone.

Only Nyx was the *last* thing I was thinking of as Cai leaned down to kiss the scar and sent a wave of searing heat washing over my whole body, head to toe. When he lifted his head, his eyes glinted wickedly at me.

"There's another one just like it on the other side," I whispered, my voice gone husky.

Cai brushed my hair away from my other shoulder and kissed the second scar. "You're acquiring quite a collection," he murmured against my neck.

"Me?" I said, a bit breathless. "Do you mean to tell me that the only adversary who ever left a mark on *you* was a bear?"

"Oh no . . ." He grinned. "See, here, these marks on my knuckles."

"I see."

"First fistfight I ever got in. It was with a wall . . ."

"A fierce opponent, no doubt." I lifted his hand and, just as he had done, kissed the pale marks one by one. I felt his fingers tighten convulsively on mine and smiled. "Is that all?"

"No . . ." He showed me a long thin line running the length of his right forearm. "That was from a tribal rebellion on the Germanic frontier. My first real engagement. Now that I recall, I think that warrior had worse breath than the bear."

He was trying to keep his tone light, I could tell, but his voice grew ragged as I dropped a line of kisses all the way along that scar.

"And is that the extent of your wounds?" I asked.

"Well . . . you have yet to leave a *visible* mark on me." He moved closer. So close our noses were almost touching. "But I've a rib that aches in wet weather, thanks to you. And a deeper ache"—he grasped my hand and pressed it to the center of his chest—"here."

I could feel his heart pounding beneath my palm, strong and steady.

"Have you asked your army physicians about it?" I whispered. "It might be something serious . . ."

"I think it's definitely serious. Probably fatal if left untreated."

If by treatment he meant kissing, then I suspected he'd more than survive the next few moments at least . . .

Or maybe not.

Thanks to Quintus the second.

Cai and I were far too occupied to hear him right away, but eventually his throat-clearing and gravel-crunching caught at the edge of Cai's attention, and I suddenly found myself kissing air.

"Quint!" Cai rose to his feet and stalked toward his friend. "What in Hades are you doing here?"

I stood too, tugging my tunic straight and smoothing my hair, trying unsuccessfully not to blush furiously. Quint tossed me a wave over Cai's shoulder.

"Game ended earlier than expected," he said.

"What happened?" Cai asked.

"I'm a *good* gambler." Quint shrugged apologetically. "I won all their money. Faster'n I expected. I offered to keep playing for fun, but by that time they were rather drunk and cranky and declined the generosity."

"Drunk?" I raised an eyebrow at him. "Sorcha's men?"

"*That's* why I'm such a good gambler," he explained. "I kept pouring them wine and me water—just enough to get them a bit wooly in the head—and it makes for much better odds."

"A little *too* good in this case." Cai frowned at him.

"Sorry." Quint offered him a rueful grin. "At any rate, they're all back out on patrol and probably looking for someone *else's* night to ruin. So if I were you, I'd escort the lovely gladiatrix to her quarters and get yourself back to ours. Me, I'm going to make myself scarce until morning."

Cai sighed heavily and picked up the jug of wine we hadn't even gotten around to opening. "For your troubles," he said and tossed it to Quint. "Such as they were."

Quint caught it deftly and tucked it under his arm, chuckling. Then he threw us a salute as he loped off into the darkness. Cai packed away the goblets and platter into a linen sack and slung it over his good shoulder. He held out his hands to me, and I stepped into the circle of his embrace.

"I wish your father didn't want you back so soon, even if I understand now why he does." I shook my head at him and ran my fingers over his tunic where it covered the claw scars on his shoulder.

Cai rolled his eyes. "He worries too much."

"He's right to do so."

"I'm just hoping he didn't go and sacrifice a white bull to the healer god Aesculapius or anything so ridiculous . . ."

He made light of it, but I knew that in his heart, Cai revered his father. Decimus Varro was like a Roman version of my father, Virico. Both big, strong, handsome men, devoted to their families and used to being in command. The senator had been a hero in the legions in his youth, and his son aspired to be just like him in much the same way that, growing up, I had aspired to be like my mother and my sister. I thought of my own father then, and how he had done all the wrong things to try to keep me safe. I'd come to accept that my father's actions had come from a place of love, but at the time they had wounded me deeply. I was glad for Cai that his father seemed to be rather less destructive in his overprotective tendencies.

"He just wants to see for himself that I'm still in one piece." Cai reached for both my hands, clutching them tight to his chest. "And then he'll be off to Brundisium and away on his trade mission, and I'll be back here at the ludus before you know it."

"Of course you will." I leaned in to him. "You need my help with your technique."

His eyes flashed and he bent his head to kiss me. A long, slow, teasing kiss that made my lips tingle and turned my skin to fireflies and feathers.

"I look forward to our practice bouts," he murmured.

I was virtually breathless but managed a raspy "So do I . . ." in response before he stepped back and, glancing around to make sure there were no guards to see us, led me back toward the main buildings of the compound. He kissed me one last time at the fork in the path that led one way to the gladiatrix barracks, the other to the stables.

My bed one way, and his the other.

In that moment, I was suddenly, painfully aware that there was still a sharp divide between someone like Cai and someone like me—like the person I'd become. Somewhere deep inside, the Cantii princess stirred to life and protested that she should, by all rights, be sleeping where—and with whom—she damned well pleased. The gladiatrix told her to shush and be proud of her place as an equal among her sister warriors, with the freedom to stay or go *and* the obligation to abide by the same rules if she stayed. Even in Sorcha's new order, that was the way things would remain. I'd have to learn to accept that, as long as I remained an Achillea gladiatrix. Which, because of my deal with Caesar, was for the foreseeable future. I sighed, and Cai seemed to sense what I was thinking.

He wrapped his arms around me and kissed the top of my head. "One day," he murmured. "One day, I will have you all to myself for as long as you'll let me, Fallon. No rules, no ranks, no campaigns or competitions or other people's ideas of what should or shouldn't be to come between us. No decurion and gladiatrix, no slave and soldier—or even princess and patrician—just us."

"Just Cai and Fallon." I sighed. "I like the sound of that."

"And we'll each leave our weapons behind."

"Now you're just being silly."

He looked down at me and grinned. "You're right. But that day will come. I know it in the core of my heart. For now? Sleep." A last lingering kiss. "Dream of your fierce goddess, dream of me, and keep a blade tucked under your pillow just in case you get into a fight with either one of us."

V

WRAPPED IN THE memory of Cai's embrace, I fell back on my bed and drifted off to sleep. In hindsight, maybe I *should* have put a blade under my pillow that night, like he said. Maybe such a talisman would have warded away the disaster that was to come, heralded—as Cai had unwittingly predicted—by a dream.

In my dream, I wandered through a hazy portal and found myself standing in the fragrant and manicured courtyard garden of the Ludus Achillea. The statue of Minerva, Roman goddess of battle, stood motionless in the moonlight, pale and perfect. But that night as I approached her in my dream, something was different. When I stepped closer, my bare feet making no sound on the pebbled path, I saw that it wasn't Minerva at all who stood there. It was my sister, Sorcha. And she wasn't dressed in the helmet and stola of the Roman goddess but, instead, she appeared in the guise of the Morrigan, dressed in a long cloak of feathers that swept the ground. No, I thought. Not feathers . . .

Iron.

Her cloak was made of dagger blades. They rang like chimes as she lifted her arms and the cloak fell away. In the moonlight, the blood that dripped from them was black. And then I saw, sitting crouched at my sister's feet, Uathach. My first fight. My first kill. I hadn't dreamt of her in months.

The Fury lifted her head. She smiled up at me. And then down at the body that lay, wrapped in the folds of what looked like a toga with a wide purple stripe. No. Not purple . . . red.

"Victrix," she said in her raven's-croak voice.

And then one other word that made my blood run cold.

"Vengeance."

I bolted awake, soaked in sweat and wondering why the light from my oath lamp was crimson. But then I realized that it wasn't my lamp. It was the light coming through my window. And then I heard it—the sound of horses screaming.

The stables were on fire.

The stables where Cai and his two friends were sleeping.

I threw on a cloak and ran down the hall, pounding on the doors of the other girls' rooms as I ran. Servants were already stumbling out into the yard by the time I got there, half-asleep and calling for buckets and water. Cai was there too, leading a pair of horses from the stalls under the pall of smoke, and I gasped with relief at the sight of him. When I glanced over my shoulder, I saw that most of the other girls had come running from the barracks behind me.

I hurried to untie the donkey from his post in the yard and saw Antonia lugging a heavy pail of water with her one hand across the yard. Cai ran by with another pair of terrified chariot ponies, Quint and Tully following right behind with more. Then Kronos was there, directing the kitchen staff to form a bucket line, but I couldn't see Thalestris anywhere. Elka ran past, blonde hair streaming on the wind, as she hurried from stall to stall, throwing open the doors to let the panicked horses out. I saw Neferet carrying a wicker cage that held a squawking young raven—once nailed to my door in an attempt to frighten me—that she'd nursed back to health and kept as a pet in the barn. My mind flashed back to the dream. My sister wearing a cloak of iron raven's feathers . . .

Sorcha was nowhere in sight.

"Go!" Kronos shouted when he saw me. "Find the Lanista!"

My heart in my throat, I ran for the main house.

As I pounded up the path, I noticed out of the corner of my eye that the guest barracks, in the far west quadrant of the compound, were eerily silent and dark. When I reached Sorcha's chambers, I found the place had been wrecked. Couches and tables were overturned, goblets smashed, and oil lamps spilled and smoldering on the finely woven rugs. Scrolls and the copper tubes they were stored in were scattered everywhere. One tube had the wax seal destroyed and was lying on her desk, empty. The tapestry of Achilles and Penthesilea on the wall had been torn in half, leaving only the dying Amazon queen hanging to stare down impassively at a pool of blood that was spreading in a slow creep across the tiled floor.

And Sorcha was gone.

I turned and bolted back out the door, a horrible foreboding writhing in my stomach like a nest of snakes. Back out in the courtyard of the ludus, it was chaos. Firelit darkness and shrieks, human and animal, tore the night air. On the sentry walkway that ran along the top of the compound's outer wall, I saw figures dressed in black cloaks and helmets. The guards from the Ludus Amazona. For a confused moment, I thought they were helping defend us from attack . . .

But then I saw that the front gate was already open.

And the guards were faced inward, their weapons trained on us.

On my friends, my fellow warriors, some of whom lay bleeding on the ground, while others fought fiercely— most of them barehanded—against the girls of the Ludus Amazona, who were all dressed in dark tunics and armed to the teeth. My mind reeled in confusion at the betrayal. The ludus *had* been attacked, I thought, but like the old tale of the Trojan horse, the enemy had come from within. And opened the door to our downfall.

There was an unfamiliar chariot standing just inside the outer courtyard, and I knew, instinctively, who it belonged to. I didn't even need to turn to see him stalking the perimeter of the chaotic scene to know he was there. I could feel his presence like a cold, oily fog, poisoning the air. Pontius Aquila. The Collector. My mind flashed back to that horrible night at the Domus Corvinus, to the memory of the men in black masks devouring the heart of a fallen gladiator in the caverns beneath Aquila's mansion, and I felt the bottom drop out of my stomach.

The only thing other than Aquila's presence that could have made this night as terrible as that one was . . .

"Gladiatrices!"

A familiar female voice, harsh and harrowing like the shriek of an angry crow, rang out in the darkness.

Nyx.

As if conjured out of the night by my very thoughts, Nyx leaped down from the sentry walk, cloak spread wide—darkness against the dark sky—like the Raven of Nightmares to land in the courtyard not thirty paces from me. In one hand, she carried the chariot whip she'd once used as a weapon against me. The braided leather rope hissed along the ground in her wake, writhing and twitching like a venomous serpent. One by one, the Achillea girls turned to stare, uncomprehending, at the girl who'd once been one of us.

"Rebels!" she continued, cracking her whip. "I call upon you to throw down your weapons!"

What rebels? What weapons?

The alarm raised by the barn fire had brought us all tumbling out of our beds and into the night without a thought to reach for swords and spears first. Which, I realized, had likely been the point of that blaze. The Amazona girls and their guards were armed, to be sure, but the only ones from *our* ludus who'd had weapons at the ready were the night watch. And they all—to a man—lay dead upon the ground. Nyx, as she spoke, was obliged to step over a prone body as she made her way toward us.

I wondered if Quint's gambling and drinking had dulled their reactions.

I wondered if Cai and I were to blame . . .

I glanced around wildly for him then and saw Cai standing with Quint and Tully, all three of them with soot-blackened faces from leading the horses to safety. Four of the Amazona guards prodded them forward to join the defeated clump of gladiatrices at the center of the yard, and Quint suddenly lunged for one of the guard's weapons. I gasped in horror as an archer up on the sentry walk spun and aimed, loosing an arrow, at the same time as Cai shouted for Quint to stop and threw himself forward in a tackle that brought his second in command to the ground. The arrow grazed past Quint's cheek . . . and lodged in the breast of legionnaire Tullius, who was right behind him and never saw it coming.

All Tully had time for was a moment of surprise before he sank to his knees and toppled forward motionless onto the ground. The look on Cai's face as he slowly got to his feet spoke murder. He glared at the man who stood framed by the archway that led to the main house, draped in a toga of indigo-dyed wool.

On the ludus circuit, he was known as the Collector, for his rapacious drive to own only the best fighters. I knew him as the leader of the Sons of Dis, a depraved and cult-ish secret society dedicated to the sacrificial worship of a god of the Underworld. The rest of the Republic, blissfully ignorant, knew him as the respected citizen and politician, Tribune of the Plebs, Pontius Aquila.

Heron and Kronos, along with the domestic staff, were nearest to him as he came forward. They gaped at the Tribune in disbelief as he strolled at a languid pace into the chaos of the courtyard, looking as if he owned the place.

We were about to learn, to our horror, that he did.

"It pains me," Aquila said, in a voice loud enough to be heard by all, "the circumstances that dictate the manner in which I must now present myself to you."

"And what manner is that?" Heron asked.

"This ludus," Aquila continued, "is an extremely valu-able asset to the Republic. A treasured facility wherein you"—he gestured to the ragged, angry gathering of glad-iatrices—"who should be joyful servants of the citizens of Rome, have learned and honed your craft. Rome needs you, ladies. Rome treasures your ongoing contribution to her vital and vibrant culture. You are to be safeguarded. But you have clearly been led astray and therefore must also be instructed in the errors of your ways . . . and reha-bilitated accordingly."

"What in Hades are you talking about?" Kronos snarled. "What errors?"

Aquila regarded him with a studied expression of mild disdain. "Why, this rebellion, of course."

"*Rebellion?*" Heron was aghast. "Are you mad?"

"Have a care, physician," Aquila warned, glaring at Heron down the length of his nose. "It is clear to me that there has been an attempted revolt at this ludus." He gestured at the lot of us standing there in sleeping shifts and bare feet, weaponless, defenseless . . . vulnerable. If *this* was his idea of a revolt, it was the furthest thing from the meaning of the word as I'd learned it.

And where in the wide world was Sorcha to refute such a ridiculous claim? I felt a sharp twist of fear in my guts and tried to tell myself the blood on the floor of her quarters didn't mean what I thought it might . . .

"I am here to tell you," he continued, as if we weren't all staring at him like he was speaking Germanic, "in no uncertain terms that the Republic will brook no Spartacus-inspired rebellion. The Servile Wars are still fresh in the memories of loyal Romans and will *not* be repeated as long as there is breath in my body."

The look on Kronos's face told me that he would cheerfully arrange for that not to be an issue if he could. "What exactly brought you out this way, Tribune?" he asked, barely leashing the anger in his voice.

"A simple errand to escort my own fine warriors home in the wake of their performance at Cleopatra's naumachia."

His mouth twisted as he spoke the Aegyptian queen's name, as though he tasted something bitter on his tongue. And how convenient, I thought, that he just happened to have a contingent of archers with him for his "simple errand."

"Fortuitous, really." Aquila shrugged. "I thank the gods they were here, and able to help quell this shameful uprising." His expression turned stern and stony. "Now, in the wake of the untimely demise of she who was Lanista of this ludus—"

The twist of fear tightened into a knot in my stomach.

"You're lying," I said, choking on the words that came out of my mouth. "She's *not* dead. She can't be! You're lying—"

"And what reason would I have to lie to you?" he said coldly. "Do you see the Lanista here among you?"

He spread his hands wide and turned in a slow circle, as if waiting for my sister to step out of the shadows. When she didn't, he shrugged and dropped his hands to his sides.

"Were the Lady Achillea alive," he continued, "I can assure you, I would be most happy to have her taken into custody for her obvious dereliction in the management of noble Caesar's facility." The word "noble" bent under the weight of Aquila's sneer. "But only the gods themselves know when—or even if—the Consul will return from the field, and so, in the interim . . ." He paused, seemingly for dramatic effect. ". . . I, Pontius Aquila, take due and rightful ownership of this facility and all those who reside within it. On behalf of the Republic, of course."

"You can't do that!" I cried.

"Who's to stop me?" he asked. "You?"

Sorcha . . .

But I had seen the blood in her wrecked scriptorium.

I glanced around wildly at the other girls, at the ludus trainers, at Heron, silently pleading for any one of them to tell me they'd seen my sister. That she was alive. Hurt, maybe. Hidden. But *alive!* Face after face told me the same thing. Everyone standing there knew Sorcha and knew that if there was even a single breath left in her body she would have been there. Fighting for us. That she never would have let this happen in the first place. All I saw in the eyes of my friends was the terrible realization that it *had* happened. And Sorcha wasn't there.

I felt a rush of blinding red rage wash over me and felt my fists clench into stones at my sides, all of my muscles tensing . . . But then I saw Cai staring at me, his own anger masked behind a warning expression, aimed pointedly at me. Tully was dead—right there at Cai's feet—the guards were dead, there were arrows trained on all of us, and we were utterly defenseless. I didn't care. No . . . I didn't *want* to care. But I had to.

The Ludus Achillea was more than just me. More than just Sorcha. And what would my sister do if *she* was the one standing there in that moment instead of me? I could almost hear her voice in my head: *Think first. Grieve later. Go down fighting only as a last resort.* I spun back around to face Aquila.

"I know you Romans," I spat, trying to think past my anger, past the cruel ache in my heart, to what Sorcha would have done and said. "I know how scraps of parchment bind you like blood oaths. And I know that even if something *has* happened to Achillea, then the ludus passes into the ownership of Thalestris!"

Heron gaped at me in surprise. But he was one of the Ludus Achillea's trusted administrators, and I saw in his face that he was fully aware of that provision in Sorcha's will too. He was simply astonished that *I* knew about it.

He took a step forward.

"The girl is correct, Tribune Aquila," he said. "I will vouch for it upon my soul's oath until such time as the document can be produced. With all respect, I must assert that the rightful ownership of this ludus passed from Julius Caesar to the Lady Achillea—the arrangements and transfers of monies finalized just this morning—and I myself have seen the further testament she herself signed, willing it unto Thalestris in the event that—"

"*This* testament?" Aquila interrupted, withdrawing a vellum scroll from a fold of his toga, as if he'd held it there in anticipation of such a challenge. "Ah. Yes . . ."

He unrolled the vellum with a snap of his wrist, and even in the darkness, I could see the bold black hand—words stroked across the document beneath my sister's careful script—that had been added to the document. There was a signature beneath it, and the blob of a wax seal. I recognized it as an imprint of a coin Thalestris wore around her neck on a chain, bearing the likeness of winged Nemesis. The goddess of vengeance.

My dream came back to me, and Uathach's voice whispered a dread warning in my mind. *Vengeance . . .*

"I believe, physician," Aquila continued, pleasantly conversational, "insofar as you are a learned man, you would find everything in order were you to read this document in full. Your former Lanista's legal—and *binding*—pledge that, in the event of her demise, the Ludus Achillea passes without limitation into the keeping of her primus pilus and longtime comrade, Thalestris the Amazon. And *here*"—he pointed to the heavier-handed script at the bottom of the document—"you would see Thalestris's subsequent—and *equally* binding—pledge to deliver those same goods and chattels over into *my* ownership for the sum total of one silver *denarius*. Which I paid the Amazon in full not more than half an hour ago."

"And where is Thalestris now?" Heron asked the Tribune, his gaze narrow and piercing.

"Who can say, really?" Aquila smiled thinly. "Probably halfway across Etruria by now, I dare say. Poor thing was utterly unnerved by the savagery of this attempted rebellion of yours."

Thalestris. Unnerved.

Impossible.

The only thing I could think—the only thing that made any sense—was that Thalestris, as fiercely loyal to my sister as she'd always been, was dead too. Pontius Aquila must have taken the seal from around her neck. Forged her signature or forced it from her hand before ending her life. My sister and her primus pilus—the two fiercest warriors I'd ever known—gone.

Aquila shrugged and carried on, weaving his ridiculous fiction as if rehearsing what he would say to the courts when he returned to Rome with Sorcha's will clutched tight in his grasping fingers. "Whilst my people subdued the uprising, Thalestris begged me to accept her offer in the hopes that I could restore order where she, tragically, could not. I graciously accepted, granted her clemency, and released her back into the wild." He uttered a brief laugh at his humorless joke, before his expression went flinty again. His eyes were black and bleak and hungry as his gaze raked over us where we stood, horrified. "The rest of you, however," he continued, "won't benefit from such leniency. You'll all need to learn the kind of respect and obedience toward me, as your new owner, that the Lady Achillea so very clearly neglected to instill in you."

I saw Heron grow pale.

This was no misunderstanding. No error of perception on Aquila's part that could be cleared up in a matter of moments with the right words from the right people. This was a runaway cart that had been set in motion a long time ago and had finally picked up enough speed to carry us all hurtling over a cliff. And while no one who was a passenger in that cart felt they deserved to be there, it was Lydia who was the first one to protest—by throwing the rest of us under the cart's wheels, as if there was a chance it could save her neck.

"I'm not one of them!" she suddenly blurted, lurching out into the center of the courtyard, wild-eyed, her hair waving in a cloud around her face.

"Lydia—"

"*Shut* up, Fallon!" She ran to Aquila, bare arms outstretched, her pleading shaded with a kind of desperate, wheedling flirtatiousness. "*She's* one of their leaders, you know—she's probably the one who murdered the Lanista! *I'm* loyal to the Republic!"

Pontius Aquila's gaze swept unblinking down upon her like she was a beggar in a back alley. Beneath contempt. I winced, sensing what would likely come next. Lydia seemed to sense it too. She was shallow, but she wasn't stupid.

She took a step back, eyes darting side to side, like a cornered animal.

"Nyx, my *dear* friend . . ." She turned her pleading to the girl who'd spent their time together treating Lydia more like a lackey than a dear friend. "You know I'm just like you. I'm on your side! Tell the Tribune—"

That was as far as she got.

The crack of leather echoed across the yard.

Lydia screamed and dropped to the ground as Nyx's whip caught her on the side of her face and blood poured onto the sand from between her fingers. I saw Gratia clamp a hand over her mouth as, between one breath and the next, the whip cracked again as it sliced across Lydia's shoulders, rending the fabric of her thin linen sleeping shift and drawing an arc of bright blood. She shrieked again in agony, and before I'd really thought about what I was doing, I put my head down and ran at Nyx.

When she'd been at the ludus, Nyx had been very good at dishing out punishment with a chariot whip. It seemed she'd gotten even better at it in the intervening months. But that was with a target more than an arm's length away. In close quarters, it was a useless weapon. If Nyx couldn't get a windup, she couldn't crack the whip to devastating effect, and that was what I was counting on. I ducked under her arm and tackled her to the ground.

I'd thought only to keep her from killing Lydia. I hadn't anticipated what would happen next: Nyx went utterly mad. I heard her growl like an animal as she thrashed beneath me. She brandished the heavy butt end of the whip like a club and caught me on the side of the head with it. Stars burst in front of my eyes, and I reeled back. Nyx was on her feet in an instant. The whip in her hand cracked again, the lash slapping viciously into the dirt beside me as I rolled frantically, half-blinded by the blow to my head. I tried to crawl, but Nyx slammed the whip across my back like a truncheon. Then again. And again.

How many nights had she lain awake, dreaming of the kind of revenge she would take on me for that moment in the arena? The moment when I'd ruined her life. I'm sure that's how she'd framed it in her mind.

I'd thought, at the time, that I'd been trying to *save* her life.

Did you really? a voice in my head asked, muted by red fog. *Or did you just want the satisfaction of seeing Nyx driven out of the one world she'd ever known? The only life she'd ever thrived in?*

Nyx didn't give me time to answer my own silent question.

A kick from her hobnailed boot lifted me off the ground and drove the breath from my lungs. I heard Cai shout and then the dull thud of a landed punch. Out of the corner of my eye, I saw two of Aquila's men dragging him back, semiconscious and struggling. My pulse roared in my ears. Nyx's boot made contact again, this time with my shoulder.

I think she'd been aiming for my head, but the kick went wide—a glancing blow, but still another burst of blooming pain. I clenched my hands into fists full of sand and threw it in her face, reaping curses—and a momentary reprieve—as my reward. It was enough so that I could scramble up to my knees and ready myself for her next attack.

But my only weapons were my fists. I made what use of them I could, and felt her nose crumple beneath my knuckles as we brawled. I'm not even sure she noticed. The blood flowed, painting the lower half of her face in a red mask.

"Where is my sister, damn you, Nyx?" I panted, grasping at the front of her tunic.

She grinned at me through red-painted teeth. "On her way to meet the Goddess."

"What happened to her?" I demanded, hauling her closer. A mistake.

"Did you know I never actually killed anyone in my time as a gladiatrix?" Nyx hissed, ignoring my question. "I'm starting to think that was an oversight . . ."

I'd been so focused on her whip, I'd failed to notice the short, sharp dagger she carried in her other hand. I don't think anyone else saw it either, but the shock of the knife blade piercing my side was like a sudden, heavy numbness. The icy-hot sensation that followed told me I was in trouble as I sank backward onto the ground. I expected Nyx would finish me off there and then. But, suddenly, I heard more shouting and looked up to see one of the black-clad Amazona guards hauling Nyx away—kicking and struggling, snarling through bared teeth like a rabid animal.

Pontius Aquila strode forward and backhanded her across the face, knocking some of the battle fury out of her. She glared up at him, panting.

"Control yourself, you wretched girl," he snapped. "Or you'll never see the inside of the arena again, and I'll assign *that* one's prodigious fate"—he jerked his chin at me—"to someone who deserves it."

That was enough to snap Nyx out of her rage completely. What was left behind in the expression on her face told me everything about her in that moment. When I'd first arrived at the ludus and Nyx had discovered the secret of who I was—that I was the long-lost sister of the Lady Achillea, the woman Nyx had devoted her mind and heart and considerable martial skills to since the day she'd been chosen to swear the oath—she'd been bent on my destruction. Not my humiliation, not my dishonor—my death. Achillea had been her hero. Her surrogate mother. Someone to aspire to emulate and make proud. And I had taken that away from her, just by showing up.

Under other circumstances, I might have felt sorry for Nyx. Because I'd grown up thinking exactly the same thing about Sorcha, and it had hollowed me out inside. Made me lose sight of the things that had been truly important to me. In that moment, however, the thing that was most important to me was that I was on my hands and knees, bleeding from a knife wound.

The pain had yet to fully register, and I clamped a hand to my side beneath the dark stuff of my cloak, hoping desperately that Pontius Aquila wouldn't notice that I was hurt.

The voice of the Morrigan hissed inside my head, whisper-ing a warning against showing weakness. I silently, fer-vently agreed. If he thought I was badly injured, the noble Tribune might just relent and let Nyx finish the job.

And I wouldn't be able to stop her.

Lydia still writhed on the ground, whimpering in agony, ignored by Aquila and his people, and I feared for what would happen to her once he remembered she was there.

I could feel the sweat breaking out across the back of my neck as I struggled to rise to my feet. The black-clad guards stood with weapons drawn in front of the clustered Achillea girls. Cai was pinned on the ground by one of the guards, his arm behind his back. There was blood at the corner of Cai's mouth, and his teeth were bared in a snarl.

I stood there, swaying, defiant, as Aquila gestured one of his men forward. Even with the feature-obscuring helmet he wore, I recognized him as one of the Ludus Achillea's former trainers—a thick-necked brute with bare arms that bore the scars of many fights, he was an ex-legion soldier named Ixion. Sorcha had dismissed him shortly after I'd arrived at the ludus because of his penchant for excessive violence. I'd thought at the time that, in a school where we were being trained to kill, that was saying something.

"This . . . gladiatrix needs some time alone, I think," Aquila said. "Take her somewhere quiet where she can clear her mind and ponder her future."

Ixion grunted and grabbed me by the arm. I shot a glance over my shoulder at Elka, whose face was rigid with fury, and shook my head. Cai had been right to warn me against action earlier. The only thing for me—for any of us—to do in that moment was cooperate. Defiance would come later. But only if we survived long enough. Dead or disabled, we were no good to each other. After a moment, Elka seemed to realize it too, and took a half step back.

I walked ahead of Ixion, one hand clamped to my wounded side, as he prodded me in the back with the butt of his sword. He steered me away from the barracks buildings and in the direction of the angry orange glow that still licked upward in the farthest corner of the ludus compound, where the stables still burned. He stopped when we reached a squat stone building that I'd never really given much thought to before that moment. I'd always assumed it was a storage shed for livestock fodder. There were steps dug down into the earth in front of the heavy ironbound door, and Ixion preceded me, producing a ring of keys from the worn leather pouch hanging at his belt.

My mouth went dry when I saw it. It had belonged to Thalestris.

So she really has left us, I thought.

Anguish for my sister surged through me again. And helplessness.

Ixion shuffled through Thalestris's keys until he found the one he wanted—a heavy black thing that looked like a claw—and inserted it in the lock. It uttered a groaning screech as he turned it, and the door swung ponderously open. He reached over, grabbed me by the shoulder, and wordlessly shoved me inside. I stumbled down another few shallow steps, gritting my teeth at the pain in my side, which had gone from dull throbbing to a searing burn. In the darkness, all I could see was a brief black corridor ahead, like a yawning maw waiting to swallow me. It terminated in a tiny cell, with a cage of bars for a door. My heart in my throat, I glanced over my shoulder at Ixion.

"I always wanted to lock one of you upstart bitches away to rot here in Tartarus," Ixion said, grinning. "Bloody shame this place was never made proper use of while Achillea was in charge."

Tartarus. Named after the mythical underworld dungeon.

I'd almost thought it was just a rumor. A thing to frighten the less tractable girls at the ludus into better behavior. Sorcha had never found the need to use Tartarus on anyone—not even Nyx—as a punitive measure. Not even me. Ixion reached for another key hanging on the wall outside the cell and opened the barred door. Wordlessly, he gestured me inside.

It was cold and dank, the air stale and heavy. The walls were rough-hewn stone, the floor dirt, and there was a single, tiny barred window smaller than my head set near the low ceiling that looked out onto a forgotten, weedy enclosure behind the stables. What *used* to be the stables.

Ixion pulled the cage door shut with a clang and hung the key back up, turning on his heel to disappear without a word. When he closed the outer door, I felt the tiny, tearing claws of panic begin to climb upward from the pit of my stomach, savaging the back of my throat. I swallowed hard to force the bile back down and shook my head to clear it.

First things first, Fallon, I thought.

Light from the guttering flames of the dying stable fire filtered through the tiny window, and in the dim orange glow, I pulled back my cloak and peered at the blood-soaked fabric of my sleeping tunic with a kind of shocked detachment. The tear in the material was small and neat— just the size of Nyx's knife blade—and I had to tear it and make it larger so I could get a good look at the wound she'd made.

Another small, neat hole. In my flesh.

I'd been wounded before—cuts, bruises, all manner of hurts that had healed and left the marks on my skin that Cai had so deliciously mapped earlier that night—and I knew that the immediate order of business was to stanch the flow of blood that still oozed. I didn't know how deep Nyx's blade had pierced or whether she had damaged anything vital. If that was the case—if there was organ damage—I was probably already dead and just didn't know it. But I wasn't coughing blood, and that was a good sign. I lifted the hem of my cloak and, with fumbling cold fingers, tore off a wide strip. Then I carefully bound that as tightly as I could about my torso, wrapping it as many times as it would go and securely tucking in the loose end. I was sweating and panting by the time I was finished.

But I wasn't dead. And I wasn't giving up.

Brave thoughts, as I wavered and leaned against the wall, sliding down to sit on the dirt floor, my knees tucked up for warmth. My eyelids drifted shut, and I don't know how long I stayed like that, a knotted lump of misery crouched in the darkness, before I heard a noise.

I looked up to see Pontius Aquila standing on the other side of the cage door. A single torch burned in a sconce on the wall, reflected in his dark gaze that was fixed upon me, unblinking. I don't know how long he'd been standing there, but when my gaze met his, he smiled—a reptilian stretching of his thin lips, devoid of warmth.

"There she is," he said. "My *genius* of the arena sands. My goddess muse of the blade and shield . . ."

I remembered back to the day I'd been sold in the Forum of Rome. When Sorcha had offered an exorbitant sum in order to wrest me from Aquila's clutches. I hadn't even known who—*what*—he was that day. I'd only known that I'd been instinctively, profoundly grateful that his bid had not won. I'd given thanks to the Morrigan and thought that she'd accepted it. That she'd shown me favor. Why then did the goddess see fit to punish me with this fate now?

Why take Sorcha from me and give me back to him?

"You're *my* Victrix now." Aquila took a step toward the bars, his eyes fever-bright.

Victrix. The name I'd borne so proudly since the Triumphs.

Was that it? I wondered. Had the Morrigan forsaken me because I'd pledged my warrior's gifts in service to Caesar?

To the enemy? I'd sought only to bring honor on the ludus. On my sister and myself. To help fulfill Sorcha's dream of creating a place where the girls I'd fought and bled with could choose for themselves the lives they wanted to lead. That I'd had to make a deal with Caesar to do it shouldn't have mattered, should it? I refused to believe that the goddess would consider him somehow more abhorrent than the man who stood before me . . . holding something in his hand. I squinted against the darkness to see what it was, and my blood ran cold in my veins. Between his manicured fingertips, Aquila held a single, slender feather wrought in silver. It gleamed red in the torchlight.

"What did you see?" Pontius Aquila's voice was soft and breathless with genuine curiosity. "That night, at my domus. What did you *see*, little raven?"

What had I seen? The memory of that night, even twisted and distorted by a swirling fog of mandrake wine, was burned into my soul. Ajax, the gladiator, lying on the stone table in the underground cavern. Men in feathered masks crowding around his split-open carcass, greedily devouring the heart that had beat so strongly within his chest only a handful of moments earlier. It must have still been warm as they put it on the scales dish to weigh it against a silver feather.

The same silver feather that Pontius Aquila held up for me to see. I shrank back from it, pressing myself into the farthest corner of the cell as he ran the feather back and forth across the bars of my cage. The metallic edge made a sound like strumming the strings of an out-of-tune lyre.

"Caesar doesn't know what he has in you," Aquila said. "If he did, he never would have given you the chance to win your freedom. Not even the glimmer of that hope. No. He is a fool. *I* am no fool. I see you. I see your spirit. The power you have . . ." His voice stretched tight and thin as he spoke, skirling higher with a kind of feverish intensity. "The touch of your blood goddess on your soul . . . I can *see* her mark on you. You were *born* to kill, Fallon ferch Virico . . ."

The shock of hearing my full royal name on Aquila's tongue filled me with a revulsion that must have shown on my face. Aquila took a step back from the cage bars, a sheen of sweat on his brow. He took a slow breath in through flaring nostrils, and his mouth quirked upward in an ugly smile.

"You're surprised that I know your name," he said. "I know all about you. More, perhaps, than you even know about yourself. I know how powerful you are . . ." He ran the feather back and forth across the bars of my cage again, drawing discordant music from the delicate silver thing. "And when you die," he continued, "I will take that power and I will make it my own."

"You'll have nothing of me that I do not give you willingly," I said through a tight-clenched jaw. "And that will never happen."

"Huh." The feather paused and Aquila turned his full, baleful gaze on me. "Even when that same generosity of spirit was once bestowed upon *you* in the arena? Tell me . . .what did it feel like when you ended the Fury's life?"

I swallowed hard against the flood of that memory, trying to will it away.

Aquila's gaze burned into me. "Did you feel the strength of her rage," he hissed, "the surge of her divine madness, flow from her body into yours?"

I looked away.

"It was a great gift she gave you. You felt that, I know. You had to have."

What I'd felt, in that moment, was sorrow. Regret.

And nothing else?

I fought silently to deny the memory and lost. My first kill—my only kill—was the woman who'd called herself Uathach. The "Terrible One." Everyone else had called her the Fury, and she had, in her dying moments after my swords had pierced her heart, pressed her hand to my breast—to *my* heart—and whispered words meant for my ears alone.

"It's yours now," she had murmured. *"Thank you . . ."*

She'd smiled. And then she was gone.

I'd tried to convince myself that I never truly understood what she'd meant. But I did. I knew exactly what she'd had given me. Death. Her death. My life, fueled by that victory, had hurtled forward from that moment on with all of the Fury's mad will to live free or die wrapped around me like invisible armor. She had given me a terrible gift even as I had relieved her of a terrible burden. Or was it the other way around?

"You understand," Aquila said. "I knew you would. You and I were meant to find each other, Fallon. I've known it ever since your sister first spoke of you. It was as if I felt the brush of feathers against my cheek." He lifted the silver feather and ran it down the side of his face as he spoke, and

I shuddered, repulsed by the wolfish hunger, the bloodlust I could see lurking in his gaze. "I know you were responsible for the death of a young warrior of your tribe. Maelgwyn Ironhand? His brother, my gladiator Mandobracius—I believe you knew him by the name of Aeddan—told me the story of what happened that night."

The night my life had collapsed into a bottomless black pit.

"You're wrong about me," I said. "Didn't Aeddan tell you that it was *his* blade that ended his brother's life?"

"Because of *you*, yes." He nodded, smiling. "*You* are a harbinger."

No. I wasn't. I couldn't be. Aquila was lying . . .

"And your sister now dead too. It seems that anyone who loves you, Fallon, is fated to die. I'd have a care for that decurion who seems so fond of you—"

"*Shut up!*" I snarled, lunging for the bars, my hands reaching to claw at his face. "Shut your evil mouth—"

He caught me by the wrist and held me there, his grip surprisingly strong.

"That auspicious night," he hissed, "that spilled a brother's blood drove you to this place. To this moment. *To me.* Don't you see, Fallon? Your goddess has laid out your fate's path to lead right to the doorstep of my god. Dis and the Morrigan are kindred. As are we."

His smile turned poisonous and he drew the edge of the feather across the soft, white underside of my forearm. It was razor-sharp, and blood welled up, seeping from the curved lines he traced, lines that formed the symbol of a feather on my skin. I gritted my teeth and clamped down on a hiss of pain. When he was done marking me, Aquila let go of me, and I snatched my arm back, cradling it to my chest.

"You're mad . . ." There was a tremor in my voice.

"Am I?" He laughed, tucking the feather away in the folds of his cloak. "What fate, then, drove Aeddan to my ludus? You were there the night he ended Ajax's life. You bore witness. He is my strongest gladiator." Aquila tilted his head. "And what about the Fury? I'd watched her fight for years. Undefeated, undefeatable . . . until you, Fallon. Victrix. Achillea didn't have your strength. She never did. That is why your goddess cursed her to fall under the wheels of a chariot whereas, in the same arena, performing the very same act, she gave *you* wings."

Would that she had, I thought. *I would use them now to fly away from this whole horrid nightmare.*

"Fight for *me*, Fallon!" Aquila suddenly gripped the bars and thrust his face close, as if he would squeeze between them into my cell. "*Win* for me."

A chill crept over my skin. Aquila's words were a dark mirror to the conversation I'd had with Caesar in his villa, the day he'd chosen me as his Victory.

"I will never fight for you," I whispered, my mouth gone dry as dust.

"Then you will never leave this cell. And that would be a great pity. Think long on your decision, my dear. And when I come to ask you again, have a better answer. For both our sakes."

VI

THE LIGHT CREEPING in through the tiny cell window shifted and changed as I huddled against the wall, drifting in and out of awareness. Beneath the torn strip of cloak I'd wrapped around my torso, I could feel that the skin surrounding my wound had grown tight and hot. But the rest of me was cold, clammy, shivering . . .

"Bright thing . . ."

I struggled to open my eyes. The voice was quiet.

Faraway sounding . . . familiar. I squinted, but everything was blurry.

"Wake up, bright little thing . . ."

The smell of stale wine filled my nostrils.

"Arviragus . . . ?" I blinked in confusion.

The mighty Gaulish chieftain the Romans called Vercingetorix sat on his haunches on the floor of my cell, waiting for me to wake. For a moment, I thought I saw him in the glory of his youth. When he'd visited my home of

Durovernum and taught me how to wrap my child's hands around the hilt of a sword. His mane of auburn hair spilled over his shoulders, and a neatly trimmed beard framed his handsome face above a thick gold torc that circled his neck. He held a sword in his hands, and the hilt glinted in the pale wash of light through the window.

I squeezed my eyes shut and opened them again.

No. Not a sword. A wine cup.

And his hair and beard were grown wild and tangled, his face lined with defeat. But his eyes. They hadn't changed. They burned with an intensity that made it feel as though Arviragus could look right through me and deep into my soul. And why not?

Arviragus was dead.

At the end of Caesar's Quadruple Triumphs, the mighty Roman general had paraded the proud Gaulish chieftain through the streets of Rome, so that all the people of that great city could marvel and jeer at the most fearsome of Ceasar's adversaries. I remembered Sorcha telling me how then, after the spectacle, Arviragus would be taken away and strangled out of view of the mob. A small mercy, that, I thought at the time. Leaving the last shreds of his dignity intact . . .

And yet, here he was. Watching me keenly through hard, glittering eyes as I struggled to make sense of the moment. When it seemed he was sure that I was fully conscious, he grinned at me and raised the wine cup in a mocking salute.

"Ave, Victrix," he said, in a voice of gravel and rust. "All hail the conquering hero."

"I don't feel very heroic," I murmured.

"Quite right. So you shouldn't." He turned and spat in the dust. "You didn't see this coming? Neither you nor your sister? I thought I taught you better than that, bright little thing . . ."

My head swam dizzily.

I felt the heat from a shaft of sunlight falling on my face . . .

I heard laughter and looked up to see a vision of my sister, lithe and lovely and young as a dappled fawn, holding out her hand to help me stand. She grinned down at me, her freckled face framed by a cloud of flyaway hair, and in her other hand she held a wooden sword. The laughter I'd heard was low and musical and came from the handsome young man with auburn braids who sat on a stump, watching me and my sister fight.

He stood and walked toward us, stopping to pick up my sword where it lay in the grass. It looked like a tiny toy in his great hand as he bent down to give it to me. "Better," he said, his eyes twinkling with amusement.

"But I still lost," I grumbled, snatching the sword from his hand with my baby-chubby fingers.

"And why is that?" he asked.

"Because . . ." I frowned, thinking hard about how my sister had beat me. "Because I started watching her sword . . . ?"

"Good!" Sorcha beamed at me. "You're learning."

Young Arviragus nodded, pleased, even though I'd been defeated. "Bright young thing!" He tousled my hair.

"While the weapon does one thing at a time, the wielder does many. And they will *tell* you what they're doing—and what they're going to do—but you must pay attention. To their feet, their shoulders, their eyes . . . That way, you'll always know what's coming. In a fight, you always need to look six, seven, eight moves in advance. Remember that. And remember *this*—it's never over until your enemy is dead at your feet. Never—"

"Ha!" I barked a baby battle cry and ducked under his arm, catching Sorcha by surprise and slapping her sword out of her hand with mine. She yelped as I jumped to tackle her, and together we fell to the ground, rolling and laughing and play-pummeling each other with our fists as Arviragus cheered both of us on . . .

The memory faded.

I found myself back in the dank gray confines of Tartarus, with a ghost.

"Sorcha let herself grow soft," Arviragus said in a ragged growl.

"She didn't—"

"She's dead, isn't she?"

My throat closed on a sob and I couldn't answer. Couldn't find the words to deny it. My heart ached for the sister I'd found after so many years only to lose again. I shook my head sharply to banish my fevered delusion, but that only made the walls swim before my eyes. Arviragus stayed put.

He sighed and drank from his spectral cup. "You, though," he continued. "I thought *you* had an edge that would keep. Did the adoration of the crowds go to your head, little one?"

"If it did, it's your fault," I snapped, in no mood to be lectured by a delusion. "You were the one who told me to charm them. Beguile them. Seduce the mob, you said."

"That's the thing about seduction, Fallon." Arviragus leaned forward, the wine stench rolling in his wake like fog. "Never get seduced in return." He chuckled mirthlessly. "What else did I say?"

I struggled to remember the advice he'd given me that day. It seemed so very long ago . . . Ah. Right. *"Be brave, gladiatrix,"* Arviragus had counseled. *"And be wary. Bright things beget treachery. Beautiful things breed envy. Once you win Caesar's love, you'll earn his enemies' hate."*

Hate. Or desire. I hadn't listened. I'd earned both, and there was nothing I could do about it now. "Go away, old man," I muttered. "You're dead."

He laughed. "I'm not going anywhere," he said. "But you are."

"Are you here then to guide me to the Blessed Isles?"

"Eh? Oh no." He paused in the middle of drinking to wag a finger at me. "You're not wriggling off the fishhook that easy. The Morrigan's not done with *you* yet, bright little thing. Not by half. So if I were you, I'd start thinking of a way out of this mess you've got yourself into."

"What am I supposed to do? I'm in a prison cell."

Arviragus laughed. "You're whining to the wrong man on that score."

"How did *you* escape?"

"The wrong way," he said, lifting his cup and tapping the rim. "Maybe one day, I'll escape the right way . . ."

A fresh wave of shivering washed over me, cold then fever-hot, and when it had passed, I was alone again. Arviragus was gone, and I would die there in Tartarus— forgotten, defeated, a pile of dust and dry bones with no funeral pyre to carry the embers of my soul to the Blessed Lands of the Dead when I was gone. The Morrigan had truly forsaken me . . . No. The goddess was good. She hadn't lost faith in me—I needed to believe in her. I closed my eyes and whispered her triple name in my mind over and over. *Macha, Nemain, Badb Catha . . .*

Then I heard the rustling of wings above me.

I glanced up to see a crow perched on the sill of the tiny barred window, tilting its head to stare at me with one bright black eye.

"Fury!" I exclaimed, and the bird answered with a soft caw.

In the days leading up to Caesar's Triumphs, I had been the target of a series of nasty pranks culminating in someone nailing a live crow to my door to try and frighten me badly enough to drop out of the competition. The intimidation had failed, and the bird, poor thing, had been nursed back to health by Neferet. The girls had adopted her as a kind of pet and called her Fury in honor of my first-ever opponent.

"Fury," I called gently, scrambling to my feet and lifting my arm. "Come. Come here, girl . . ."

She tilted her head this way and that, croaked at me,

and then hopped down off the sill onto the wrist of my outstretched arm. A spark of hope flared in my chest as I carried her over to the barred door to the cell. It was locked from the outside, and only the iron key—hanging on the opposite wall from a hook above a shelf, so tantalizingly close and just out of reach—would open it. Without that key, I wasn't getting out of that cell, let alone out of Tartarus.

One of the things we learned about Fury, once she'd healed, was how clever she was. She easily learned tricks and seemed to delight in performing them for us. One of those tricks was fetching things. I nudged the bird off my wrist and onto the crossbar of the cell door. She twitched and ruffled her wings and looked at me expectantly.

"Fetch, Fury," I said, and stared pointedly at the key.

The key was fashioned in the shape of an owl, the sacred bird of the Roman battle goddess Minerva, and I sent up a silent desperate plea to the Morrigan in the hopes that the two goddesses—and their creatures—were on friendly terms. I stretched out a hand, reaching with splayed fingers toward the key hook. The reach made the wound in my side burn fiercely and pulled at the thin lines of the cuts Aquila had carved on my arm, drawing fresh beads of bright blood welling to the surface through the rust-dark scab that had already formed there.

I wondered just how long it had been since I'd been locked away in Tartarus. Hours? Days, even, maybe . . . Elka and the others probably thought I was already dead.

Fury was my only chance.

"Come on . . ." I cajoled her in a singsong rasp. "That's it . . . the key, Fury . . . pick it up and bring it here. Bring it to me, Fury . . ."

She tilted her head, swinging it from side to side, her bead-black eyes looking from me to the key. I held my breath as she took a few little hops and flapped up into the air to land on the little shelf beside the key hook. I felt a surge of giddy hope.

The Morrigan *was* still with me. She'd sent her servant to help me . . .

Fury shifted back and forth from foot to foot.

"Come on . . ." I encouraged her. "Get the key . . ."

She pecked about on the ledge with her sharp black beak.

"Good girl . . . good . . ."

A rustling in a dark corner suddenly caught her attention, and she launched herself off the ledge, swooping down to catch a mouse in her talons. Then she flapped through the bars of the door, past my head, and back out the window grate to enjoy her repast in the yard.

"Oh, Lugh's *teeth*!" I cursed as she disappeared from sight. "You *stupid* bird!"

Sent by the Morrigan, indeed.

Fury was only a crow, doing what crows did. Hunting, not helping. And I had only myself to berate. She was a bird, that was all. Not some kind of mystic messenger, not my salvation, just a bird. I fell back against the wall. The crushing weight of aloneness felt like a suffocating blanket, and the silence left behind in the wake of Fury's ruffling wings was deafening. In my despair, I half hoped Arviragus would appear to me again.

He didn't.

My heart sank. But then a key scraped in the door lock at the end of the gloom-dim corridor, and it leaped back upward into my throat. I froze as the heavy door swung open and a pale wash of starlight silhouetted a soldier's helmet and cloak.

Cai! I thought, pulling myself up to my feet. *He's found me!*

No.

The shadowed, featureless figure stepped forward and I saw not a crimson helmet crest but a spray of black feathers. Not a red decurion's cloak but a soot-black drape of cloth hanging in deep folds. One of the guards from the Ludus Amazona, come to take me to Pontius Aquila or end my life. The cloak billowed in his wake like wings as he strode swiftly down the hall toward my cell, and I skittered back into the far corner at his approach. He reached for the key I hadn't been able to cajole Fury into delivering to me, and unlocked the door.

When I didn't move, he huffed impatiently.

"What's the matter with you?" he snapped. "Come on!"

I blinked at the sound of words spoken in my own language.

"Aeddan . . . ?"

He seemed to realize, then, that the helmet he wore

obscured his features. Aeddan reached up and pulled off the headgear. Beneath it, he still wore his dark hair long, but his face was more angular than I remembered it.

"Do you want rescuing or not?" he asked.

For a moment, I didn't think I'd heard him right. "I—what?"

"I'm rescuing you. What do you think I'm doing here?" He stepped over the threshold of the cell and took me by the wrist, but I shrugged angrily out of his grip.

"I'm not going anywhere with you," I said. "You'll only take me to him. To Aquila."

"That was the furthest thing from my mind."

"You work for him."

"He thinks I do."

"He trusts you." I pointed to the key ring still clutched in his hand. "How else would you have known where to find me? How did you get those keys?"

"He trusts me because he assumes I bear a grudge against you," Aeddan said, visibly struggling to curb his impatience. "I can't think why—I mean, you only rejected me as unworthy of your hand, set me and my brother against each other, humiliated me in front of the entire Circus Maximus during the Triumphs . . ." He shook his head and looked for a moment as if he'd talked himself out of my rescue. "As for the keys, I found them in the desk in the Lanista's scriptorium. I took them when Aquila was busy rifling through her documents."

He held them up and I realized that they were, indeed, Sorcha's ring of keys and not the ones belonging to Thalestris.

"What happened to my sister, Aeddan?" I asked. "Did you—"

"No!" Aeddan turned a withering stare on me. "No, Fallon. I've only killed my *own* sibling. But thank you for reminding me of just how much a monster you think me."

"I—"

"We have to go." He glanced down the corridor, then back at me. "Now."

Still I hesitated.

"Do what you will," he said, throwing up a hand in frustration. "But if you want out of here, I'm sorry to say that it'll either be with me . . . or with Ixion. One of us will most definitely take you to Aquila. Eventually."

That was all the motivation I needed.

I was still half-convinced Aeddan was lying. But I was also half-convinced that this was the moment Arviragus had prepared me for. My one chance for escape. I glanced back over my shoulder as I ducked out into the corridor, but the cell was empty. Of course it was.

He's not there, Fallon, I thought. *He was never there. Arviragus is dead.*

I knew that. But it still felt as though I was leaving him behind. Again.

I tugged my cloak close about me to hold myself together—mind and body—and stumbled out of Tartarus behind Aeddan. Once out in the yard, he put an arm out to stop me while he checked around the corner.

"As for your question on how I found you," Aeddan continued in a low murmur, "the Morrigan showed me the way."

He nodded down at the tiny half-moon opening at the base of the stone wall we were pressed against. My cell window. I saw Fury, hunched there in the weeds, making short work of the unfortunate rodent she'd caught. When she saw us looking at her, she uttered a breathy little croak and flapped into a nearby tree.

"I'd almost given up on looking when that crow there came flapping through that grate," he said. "It caught my attention, and that's when I heard *your* curses coming from inside that building. I tried my luck with the key ring, and . . . Fallon?" He shook me by the shoulder. "Fallon—are you all right? It's only a bird. I was joking about the Morrigan."

"I know." I knew he was joking. But Fury *had* saved me. The Morrigan had heard my prayers and given me this chance. Now it was up to me to make the most of it and prove her faith in me wasn't misguided. "I know . . ."

Aeddan frowned at me in concern, then shook his head. "Come on."

The air was cool and wet, and I could smell the tang of charred wood as we hurried past the blackened stumps of timber supports, the only thing left of the stables. The ludus chariot ponies were all picketed on a line out in the yard, and one lifted his head and whickered softly when he saw us. We froze at the noise, but other than the horses, the stable yard was deserted.

Aeddan grabbed me by the wrist then, dragging me stumbling after him. We made our way across the midden yard and down a servants' corridor, toward the gate that led out to Lake Sabatinus. All the buildings were dark, including the barracks, off to our left. I pulled Aeddan to a stop and shrugged out of his grip again.

He glared at me, then glanced around to make sure we were still alone and unseen. "What?"

"I'm not leaving without the others."

"Fallon—"

"I'm *not* leaving without the others."

Aeddan knew me, well enough to know that arguing was of no earthly use. He would either have to help me help my comrades or sound the alarm and have me thrown back in Tartarus.

"Where is everyone?" I asked. "What's the present situation?"

"The ludus domestic staff were allowed to keep to their quarters," he said. "Aquila doesn't consider them a threat. But your friends and those two legionnaires are being held all together in the infirmary. Under guard. Aquila has returned to the capital and left Nyx and that brute Ixion in charge, along with a handful of guards. But they're spread thin between guarding the Amazona gladiatrices and the Achillea ones."

I nodded, trying to clarify my thinking through the fog of pain that still wrapped around my brain. I could picture Nyx luxuriating in the Lanista's private quarters, gorging herself on food and wine and lording it over the ludus staff. I didn't think I'd have to worry much about her.

"What else can you tell me?" I asked Aeddan.

Aeddan hesitated for a moment, his expression bleak. Then he said, "The reason the Tribune has gone to Rome is that he is arranging for a very lavish, very private *munera* to be held here at the ludus."

"Like the night at the Domus Corvinus."

Aeddan nodded. "Only this time, instead of a pair of gladiators fighting to the death, they'll have their pick of a whole crop of talented young gladiatrices to pit against each other. On the night of the next new moon—when the gods turn their blessed light away from the world— Pontius Aquila will return here with all of his rich, twisted friends, and . . ."

"And the Sons of Dis will bathe in the blood spilled on the Ludus Achillea sands." My mouth went dry at the thought.

Aeddan nodded, grim-faced.

Without another word, I turned sharply and headed toward the barracks. Aeddan made a grab for me, but I shrugged him off and kept walking. He had to almost jog to keep up.

"Fallon!" he whispered. "I *told* you—the other girls aren't in their cells."

"I know," I said. "I need my things. I'm not leaving without the others *and* I'm not leaving without my swords."

The barracks were deserted. As Aeddan kept watch at the door of my cell, I slipped a clean tunic on over the torn and bloodstained one I already wore, and belted it loosely. I didn't need anyone to know I'd been wounded. Not until we were well gone from the ludus and there was time for such things. Then I slipped on my boots, trying not to wince as I bent over to wrap the laces around my calves, and refastened my cloak around my neck.

I stuffed my swords, a dagger, and a tool kit into a travel bag. I had few treasured possessions, but I hesitated a moment, looking up at where my oath lamp sat on the windowsill. I picked up the lamp and set it down in the middle of my neatly made bed.

A message to Nyx. And a promise.

I will be back.

She would find it, I knew. She would find it, and she would understand.

I took a last look around the tiny room that had become my world and tried to memorize every small detail. The image of the place wouldn't fade in my mind, I vowed. I wouldn't let it. I would return before it had the chance.

That, I swore on my soul and on my swords.

VII

IF IT HAD been daylight, I don't know that I could have done it. Facing off in an arena against opponents who knew you were coming, who could defend themselves against you, was one thing.

Cutting a man's throat from behind was another.

But as Ixion's heavy dead body sagged away from me, I reminded myself that if he had seen me coming, I would be the one lying there, bleeding out into the dusty ground. I didn't know if the man's capacity for casual cruelty warranted such an end. All I knew was that, in that moment, the only thing I cared about was freeing Elka and the other girls. And if Ixion's life was the price for their freedom, I'd gladly carry the debt of guilt for causing it. Never mind that my hands were shaking as I wiped clean my blade on the dead man's tunic.

"Fallon?" Aeddan frowned at me in the darkness,

stepping over the body of the other guard he'd dispatched. "What's the matter?"

"Nothing," I lied. "I'm just not used to murder, that's all."

"You're pale and you're sweating." He grabbed me by the arm and turned me to face him. "Are you hurt?"

"No." I jerked my wrist out of his grip and put the tip of my sword up an inch from his nose. "I'm fine," I said. "And if you even try to suggest otherwise in front of the others, I'll find it within me to *get* used to murder."

He blinked at me and frowned, but stepped back a pace.

We dragged the bodies out of sight and made our way into the infirmary. The long, torchlit room felt like the inside of a hornets' nest that some very foolish person had thrown rocks at. The very air hummed with a defiance I could feel buzzing against my skin. My ludus-mates were gathered in small, tight groups, and I took the moment before they noticed me to look around, my heart swelling with pride.

They were angry. Not afraid.

And they clearly hadn't gone quietly to their make-shift incarceration after I'd been hauled away to Tartarus. Elka sported a livid black eye, and there were rust-colored blood splotches down the front of Gratia's tunic that, judging from her *two* black eyes, were the result of a broken nose. Others wore an array of bandages, and over on a far cot, I could see the shape of one of the girls lying on her side, covered by a bloodstained sheet.

I felt my knuckles crack as my fists knotted at my sides.

At the far end of the room, Cai and Quintus—male and military and therefore, presumably, the only *real* threat—were shackled and chained to a stone column.

I understood why the infirmary had been chosen as the place to gather the girls together. The barracks had dozens of cells, but multiple entrances and no locks on the doors. Here, though, there was only one door, and the windows were high and too small to climb through. And there were plenty of beds, along with Heron the physician to tend any injuries the girls had sustained. He was there now, crushing herbs in a mortar and muttering to himself. And he was the first one to notice me as I stepped further into the room.

"Fallon!" he exclaimed, and set the mortar down with a clatter.

Cai's head snapped up and his jaw dropped in surprise as our eyes met for a brief moment. I held up the key ring so he could see it, rattling the keys, and he smiled that slow smile I'd grown so fond of and missed so much. But before I could move to unlock him and Quintus, Elka was across the room and grabbing me by the shoulders, grinning savagely.

"I knew it!" she said. "I knew you'd find your way back."

"I didn't. Not without help, at least . . ."

Aeddan moved out from behind me, and everyone else went statue-still. I glared pointedly at the black feather-crested helmet he still wore. He winced and reached up to remove it. Tucking it under his arm, he said, "The main house is still quiet, but we should make haste . . ."

Aeddan's words trailed off as he realized Elka was staring at him, the fire in her eyes gone ice-cold. She took a
single step forward. "What is *he*—"

"I'll explain later." I put a hand on her shoulder, forestalling any immediate violence, but Elka's hands were
clenched in fists and stayed that way. "Right now, we have
to figure out how to get out of here. All of us."

I left her standing there facing Aeddan, the two of
them engaged in a silent battle of wills, as I made my way
over to Cai and Quint, murmuring greetings to the other
girls as I went. I fumbled through the keys and, finding
one that looked like it would fit, turned it in the shackle
locks. The chains fell away, landing in a rattling heap on
the floor. Quint nodded his thanks, and Cai reached out for
me, drawing me into an embrace—but I stopped him with
a hand on his chest. He nodded, taking it to mean that there
would be time for that later, but in reality I just didn't want
him to know I was hurt. I couldn't afford either affection or
sympathy in that moment if I was to stay strong and keep
from breaking like a dry reed.

I turned back to the others as they crowded around,
asking questions.

"This is madness, Fallon . . ."

"Where have you been?"

"What's going on? Was there really a rebellion?"

"Why are we being kept locked up?"

"Is the Lanista really dead?"

I held up my hands, swallowing hard against the knot
in my throat at that last question. "All I know for certain," I

said, "is this: Pontius Aquila has taken control of this ludus. And that means he's taken control of us. If we stay."

"*If?* What do you mean, 'if'?" Damya gaped at me. "We're prisoners!"

The girls all fell silent, and Cai took a step forward.

"Where are the guards, Fallon?" he asked quietly.

We locked eyes for a moment. "Indisposed."

Ajani nodded decisively. "Then now's our chance."

There was a loud murmur of assent from all the others. *Almost* all the others.

I looked toward the one silent corner of the room. "Tanis?"

The other girls turned to where the young archer leaned against the wall, her arms crossed and her mouth in a tight line.

"You're coming with us," Ajani said, stepping forward to put a hand on her fellow archer's shoulder. "Aren't you?"

Tanis shrugged out of her grip. "We're no safer out there than we are in here."

"That's not true," I said.

"First you want to leave and now you want to stay," Gratia said, her lip curling in disgust. "Which is it, gladiolus?"

"It doesn't matter what I want! What any of us wants—it never did. Don't you get that?" Tanis looked at Gratia like she was simple in the head. "We're not free. We were stupid to think that we ever would be. Who cares how he took over the ludus?"

"I care," I said. "He murdered my sister."

The words dropped from my mouth like stones down a well, cold and dark and echoing. The room went silent for a moment, and then Tanis shook her head.

"You don't know that," she said. "What if he was telling the truth? About the rebellion attempt? We're not all pure and good here, Fallon. No matter how much you like to think we are." She glared around the room, the heat of her gaze lingering on Meriel and Gratia and a few of the other girls. "Any one of *us* could have—"

Meriel took a swing at her, and the room erupted into a chaos of shouting. Until Aeddan finally stepped forward, imposing in his black cloak and armor, and drew his sword. "Shut up!" he snarled. "All of you."

"Aeddan!" I pushed toward him through the tangle of girls. "Put that sword down or someone's going to get hurt!"

That someone was probably going to be him. The girls surrounding him might not have been armed, but they were the embodiment of strength in numbers. I just wished Tanis could see that.

With a huff of frustration, Aeddan slammed his sword back into its sheath. "If you stay here, you will die," he said.

"It's a ludus." Tanis kept up her sullen argument. "Dying's pretty much the point, isn't it?"

"No," I said. "Fighting is the point. At least, it *was*. Pontius Aquila is different."

But some of the younger girls had begun to frown and shift uneasily. I couldn't blame them. All they knew—*really* knew—about the situation was that something had happened to the Lanista, and a rival ludus owner was now in charge of the academy. Nyx had gone on to fight for him, and Nyx had been one of us. How bad could it really be? I realized, then, that I was the only one of the Achillea gladiatrices who understood just how dire the situation was. Cai and Aeddan knew, but I'd never spoken to any of the other girls about the horrors I'd encountered in the Domus Corvinus. I hadn't even told Elka. I'd never wanted to relive those memories.

"Fallon is right," Cai said, stepping forward. "And so is he." He nodded at Aeddan. "Pontius Aquila is a respected citizen. He is the Tribune of the Plebs and an influential politician. He is also mad and dangerous. And utterly ruthless."

Even Tanis went still at *that.*

"The arena games aren't just sport to him," I said, my voice ragged in the sudden silence. "They're . . . rituals. Twisted blood rites. He belongs to a secret society of men who stage private munera where the fighters are nothing more than sacrifices to a dark god they call Dis."

I looked up to see Elka's gaze fastened on me. "How do you know this?"

They all stared at me, wide-eyed and skeptical, waiting for some kind of an explanation that would make sense of what Aeddan was saying. I took a breath and told them all what I'd experienced after Elka and I had been lured by Nyx to the Domus Corvinus with the promise of an evening of harmless—if forbidden—fun. It had turned out to be quite the opposite. "Forbidden" in reality was more like "outlawed," and "fun" translated horribly as "nightmare."

I told them what I'd witnessed in the catacombs of the palatial house that night while the rest of the party guests carried on, reveling in the thrill of a gladiatorial duel that had proved salaciously lethal. The guests didn't know that the loser of the bout was taken away and laid out on a marble slab, like a sacrificial altar to a dark god. They didn't know that his chest was split open like a roasting carcass, his still-warm heart torn from the cavity and weighed on a golden scale. And they most certainly did not know that, after that, it was consumed by masked men who called themselves the Sons of Dis. Devoured in a bloody, horrifying ritual. But I knew. I'd seen it happen with my own eyes.

Dis, I'd later learned, was the dark incarnation of the Roman god Saturn—ruler of the Underworld, a pitiless deity who could grant his worshippers strength and power but would only be placated with blood. As I told my friends the tale, Aeddan stood at my side, his face pale and his jaw tight, nodding confirmation of everything I'd said.

"They . . . *ate* the heart of the man you killed?" Tanis asked, one hand creeping up to cover her own breastbone.

Aeddan nodded.

Heron ran his fingers over his beard, regarding Aeddan with scholarly detachment. "And yet, you still fought for Aquila," he said.

Aeddan met the physician's gaze with an unblinking one of his own. "At the Ludus Saturnus. I did. Until he made me a member of his elite guard."

Heron nodded, and said nothing more. The girls stared at Aeddan with varying expressions of wariness, curiosity, and revulsion. I had my own ideas as to why Aeddan had stayed in close proximity to Aquila. He wasn't a slave. Even if he wasn't welcome in our own land, he still could have left at any time. But if he had, he wouldn't have been at the Ludus Achillea now. And I'd still be locked up in Tartarus.

I turned away from him to find Elka staring at me.

"I had no idea," she said. "That night . . . after I lost track of you. That's . . ." She trailed off, unable to put into words what she was thinking.

"Evil," Neferet finished her sentence for her. "What they did was evil. In Aegypt, when we die, Anubis, the god of the dead, carves out our heart and weighs it against Ma'at, the feather of truth."

My hand went to the wound on my wrist—the one Aquila had carved with *his* feather—and a shiver of dread ran through me, scalp to sole.

"But Anubis is a god," Neferet continued. "And only a god has that prerogative."

"Aquila thinks of himself like that," Aeddan said. "He thinks the heart of a warrior gives him strength. Power."

Ajani stepped forward. "The hearts of *these* warriors"— she gestured to the girls gathered around—"will *not* give him power. We will give him nothing but pain."

When I'd told Aeddan that I wasn't leaving without the others, I think I knew that the likelihood of *all* of us escaping was a remote possibility. The Amazona girls and their guards outnumbered us, and unless all the luck and every benevolent god who chose to turn an eye on our plight was with us, some of us simply weren't leaving the ludus that night.

"I wish you good fortune, Fallon," Heron said, pulling me aside after we'd come to a mutual decision to take our chances outside the ludus walls. "But I can't come with you."

"What?" I asked. "Why not?"

He led me over to the figure lying on the cot and lifted the sheet. Lydia lay beneath it on her left side, her shoulders seeping blood through the bandages Heron had applied. She moaned quietly and her eyelids fluttered, but that was her only response. The skin on the right side of her face, where the lash of Nyx's whip had scored, was split to the bone. Heron had done an admirable job of sewing her up with neat, tiny stitches, but Lydia would carry a livid scar for the rest of her life. The cot beneath her was stained with the blood from her wounds.

In spite of myself, I felt a twinge of pity. I quashed it as best I could.

"As you see, Lydia isn't going anywhere," Heron said. "Not anytime soon."

"Leave her behind then," I said.

"Fallon," he chided me gently. "You know I can't do that. I swore an oath to care for the girls of this ludus. Even the ones who might not entirely deserve it. Aside from the soft-tissue wounds, her cheekbone is broken. Without the poppy draughts I've administered, the pain would be overwhelming. If I don't keep her in a stupor for the next few days at least, she'll howl herself mad."

"What if I . . . what if *we* need you?" I asked.

My own wound—the one from Nyx's blade—had begun to throb again beneath my cloak, and I clenched my fists to keep from putting a hand to my side. If Heron realized I was hurt, he would have done whatever he thought he needed to—for my own good—to keep me in his infirmary. Even if it meant alerting Aquila's guards.

"I can take care of it," Neferet said. "Of us."

I looked back and forth between them. Heron frowned, clearly torn. But then he nodded and walked swiftly over to a long cupboard. He took a bulging leather satchel down from a shelf and handed it to Neferet. "I pray you won't need it," he said. "But if you do, this should see you through most injuries or illness."

Neferet took the bag solemnly, as if it was filled with precious treasure. She looped the strap across her shoulder and gave Heron a swift, spontaneous hug. The physician's usual dour expression crumpled slightly as he squeezed his eyes shut and returned the embrace.

"Go," he said, pushing his apprentice to arm's length. "Remember what I've taught you: that in medicine, sometimes *this*"—he tapped her chest, just above her heart—"is a wiser physician than *this*." He tapped her forehead.

She nodded, her dark eyes wide and unblinking in her small, serious face. "I will strive to honor your teaching."

He snorted. "I'd be happy if you just strove not to let any of your comrades turn septic when they get hurt.

Because as sure as the sun climbs the morning sky, they will get hurt." He raised an eyebrow at me.

I ducked my head and turned away. Of course, he didn't know that I was already in need of Neferet's ministrations—once we got somewhere safe—but he knew that I was endangering the others. And when it happened to one of them, it would be my fault. And my responsibility.

On the other side of the room, Cai and Quint were plotting our escape. Aeddan stood by, arms crossed over his chest, listening.

"Our best bet, if we're to make a break for it as a group, is to put the horses in the yard to strategic use," Cai was saying as I approached, Elka following in my wake.

Quint nodded. "We saddle only the cavalry mounts," he suggested. "They're trained to act as shields and rams in a crowd. And hitch two of the light passenger carts to the fastest horses. That's about all we'll be able to keep control of in a running fight through the front gates. Any more than that, and we risk getting hemmed in by our own people. If that happens, they'll cut us to pieces."

"What about the rest of the horses?" Aeddan asked. "You can't leave Aquila and his thugs any means of pursuit."

Cai hesitated. Elka didn't.

"We'll have to lame the chariot ponies." She said it matter-of-factly, but I saw her throat muscles working as if trying to keep those words out of her mouth.

I wasn't about to entertain *that* thought for even an instant. "I know what you're thinking, Elka, but no. No cold-blooded Varini tactics!" I put a hand up, forestalling her objections. "I remember what you told me about your tribe and leaving nothing behind for the enemy to use once you move on, and I remember thinking that, yes, that made a certain amount of sense. But we're *not* moving on. And those horses are as much a part of this place as we are."

Elka raised a pale eyebrow at me. "You mean the place we're abandoning?"

"We are *not* abandoning the ludus," I said emphatically, only just realizing, myself, what I'd actually said. "This is . . . Cai? What is this?"

"A tactical retreat?"

"Yes!" I nodded. "A tactical retreat."

Elka's expression conveyed her skepticism, but she put up her hands and didn't argue. I looked back at Cai and Quint, hoping they had another solution. Cai thought for a moment, then nodded.

"We'll cut all the saddle girths and bridle tack, then. That should slow them down at the very least." Cai looked over at Aeddan. "Unless you think any of those brutes can actually ride bareback?"

Aeddan shook his head. "From what I've seen of Aquila's men, I'd be shocked to learn any of them could ride even *with* a saddle."

"That should take care of that, then," Cai said.

"What about the chariot ponies?" I asked. "What about Nyx? She's the best driver we ever had."

"Smash the spokes on all the chariot wheels," Quint suggested. "Those can be rebuilt, but not without time and effort. All we need is a decent head start."

Cai nodded. "Agreed."

Elka accepted the solution, her mind already turned to other issues. "We can't go back to the barracks for our own weapons," she said. "Crossing the compound is too risky."

She was right. I silently thanked the Morrigan that I'd had the foresight to retrieve my own swords. "If we can get to the equipment shed, we can at least pick up some gear there," I said, "but there's no guarantee we'll make it even that far before we're detected. In the meantime, you and the rest of the girls had best arm yourselves with anything you think might be useful."

Elka cast a searching glance around Heron's workroom, and I saw her eyes light up. She crossed over to a cabinet and plucked a wicked-toothed bone saw off a hook. She hefted it and nodded in satisfaction. I heard Quint sigh. When I looked over at him, he was gazing at Elka with utter devotion.

The other girls swiftly followed her example, snatching up anything off a shelf or from a hook that could be used to stab, slice, or bludgeon. Damya broke apart a wooden stool with her bare hands and distributed the legs as clubs. Ajani gathered up Heron's surgical knives and shoved them through a strip of bandage cloth she'd looped across her torso so she could access the blades with ease. Gratia hefted a tall bronze lamp stand, and Meriel gripped a pair of pointed metal surgical implements in both hands. I couldn't have even guessed what their intended purpose was, but was fairly certain Meriel would put them to good use. Even Tanis had found a weapon for herself—a corpse hook.

I let that pass without comment. Apparently, the prospect of having her heart torn from her chest and devoured had unearthed a previously unmined vein of courage in the young archer. At least she seemed resolved to join us.

Together with their makeshift weapons, the Achillea gladiatrices ranged around me in a loose circle, bruised and battered. But also quiet, competent, and very, *very* angry. Pontius Aquila, I thought, was operating under some fairly profound misapprehensions. He thought *I* was a fighting spirit?

I was one of many.

One of a defiant sisterhood.

"Antonia?" I said, glancing over at where she had drifted away from the rest of us. She looked on the verge of tears suddenly. "What is it?"

"*My* weapon . . ." She gestured to the stump of her arm, clad in the plain leather sheath she wore outside of the practice arena. "It's in the trunk in my room, and, as you say, we can't risk going back to the barracks. But I'm useless without it. The rest of you can make do, but I can't. I can't fight without my own blade, and I'll only be an impediment. You might as well leave me behind with her." She jerked her head at Lydia, where she lay unconscious on the bed.

My heart ached for Antonia—for her bitter frustration in that moment—but Neferet shook her head and sighed dramatically.

"What?" Antonia glared at her.

"Well . . ." Neferet exchanged a glance with Heron. "I *was* going to save this as a surprise for a special occasion."

Antonia frowned in confusion.

"But since you're making such a fuss . . ."

Neferet went over to Heron's workbench and knelt down before a basket stacked with neatly folded lengths of linen. In spite of the gravity of our situation, I noticed the hint of a smile playing at the corners of Heron's mouth.

I looked over at Elka but she just shrugged.

Neferet lifted the piled cloth and reached underneath to retrieve something that looked like a cross between an armored greave and one of Heron's more diabolical medical instruments, crisscrossed with a web of leather straps and buckles. The leather was supple and polished to a deep sheen, and all of the metal fittings gleamed.

"I was just putting the final touches on it," Neferet said, holding it out to Antonia. "Here. Try it on."

Since the day Antonia had decided she wasn't going to let her injury keep her out of the arena, she'd been experimenting with different apparatuses—various kinds of rigging so that her truncated arm could function as a weapon. She'd gone through a series of modifications, each one honing the device to give her more control and mobility. And clearly Neferet had been paying careful attention to what had worked and what hadn't.

Antonia slid her arm into the leather greave. It ended in a half-moon-shaped blade that looked like it could cut through the toughest boot leather with ease. Neferet adjusted the straps and stepped back, her face splitting into a wide smile as Antonia took a few tentative swipes through the air in front of her.

"Just be careful," Heron said. "It's sharp." An understatement.

Antonia lifted an eyebrow at him, grinning dangerously. Then she whirled in a full circle, the curved blade dancing through the air in an intricate series of attack patterns that culminated in an overhead arc. The blade whistled as she swept her weapon arm high overhead and down, burying one wickedly honed point of the blade a thumb-length deep into the wooden surface of his workbench.

Panting a bit, she pushed the hair out of her eyes and yanked the blade free. She turned to Neferet, eyes shining, and said, "It's perfect."

Antonia held out her hand, and Neferet reached to take it. "Then it's good enough for you."

This, I thought. This is what we were about to start fighting for. Our lives, our happiness. Each other. Sorcha had dreamed of this for us—and now it was up to us to find a way to keep that dream alive.

"What time of night is it?" I asked Heron.

The physician checked the device he called a *clepsydra*—a Greek contraption that measured time with water—and said, "Sunrise is in four hours."

I nodded. "Then I want us to be ready to go in two."

Cai and Quint enlisted a handful of the girls and led them, with all possible stealth, to the outbuilding where the chariots and wagons were kept. There, they went to work malleting through the spokes of every wheel they could find. At the same time, Elka and I, along with Meriel and Damya, headed to the tack shed, where we sawed through all of the saddle girths, reins, and bridles hanging from hooks on the walls. Then once we were done, it was out to the yard, where we still had the cover of darkness to help hide our little insurrection.

The horses picketed out in the yard were restless, not used to spending nights outside of their stalls, but they calmed under Ajani's gentle hands and soothing whispers, enough so that we could hitch the two fastest pairs to the carriages while Cai and Quint saddled their cavalry mounts. My fingers fumbled with the harness buckles, palms sweat-slick, and at every moment I expected we would be caught out. I kept glancing nervously over my shoulder to where Aeddan stood beneath the stone arch leading to the main house, watching for any movement.

There was none. And that made me even more nervous.

I reminded myself that Aquila was no military man. His guards, no soldiers. And his gladiatrices were more used to being guarded than guarding. They were fighters, not strategists. And with me safely—supposedly—locked away in Tartarus and with the only two "real" soldiers chained up in the infirmary, they clearly weren't expecting escape attempts. An oppressive silence lay heavy on the ludus in those dark hours before the dawn.

It wouldn't stay that way for long.

"The goddess keep you all," I said when we were done and all the girls had gathered around, awaiting orders. "When this happens, it's going to happen fast. It will be chaos, and that's what we'll need if any of us is to escape. Whoever gets out, gets out. Whoever gets left behind . . . Don't give in. Don't give up."

Cai glanced skyward suddenly and said, "Rain."

"Good," said Quint. "The more impediments, the better for us."

I desperately hoped so. The wide sand road that led to the main gate—and freedom—had gone from raked smooth to pockmarked as the raindrops began to fall. Clouds scudded over the face of the moon, and a gust of wind blew the wetness in under the eaves where I stood, cooling my fever-heated skin . . . and then making me shiver.

The driving purpose that had sustained me in the hours since Aeddan had freed me from Tartarus was beginning to wane. I could feel it. If we didn't make our move soon, I didn't know that I would be able to move at all. Slowly, with strips of Heron's linen bandages wrapped around the horse bridles to muffle the noise, we moved out, pausing beneath the wide stone arch that opened into the main courtyard . . . our gateway to freedom.

I held my breath as the guard in the watchtower suddenly stuck his head out into the open. We all froze, staring up. Feeling the first drops of rain, the guard cursed—a small, faraway sound in the night—and stepped out onto the causeway to relieve himself over the side of the wall before the shower became a downpour. As he stepped up on a block of stone and hitched up his tunic, I signaled to Ajani. She didn't have her bow, but when she'd raided Heron's store of surgical knives, she'd picked the ones best balanced to throw.

Cruel to take a man's life in a moment like that, but the opportunity presented itself, and I wasn't about to let it escape our use. Neither was Ajani. The blade sliced through the rain, spinning end over end, and the man toppled soundlessly over the ludus wall. We all stood like statues for a long moment, waiting for the alarm to be raised.

Nothing.

Just rain and darkness.

"Let's go," Cai said, nodding to Quintus and waving me forward. I sprinted across the yard to where the massive sliding lock-bar was secured with a great heavy lock. There was only one key on the ring I carried that was large enough to fit, but my fingers fumbled with it, numb and unresponsive, slick with rain and sweat. My heart hammered in my ears. My knife wound was on fire and—I was almost certain—bleeding again. And the mark Aquila had carved on my arm seemed to hiss and tingle, sending sparks shooting up and down my limb.

"Come on, Fallon," I muttered to myself. "Come *on* . . ."

And then, overhead, I heard the hammering of feet on the guard walk.

"Felix?" shouted a voice. "Where are you?"

There was silence, then a burst of cursing. When I looked up, it was to meet the gaze of a second Amazona guard who'd come to check on his fellow. He'd seen the body lying on the ground below, and now he was peering down directly at me.

We had no time left.

I tore my gaze away from his astonished face and went back to work on the gate lock. The key rattled in the hole, and it took all my strength to make it turn. But then the latch sprung open and the lock fell to the ground with a dull clank. Ajani threw another knife, but the second guard had already ducked back behind the parapet and was yelling for help at the top of his lungs. I shouted for Cai and Quint to come help with the slide bar, but Gratia got there first and shouldered me aside, straining as she hauled on the thing, and managed it single-handed.

Then, Cai and Quint were there to haul open the doors.

"Go!" Cai barked. "Both of you—back to the wagons! We've got this . . ."

I turned and ran, but I could already see light in the main house. Torches flared, guttering and smoking in the lashing rain as Aquila's men came running. And not just his men. The Amazona girls too. I saw Nyx sprinting across the yard, her black hair flying loose behind her. *Not this time,* I thought. I wasn't about to let her get close enough to finish what she'd started with me.

I signaled to the Achillea girls, and they started yelling and clashing makeshift weapon against weapon. The unpicketed ponies panicked and began to rear and scream—lashing out with hooves and teeth as the girls drove them to form a barrier between the others and us. Already on edge from the fire that had destroyed their barn and the time spent kept outside in unfamiliar conditions, the animals were easy to spook, and we used that to our best advantage. Once Cai and Quint were mounted on their cavalry horses and herding them toward the Amazona gladiatrices—none of whom looked excited at the prospect of attempting to breach a wall of panicked horseflesh—we had our opening.

Gratia was at the reins of one of the two wagons, somehow managing to keep her horses under control. Arm muscles bulging, she hauled the reins up short and shouted for the girls herding the other horses to hurry up and run for the cart. I ran for the other one, sprinting for the bench seat up front, where I could help Elka drive if needed. It was the very same cart I'd first ridden to the ludus in—a slave on the way to what, at the time, had seemed a fate worse than death—and now it was my chance at salvation.

I put my foot up on the rail and grabbed the sides of the wagon, hopping on one leg as I tried to gain my balance. But the movement of the cart wrenched my arm. Pain bloomed and I felt a wave of nausea sweep over me. I tried again and was startled when I looked back into the cart bed. One of the faces I saw there, staring up at me, was Leander's. It was the first I'd seen of him since the ludus had been attacked. He must have heard the commotion and scrambled away from the kitchens, jumping into the cart bed in the confusion. Clearly Leander wanted about as much to do with an Aquila-run ludus as we did.

His face was white with fear, but he reached out a hand to me as I clung to the side of the cart, my feet scrabbling for a foothold.

"Domina!" he said. "Let me help you—"

I tried to grab hold, but his fingers slipped through my grasp.

And then, suddenly, Nyx was there. Reaching up for me. Mouth open and eyes blazing hatred, she grabbed my arm and threw herself backward, dragging me down into the mud with her. Elka didn't see—she must have thought I was safely aboard—and slapped the reins, shouting for the horses to move. I lost my grip entirely. The cart surged forward, thundering through the main gate as I fell.

I landed on top of Nyx, and that was the only thing that saved me. My knee jammed up under her rib cage, and I heard the breath leave her lungs in a great *whoof* of air. I kneed her again for good measure and staggered up to my feet, leaving her there, lying on the ground and gasping for breath.

There was still a clot of Achillea girls dodging the black-clad guards in front of the gate as they struggled to swing the heavy doors closed again. Tanis, with her corpse hook, was one of them. She screamed my name and took a step toward me, faltering on her leg that still bore the marks of the rope burns she'd suffered in the naumachia. I started toward her, but Nyx—chest heaving and fury in her eyes— suddenly stood in the way.

Her whip cracked through the air, sending one of the draft horses bucking and rearing between us.

"Fallon!" Tanis cried frantically out over the mayhem. "Help me!"

The gates were closing. I'd never make it, I thought— with or without Tanis—but in that moment, a stray, white-eyed chariot pony skittered out from behind a wall buttress right in front of me. One of the smaller mares, used mostly in practice, but swift-footed and agile . . .

"Fallon! Don't leave me!"

. . . and my last chance at escape.

Run! the Morrigan whispered in my ear. *Live! Return to fight another day!*

Or die. There was nothing else for me to do. I leaped for the horse.

"Fallon!"

Tears of helpless frustration burning my cheeks, I bent low over the little mare's back and slapped her shoulder. With a burst of speed like a champion racer, she surged through the rapidly closing gap between the ironbound oak doors. I looked back over my shoulder at the ludus as we pounded down the road and saw that there were still girls caught on the wrong side of the doors. Too many of them.

The last thing I saw was Tanis. Her face, moon-pale, eyes wide and dark and blankly terrified. Staring after me as if I'd viciously betrayed her in that moment. Which, I suppose, I had. I told myself I didn't have a choice. That it couldn't be helped. That I'd go back for her . . .

In the last sliver of space between the gate doors, I saw one of Aquila's men stalk toward her, and Tanis saw him too. The corpse hook fell from her hand and she dropped to her knees in the mud, lifting her hands above her head in surrender.

Lightning cracked the sky, and the rain began to fall in torrents.

VIII

I BURIED MY face in my pony's mane. Hanging on blindly, I let her run for all she was worth as those of us who'd managed to escape galloped south down the Via Clodia. Lightning lashed the bellies of lowering clouds, and mud splashed up in great thick spatters. We traveled hard and fast in the darkness and the unrelenting rain, pausing only briefly to let the horses catch their wind at the side of the road.

The farther we got from the ludus, the better I should have felt. But I didn't. Instead, Tanis's cries for help rang in my ears. And dread thoughts of Nyx at our heels, or Aquila waiting for us in Rome, wrapped around me in a suffocating embrace. Cai tried to calm me, to make me rest for a moment, but I couldn't. I needed to keep moving or I would crumple. Fold in on myself and wilt into fevered oblivion. The bandage beneath the tunic covering my wound was damp, sticky, and hot to the touch. Only the darkness and my cloak concealed the fact that blood was running down my flank, collecting in my boot. The breath rasped in my lungs, and my vision blurred and sparkled with flickering red fire at the edges.

"How many?" I asked Elka during a rest, dizzy and nauseous, unable to make myself do a proper head count. Or maybe it was just that I didn't want to know who'd been left behind. "How many of us are there?"

"Twelve," she answered. "Thirteen if you count that ridiculous kitchen boy. Plus the soldiers, and your gloomy friend from Aquila's own ludus."

"That's all?"

She bit her lip. "The others didn't make it out."

"Help me, Fallon!" Tanis's voice cried out in my head.

I squeezed my eyes shut and wiped the rain from my face. Then I turned and called for everyone to mount up. Before our escape, Elka had asked me where we were going to go, and I hadn't been able to give her an answer. Rome was, we decided, out of the question entirely. Pontius Aquila had a home there, the vast, sprawling Domus Corvinus. He had servants. Friends. The Sons of Dis. Eyes and ears everywhere . . . and even in the twisting streets and tangled districts of Rome, there was nowhere any of us could think of to hide. The townhouse where the Ludus Achillea lodged our gladiatrices when in Rome was the first place Aquila would look for us. Caesar's estate across the river might have been an option if Caesar was there, but of course, Caesar and his Populares were halfway across the wide world fighting wars with the Optimates, wars that had angered his fellow

Romans—one of the reasons *we* were now fugitives. Charon the slave trader, my patron in the arena, had a house in Rome, but I had no idea where or how to find it. Neither did Cai.

Together, we'd come to the conclusion that our best bet was to try to skirt the eastern edge of the city heading south. If we could just outrun the news of our so-called "gladiatrix rebellion" long enough to make it to Neapolis, or even as far as the province of Sicilia, we might stand a chance. It was decided. But all that changed as we approached the walls of the city.

The rain had begun to ease and a haze of mist seeped up out of the ground. In the distance, I could just make out the contours of the Seven Hills of Rome, dotted with villas and temples, crisscrossed with roads and meandering open markets and gathering places. A teeming hive of humanity that, the closer we rode, looked like an empty cursed place, the windows shuttered against the hour and the weather and not a soul on the streets.

Not a soul except for one . . .

Riding in a chieftain's war chariot a hundred paces ahead of me.

A voice called to me on the wind with the sound of a whetstone on rust.

"Fallon . . ."

I lifted a shaking hand to wipe the rainwater from my eyes.

It was him. Arviragus.

I peered into the fading darkness and could only just make out his forest-green cloak and auburn hair, spread wide on a ghostly wind generated by the passage of his ghostly chariot. He didn't so much as glance over his shoulder at me, but I knew why he was there.

To lead us to a safe haven . . .

The Morrigan had sent his shade back from the Lands of the Blessed Dead to lead me and my friends. And I would follow. Head swimming, vision blurring, I wound my hands tightly in my horse's mane to keep from falling off, and urged her from a canter to a gallop as the chariot began to pull away just outside the city gates.

Behind me, I heard Cai frantically shouting my name as my horse broke away from the rest, asking me where in Hades did I think I was going. I started to laugh. Because if *that* was where Arviragus in his war chariot was about to lead me . . . if Hades was where we were bound . . . then by the gods—his, mine, and Rome's—I would follow him all the way down.

As it turned out, I didn't have to go quite that far. I had to follow my ghost king only through the gates of Rome and down a tangle of deserted streets to a narrow twisting lane in a questionable part of town not far from the Circus Maximus. But when I turned the corner, Arviragus had vanished and the street dead-ended in front of a plain stone wall featuring only a single, heavy door set with a small grated window.

I dismounted—which is to say, fell off my horse—and lurched through the ankle-deep mud toward the door to pound on the oak planks with the butt of my sword. The war chariot was nowhere in sight. But I shouted Arviragus's name in a voice gone hoarse with fever.

"Fallon!" Elka shouted, grabbing me by the shoulders and dragging me away from the door. I think she must have been calling me for a long time. "Are you mad, leading us into the city? What are we doing here? Someone's going to call the watch and have us arrested! You don't even know who lives there."

I turned to her, my mind awash in confusion.

Live there? No one lived there. Arviragus was dead, and this had been his prison. Now it was nothing but a cold empty—

"What in the name of Jupiter do you want?" asked a gruff, angry voice.

From the *other* side of the door.

I whirled around—nearly losing my balance and pitching face-first in the mud—to see a pair of narrowed eyes peering out through the grate at us. They widened when their gaze fell upon my face. I tried to say something—anything—but the face disappeared and the grate slid shut with a bang.

I felt a helpless sob hitching its way up my throat.

Then I heard the sound of bar-locks sliding and the heavy door opening.

"Miss Fallon . . . ? Is that you?" A man dressed in a worn cloak over a legion soldier's gear reached out and grabbed me by the shoulder, pulling me inside with my weary pony in tow.

Unable to speak coherently, I put a desperate hand against his chest and beckoned behind me. One by one, Elka and the rest of the Achillea fugitives poured into the barren little courtyard, which could barely contain our numbers. Cai was the last one through, and he barked a terse command to Quint to shut the portal door. Horses and bodies milled around with me at the center, dizzy and swaying. The stone walls spun around me as I struggled to keep standing. This was the place where Arviragus had been imprisoned. The place where he'd died.

The place where he stood framed by the inner door to the prison . . .

His eyes went wide as his mouth formed the shape of my name.

After that, nothing. Only blackness and silence.

"Fallon . . ."

Something smelled strange. Not unpleasant, just . . . bracing. Pungent. Like juniper boughs fresh-cut and stacked for a bonfire at Samhain.

That must be it, I thought. *Mael is trying to wake me so I can dress for the festival . . .* Or, more likely, a round of sparring in the Forgotten Vale before the feast. *A fight would be good right now,* I thought. *There's something I ought to be fighting. Someone . . .*

"I'll be there in a moment," I heard myself murmur. "I just need to find my sword first . . ."

I could feel my hand opening and closing on the bed

beside me, searching for the hilt of a weapon. But what I found instead was another's hand. Warm and strong and calloused, fingers gently wrapping around mine, keeping me still.

"It's all right, Fallon," that same voice said. Familiar, comforting. "You don't need a sword. You don't need to fight right now. You won."

I opened my eyes to see Cai gazing down on me, the worried frown that creased his brow smoothing as I blinked up at him. "I did?"

He nodded. "You did."

"That's good," I said. "Who was I fighting?"

"Yourself."

I shook my head, fuzzy with confusion, but that just made me dizzy.

"You've been feverish and delirious for two days now," he explained. "Almost three. But thanks to Neferet and Ajani, your fever has broken."

Ah, I thought. *That explains the scent.*

Neferet had Heron's training, and Ajani was skilled at mixing salves and unguents. Together, the two of them must have treated the stab wound Nyx had given me. Now that I was aware of it, I could actually feel a cooling sensation all along my flank, under a linen bandage. And the tightness of stitches. Heron's medical bag had already been put to use. I was only sorry I was the one who'd necessitated it.

"They tell me you're going to be all right," Cai continued, his expression turning stern. "No thanks to your own damned stubbornness, I should say. You should have told me you were hurt."

I struggled to sit up, feeling as if I was waking from a long sleep fraught with strange dreams. My limbs felt soft, but my head was beginning to clear. And I was very thirsty. I grabbed with both hands for the cup of watered wine that Cai lifted from the table beside the cot I lay upon. I gulped at it like it was the finest vintage, not the thin, sour mixture that it was. I finished it and handed the cup back, looking around the dimly lit room.

"Where am I?" I blurted.

"You're a guest in *my* humble abode," rumbled a voice from the shadows beyond the foot of the bed.

My mouth fell open as Arviragus stepped into the circle of lamplight.

"And believe me when I say that I'm just as surprised as you."

No shade, but the man himself. Real as life and just as impossible.

Not a ghost. Not my imagination. *Alive* . . .

I felt the prick of tears as Cai made way for him to sit on the edge of the cot. I hugged Arviragus with all the strength I had—not very much at all—and he wrapped his great long arms around me, smoothing my hair as I wept into his shoulder.

"I thought you were dead," I sobbed.

"I was, dear girl," he murmured. "I was."

I looked up into his face. "What happened?" I asked. "After Caesar's Triumphs . . . I thought . . ."

"Yes, well." He snorted. "It seems the fearsome old general had a change of heart. Couldn't bear to rid himself of his best enemy after all."

"I can hardly believe that of Caesar."

"I can." Arviragus shrugged. "In fact, I think it's very much in character for him. So long as the world thinks I'm dead, it harms Caesar not at all to let me live and, indeed, assuages that small, deep corner of his soul that rebelled against the massacre of so many of my people. A tyrant has to find ways to live with himself. Leaving me alive was one of Caesar's, even if that life wasn't much of a step above death. That is, until you and your gaggle of gladiatrices arrived."

I swallowed the tightness in my throat. Arviragus alive was a comfort I hadn't expected. Not after everything that had happened. "Did Cai tell you of . . . ?"

"Sorcha?" The sorrow in his gaze was a deep as his compassion. He nodded. "I have made sacrifice to the goddess for her safe journey."

He held my hand quietly until the storm of my grief passed over me again and I was able to look him in the eyes once more.

"What madness led you here, Fallon, of all places?" he asked.

"You did. *You* were my madness."

I explained how his apparition had goaded me from my cell and, later, led me through the streets of Rome, and Arviragus shook his head in wonderment. "The Morrigan's will is a very strange thing sometimes," he said.

"Strange, perhaps," Cai said. "But in this case, fortuitous."

I looked up at him.

"I doubt we would have made it past the city at all if we'd kept to our original plan," he explained. "The *vigiles* were already looking for us within hours of us coming to this place. They would have most likely caught up to us on the road south to Neapolis if we'd stayed that course."

Vigiles, I thought. Rome's watch guard. "News travels that fast?" I asked.

He nodded. "We must have missed a saddle or a chariot. Or one of the guards rode bareback to send word. But word has definitely reached the local constabulary. They're said to be on the lookout for a band of escaped renegade gladiatrices from the Ludus Achillea, led by none other than Caesar's darling Victrix herself. And as we all know—"

"The Roman mob has not forgotten Spartacus," I said with a sigh.

"You've been branded a rebel and the leader of rebels." Cai shook his head in disgust. "That makes you a political liability for Caesar. It'll take a while for word to reach *him* of that, but when it does . . ."

"How do you know all this?"

"I have a friend, remember? One who is privy to the secrets of the city. And its men of power." Cai poured another cup of watered wine and handed it to me. "I sent word to Kass about what had happened and asked her if she had any insights into our situation."

Kassandra, I remembered. She had been kind to me—rescued me, really—on more than one occasion. A brothel slave, she was also a secret informant for Julius Caesar. A dangerous profession—in both respects—but she somehow managed to navigate that world with grace.

"What did she have to say?" I asked.

"She gave me the political lay of the land, and we're in more trouble than I thought." Cai sighed bleakly and I waited for him to continue. "There is a deep unrest brewing in the Republic, Fallon. The Optimates—the men Caesar is fighting right now—and the Populares, the ones who support him in this war . . . they are the public face of the conflict. The two major factions in the power struggle that everyone sees and knows. But, according to Kass, it is the Sons of Dis and those like them who are the monstrous visage lurking beneath."

"The blade cuts both ways," Arviragus mused. "The political climate is the very reason *why* men like Aquila suddenly feel they have the kind of agency to promote things like the Sons of Dis and get away with it. Public perception is everything to the Roman mind."

Cai nodded. "And people like you and Sorcha, Fallon—the champions of Caesar, his stars of the arena, and favorites of the plebs—you're only pawns in a much greater game here. A distraction and a bargaining chip, both."

"And in Aquila's twisted mind, a source of arcane power," I said, looking down at my arm, where the cuts he'd made were healing, slowly becoming the thin white scars I would carry so long as I lived. "Let's not forget that."

Cai shifted uncomfortably at the thought, but nodded. "Yes," he said. "In his mind. And the minds of his followers."

"And now Sorcha's dead because of it," I said, crushing the renewed swell of agony that saying those words caused me. "Forget Aquila's sick agenda. Even if he were to vanish from the earth right now—and what a pleasant thought *that* is—the way things stand, we're going to have to find a way to clear our names. All of us. Or we'll all live as fugitives for the remainder of our days. Numbered as they are."

"We'll find a way," Cai said. "Don't worry about that now."

"Aye. You will." Arviragus reached out to squeeze my hand, his expression one of commiseration. But I saw in his eyes just how likely he considered that possibility. "In the meantime, you'll need your strength back. I'll go scare up a bite for you to eat." He nodded at Cai and left us alone.

We sat silently for a while, just sitting and staring at each other, and then Cai reached over, taking my hand in his.

"You gave me quite a scare, Fallon," he said.

"I gave myself one." I smiled at him wanly. "Several, in fact. I thought I was going to die in that cell."

"But instead you found a way out."

I shook my head. "No. I didn't. Aeddan found me and led me out."

I could see a wealth of things in Cai's face that he wanted to ask me about that, but he confined himself to just one question. "Do you trust him?"

I thought about that for a long moment. Cai knew about Aeddan—and Mael—and he must have been wondering how I could even stand to look at the man who'd murdered my first love.

"Trust him?" I hesitated, but I already knew the answer. "Yes. I do."

Cai waited.

"But that's a world away from forgiving him, believe me." I sighed. "*Several* worlds."

"Good." He nodded. "Then it should be no problem for us to thank him for the rescue and turn him out into the city to fend for himself."

I frowned. "And what if they find him? He's a well-known gladiator, and he's defected from Aquila's ludus—they must be looking for him too. No." I shook my head. "If we turn him away, it might lead the vigiles straight back to us."

Was that really it? I asked myself. The reason I was reluctant to rid myself of Aeddan? Or was it just a way of torturing us both for what had happened to Mael? A kind of dual penance? I honestly didn't know. There was so much I was unsure of, not the least of which was—what now? I didn't know where we would go or what we would do. How we would clear our names. But what I did know, deep in my heart, was that wherever we went, whatever we faced, we would need every advantage we could lay our hands on.

"He's good in a fight," I said. "And I fear we're going to need that too."

"I hope you're right." Cai nodded, accepting my decision even if he didn't like it much. "About trusting him, that is. But if he becomes any kind of a problem, you only have to say the word, Fallon, and I'll happily run my swords through his guts without a second thought."

I gave him a look.

"Or"—he shrugged, grinning—"I suppose I could just stand aside and watch you do it first."

"We could draw lots." I grinned back. "And I know Elka would love to take a crack at him too."

Cai laughed. "That she would. She almost did—a couple of times—while you were in your fever." He glanced over his shoulder at the door that led to the outer yard. "She cares about you a very great deal. They all do."

A sudden blush of shame burned my cheeks as I realized that I'd been avoiding asking after the others. Elka and Ajani and the rest. I didn't even really know, beyond the number Elka had told me on the road, who'd made it out. And who hadn't. I squeezed my eyes shut and saw Tanis's stark white face as she dropped to her knees in the mud. But then I shook my head and opened my eyes again. I couldn't stay hiding in the darkness of Arviragus's prison home for the rest of my life. The whole mess was my fault in the first place. My fault, and my responsibility.

So I might as well pull myself together and face my friends.

And tell them what?

I hadn't exactly figured that part out. I asked Cai for a few moments alone to collect myself, and told him I'd meet him in the yard, where the others waited. Because of Kassandra's warnings, no one had gone about in the streets of Rome since we'd arrived, Cai told me. No one except Leander, who knew every back alley in the city and how to make himself invisible. As much as it had angered me on the wild ride down the Via Clodia to think that he had stolen a place in the wagon that could have gone to one of the gladiatrices, from what Cai told me I had to admit that, in short order, Leander had proved himself invaluable to our fugitive cause. Whatever that cause might ultimately prove to be.

He'd even procured a clean tunic and cloak for me to wear.

I dressed and combed my fingers through the tangles of my hair as best I could. Then I headed out into the yard to meet my ludus-mates. They'd been industrious over the days I'd lain tossing in fever. The yard had been set up with tent-like awnings for shelter against any more rain, and the girls had done their best with what provisions Arviragus's accommodations and Leander's stealthy sojourns had provided in such a short time. The atmosphere reminded me of the days we'd spent traveling around on the ludus circuit, in the lead-up to the Triumphs. There were sleeping mats and rugs laid out beneath the awnings, and two cooking fires glowing, one with a roasting fowl set over it and one with a pair of rabbits turning on a spit.

The girls themselves sat scattered about, conversing in low tones or tending to chores. In the far corner of the yard, Aeddan sat alone on a bench, sharpening a knife on a whetstone with all the focused purpose of already knowing who he planned to use it on.

I walked out into the yard on wobbling legs, blinking against the shafts of sunlight that streamed between the awnings. Gratia was the first one to notice me, and she hailed me from across the yard, a wide smile splitting her face. One by one, the others turned to greet me too. I felt a surge of relief when I realized that not one of them actually seemed to blame me for what had happened. Neferet and Antonia were there, side by side as usual. Ajani and Elka. Meriel.

No Tanis or Lydia, of course . . .

"Where's Damya?" I asked, looking around.

Gratia shook her head. "She didn't make it out."

"Oh . . ."

I looked around at the others who had made it that far.

Over near one wall sat a girl I'd once thought of as "Wolf" because of the design on the shield Sorcha had given her at our oath swearing. Her name was Hestia, and over the last several months, I'd watched her fighting thraex-style with a methodical determination that won her more bouts than not. She was sitting with a Greek girl named Nephele who'd grown up a beggar on the streets of Athens until she'd been taken and sold. She never stopped smiling—which was a mystery to me—and her smile brightened as our eyes met.

I looked away from her to the other girls. Beneath one of the awnings sat Vorya, a girl from a neighbor tribe of Elka's own Varini, who'd been with us since those first days traveling in a slave caravan, but who I couldn't remember having had a lengthy conversation with. At the same fire were Kore and Thalassa, both of them from the isle of Crete; and a Germanic girl named Devana. Tending the rabbits was a North African girl whose given name I'd never known. She'd called herself Anat—after her tribe's war goddess—upon arrival at the ludus and refused to be referred to as anything else.

I didn't know any of them nearly as well as I wanted to. As I should have.

I promised myself that would change.

"Damya and Tanis and some of the others might not have made it out, Fallon, but *we* did," Ajani said firmly. "And we wouldn't have, if not for you."

"Right." Elka nodded. "So. Seeing as how you've stopped babbling and sweating, let's get on with it. What do we do now?"

I'd rather been hoping I'd have a few more moments upright before that question reared its head. Of course Elka's cheerfully dire pragmatism would allow for no such thing. Move on, don't look back. There's always something in front of you that needs fighting . . . And there was one thing in front of me I definitely needed to fight. Pontius Aquila.

"I'm going back," I said.

"Back?" Ajani tilted her head as she looked at me. "Back where? Home?"

"Yes," I said and felt my hands knotting into fists. "Home."

"To Britannia?"

"No." I looked around at the gaps in our company that should have been filled with the girls we'd left behind. "I'm going back to the Ludus Achillea."

"Didn't we just leave that party?" Gratia snorted.

Elka's eyes narrowed. "When you said 'tactical retreat,' I didn't think you really meant it."

"Of course I meant it," I said. "Sorcha gave everything—even her life—to secure the ludus as a safe haven for us. I intend to find a way to take that haven back."

"Might be helpful if you find out how it was taken so easily in the first place," Aeddan said, from where he sat apart from the others. Just loudly enough so that we all turned to look at him as he sheathed his blade and put aside the whetstone.

"What are you saying, Aeddan?" I asked.

He looked at me. "Pontius Aquila had to have had someone inside the ludus working with him."

"You mean someone other than *you*?" Elka cast a laden glare at the black feather-crested helmet that sat beside him on the bench.

"I mean," Aeddan said, ignoring the glare, "someone he could plan an attack with. Well before any of the Amazona gladiatrices, or their guards—including me—ever set foot inside the gates of your compound."

As he spoke, he reached beneath the helmet and pulled out a red leather pouch. He hefted it in one hand, and it made a muted jingling sound. Coins. A lot of coins. Elka frowned and everyone else went very still.

Everyone except Leander.

He'd been crouched by one of the cooking fires, turning the spit on the roasting fowl. But he took that moment to shuffle awkwardly away from the fire, as if he would get up and leave. But to go where, I didn't know. There was nowhere *to* go.

"What do you think, slave?" Aeddan called out in a casual tone. "Is there anything you'd like to share with this gathering?"

Elka snorted in derision. "You can't be serious."

I was tempted to agree with her. "Are you actually saying Leander is some kind of . . . what? Conspirator?"

"No." Aeddan shook his head. "He doesn't have the wits. But I'm fairly certain he knows who *does*. And he's so far chosen to keep his mouth shut about it."

Aeddan tossed me the leather pouch. It was heavy in my hand as I caught it.

"I found *that* in the bottom of his traveling pack," he said.

Gratia scowled at Aeddan. "You searched through his things?"

"I searched through all your things."

"You don't trust us," Neferet said, shaking her head in disgust.

"I don't trust anyone," Aeddan snapped. "Neither should

you. But *he* was the only one who had a pouch full of money stowed in his gear."

Cai turned from me to Leander. "Where does a slave get that much coin?"

"The . . . men. The men on the—the boat . . ." Leander stammered, wide-eyed. "The ones who paid me to chop down the mast—"

I upended the pouch and poured out a stream of gleaming coins onto the ground. There was a small fortune in sestersii. More than a top gladiatrix would make winning a prime festival bout in the Circus Maximus.

Ajani turned to Leander, a dangerous snarl curling her lip. "Liar," she said. "Those curs wouldn't have paid you half that much."

A sheen of sweat had broken out on Leander's brow, and his eyes darted wildly, as if seeking any means of escape. "The Lanista . . ."—he tried again—"she also rewarded me for—"

"Don't." I took a step toward him.

"Domina . . ." he said, and swallowed nervously. "Please . . ."

I loosened the sword that hung on my right hip. "Sorcha didn't give you those coins."

He shook his head. "No."

"Who did?"

"She . . . it . . . it was for my silence," he said in a rush. "She gave me the pouch and told me to keep my mouth shut. Forgive me—"

"*Who?*" I asked.

"Thalestris." It came out in a ragged whisper. "I was to keep quiet about the Lanista. Your sister, domina . . . She's not dead. At least . . . not yet—"

With a snarl, I shoved Leander up against the stone wall of the courtyard, and thrust the tip of my sword up under his chin.

"*What do you know?*" I asked through teeth clenched tight.

"On the night the ludus was taken," he said, naked fear in his eyes, "I was asleep in an alcove in the kitchen. I awoke to the sounds of Thalestris dragging the Lanista out through the service gate in chains. She was unconscious, and there was blood on her sleeping shift—but even more blood on the Amazon's tunic. I think Thalestris was hurt, from the way she moved. And she was in a hurry. Desperate. When she saw that I was awake, she gave me the coins to buy my silence."

"You treacherous little—"

"I was afraid!" he screeched. "She told me that Pontius Aquila would further reward me—but I *know* what *that* means more often than not. It's why I decided to leave the ludus when you all did."

I felt the breath heaving in and out of my lungs as if I'd just run a mile. My pulse roared in my ears, and I held Leander pinned to the wall almost as much to keep myself standing as from anger.

Thalestris wasn't dead.

She was alive and—there was simply no other way to frame it in my mind—in league with Pontius Aquila. And she had my sister. The naked betrayal of it staggered me. But I could barely even think of it beyond that one simple fact.

"My sister isn't dead . . ."

Leander shook his head.

I felt a touch on my shoulder as Cai stepped up beside me. "What makes you think the Lanista is still alive?" he asked, his fingers tightening, as if he expected I might try to carve answers out of Leander's flesh in chunks.

"Because Thalestris wants more than just her death," Leander said. "She wants blood vengeance."

Why? I wondered. *For what?* And then, in the next breath I knew.

Even as Leander said it out loud: "Vengeance for the death of her sister."

I released Leander and stepped back, reeling.

Suddenly it all made sense. Thalestris wasn't just a pawn in Aquila's game. She'd been playing her own all along. I remembered the day I'd found the crow nailed to my door and had been convinced Nyx had been behind the evil prank. Even when she'd denied knowing anything about it. But Thalestris had been there, as I'd cleaned the blood from my door, and she'd told me how it was a warning I should heed. For Sorcha's sake.

"Think on this," she told me, *"it would break the Lanista's heart if she were to lose her beloved sister. Believe me. I know."*

It had broken Thalestris's.

In the wake of the fateful battle that claimed her sister Orithyia's life and secured my sister's place as Lanista of the Ludus Achillea, Thalestris had donned a mask of forgiveness—of dearest friendship, even—but deep down, she'd harbored an implacable revenge for years.

Nurtured it, fed it and coaxed it to grow . . . and I understood.

I'd spent years of my life thinking my sister was dead. I could still feel the coal of hatred that had burned in my heart for Caesar, the man I'd thought responsible for her death. But how Thalestris had managed to hide her true feelings from Sorcha for so long . . . *that* was impossible for me to understand. My sister's primus pilus and closest confidante, she could have killed Sorcha a thousand times in a thousand ways. In a sparring bout, in the dead of night, with a draught of poison . . . but no.

She wanted her broken.

Suddenly, I understood. Sorcha would know, before she died, that Thalestris had killed her dreams too. Her fight for the freedom of the Achillea gladiatrices—a dream that Thalestris had so very maliciously delivered into the grasping hands of Pontius Aquila. Along with Sorcha's baby sister. Me.

The ultimate act of poetic vengeance.

I turned back to Leander. "How do you know all this?"

"One of the advantages of being a slave, domina." He grinned bitterly. "No one ever thinks you're listening."

"I'm listening now," I said and lowered my sword.

"When Nyx was sold to Aquila before the Triumphs," he said, "I packed a cart with her gear while she and Thalestris talked. About you, domina, and about the Lady Achillea. Nyx was furious. She felt betrayed, she said. Thalestris told her not to worry—that Nyx would soon have her revenge on you . . . and that *she* would have her revenge on the lady."

In his time at the ludus—sweeping, serving, bending his head, and averting his eyes—Leander must have heard, and seen, a great deal. I remembered then that the night Nyx had led me and Elka and Lydia to that cursed Bacchanale at the Domus Corvinus, it had been Leander who'd procured the key to the door to let us sneak out. And I remembered something else. He'd been whipped for it.

"You never told anyone what they said?" I asked. "You never told Sorcha?"

"I thought at the time that it was just talk." He shook his head, and I could see genuine regret in his eyes. "Nothing but talk. I forgot about it almost as soon as I heard it, just like most things."

"Why didn't you say anything about the Lanista's abduction earlier?" Cai asked. "That was far more than just talk."

"Because Thalestris didn't just give me coins." Leander turned to him. "She also gave me a promise. She said she'd kill me if I so much as breathed a word of what I saw that night. She told me she would find me—hunt me down wherever I was—and split me open to spill my guts for the vultures. She was very convincing."

I fought against the surging tide of desperate hope that swept over me. If I was to help my sister—*save* her—then I had to keep my wits about me. *Listen to your head, not your heart*, I could almost hear her say. *Truth before hope. Strategy before passion.*

"Aeddan—did you know Thalestris was still alive?"

He shook his head. "Pontius Aquila may have trusted me enough to think I wouldn't turn against him, but that doesn't exactly mean he considered me a close confidant. I didn't know it was the Amazon who was working with him, and I saw nothing of what happened to her, or your sister, on the night of the ludus attack."

I turned back to Leander. "Did she say anything else? Thalestris?"

Leander nodded. "When she was dragging the Lanista out through the kitchen—before she saw that I was awake—she was ranting. Laughing to herself and saying how she would take the Lanista away and make her pay. That she would sacrifice her to the goddess of the Amazons under the light of the Huntress Moon. How spilling of her blood would make their tribe mighty again. I think she has gone mad, domina. The goddess Nemesis has infected her mind."

Maybe so. But at the very least, Sorcha was still *alive.* There was still a chance.

"Huntress Moon . . . the next full moon," I turned back to Cai and the others, looking from face to face, unable in the wake of my fever to even think for myself what day of the week it was. "When is that? Does anyone know—"

"Fifteen days," Neferet said. "Lucky for Achillea, there's still time."

"Depending on where Thalestris has taken her," I said. "Leander?"

"Right . . ."

"Where?"

He nodded and held up a hand, and I could see him struggling to remember. The muscles of his throat worked as he swallowed hard, concentrating. "Corsica!" he said finally. "They've sailed to the island of Corsica."

In the middle of the Mare Nostrum, I thought. And I felt my heart sink like a ship in those deep waters that I had no way to cross.

IX

I HEARD QUINT groan and looked over to see a pained expression on his face.

"Quintus?" Cai asked.

He sighed. "I was afraid he was going to say that."

I remembered then that Cai had told me Quint was from Corsica. I struggled to remember what else I knew about the place, and the only thing that came to mind was something Cai had told me as the slave transport ship we were on sailed past the island, on that long-ago day when I'd been on my way to being sold in the marketplace of Rome.

He'd told me then that Corsica was inhabited mostly by . . . what was it? Right. I remembered: *Sheep. Bees. A few ill-tempered natives too intractable even to be useful as slaves.* That sounded like a fairly accurate representation of a tribe of Amazons . . .

"Why 'afraid,' Quint?" I asked.

"I was born in a fishing village on the east coast of Corsica," he said. "Youngest of five boys—hence the name: Quintus. My mother sent me and two of my brothers away to the mainland when I was ten."

"Why did she send you away?" Elka asked.

He paused and glared at the ground between his feet, a strange expression that was half regret, half anger crossing his face. "Because she didn't want us to be taken," he said. "Like one of her other boys had been. My brother Secundus . . ."

"Taken by who?" Elka asked.

Quint lifted his gaze to meet hers directly and said, "The Amazons."

Cai and I exchanged a glance.

"That's what they call themselves," Quint continued. "They're *not* really—everyone knows there haven't been any real Amazons for over a century—but don't tell them that . . ." He looked about, the muscles of his jaw working. "Is there any drink left around here?"

Arviragus silently went and fetched him a mug of ale. Quint took a deep pull and huffed a sigh as the rest of us gathered around to listen to his story.

"In the early days, a hundred years ago or more, when the Greeks first sailed the Mare Nostrum and discovered Corsica, they colonized it," he began. "No one else had really paid it much attention before that time, but they thought it might be worth establishing a trading port or two in the coves where the marsh flies weren't so bad. They brought slaves with them, of course, and some of those slaves were, to my understanding, Amazons. Real ones. Or the daughters of them, at least."

I remembered Gratia saying something similar about the real Amazons having died out long ago as we sat around the fires on the beach after the naumachia. And when Quint told his story, it sounded like part of a long-forgotten legend. I forced myself to listen, not to give in to the urge to do something—*anything*—in that moment that would do nothing to actually help my sister and would only put myself and my friends at risk.

The Huntress Moon, I told myself. *There's time . . .*

"Corsica is a rugged land," Quint was saying. "Mountainous where it's not treacherous bog, full of ragged peaks and hidden valleys . . . and, well, it proved the perfect place for those ladies to one day defy their masters. They rose up, rebelled, escaped, and set up a cozy little settlement of their own, hidden away on the other side of the island." He laughed a little and swallowed another mouthful of ale.

"And no one ever hunted them down?" Hestia asked, skeptical.

"Their Greek masters decided—wisely, I suspect—that they were more trouble than they were worth and let them be," Quint said. "The Roman settlers who came after—my folk—decided to adopt that policy. And so they've remained there ever since, spearing fish, brewing honey mead, telling tales of bygone glory . . . *and* occasionally swooping down out of the hills in a midnight raid to steal a few of the young fishermen—my brother, for example—from the villages on the other side of the island to keep their population from dying out entirely. Probably explains my predilection for cold-hearted warrior women," Quint muttered, casting a laden glance at Elka.

She grinned back at him. Cold-heartedly.

"The only time we ever got any retribution," Quint continued, "was once when my brother Tertius was a raw recruit with the legions and our village begged Rome for protection. They feared the time was coming round when the Amazons would be back. He was sent over with a detachment to the village and, sure enough, there was a raid all right. Chaos and casualties. But they captured a handful of those wild women and sold them at auction in the Forum. I'm betting your Thalestris and her sister were two of those."

"And we all know the rest of how *that* story ends," Cai said, grimly.

"No," I said. "We don't. Because it's not over yet."

A spark of anticipation flared in Quint's gaze.

"Can you take me there?" I asked. "To their settlement?"

He nodded, and a slow smile spread over his lips. "Aye," he said. "I can lead you right to their bloody doorstep."

I turned to Cai. "We're going to need a boat."

Antonia stood up. She was back to wearing the plain leather sheath over her arm, her crescent blade carefully oiled and set aside. "One big enough for all of us," she said.

"I can't ask that." I shook my head. "I don't know what risks we'll be taking—"

"You don't have to ask. Achillea could have turned me out of the ludus after the accident." She gestured to Neferet, who stood beside her. "Both of us. But she didn't. We owe her our loyalty, Fallon. And you too."

"Me?"

Neferet nodded. "You could have easily left us at the ludus and escaped on your own. You didn't."

Gratia stepped forward. "We're with you, Fallon. To be honest, I want to be there just to see you pummel Thalestris's treacherous arse into the dust." She rolled her muscled shoulders, grinning, and cracked the knuckles of her fists. "And maybe give a hand, if the opportunity arises."

I looked around at all of their faces. Each one—from Elka, my closest friend, to Devana, who I barely knew—bore a look of fierce determination. Of purpose. Even Aeddan's expression told me that he would follow me to Corsica to rescue my sister.

I felt a swell of gratitude. For all of them.

Leander stepped forward. "Please, domina, let me come with you too. All my life, I've pretended I was the hero in my own epic tale. But you, all of you, are real heroes. Give me the chance to win back your trust—to prove myself more useful than pilfered fish and wine."

"And the bag of coins we're not giving back to you," Elka said.

His shoulders sagged for a moment at that, but then he turned back to me. "Let me help you bring the Lanista home," he said quietly.

I raised an eyebrow at Cai.

"Better bring him along," he said. "Who knows what kind of trouble he'll get himself into if we leave him behind."

"All right then, hero." I nodded. "You're with us. One of us. But I swear on the breath of the Morrigan, if you even think of betraying us, I'll make you wish for Thalestris to find you before I do."

It was decided. Now, like one of Leander's epic tales, all we had to do was journey to a land across the sea, descend into the Underworld to rescue my sister from the clutches of death, and . . . if we somehow managed to get *that* far, I thought silently . . . return with Sorcha and together liberate our home from the evil that beset it.

The Ludus Achillea might have been named for the legendary hero Achilles, I thought, but even *he* might have second-guessed undertaking such a journey.

My next thought was *To hell with Achilles!*

He was famous for defeating one Amazon.

I would defeat them all, if it meant getting my sister back.

We were all in agreement then. Pontius Aquila could wait. Rescuing Sorcha was the first order of business for our merry band of renegades. There were dozens of arrangements to be made before we set out on our quest, not the least of which was procuring transport, but there was, at the very least, a real sense of purpose among us. Even Arviragus's longtime guard—Junius was his name—had been converted to our cause and was bustling about like a man with newfound direction in life. A focused, palpable urgency had turned Arviragus's prison cell and courtyard into a hive of activity. Most of it having to do with weapons. And war paint. The girls had collectively decided that if we were to take on a gang of so-called Amazons, we would do it in fearsome, Ludus Achillea style.

Back on the night of our oath taking, when Sorcha had first appeared to the new gladiatrices, she'd done it dressed in the full regalia of a Cantii warrior princess, complete with intricate designs painted on her face and limbs with woad—the bright blue skin paint the Cantii and other Celtic tribes wore into battle. My companions had taken inspiration from it and, to that end, most of them were inside that morning, crouched over braziers and experimenting, mixing pots of salves with pigments Leander had procured at the market—with Thalestris's coins—to produce an equivalent shade of blue. They tested out the results on Quint, who was only too happy to sit there, captive and flirting.

I could hear the laughter even when I stepped outside for some air. It made my heart feel less like a knotted bruise throbbing on the inside of my chest every time I thought of Sorcha. I prayed almost constantly that Leander was right, and that the Morrigan—and Thalestris—would keep my sister alive at least until the night of the Huntress Moon.

Meriel was sitting alone out in the yard.

I figured she had enough permanent woad tattooed onto her skin that war paint wasn't really a priority. I sat a ways off from her and went about sharpening my swords. After a while, I shifted on my haunches, still aching a bit from my wound, aware that Meriel had been staring silently since I'd come outside. I sighed inwardly and turned to stare back.

"Something on your mind, Meriel?" I asked, as pleasantly as I could.

She was silent for a long while, as if deciding whether it was worth telling me what that something was. But I'd never known Meriel to shy away from confrontations— real or imagined, large or small—so it wasn't a surprise when she did open her mouth.

"I don't like you, Fallon ferch Virico," she said finally, speaking my full name with deliberate emphasis. She spoke in her native tongue, which I understood—barely— because of the similarities to my own, fogged as it was by the thick burr of a harsh northern accent.

I nodded. "I know. Back at the academy when Nyx and—"

"*Hang* Nyx." Meriel glared at me bleakly. "I didn't need Nyx to tell me how to feel. I didn't like you before I was born."

"That seems a bit extreme," I said.

"My tribe are the Coritani."

"Ah."

That explained a lot. Everything, really. In truth, I'd always suspected as much, based on the tattoos and accent. The aggressively bad temper. And it was more than enough reason to hate me. There was a blood-deep feud between her tribe and mine, a grievance that had spanned tens and tens and tens of years before I was even a wisp on the wind . . . Long enough that most had forgotten the reason behind the thing, but not the thing itself. I'd grown up hating Meriel too, I suppose. In principle, anyway. When my driving passion in life had been to join my father's royal war band, I'd always assumed that hers was one of the tribes I'd go into battle against when the time came.

When the time came . . .

It never did. For either of us. And now here we were.

"So. I didn't like you before I met you." She shrugged. "Making your acquaintance did nothing to alter that."

I laughed. "Fair enough."

"Now, Nyx, I like," Meriel continued. "She's a cold-hearted, poison-eyed bitch, and she'll stab you in the neck at breakfast for a second bowl of porridge if she's peckish. I like that. I understand it . . . But I don't trust it." She turned back to me, her expression serious. "I trust you."

That surprised me. "You do?"

"What choice do I have?" She snorted. "You're honest and honorable. All the things I'm not. I'd be a fool not to trust you."

"Thank you. I think."

She nodded her chin toward the cell house where the others were. "These girls . . . I've known most of them longer'n you. I don't like most of *them* either. But we're sworn to each other—to fight and die for each other—and Nyx never understood that. Porridge is one thing. Blood's another and thicker even than that. We all swore a blood oath to look after our ludus-mates. And I know *you'll* uphold that. You and your Lanista sister—damned if I'd known I was fighting for the great Cantii bitch-goddess

Sorcha ferch Virico all those years at the academy! Lugh's teeth. I might've killed her in her sleep before you were ever taken from home. And now look at me. Off to go save her precious neck. It's an odd old world the gods have given us, Fallon, and that's the truth of it."

We laughed together, quietly, and then Meriel went back inside. I told her I'd follow, but I still wasn't up to much company. Instead, I went and sat in a corner of the yard, hidden from the brightness of the high sun beneath one of the makeshift awnings, and started sharpening my swords again. If we didn't leave soon, I'd sharpen them down to meat-skewers. I wished Cai was there to distract me, but he'd gone out into the city, incognito, to arrange for a ship. The thought had barely crossed my mind when I saw Junius issue a challenge through the iron grate of the outer courtyard door. It was Cai, dressed as a merchant, with a cowl drawn up around his face. Junius opened the door just enough to let him through, and as he was closing it, I saw Cai hesitate and turn back.

Someone had called his name from the street.

For a brief, panicked moment, I thought maybe the vigiles had discovered our hiding place. But then I saw a slender, cloaked form slip through the gap across the threshold in Cai's wake. Not a soldier or a watchman, no. A girl.

Kassandra.

Cai strode back to her as she pushed the palla shawl back from her face. Her hair was loose and tumbled about her shoulders, and her cheeks were flushed. It looked as though she'd been running. She spoke in low, urgent tones, but I was too far away to hear what she said. Cai listened at first, his head bent in concentration. After a few moments, he shook his head and uttered a bark of laughter. But Kassandra clearly wasn't joking, and she wasn't finished. She made a grab for Cai's arm but he shook her off, suddenly angry.

I still couldn't hear the argument but I'd rarely seen Cai so upset. He put a hand up and—this I *did* hear—told Kassandra to shut her mouth and never speak such a lie to him again. Not to him, or to anyone. Then he turned on his heel and stalked off into the prison house. Kassandra called after him, but her cries fell on deaf ears. The door slammed in his wake, and she stood there, staring after him, her hands clutched together.

I remembered thinking once that there had been something between the two of them. I'd long since laid that fear to rest but, suddenly, the ghost of it was there, hovering over my shoulder, whispering in my ear. I shushed that whisper mercilessly and, sheathing the sword I'd been sharpening, walked over to Kassandra. It took a moment for her to even realize I was there. When she did, she turned to blink at me blankly, her mind a mile away from where she stood.

"Kassandra?" I asked. "What is it?"

"I . . ." She hesitated for a moment and her glance flicked back and forth between me and the direction Cai had gone. Whatever she'd been about to say died on her lips and she shook her head, lapsing into silence, her brow creased into a deep, anxious frown. I noticed then that, beneath the flush of her cheeks, she was pale and drawn, her features more sharply defined than the last time I'd seen her, as though she'd lost too much weight. And there were circles under her eyes.

"Kass . . ." I put a hand on her arm. "Are you well?"

She looked at me, blinking, as if she'd half forgotten I was there.

"No," she murmured. "No, I'm not."

"What's wrong? Can you tell me?"

She laughed harshly and shook her head. "No. Only . . ." Again her glance drifted off in Cai's wake. "Only this: I . . . dream, Fallon. Terrible dreams where the statues of the Forum are thrown down and shattered and the streets of Rome run with blood. I fear that something terrible is about to happen. To the Republic . . . to those loyal to Caesar. Maybe to all of us. I fear a dreadful turmoil approaches."

In the brief time I'd come to know her, I'd learned that Kassandra was a sensitive and generous soul, for all that she'd likely seen the worst of humanity in her life. And now . . . bad dreams? Ruinous premonitions? She'd already told me poppy wine—and worse—flowed freely in the House of Venus. Maybe she'd fallen into the habit. I could hardly blame her. The life she lived . . . I probably would have tried to numb myself too.

I wondered why she would have felt the need to tell Cai of her fears—and why he would have reacted so. Then I wondered if maybe Kassandra didn't secretly have feelings for Cai. Was that why she'd come to see him? To try to convince him to leave aside the reckless danger I seemed to be leading him into? I couldn't find it in myself to blame her for that. But I could also see how that would anger Cai.

"Kass . . ." I had to shake her arm to get her to focus on me again. "Why don't you stay here? With us? Join me and the rest of the girls and—"

"And learn to fight for my life?" She laughed. It was a hollow sound. "I'm already doing that, Fallon. I just don't have the luxury of watching my enemies bleed."

I let go of her, and she pulled her palla back up over her head, hiding her face once more from the eyes of Rome. Junius let her back out through the gate, and I stood there for a long moment after she was gone, a confused knot of emotion sitting heavy in my chest. Was there more between Cai and Kass than I had guessed? I shook my head. No. He would have told me.

Would he? Really?

I had to believe that he would.

When I turned to go back inside, I saw Aeddan standing in the shadows of an alcove, leaning against the wall with his arms crossed and a stony expression on his face. He was close enough to have probably heard the entire exchange between Kassandra and Cai, and I waited for him to say something. But he didn't.

He just pushed himself away from the wall and walked away from me, shaking his head.

Later that evening I couldn't find Cai. He'd been a walking thundercloud ever since his encounter with Kass. Quint had told me that he'd gone back out into the city to continue making arrangements for our impending departure. I wasn't sure I believed him. But I trusted Cai. I trusted Kass, for that matter, too. Neither of them, I firmly believed, would ever do anything to hurt me, and if they had something to work out between the two of them, then I would leave them to it.

To take my mind off that possibility, I found myself later that night ruminating with Elka on the things Kass had said about the state of the Republic, and about what she'd already told Cai about the Optimates and the Populares and the secret power struggles that took place in the shadows of those two factions. I could hardly discount Pontius Aquila and his handful of depraved followers—I'd seen them with my own eyes—but was it *really* possible, I wondered, for such practices to be as widespread as Kassandra seemed to think they were? For such men to have influence over the power behind Rome herself? Even Caesar, I knew, had once been a high priest in the strange and secretive Order of Jupiter, but I still had difficulty reconciling the strategist with the mystic.

Elka, of course, had theories based on her own tribe's struggles for dominance.

"Men have always drawn power from death," she said, keeping her voice to a low murmur as she stirred the embers of the brazier between us. "And not just the death of their enemies. Sometimes the death of friends. My tribe— the Varini, and others like them—in times of trouble, they would take the war captives out into the forest and return home without them. When I was a girl, I came across what was left of one of those captives when I got lost one day gathering wood. He'd been blood-eagled. Split open and strung up between the branches of a tree as an offering to our gods and a warning to our enemies." She shrugged and reached for a mug of ale. "Sometimes, when there were no captives, they'd take one of our own. An 'honor,' it was called. And don't tell me that you Celts never do similar things. I know that you do."

It was true. The druiddyn, the spiritual leaders of my tribe, sacrificed men to the bogs to propitiate the gods. The warriors of the tribes took the heads of their enemies as war trophies. I'd heard tales that some—the Catuvellauni, mostly—even hung them from the rafters and on the doorposts of their houses as talismans of power. My father, to my knowledge, had never done such a thing. And he hadn't ever allowed it from his war band.

And maybe that's why he failed on the field of battle, I thought. *Maybe that's why he was a weak king . . .*

What if there truly was power—*real* power—to be found in the death of others? Or was it just the way small men made themselves feel larger? I thought about the Morrigan and the demands *she* made of her faithful, and I wondered. What if, one day, the goddess demanded that kind of sacrifice from me? The life of another for something as base as political gain?

She wouldn't do that, I argued silently. *Would she?*

Not even here, in Rome? Not even if it meant gaining power over Romans and their gods? I honestly didn't know. But the thought was enough to give me a chill on my skin that even the fire's warmth couldn't banish.

Word came the next morning—finally—that we had a ship. Cai gave me the news himself, and I noticed that his brooding mood had seemingly lifted overnight. My own foreboding vanished too, in a freshening wind of fierce anticipation. We would leave Arviragus's prison house that very day, at dusk.

"I'd like to come with you."

I jumped down from the back of the wagon Cai and I had been loading with gear and stood staring up into Arviragus's bearded face, not knowing quite how to respond.

"That is, if you think you could use an old warrior," he said.

"Uh . . ."

Until that moment, it hadn't even occurred to me that he'd *want* to come with us. But there was a naked apprehension in his gaze—I think he was actually afraid we'd leave him behind—and I didn't know what to say. True, since we'd descended on his prison home, I'd only seen him drunk once or twice—and not dead drunk or raving drunk or sick drunk—but he certainly wasn't the warrior he had been all those years ago. Not close to it. And he didn't exactly cut the most inconspicuous figure. It would be risky even getting all of us to the docks and aboard ship without the vigiles catching wind as it was.

"You are somewhat . . . recognizable, lord." Cai delicately voiced at least that much of what I was thinking.

The look on Arviragus's face broke my heart when he nodded and began to turn away, shoulders slumping. I reached out a hand, but Junius had heard the exchange and came over to us.

"I think I can help with that," he said.

Arviragus peered at him suspiciously.

"I've my soldier's shaving kit and a stash of civilian garb in my trunk," he said. "The tunic'll be a mite tight and the cloak a mite short, but if you stoop and keep your head down, you won't look like the thundering great backwater barbarian you are. Come on."

I watched them walk back into the cell where Arviragus had spent the last seven years of his life. Where he would spend who knows how many more until his great heart gave up beating and his soul escaped, finally, to the halls of the valorous dead in the Blessed Isles of the afterlife. If we left him there.

Cai was watching him too.

"You don't think this is a good idea," I said.

"His hands shake."

I lifted my arm and held out my hand, fingers splayed wide. "So do mine."

Cai took my hand in his. "*Your* strength will return."

"So will his."

"And if it doesn't?"

Then it didn't, I thought. And Arviragus the legend became Arviragus the liability. But I knew I'd already made my decision. "I'm not leaving him behind," I said. "Like I left Tanis and the others . . ."

"You said it yourself, Fallon." He smiled at me gently. "That was only a tactical retreat."

"Right." I nodded. "And Arviragus is a masterful tactician. His experience could come in handy."

I knew I was concocting the thinnest of rationalizations for bringing him along, but I didn't care. Arviragus had earned my faith in him. And if that faith was misplaced, then . . . what? Was I willing to risk the fates of many for the benefit of one who'd had his chance at glory a long time ago? Whose name was already, forever, a shining silver thread woven into every bard's tapestry of songs? I wondered what Sorcha would do if our situations were reversed.

Would she risk my life to save his?

I already knew the answer before I even asked the question: Yes.

And the Morrigan alone could judge the rightness of it.

Right or wrong, Arviragus was a sight to see when he reappeared, shorn of his tangled mane and beard, and dressed in a plain tunic and cloak. Even Cai looked twice, a hint of a smile tugging at his mouth. Arviragus could have almost passed for any merchant or a farmer from the provinces come to Rome to trade. Nothing could completely hide his warrior's carriage, but I hoped that it would simply make men avoid eye contact, thinking him an ex-soldier or mercenary.

Mostly, I just hoped he would keep his hood up, and his drink down.

"Will *you* come with us, Junius?" he asked his longtime jailer. Seeing as how there would be nothing left to guard after he was gone.

"I've been hovering over you for the better part of the last seven years," Junius snorted. "You'd think you'd be glad to see the back of me. No, I'll stay here. My relief isn't scheduled to take over for another week. That'll give me time to think of something to tell him. Probably that you drank yourself to death and I had to bury you in the yard."

"He'll believe that."

"Oh, aye. And keep it a secret, because he wants his legion pension."

The two men clasped each other by the wrists.

"Goodbye, old friend," Junius said.

"Farewell, old enemy," Arviragus growled.

My heart swelled a bit at the straightness of his spine and the flickering fire I could see kindled to life somewhere deep behind his eyes.

X

THE CLOAK LEANDER had found for me was a shapeless, featureless thing with a deep hood—useful for conveying anonymity, which I desperately needed. As Caesar's vaunted Victrix, I'd been seen by at least half of the citizens of Rome on more than one occasion, and there was a good chance someone would recognize me if I went about in the streets bareheaded.

And not just me.

We had to tie Elka's long blonde braids up and hide them beneath a drab shawl she wore over her head. We hid Ajani's distinctive features beneath a veil. The other girls were likewise disguised, and Cai and Quint both had to stow their legion gear in a trunk and dress in garb befitting merchants, hoping no one would scrutinize their military-short haircuts.

We made our way down to the docks on the River Tiber in pairs and small groups and, once there, used the cover of the merchant stalls and the constant, crowded flow of foot traffic to our best advantage, boarding the craft Cai had procured at inconspicuous intervals. The vessel was a low-slung, dragon-prowed affair with a tattered, faded sail that looked as though it had once belonged to some less-than-prosperous northern raiders. Its side rails were festooned with the ragged-edged sea-bleached shields of its former shipmates, and it looked thoroughly disreputable and barely seaworthy. I suspected that no one would think to look twice for a gaggle of fugitive gladiatrices sailing aboard her.

Still, I would breathe a sigh of relief only once we'd made our way past the docks of the port city of Ostia, with wind filling the sails and the boat bounding through the waves of the Mare Nostrum, heading west toward Corsica. And, I prayed to the Morrigan, my sister.

We'd agreed before setting out that Elka, Ajani, and Gratia would each take a couple of the newer girls. Elka, her tattered palla pulled up over her head, walked bent over like a crone, accompanied by Devana and Nephele. The disguise gave Elka an excuse to lean heavily on a "walking stick"—a long wooden staff that, in her hands, was almost as lethal as her customary bladed spear. Just in case she and her charges ran into any trouble.

Ajani took Kore and Thalassa and had to hide the small bow Leander had found for her beneath the heavy veils she wore. It was a cheaply made thing, almost a child's toy, but it was accompanied by two full quivers of arrows. Ajani had spent days oiling the bow and sharpening the arrows, gently straightening every single shaft over a brazier so they would fly as true as her aim.

Gratia, accompanied by Vorya and Anat, went unequipped. In a street brawl, her bare hands would probably be just as effective as anything else, I reasoned. Whatever other weapons we'd amassed, the girls hid them in boots or packs or under wraps. It wasn't hard—we were still light on arms all around, and what we'd been able to scrounge were mostly long knives and short swords. I counted myself extremely fortunate, under the circumstances, that I had my oath swords, strapped to my hips under my cloak.

The day grew long and I fidgeted with the hilt of one blade, leg muscles cramping from stillness, as Meriel crouched beside me in the shadows of a cloth merchant's stall. She carried only a thin-bladed dagger tucked away in her boot, and I desperately hoped she wouldn't have the opportunity to use it. Because whoever she bloodied with that blade would have to be less than her arm's length away. I shifted uneasily at the prospect of a fight. We'd been lucky so far. Over the course of the last hour or so, as the sun sank toward the hills across the river, she and I had waited.

I glanced back toward the wharf. It was close to deserted now, save for a few late cargo porters and a scattering of gulls searching for scraps. I looked to the ship but couldn't see Cai or Quint in the prow yet. At irregular intervals, one of them—both still dressed like merchants—would appear standing in the prow of the docked boat, and that would be a signal for one of our little groups to make their way onboard. The bustle of the wharves, even that late in the day, helped mask the activity. Our little bands of travelers blended into the crowds, only to disappear up the gang-plank onto the ship, where they stayed out of sight.

Meriel and I were the last, waiting out of sight in the gathering purple shadows as dusk gave way to a deeper dark and the first stars pricked their holes in the fabric of the sky. Antonia and Neferet, along with Leander and Arviragus, had gone aboard not long before. Now the wharf traffic was almost down to nothing, and it wouldn't be long.

Meriel nudged my shoulder. "There's our signal."

"Let's go."

We were so close. A spear's throw—less—when they came out from between the pillars of the merchant's guild pavilion. A half dozen vigiles, all bristling with armor and waiting, clearly, for me to show before they made their move. We'd walked right into a trap.

"That one!" one of them shouted, pointing at me. "It's her!"

We ran, Meriel turning the air as blue as her tattoos with curses. "I'm useless with only this bloody cheese knife!" she exclaimed, brandishing the little blade she carried as her only weapon.

Within a stone's throw of the ship, three more vigiles stepped out from behind a stack of crates—blocking the way between the gangplank and us. Between freedom and us. Meriel skittered to a halt and turned to me, eyes white-rimmed. I drew my swords and offered her one.

She reached to take it—and then lunged past me, shouting, "Never mind!"

"Meriel!"

"Better idea!"

The docks were full of ships and boats and all manner of associated paraphernalia, including fishing gear. A neat stack of it: crab pots, nets, and a bundle of fishing spears. In the arena, Meriel fought retiarius-style, with a trident and net. The spear she snatched up had only two tines instead of the three, and the net was hung with bits of seaweed, but I don't think she cared in the moment. She turned to jam her shoulder up against mine, and together, we faced the advancing vigiles.

As constables of Rome, the vigiles were tough and they were brutal, an effective force in keeping the peace in the city. But when they fought, they fought like thugs. A few of the senior officers were legion-trained, but the majority of the men who patrolled the actual streets, navigating the treacherous rivalries of the district merchant guilds and their gangs of enforcers, were simple brawlers. Big, strong, they outweighed and outmuscled us.

And two of them went down like sacks of grain the instant they attacked.

I didn't have time to think about how it felt to have to wrench my sword out of human flesh again, twisting as I did to avoid slipping in the hot, red rush of blood that followed, painting the cobbles beneath my sandals. I only thought about the lives of the girls on the boat behind me. Of Sorcha waiting for rescue . . .

"Fallon!"

Meriel shouted and I ducked without thinking, slamming my knee painfully onto the ground and rolling over onto my back. The setting sun flashed red on the blade descending in an arc toward my head. I thrust out an arm to block the coming blow but suddenly the sword was gone, caught in the barbs of Meriel's fish spear and swept aside. The blade flew through the air, and its wielder cursed and lurched after to retrieve it.

I sucked in a breath and scrambled clear of the melee, gasping a thanks for the save. Meriel grunted in response and grasped my wrist to drag me up to my feet.

"Down, Meriel!"

I shouldered her aside and slashed my swords overhead as the vigile behind her raised an axe over his head, screaming as he swung the weapon back for a killing blow. He screamed louder when he realized that he no longer had an axe—or an arm—to swing.

Another constable, maybe twenty paces ahead, hauled up short at the sight of his armless fellow, the look of fleeting horror on his face swiftly replaced by one of scorching fury. He brandished a short curved sword and charged at me. I braced for the impact of his blow, but it never landed. Instead, an arrow grazed past my ear and pierced his shoulder. The missile came from the direction of the docks—someone on the ship must have realized we hadn't made

it aboard yet and come up on deck to see the commotion—
and it slammed into the vigile, spinning him around in
a grotesque dance before he fell to the wharf, howling in
pain. If Ajani'd had her proper bow, I thought, he wouldn't
be howling. He'd be dead.

Three more arrows flew in rapid succession, two of
them striking flesh, and in a matter of moments, the circle
of constables that had been advancing on me and Meriel
had scattered in all directions. That earned us a respite to
take cover behind a stack of empty wooden fowl crates.
We crouched there, side by side, both of us gripping bloodied weapons and gasping for breath. I peered between the
slats of a crate to see if I could assess our situation. The
vigiles' numbers had dwindled, but an alarum had been
sounded somewhere, and the faint hope that Meriel and I
would both make it to the gangplank unscathed suddenly
vanished with the last light of the sun beyond the horizon.

The crack of a whip made us both turn back toward the
merchant stalls.

I heard Meriel whisper an oath. And a name: "Nyx."

Like winged Nemesis she came, soot-black cloak and
midnight armor, thick lines of kohl circling her eyes like
war paint. Teeth bared in a snarl, Nyx cracked her whip
again. Her eyes scanned the deserted wharf, and she
shouted for the vigiles who followed in her wake to cut off
access to the docked ships. Another few moments and we
would be hemmed in, with no chance of escape.

I moved to step from behind the crates, but Meriel
grabbed me by the shoulder and hauled me back. "You

walked away last time," she said. "She's not going to let that happen again. She'll kill you."

"She can try—"

"But she won't kill *me*," Meriel said, silencing my attempted bravado.

"Meriel—"

"Don't be stupid, Fallon! Everyone knows—in all the ludus, there was only one fighter you never beat outright. Not without help. Nyx might not be *better* than you, but she knows how to *beat* you."

She wasn't wrong.

"I'm the closest thing she had to a friend at the ludus. If either of us is going to face her, it should be me. Go," she said. "I'll hold her off as long as I can."

I shook my head. "I'm not leaving you."

"Then neither of us is leaving," she snarled. "Don't be a fool—go!"

The sounds of shouting registered from over my shoulder, and I glanced around to see a flurry of activity onboard the ship as the sailors rushed to cast off before the vigiles could reach them. At the rail, Cai and Elka were shouting for us to hurry. And Ajani had another arrow nocked in her bow. I hesitated, turning back to Meriel.

"Go, Fallon!" she urged again. "They need *you* on that ship, not me. And the Lanista needs you most of all."

"Meriel—"

"*Go!*"

And then she stepped out from behind the crates and

calmly strode toward Nyx. With a snarl of frustration, I
slammed my swords back into their scabbards. There was
nothing to stop me from stepping out with her. Nothing
except the thought of my sister. And the boatload of fugitive gladiatrices who'd sworn to risk their lives to help save
her. Like Meriel was doing now.

"I don't have a problem with you, Meriel." Nyx's voice
carried to where I was still hidden.

"Yeah, Nyx," Meriel answered. "You do."

I heard her shout a Prydain battle cry, and I heard the
crack of Nyx's whip. Fighting every urge I had to the con-
trary, I turned and ran for the ship. The sailors had already
cast off the lines, and the vessel was swinging out away
from the jetty. I saw the gangplank teeter and fall into the
water as the gap between the boat and the wharf widened.
The ship rail was lined now with faces—all open-mouthed
and urging me to run *faster!* I put my head down, arms and
legs pumping, and when I reached the edge of the stone
jetty . . . I leaped.

I almost didn't make it. My foot hit the deck railing and
I pitched forward, flailing wildly for something to hold on
to. And then Cai was there, holding on to *me*. He pulled me
onto the deck and crushed me to his chest. I stood there a
moment, the breath heaving in my lungs, before I twisted
away from him and turned back to lean out over the railing.
Back on the dock, Meriel was still on her feet, still fighting.
I'd marveled before at her skill—at how it always seemed
like she was dancing with the retiarius gear—and if it was

the arena, I would have stood there cheering. Instead, my heart was in my mouth as our boat picked up speed and we sailed away from her.

When she went down, finally, under a heap of constables, I could only stand there and watch, numb with horror. Nyx was too far away for me to see her face clearly as she stepped away from the downed girl, but I saw her walk to the very edge of the wharf and stare after our retreating ship.

I imagined her standing there for as long as I did.

I could feel her staring after me. We had not seen the last of each other, but I knew in my heart I had seen the last of Meriel. And it felt like a stone in my chest.

"You lose some along the way," said a voice at my elbow. "It's not your fault. But you should know, you'll probably lose more if you keep to this path."

I turned to see the ship's master standing with his arms knotted across his chest, staring at me with dark eyes. Charon the slave trader. The man who'd captured me and sold me, saved me more than once, and now risked everything to help me save my sister.

"Is it the right path?" I asked.

"You're asking the wrong man." He shook his head. "I'm a slave trader, Fallon. I can speak to the right and wrong of a thing out of both sides of my mouth. It's how I sleep at night."

"They'll follow us." I nodded in the direction of the wharf—and the girl—we'd already left far behind. "Won't they?"

Charon laughed a little. "They can try," he said. "But they won't catch us. Or have you forgotten? I have a long history of leaving ports in a hurry under cover of darkness."

He reached out and gently squeezed my shoulder. Then he left me alone, calling softly out to his crew, who bent to his orders and guided us stealthily down the wide black river. The ship sailed on, a dark silent sea creature riding the deeper darkness of the Tiber's waves. All around us, lamps in windows flickered like fireflies, growing fewer as we left the city far behind.

The vessel was manned by a sparse crew, and so Cai, Quint, Aeddan, Leander, and Arviragus were all pressed into rowing service until such time as we made it out onto the open sea and could unfurl the sails. The girls of the ludus offered to help, but Charon's sailors were already uneasy with so many females on board, let alone ones who could handle the duties of men just as well as they could. They muttered darkly about women and bad luck, but I wondered if some of them just didn't want to be shown up by the likes of Gratia pulling at the oars.

I said as much to her, half-joking, when I found myself standing next to her in the stern of the ship, staring back toward a Rome that had long since disappeared in the distance. Gratia didn't laugh, but I didn't really expect her to. Neither of us was in much of a mood for levity. Not after watching Meriel go down.

"We've left a lot of girls behind," Gratia mused, echoing Charon's sentiment earlier. "A lot of friends."

I felt the dull-edged knife of guilt twist in my heart. "I know. I'm sorry—"

"No." Gratia glanced at me sharply. "No, Fallon. *You* have nothing to be sorry for. I thought Nyx was my friend. I really did. And I've lost her too. The fact that she never felt that way about me—about any of us—doesn't make it hurt any less. What she did to Lydia, to Meriel, those were betrayals. What she's done to you? Unforgivable."

"She thinks I took something from her. Something precious."

"Status. Reputation."

"Sorcha."

"Well, that's something Nyx should have learned by now. You don't own people." She snorted—at the irony, I think, of those words spoken from one slave to another. "Not their hearts, anyway. And if you lose them, then you weren't strong enough or worthy enough to keep them."

I turned to look at Gratia, surprised and a little ashamed that I'd never really considered her disposed toward those kinds of thoughts. Those kinds of *feelings*. I'd only ever thought of her in terms of her bluntness. Both as a fighter and as a person. I guess I'd always known there was much more to her—to all of the Achillea gladiatrices—than just the skill and will to survive. But when you spent your days facing off in the arena against the same people you broke bread with every morning, there was a natural tendency to reduce them to just that: the block of marble, not the finished sculpture.

I reminded myself again of what Sorcha had been striving for with her ideas of a Nova Ludus Achillea. A place where we could be more than just rivals. We were people. Individuals. Creatures of heart and mind, not just flesh and bone, and we deserved a chance to live our lives fully. I wanted that. For me, for Gratia. For all of us. For my sister and my sisters.

Corsica, I vowed silently, would not be the end of it.

It would be the beginning.

After Gratia bid me good night, I went to find Neferet, to see if there was anything in her satchel she could give me to calm my stomach and my nerves. I wasn't the first, apparently.

"Sea sickness," she diagnosed, then gave me a cup of water that she poured a pinch of powder into. "Drink this. And then go lie down. It'll make you drowsy, and maybe a little muddled. So stay away from the ship's rails, and try to get some sleep."

I drank the soporific and wandered off to find a spot somewhere on deck where I could curl up out of the way. Tucking in behind a stack of folded sailcloth near the stern, I wrapped my cloak tight around me and pulled the hood up over my head. The deck had fallen silent, save for the creak of oars and the murmur of the sailors, and they soon lulled me to sleep.

And fretful dreams. Dreams of home . . .

"You mean Britannia?" I heard Cai say.

I tried to answer him, but my head was too heavy and my mouth wouldn't open. And then I realized he wasn't talking to me anyway.

"Durovernum," Aeddan answered. "You could send her back there."

What? No he can't . . .

The sounds of the conversation began to drift in and out, like waves on a beach.

". . . longer she stays in Rome, the shorter her life will be . . ."

That was Aeddan.

". . . draws down danger like a flower draws bees . . ."

". . . go home, back to where she truly belongs . . ."

Cai's voice was muffled. His words indistinguishable, try as I might.

". . . the life she should have had. The life of a queen."

I have the life of a gladiatrix, Aeddan, I thought. *The life I want now . . .*

And then I heard Cai say, "I'm listening."

What? Why? Don't listen to him, Cai . . .

I wanted to stand up and confront the two of them, but the dream wouldn't let me. I was paralyzed. I could only lie there while they discussed what was to be done about me. Their voices drifted in and out of my ears, shifting and modulating, catching in the sails and echoing off the wind and the waves.

". . . with her sister or without . . ."

I heard myself moan in denial. There would be no "without" Sorcha.

"... a queen ... want for nothing—"

"And we both know she won't go willingly."

"She will," Aeddan said. "If *you* tell her to."

Like hell I will ...

"... tell her that you don't want her here." Aeddan's voice grew clearer. "That you don't want *her*. If you don't love her, then it shouldn't be a problem for you. But if you do love her, Caius Varro, then *lie* to her."

I fought against the soft black fog that wrapped around me, pulling me down, struggling to hear Cai's answer—and how vehement his denial would be.

But there was only silence.

And with his silence, I felt my heart crack.

Then the darkness insisted, and I fell into a bottomless, dreamless well. When I awoke sometime later, my eyes snapped open and I sat bolt upright, glancing around wildly in the predawn gloom, scanning the deck for Cai and Aeddan, but they weren't there. The only sounds were the creak and splash of the ship. The shushing of the oars. And the echoes of their voices from my dream.

By the time the sun rose my dream had faded to a tangled, uneasy jumble, and I stood at the railing, staring out at the sea as it turned from deep cobalt to shimmering turquoise and the sky brightened to gold.

"Fallon?" Cai put a hand on my back, between my shoulders, and I felt my muscles tense at his touch. He must have felt it too. "What's wrong?"

I took a breath and turned a smile on him.

"Nothing," I said. "Just ... tired. I didn't sleep much."

I wasn't about to blame Cai for my nightmare. Unlike Kassandra, I wasn't about to start believing that my bad dream had been brought on by anything more than the stresses of the last few days. And Neferet's potent soporific. I steadfastly avoided comparing it to the visitation I received from Arviragus in my prison cell. *That* hadn't been real either, but it had been meaningful . . . in the end. Not this. Not Cai. I refused to believe that he would plot with Aeddan in such a way.

"And how was your night?" I asked. "What did I miss?"

He grinned ruefully and held up his hand, palm up. "Callouses," he said. "Rowing's worse than swordplay for them." The skin of his fingers was blistered in places, raw in others, and I winced on his behalf. "Quint's overjoyed, because it gave him the chance to go beg Elka to bind his wounds."

I raised an eyebrow at him. "Really."

"Didn't work." Cai shook his head. "She sloughed him off on Ajani, who's presently taking pity on the poor lad and slathering him in one of her salves."

I laughed—only a little with relief—and turned back to lean on the rail, looking around at a vast expanse of nothing. No land anywhere. We were through, out on the Mare Nostrum, and clear of Rome and Aquila's hunters.

"It was worth the callouses," Cai said, grinning at my expression.

"We did it," I said, only half believing what my eyes told me. "We're beyond Aquila's reach."

Cai nodded. "For now," he said. "Charon's men might be slavers—"

"And pirates and miscreants and ruthless whenever it serves them to be—"

"But they're good."

They were. And so was Cai.

If I'd been on that galley for any other reason, I could have blissfully lost myself to the warm, fragrant breeze, the splendor of the sea and sky, and the fact that we were the only ship in sight. However Charon and his men had done it, he'd been true to his word. They'd gotten us down the river, past the port of Ostia, and out onto the open sea.

I shouldn't have been so surprised. Charon was, after all, a master of stealth and secrets, and he was motivated. He'd once told me that he'd been hopelessly in love with my sister for years. I hadn't forgotten, and I'd shamelessly used those old affections when we'd plotted our escape. Cai knew it. And he hadn't objected to the blatant manipulation when I'd suggested he reach out to the slave trader for help in securing transportation.

"I hope *you're* never taken captive again," Cai said. "I'm pretty sure this little adventure will tax Charon's goodwill to the limit, and I don't know where I'd find another boat."

"But you would." I grinned. "Somehow."

Cai nodded, but I could see his thoughts had drifted elsewhere. His gaze was distant, focused somewhere toward the horizon where the hills of Rome had long since vanished behind us. I sensed somehow, without even asking, that he was thinking about his argument with Kass, and I felt my stomach clench a bit. I wondered if he'd regretted leaving her behind . . .

"Cai?"

"Hmn?" He blinked and looked back at me.

"Is everything all right?" I asked, realizing what a strange question that might have been, under the circumstances.

He smiled at me. "Are you here, now, with me?" he asked.

I nodded.

"Then everything is absolutely perfect."

He kissed me, and left me to go scrounge us something to eat. I rose and stretched and put Kassandra out of my mind. What Cai had said was true—as long as we were together, everything *was* fine. As I stretched, I felt the pull of the healing skin around my injury, but I no longer experienced any sharp pain with it. That was a relief. I needed to be in fighting trim for what lay ahead of us. Whatever that might be. The wound on my forearm—the one from Aquila's demon-forged silver feather—still tingled a bit when I thought about it, but I tried very hard *not* to think about it. My strength had not left me, and my fingers still clenched into a tight strong fist at my command. I raised that fist in front of my face and stared at my pale-skinned knuckles for a long moment. When I released my grip my fingers opened wide like the wings of a bird.

"He has no hold on me," I whispered to myself as I

shook the blood back into my fingertips. "My strength is the Morrigan's strength. She will not forsake me."

The sails had been raised and the oars shipped once we'd reached the open sea. They snapped and billowed above my head. There was a water barrel on deck, and I went to quench my thirst, passing Arviragus, who stood at the railing on that side of the ship, staring out at the horizon and lost in thought. I noticed his complexion, already pale from years of imprisonment in his sunless cell, was tinged with a slightly greenish cast. But there was also a new, sharp glint in his eyes, and the way he lifted his head to the freshening wind and gulped at it—like a long-kenneled dog let loose on the hunt for the first time—made me offer a silent prayer of gratitude to the Morrigan for leading me to him in my delirium. He was free again. And whatever else happened, *that*, in itself, was a gift I'd never expected to be able to give.

I smiled to myself as I wandered back to settle down on the stack of folded sailcloth I'd slept next to, waiting for Cai to return with breakfast. My stomach actually growled at the thought of food, and I took that as a good sign for my returning strength.

The other girls were scattered in small groups spread out along the deck. Some of them, I suspected, had never been out on the open sea before. And even for those who had—myself and Elka included—it was a disconcertingly foreign experience. Not just the motion of the ship on the waves, but the fact that the land had disappeared behind us, with nothing to indicate that there was anything but water and more water ahead. I saw more than one fearless gladiatrix glance nervously out over the rolling waves, searching for terra firma.

Eventually, though, the unease gave way to mere queasy boredom.

"What's the matter with them?" Cai asked me once we'd finished breakfast and the sun had climbed high into the sky. He too had sensed the growing restlessness among my fellow gladiatrices.

"I think they need something to keep them occupied," I said.

Cai pondered that for a moment, then said, "I have an idea."

He gestured me over to the side of the ship and reached over the rail to hoist up two of the round shields that decorated the sides. I laughed and shook my head. "Do you remember what happened the last time you and I fought and there was a shield involved?" I asked.

"You cracked my rib." He grinned back at me. "How could I possibly forget?"

"And you want to risk that again?"

"I do not." He shot me a look from under a raised eyebrow. "Between you and that bear, I've recently found myself inclined to watch *others* hurt themselves instead."

"Oh, I like the sound of this," Quintus said, wandering up.

I'd noticed Quint had no trouble with his sea legs. Likely the result of having come from a Corsican fishing village, where he'd probably learned to ride the bobbing waves astride a skiff before he could walk on land.

"You like the sound of what?" Elka asked, pushing herself up from where she'd been dozing fitfully on a deck bench.

"Fighting," Cai said. "Us against you. Well, Quint against you."

Elka snorted and knotted her arms across her chest, eyeing Quint up and down. "Your kind doesn't fight, soldier boy," she said. "You just hide behind your shields and wait until the real warriors tire themselves out."

"That's not true!" Quint protested. "Also? It's called strategy. And it's not as easy as you'd think."

One by one, the other girls wandered up to join us, drawn by battle talk.

"You fight like insects," Vorya sneered. "It's mindless. Boring."

"I didn't know war was supposed to be entertaining," Quint countered.

"Then you've never seen *us* fight," Kore said, and earned a shoulder punch from Thalassa. "Or you wouldn't say such a thing. We'd get your blood pumping, that's for sure!"

Elka and I exchanged a glance, and I hid a grin behind my hand. The two of us had been fighting as gladiatrices for less than the span of a full year, but the younger girls on that boat were a whole new generation of firebrands, eager to prove themselves out on the sand. Nephele was nodding in vigorous agreement, and I was pretty certain she'd taken her oath only two months back. She hadn't even seen real exhibition combat yet.

In the face of Quint's argument, that didn't seem to matter. And he remained undaunted in his debate. "That's the *thing*, though," he said, responding to Kore's assertion. "Isn't it?"

"What thing?" Devana asked.

"His pumping thing?" Anat said with a feigned innocence that turned Quint scarlet with blushing. "What about it?"

"The *thing* I'm talking about, you ridiculous creatures, is discipline. *Teamwork*. It's all very well and good to get out there and face off in single combat. But what if you've got a whole army coming at you?"

Devana shrugged. "You fight? Same as one-on-one."

"But it's *not*!" Quint said, gesturing triumphantly, as if she'd just clearly and succinctly made his point for him. The girls just looked at each other, shrugging, and Quint huffed a sigh and tried again. "Look," he said. "You've got attackers coming at you from all sides. There're arrows and slingshot raining down from above. Men behind you, men in front of you, men to the right, to the left; if you fall, your own army'll walk right over you. So you'd better not fall."

"Sounds horrid," Hestia said. "Dishonorable."

"How does anyone survive?" Devana asked.

Quint hefted the shield. "Defense."

"I prefer offense," Gratia said, holding out her arm and curling her fingers into a fist with a loud succession of knuckle pops.

"Then I'll see you again on the banks of the River Styx," Quint said, and swept the shield suddenly to the side, knocking Gratia's fist away as if it were a bothersome horse-fly. "But you'll get there a long while before me. Because I'll be going home and straight to the taverna for a cool jug of wine after a successful campaign. And another. And another. And you'll all be bleached bones in a meadow."

The girls shifted uncomfortably, and Quint relented.

"You think it's mindless, I know," he said, with a sigh. "A soulless way to fight. It's not. It's training. Just like you train. Right, decurion?"

"My second would not lie to you ladies," Cai said, gesturing magnanimously. "And he has trained some of the finest soldiers that were under my command. Why not give him a chance?"

There were glances back and forth, shoulder shrugs, and then Ajani stood and said, "Well, I've got nothing better to do until my feet hit dry land . . ."

"Good!" Quint slapped his palms together. "Everyone, fetch a shield."

The girls moved to the ship side rails, where the sea salt–weathered round shields hung from hooks in all their faded glory. I hefted one along with all the others, wincing a bit at the heavy awkwardness of the thing.

It didn't go unnoticed. Neferet was on me like a mother duck on a wayward hatchling. "Not you, Fallon," she said. "You'll pull your stitches out, and I refuse to put them back in."

"Come on," Cai said, grabbing my hand and leading me off to the side. "We can sit and watch the battle from afar, like the great generals do."

Reluctantly, I went with him, placated somewhat by the arm he snaked around my waist as we sat side by side. I'd forgotten how good it felt to just lean into him sometimes, and I relaxed for the first time since I'd woken up that morning.

Over on the opposite guardrail, I saw Aeddan and Arviragus settle themselves, cross-armed, to watch the exercise. I wondered what Arviragus must be thinking, observing as a group of young warriors trained in the techniques that had decimated his tribe. I wasn't sure about it myself. But the Cantii had never lost in the way the Arverni had. Not many tribes had, really.

Quint challenged the girls not to fight but rather to defend. His aim was to see if we could work as a unit the way the legion did, responding to commands as a single entity. And he was right in what he'd said. Legion shield work *wasn't* anywhere near as easy as it looked. He started off instructing his gaggle of gladiatrices in the formation of the *testudo*—the essential legion "tortoise" defense— where soldiers in the front line of a fighting unit held their shields out as a solid defensive wall, while those in the ranks behind held theirs overhead, forming a defensive shell. The round shields offered less coverage than a heavy rectangular legionnaire scutum would have, but the lighter weight was to the girls' advantage. Still, they had to learn to move as one, like dancers in a chorus, as Quint would blow a series of notes on a whistle he carried to indicate the formation changes.

"See?" Cai said, as he pointed out the finer points of the defensive maneuver with his sword. "The footwork is key, just like in a duel—Elka! *Right* foot!—otherwise you get all tangled up. Good, Hestia! Neatly done . . ."

"Vorya was right—they *do* look like an insect!" I marveled. "Like one of those segmented things with all the legs."

"Exactly." Cai grinned at me. "And you know how hard those things are to squash!"

I did. We'd been plagued with them for the better part of a hot month at the ludus, and whacking them repeatedly with a sandal did almost nothing to deter the little monsters. I could see how it would be much the same with the testudo formation, properly executed. I watched Quint running up and down the line of shields, probing for weakness, slamming them intermittently with the flat of his blade to indicate gaps that needed closing. It was a fascinating lesson in legion discipline, and I felt like I did when I was a girl, watching Sorcha learn some new technique that was exciting and mysterious to me—until I discovered the tricks behind it.

"That's it," I muttered when Quint called a brief break.

I jumped to my feet and took up a spare shield, no longer able to sit idle when there was a new way of fighting to be learned. Just like when I was a girl, I needed to know the tricks. Neferet looked about to squawk at me again, but I stopped her.

"If I can't fight here," I said, "I'm not going to be able

to fight when we find Sorcha and Thalestris, now, am I?" I shrugged the shield straps up my arm and joined the line. "Better to know that sooner than later."

She couldn't really argue with my reasoning and contented herself with the sort of annoyed, professional grumbling that she must have picked up from her time spent with Heron. I grinned, ignoring her, and tested my strength, turning my concentration toward Quint's instruction. As both a Cantii warrior and an Achillea gladiatrix, the legion way of fighting felt—at the beginning—utterly foreign.

Not just to me, but to all of us.

It took some getting used to. To put it mildly.

For the first hour of Quint's drills, we fell all over ourselves, bashing each other with the shields and, as Cai had predicted, tripping over each others' feet. There was a lot of swearing—and a lot of laughing—and then, gradually, we started to move from testudo to hollow square to staggered formation and back again with a degree of precision. By the time we finished the drills, all of us were sore and sweating and congratulating each other on our newfound defensive prowess.

Cai dubbed us "Legio Achillea," and Quint stood in our midst with his hands on his hips, looking extravagantly pleased with himself—especially when Elka affectionately punched his shoulder as she went past on her way to stow her shield.

The distraction had transformed the mood of the ship. Most of us seemed to have even forgotten we were sailing out on the open sea without a stitch of land in sight. It felt more like we were gliding along on a pleasure barge crossing a placid lake. The lightness hadn't touched all corners of the ship, though. Arviragus had disappeared belowdecks—to nurse his seasickness with a draught, Leander said, but I suspected it had been a bit too painful a reminder of his own defeat by those same maneuvers. Aeddan brooded silently from his perch in the stern of the boat, watching everything through his hawk eyes and scowling. And as the girls dispersed, I glanced over my shoulder to see Charon standing in the bow, arms crossed over his chest and a far-away, pensive look shadowing his handsome face.

I gave Cai's arm a squeeze and crossed the deck to talk to the slave master.

Charon nodded at me in greeting, his dark eyes never leaving the horizon in front of us. I leaned on my elbows beside him and gazed in that direction. At first, I thought it was my imagination, but as I looked, I saw a thin, dark smudge in the farthest distance that began, ever so slightly, to thicken as we sailed toward it.

"You're thinking about what we might find when we reach the end of this journey," I said quietly. "Aren't you?"

"Aren't you?" he countered.

"You mean, am I wondering whether we'll find my sister alive or dead?" I looked at him sideways and lifted a shoulder. "I am. Then again, I've spent most of my life thinking Sorcha was dead."

Charon nodded, staring out over the water. "The thought of having only just found her to lose her again must be unbearable," he murmured.

I suspected he was speaking more of himself than of me. I turned back to gaze at the growing shape on the horizon. "I do not think the Morrigan would be so cruel," I said.

"Your fearsome war goddess." He regarded me from under an arched brow. "She who—as I've been led to understand—bathes in the blood of her enemies and feasts on their eyes after the battle's done? *She* would not be so cruel?"

I smiled at him. "She led me to Sorcha once; she'll do so again."

"And what if we, weak unworthy humans that we are, are too late when we do finally find her?" he asked.

"We won't be," I said, feeling the smile fade from my lips. "But even if we're too late for rescue, we'll still be right on time for revenge."

XI

THE SEA RUSHED to meet the rugged contours of the wild Corsican coast as if it had been too long away from the kiss of land. To the north and west of us, the water was the color of the blue-green faience collars Cleopatra wore around her neck, the waves sparkling and laced with delicate nets of pearly foam. Schools of silver fish darted and danced in the shadows cast by the galley prow as we sailed in the lee of majestic cliffs. In the far distance, I could just make out the profile of another island—Sardinia, I'd been told it was called—that lay to the south of us.

We sailed between the two islands, following the Corsican shoreline, and eventually rounded a towering promontory that raced away to the east, swooping low to become a gleaming beach circling a deep, sheltered bay surrounded by forest-cloaked hills rising back toward craggy mountains.

Cai looked at Quintus. "Is this the place?"

Quint nodded. He looked over his shoulder at where Charon stood up on the captain's deck and pointed to a spot on the shore. The slave master gave the order, and the sailors steered the ship in that direction.

"Do you think they'll have sentries posted?" Elka asked Quint.

He shook his head. "No. No one comes here."

"Because of the Amazons?"

"Their reputation has been enough to guard this place and keep it safe since before I was born," he said. "There are those who say it is a cursed place."

I saw Charon wince and glance over his shoulder at the ship's captain, who'd been listening to the conversation. Charon took Quint by the shoulder and turned him away from the man. "I'd counsel you against using that kind of language around the crew, friend. Sailors are a superstitious lot."

Charon had already told us that his men would not go ashore with us when we dropped anchor. They were slavers and sailors, not fighters, and no amount of money—even if I'd had any to speak of—would convince them otherwise. But I worried in that moment that they would leave us to our business once we were gone and sail back to the mainland without us. I said as much to Charon.

He shook his head. "I'll stay behind. You'll have a ship standing by to return to, Princess," he said. "I promise."

"And *I'll* stay behind to make sure he keeps that promise," said Aeddan, joining the conversation.

Charon cocked his head and regarded Aeddan. "You don't trust me?"

"You're a career thief." Aeddan shrugged. "A scoundrel. The leader of career thieves and scoundrels. I trust you as much as I would any in your trade."

I groaned inwardly, but Charon just smiled. He turned to me. "And you, Fallon, do you trust me? Him?"

"I trust that you'll be here when I get back," I said. "Whether Aeddan is or not, well . . . surprise me."

"I'll happily take wagers on whether we come back to find him floating faceup or facedown," Elka said dryly.

Aeddan turned a flat stare on her—which she returned in kind—but that was the extent of his response, for which I was thankful. I'd resigned myself to the fact that he seemed determined to make himself "useful" on our quest and there was nothing that would dissuade him, short of one of us throwing him overboard. Maybe Elka had the right idea with her suggested wager. My dream of Aeddan's duplicity, of him trying to convince Cai to lie . . . to make me leave . . . swam up from the depths of my mind, writhing like a sea serpent, and made me wonder, again, just exactly what Aeddan's motives were. And whether or not I really could trust him.

Or Cai . . .

No. Aeddan was the only one I questioned. Even as I owed him my escape from Tartarus. I bit my tongue, frowning, and went to check my gear.

At Quint's direction, Charon's men anchored the galley in a northern curve of the bay and launched the ship's

single skiff over the side to ferry me and Cai and the others
to shore. The little craft could only hold two at a time plus a
rower, so it would take a while, and I was a seething ball of
impatience. So much so, in fact, that my nerves must have
frayed to the breaking point without my really realizing it.
Because it was only moments after the skiff turned around
and headed back out to where the ship was anchored, leaving me and Cai alone, when I turned to him.

"I . . ." My mind told me to stop. To let it go.

"Fallon?" he said. "What is it?"

"Did you . . . speak to Aeddan last night? On the ship
while everyone else was asleep?"

I half expected him to laugh or deny it. Why would he
speak to Aeddan? But he did neither, and the memory of the
conversation clouded his clear hazel gaze. I closed my eyes as
I felt my heart sink. It hadn't been a dream. Not at least that
part of it. And now there were only two possibilities. Two
answers to fill in the terrible, silent space of Cai's answer.

"It's not what you think," he said.

I shook my head and turned away.

"Fallon—"

"No." I spun back around, anger burning in my cheeks.
"*Cai*. I heard."

"You heard what?"

"I heard what you said—or what you *didn't* say!"

He gaped at me in confusion. "What—"

"You *hesitated*. When Aeddan told you to lie to me—
to tell me that you didn't love me—so that I'd leave. You
didn't tell him no."

"That hesitation you heard," Cai said sharply, "was me trying to figure out how best to explain the kind of girl you are to your tribesman without punching him in the face first. Fallon . . . if all you heard was that hesitation, then you didn't hear the most important part."

"And that was?"

"The part where I told Aeddan that he could go straight to a hell of his own choosing before I would agree to such a thing. Understand something, Fallon . . ." His expression was hurt. And more than hurt. Angry. "Something vital. I would sacrifice any chance I ever had at happiness with you if I thought that, in doing so, I would be making your life better or happier. And I'd do it with a smile on my face and a song in my breaking heart. But I will *not* lie to you. Ever. And telling you I don't love you is the most flagrant lie that could ever pass my lips."

I watched helplessly as the hurt in his gaze turned to disappointment. He shook his head sadly, and I was beginning to think I'd made a terrible mistake.

"I thought we had agreed to treat each other as equals," Cai said quietly.

"Cai—"

"You *really* don't trust me, do you, Fallon? When are you going to believe in me enough to accept the fact that I believe in you?"

"I do—"

"Back at the ludus you didn't even tell me you were hurt."

"What—" I sputtered. "I didn't tell anyone!"

"You didn't tell *me.*" There was a long pause. "Did you tell Aeddan?"

I couldn't bring myself to answer him. Was he right? Did I actually trust Aeddan more than I trusted Cai? And what in all the worlds did that say about me? That I could confide weakness to the man who'd murdered my first love, but not the man I loved now? Was I *that* afraid of what Cai would do to my heart if I ever gave it to him fully? My silence spoke volumes, apparently.

"Right," he said. There was a weary resignation in his voice. A dull, bruised ache.

"I didn't tell you because I didn't want you to think I couldn't handle myself," I said. "I just didn't want you to lose trust in *me.* To think I wouldn't be able to get us out of there—"

"But I *do* trust you. How many times do I have to tell you that?"

"Until I believe it myself."

He laughed, a mirthless weary sound. "I don't know that I have that much breath in my body, Fallon."

"Trust goes both ways, Cai."

"I don't know what you mean."

Kass, I wanted to say.

But the skiff had returned. And there was no more time for us to argue.

"This isn't over," Cai said before Antonia and Neferet stepped ashore.

I nodded and turned to the water, watching as the two of them waded through the knee-deep froth, holding each other's hands for support. Over the next hour or so, the beach began to slowly fill up with gladiatrices, and there was no chance for us to finish our argument. In truth, I wished it had never started. The uneasy feeling that I was profoundly on the wrong side of it was like a thorn against my skin, and every time I looked over at Cai, I wanted to take his hands in mine and kiss away the angry words I'd flung at him.

But it would have to wait.

Not far from where we landed, there was a river that emptied into the bay. The rich soil it carried down from the hills stained the pale beach sand, marking the place where fresh water met sea, and that was where we would begin our trek up into the forest of pine and cedar and olive trees. The sky overhead was brilliant blue and dotted with puffs of cloud, but beneath the trees, the deep green shadows raised gooseflesh on my arms. The hills rising up ahead of us were silent, and it seemed as if even the birds avoided this place.

My fellow gladiatrices ranged in a loose half circle around me, silent and formidable, faces and limbs marked with war paint. I could feel the designs on my own skin pull tight and tingle as I moved, and I shivered in anticipation of the battle to come, sensing the same coiled tension in the others. The battle readiness. Even Neferet, who'd sworn off ever picking up a weapon again, had a look to her that made me pity anyone who attempted to test her resolve regarding that oath. She shifted the surgeon's bag on her shoulder, Leander at her side. He would stay with her, behind any kind of fighting we might encounter, to help with wounded—if it came to that. Knowing she was there with her bandages and instruments and potions made me feel better about what was potentially to come. About the fact that I was dragging my oath sisters into danger to rescue my blood sister. And I refused to even entertain the thought that she might not be there for us to rescue.

Arviragus had forgone the woad, but he didn't really need it to be intimidating. And war paint would have looked a bit ridiculous on Leander—although the way he handled the blade we'd given him made me think that he'd picked up at least a few tricks, watching us all practice back at the ludus. It was almost enough to bring a smile to my lips as I watched him. The kitchen boy was finally the hero in his own tale, and he seemed determined to make the most of it.

Cai and Quint, for their part, were dressed in full battle garb, scarlet-plumed helmets waving in the breeze off the ocean. The very picture of ruthless legion efficiency. I was used to the stern, soldierly expression on Cai's face under the brim of his helmet, but it was unsettling to see Quint's gaze turned so hard.

"Thank you for leading us here, Quintus," I said, before we set off.

"Don't thank me," he said. "You're doing this for your sister, Fallon, but I do this for myself. And for the brother I never came back to save."

He turned away and started up the path, and I glanced over to see Elka watching him go, her expression pensive.

Her blue gaze stayed on Quint's back until he had disappeared beneath the trees. I waved the others forward and we followed. The path wound beside a little tumbling river, over white rocks furred with moss, beneath the branches of ancient trees. It was worn smooth from many years of use, but it was steep going in places and we were all breathing hard after a quarter hour's climb. Arviragus strode up the twisting incline in Quint's wake directly ahead of me, the unsheathed sword in his hand swishing side to side, like the tail of a hunting cat. His head was in constant motion, eyes scanning the rugged terrain on both sides, and he was the one to sense the initial attack before any of the rest of us.

I could almost see the hackles rising on the back of his neck as he turned to me, his eyes almost black in the failing evening light as he said, "I have a bad feeling—"

And that was all he had time for.

The arrow slammed into the dirt between my feet. I yelped and dove for cover behind a stout, twisty pine, shouting for the others to do the same. I saw Ajani tackle Nephele out of the way, and Kore and Hestia ducked down behind a boulder. The rest of the girls were strung out along the path, with Gratia bringing up the rear, and I hoped frantically that our archer assailant was alone. If not, the girls would be easy pickings and there was nothing I could do about it. Cai landed in a tumbling crouch beside me as two more arrows sang through the air like hornets, and Arviragus scrambled around the other side of the tree as another missile grazed his ear.

"Damn my eyes!" he cursed, his broad shoulders jamming up against the rough bark of the tree. "I used to be a lot better at this sort of thing." He reached up to touch his ear, and his fingertips came away bloody.

"I can't imagine how all those years in a prison cell managed to dull your edge," Cai said, frantically signaling Quint, who was ahead of us, taking cover with Elka.

"I think it was the wine," Arviragus muttered dryly.

I edged around the bole of the tree, peering in the direction of where the arrow fire had come from, expecting another volley. Nothing. We waited, moving back onto the path only after a good long while had passed. The forest had resumed its eerie stillness, and eventually, Elka and Quint came loping back down the trail and the other girls climbed up to meet us.

"I think it's clear," Quint said, quietly. "Whoever took those potshots at us probably ran out of arrows."

"If that's the case," I said, "they've probably run back to wherever they came from to warn of our presence. We've lost any element of surprise we might have had."

"We don't need surprise," Antonia said. "We are the House Achillea, and we'll win whether our foes expect us or not."

There was a murmur of assent from the others, and I felt my heart swell at the bravery—and loyalty—of my companions as we set off back up the winding trail. In fairly short order we discovered that we *hadn't* actually lost the element of surprise. But neither had our archer, who, it turned out, hadn't run off at all.

Although it appeared she *had* run out of arrows.

The large basket of fish came sailing out of nowhere, hitting Quint square in the chest and knocking him to the ground. It was followed close behind by a second basket that plummeted out of the sky as if flung by a catapult and headed directly for me, but my swords were already in motion. My right blade deflected the basket, and my left took the head clean off a nice-sized sea bream that tumbled clumsily through the air.

I had a moment to relish the excellence of my reflexes, before I realized that my momentum had carried me to the very edge of the path—which crumbled away beneath my feet as I dropped my swords and flailed wildly, grabbing at handfuls of nothing as I tried to keep my balance. I heard Cai shout in alarm as I toppled over the precipice, my own cry strangled in my throat, and then there was a sharp, painful yank on my arm that almost pulled my shoulder from its socket.

I dangled in midair, looking up into Elka's grimly determined face.

"I've *got* this one!" she snapped over her shoulder. "*You* lot go after the fish-lobber so she doesn't raise a bloody alarm!"

I heard the sound of running feet fading up the path.

"Men," Elka muttered through clenched teeth as she strained to haul me back up. "They hinder more than they help, *ja*? Thalassa, Nephele—get over here and grab my legs! Hold tight . . ."

Her two-handed grip on my wrist was excruciating, but

I couldn't help but gasp a laugh as I dug my feet into the cliff face and reached up with my free hand. "Aye, men," I grunted, struggling to climb. "Of course . . . I remember . . . a time when you yourself . . . would have hacked off . . . my foot . . . rather than help . . ."

"That . . . was before . . . we knew each other . . ."

One last heave and I was up and rolling onto my back on the dirt track. The other girls fell back on their haunches as Elka and I lay there, gulping for breath for a moment. She rolled her head and grinned at me.

"But," she continued, "the strength of my character saved you."

"I'll give the credit this time to the strength of your arms," I said and climbed shakily to standing. "Come on."

I held out a hand to her and then, together, we turned to help the other girls to their feet. Elka stood, pushing the sweat-damp hair back from her face with her forearm, and then we all took off running, scrabbling up a near-vertical incline to squeeze through a narrow break in a rock wall. I heard Cai shouting what sounded like orders to Quint, and by the time I was through to the other side, I saw the two of them had the fishergirl down on the ground, held there by Quint's hand on her throat. His other arm was lifted, weapon poised and about to descend.

"Quintus!" I shouted. "Hold!"

I strode forward, ignoring the fact that I was still gasping for breath. At a glance from me, Cai pulled Quint away from our assailant. Close up, I was startled to see she was barely more than a child. A dangerous child, perhaps, but she couldn't have been more than fifteen years old. Maybe younger. Younger than the girls who'd just helped Elka haul me back up that cliff. Except the look in this girl's eyes was anything but childish. She lay there, stone still and glaring poisonously up at me, and I drew my double blades, leaning down to cross them in front of her throat.

"Thalestris," I said, cutting straight to the heart of the matter. I saw no reason not to be direct, under the circumstances.

The girl's eyes narrowed.

"You know her?"

She didn't answer.

Quint stepped back up beside me and gazed down at the girl. "Just occurred to me—she might not speak Latin," he said. "Let me try something else."

I kept my swords at the ready as he crouched down in front of her. He spoke to her in Greek—I recognized the sound of the language if not the meaning of the actual words—and after a few moments, she answered him. Her replies were brief but seemed to satisfy Quint. He stood and turned to face me.

"She's there," he said. "Thalestris. She's at the *oppidum*— the settlement gathering place—and she has your sister. Sorcha is still alive. Thalestris is planning on sacrificing her this very night at moonrise to their Amazon goddess, Cybele. This girl was catching fish for the celebration rites to take place after. But she will take us around and show us a rear approach to the oppidum. She says they won't be expecting any kind of attack from that direction."

"And why will she do that, exactly?" Elka asked, wary as always.

"Because I told her if she didn't"—Quint grinned coldly—"that Fallon would carve her up into pieces too small to use even as fish bait."

"But you could have told me that yourself," the girl said to me in accented, but perfectly understandable, Latin. "Instead of having to defer to this . . . *man.*" The derision positively dripped from her lips, lifted in a sneer at Quint.

"You speak Latin?" I asked, trying not to show my surprise.

"I speak your tongue well enough." She lifted her chin defiantly.

"It's not *my* tongue," I said, crouching down in front of her. "And if you understand it well enough, you should also understand when I tell you that I defer to no man. But this one speaks the truth. I am not cruel, but I am not merciful. Not this day. Not when my sister's life is in danger. Help us and all will be well. Hinder us and you will die."

"I guess I don't really have much choice then, do I?" she said, dryly.

I admired her courage. It didn't even seem like bravado as she stood and dusted herself off. Then without a backward glance, she turned and started up the path, muttering about the waste of perfectly good fish.

Cai came up beside me. "Fallon," he said, putting a hand on my arm, a frown of worry on his brow. "Are you all right?"

"I'm fine," I said, shrugging out of his grip, even though I didn't really meant to.

His lips disappeared in a white line and he nodded brusquely. "Good."

"Let's keep moving," I said, and gestured to the others to follow.

The path angled steeper the farther up we hiked. I turned to glance over my shoulder at the line of gladiatrices following me up the hill. From my vantage point, they looked like an armored serpent, twisting its way up the path, a line of round, many-colored scales upon its back. We'd decided, collectively, to bring the shields from the ship, carrying them on our backs. Just in case. I hoped we wouldn't need them. But never again would I decline the opportunity for an advantage in a fight, and if the Amazons, like the Cantii and the Arverni and—as far as I could tell, almost anyone who wasn't a soldier in the Roman legion— fought as individuals, then our newly learned defensive tactics might come in handy.

If it came down to a fight.

And I knew in my heart that it would.

Thalestris wouldn't give up without one, but I wondered about her fellow Amazons. Were they really the fearsome fighting force of legend? Warrior women fueled by the magic of their gods, adversaries of legendary heroes? Our sullen young captive didn't seem quite so mystical. I glanced around me as we ascended—at the signs of what seemed to have been a once-prosperous settlement. There were stone ruins dotted here and there beneath the trees, but no signs of recent habitation. And then the path crested a rise and opened up before us to reveal a sweeping, terraced landscape. I could see the remains of fortifications and walls, tumbled structures and stone pillars. At the center, there was a broad, roughly circular enclosure, like a natural arena, watched over by several tall stone sentinels carved in the shapes of weapons and warriors with stern, glowering faces. From the way Quint had described it, I thought this must be the oppidum—the settlement that had been built by the original inhabitants of the island and then abandoned, only to be taken over by the Amazons once they had escaped their Greek masters.

The place looked forsaken, silent and still, long uninhabited. Except . . .

Not far ahead, Quint had stopped in front of the hollowed-out curve of a massive boulder that formed a shallow cave that might have provided scant protection from the elements. He stood staring into the shadowy niche, and following his glance, I could see why. There were cages there, beneath the low stone overhang. Empty, but big enough to have once held one or two occupants each. I watched as Elka reached out and put a hand on Quint's shoulder.

"Quintus," she said quietly. "You don't know—"

"Yeah," he said. "I do. They kept him in one of these. I know it."

"Quint . . ."

"It doesn't matter now." He shrugged off her hand. "Come on. Let's go."

I looked back at Arviragus, who had a firm grip on our young Amazon captive, and knew by the way she was staring at the cages that Quint was right. That's exactly what they'd been used for. The look on Arviragus's face told me he recognized them for what they were too.

"Where are your people?" I asked the girl.

She looked at me, her gaze flinty. "Don't worry," she said, her focus drifting over my shoulder. "They're coming."

"What?" I rounded on her. "You said they wouldn't be expecting us—"

"They're not!" she said, pointing behind me at where the pale round ghost of the full moon was just rising into the dusky sky. "They come for the sacrifice." Then she pointed at a rough-hewn menhir in the center of the main clearing, a pillar carved from a single stone darker than the surrounding rock and taller than the tallest man. In the fading light, I realized that there were ropes circling it.

Ropes that bound my sister Sorcha to the stone, holding her immobile.

The sacrifice.

Sorcha's head hung down, hair obscuring her face. I sucked in a breath at the sight of her and was suddenly assailed by a strikingly vivid memory from my childhood. When I was five or six years old, Durovernum was attacked by raiders who'd sailed in shallow-keeled boats all the way up the River Dwr. They thought themselves brave but in reality were just too stupid to realize what they were up against. The fighting had been brief, vicious, and—on their end—lethal to a man. About the only thing the raiders managed was to set fire to a grove of pine trees near the town walls. I remembered my outrage as a child, because it was one of my favorite places to play. I also remembered the smell—the sharp, potent tang of blazing pine sap.

I could taste it. Acrid green smoke. Just a hint on the breeze . . .

"Look sharp!" I hissed. "We're not alone!"

An understatement.

The moon rose before us, the sun set behind, turning the oppidum into a stone bowl filled with misty purple shadows. But in the distance, I could see thin lines of black smoke rising, and the branches of the olive trees glowed orange with the reflected light of flames.

"Down!" I whispered, gesturing. "Quiet!"

Arviragus clamped a hand over the Amazon girl's mouth and dragged her into a crouch behind a boulder. The others followed, scattering to hide themselves behind rocks and trees. I saw Quint, crouched and sprinting, disappear behind a rise of hill, and then my attention was wholly occupied by the smell of burning and the sound of many footsteps. The Amazons of Corsica streamed out from beneath the trees. Twenty, maybe thirty of them altogether. More than twice our numbers.

Too many.

Far too many of them for us to fight . . .

I felt a swell of despair in my chest as they strode out into the open. In their fists, they bore long chains from which strange lanterns swung—ball-shaped iron cages filled with pine-tar resin, the source of the green-tang smoke. They burned with roiling orange and blue flames and looked like smoldering souls captured from battlefields. As they entered the oppidum clearing and ranged themselves into a circle, some of the younger girls went around, lighting torches on poles with the lamps, and soon the clearing was bathed in an eerie, crepuscular glow.

I didn't see Thalestris among them as the torch lighters joined their sisters in a circle and, together, the Amazons began to stamp their feet on the bare earth—in time with each other at first. And then, slowly, the rhythm shifted, becoming complex with counterbeats and accent stomps that reminded me of the hide drums the Cantii warriors carried into the field to frighten our enemies. As the cadence built, growing faster and louder, the Amazons began to swing the lamp chains back and forth. Another stomp and one girl in the circle whipped her lamp over-head in a full fiery arc, followed by the girl next to her . . . and the next, until the clearing was full of roaring hoops made of flame. As I watched, open-mouthed, the shapes they drew in the air changed, and the circle they formed disintegrated as each Amazon broke out into a dance of her own—distinct from one another, and yet still a part of the whole. Individual flourishes flowed in fiery patterns from Amazon to Amazon, as if they were storytellers passing a tale from each to each. It was a mesmerizing spectacle—like nothing I'd ever seen before—and I began to understand the stories of the Amazons and their terrible war-magic, gifted to them by the gods.

The flaming cages whirled, faster and faster, painting circles of fire in the darkening air, like red and gold flowers blooming in the darkness, and the whoosh of the roaring flames sounded like the fearsome cries of wild beasts. The Amazons moved like dancers, whipping the fireballs through the air so that they would loop around necks and limbs and then double back, lashing the air like the crack of Nyx's whip and skimming past flesh by a hairsbreadth. They swung them in twisting arcs, leaping over the chains and ducking under them, and as they danced, the tempo of their feet increased until it was one great thunderous noise. The fireballs arced high over their heads to slam down into the ground in showers of sparks . . .

And then silence.

Deafening in the wake of the roaring war dance.

I blinked against the momentary fire-blindness that marred my sight, lightning traces crisscrossing my field of vision as I squeezed my eyes shut. When I opened them again, it was to see the Amazons standing statue-still in their circle, fire chains held at their sides, plumes of smoke rising from the still-burning cages.

And into that smoldering circle strode Thalestris, dressed for war.

She carried no lantern, only a slender spear in one hand and a long-bladed knife in the other. I felt every muscle in my body tense as she stalked across the circle to stand before the menhir where Sorcha was bound. I saw my sister lift her head to meet Thalestris's gaze, her eyes burning with defiance.

"Cybele!" Thalestris shouted to the skies, arms spread wide in supplication. "Black stone mother! Guardian of the boundaries between the living and the dead! Accept this blood sacrifice that we may wash the shame of our sister Orithyia's disgrace and defeat from our skins and from our souls!"

It seemed to me, in that moment, some kind of twisted version of the oath rites of the Ludus Achillea. Like something seen in a warped bronze mirror, glimpsed through a pall of oily dark smoke. Something Pontius Aquila and his Sons of Dis would appreciate . . . I shuddered at the thought.

There was a moment of ominous stillness among the women warriors gathered there, and then a battle cry errupted from their collective throats, shattering the gathering night. I felt a hand of panic squeezing my heart. There was nothing we could do in that moment—facing off against a ring of flame-wielding warrior women—that would save my sister. A direct charge of the Achillea fighters would only get them killed outright, and *that* I would not do.

So I readied myself to do the only thing I could think of. Charge them myself and hope that a single target would be harder to hit. Hope that I could get to Sorcha before—

Thalestris raised her knife . . .

The cage flames whirled again. Faster and faster . . .

And then, above it all, I heard the high-pitched skree of Quintus's signal whistle as he sounded three short blasts.

"Legio Achillea!" Cai reacted immediately, shouting in his command voice. "Form up!"

I spun around to see him standing atop a boulder— sword raised high, shield at the ready—and I was up and moving before his command had died in the air. As I ran,

I reached over my shoulder and unhooked the shield that hung on my back, drawing the sword from my left hip with my right hand. I saw the other Achillea girls leaping from their hiding places to do likewise.

The reaction from the Amazons was instantaneous. The circle of warriors spun outward, and their battle cries turned from exultant to enraged. Their sanctum had been violated, their ceremony disrupted. It wasn't a transgression they were about to take lightly.

Good, I thought, feeling the snarl on my lips crack the war paint on my cheeks. *Come on then . . .*

In the chaos of that moment our young captive shook free of Arviragus's grip and, yelping her own skirling war cry, bolted like a young deer up a twisting path to one side of the sprawling enclosure, disappearing behind one of the carved stone sentinels. Arviragus started to scramble after her, but I stopped him.

"Arviragus!" I shouted. "We'll handle the Amazons—you get to Sorcha!"

At the sound of her name, Sorcha's head came up fully and her eyes locked with mine. I saw her mouth form the shape of my name, and even though I couldn't hear her voice, I felt my sister's strength flow into my arms.

Then my view of her was cut off, obscured by a phalanx of Amazons as they moved toward us and we suddenly realized that the lamps they bore were in no way purely ceremonial. Thank the Morrigan, Quint seemed to realize it too. From his high hidden vantage point, he blew a sharp, frantic sequence on his whistle, and the Achillea gladiatrices snapped into a testudo formation as if we'd been practicing to join the legion all our lives.

It *saved* our lives.

Legion tactics. I fervently ignored the irony.

The flaming iron cage balls soared out of the darkness like stones hurled from catapults, slamming into the protective shell made from our wall of shields, and the darkness exploded into showers of sparks and cinder-bright smoke. The Amazons retreated, regrouped, and came at us again—from three sides. The whistle blew. And just like we'd practiced for hours on the boat, we shifted into position forming a defensive hollow square. Shields locked and held up and at an angle, we withstood that second frantic onslaught of the fire chains slamming into our wood-and-iron defenses. The thunder of the impact was like the gods themselves hammering against our shields.

But our shields held.

Our blades darted out like serpents' tongues, sometimes tagging flesh.

And we advanced.

Step by practiced step, shifting one way or the other as Quint's whistle signals pierced the din. With each onslaught, pine tar resin flew in thick, sticky gobs of flame from the iron cage balls at the end of the chains. Dangerous and devastatingly painful, the stuff would cling to any flesh it came into contact with and burn clean through to the bone. We weren't about to let that happen. But we couldn't hold them off forever. From behind the splintering wooden barrier, I glanced over at Cai on my left and saw that he was grimacing fiercely, his teeth bared in a savage grin.

"Is this what it's really like in the legion?" I asked him breathlessly.

"No," he said, stepping to the left as another series of whistles pierced the air. "This is much more fun!"

With each blast of Quint's whistle, we moved through the steps of the martial dance of legion formations. We wheeled and spun, locked shields and advanced, switched positions and rush-attacked, frustrating the Amazons' efforts to crush us or immolate us. Safe in formation we advanced, pushing the Amazons—who fought like the berserker warriors of legend, hurling themselves against our defenses—slowly backward, toward where the hills climbed sharply upward.

Behind our wall of shields, I looked down the line, left and right. To my right, Gratia and Elka held strong at the center of our broad wedge. Elka howled a stream of Varini curses, and Gratia's teeth were bared like a tiger on the hunt. To my left, Cai and Ajani harried the attackers with darting blades through the narrow gaps in our formation. On the other side of Ajani, I saw Antonia duck low beneath her shield edge and swipe at the legs of an Amazon with the crescent-bladed sheath weapon strapped to her arm. An ugly scream told me she'd hit her mark, and suddenly there was an easing off in attack pressure as her comrades dragged the wounded woman away from our advance.

The urge to break formation and spill through that gap was almost overwhelming. It's what the Cantii in me would have done. What the gladiatrix would have done too.

"Hold the line!" I called, deferring to my legionnaire self. "Advance on the line!"

Realizing the futility of their attacks, Thalestris and her sisters retreated behind a raised ridge of earth, and that's when the arrows began to fly. They could hold us off indefinitely from that position. Except for one thing . . .

Cai and I realized it at the same time.

The heat from the fire chains was no longer coming in waves. Instead, it had become a constant, brutal presence pressing against our faces. The shields we'd taken from Charon's boat might have been old and battered, the bright-painted designs faded and peeling from exposure to the wind and salt sea, but they were stout and well-made. They'd withstood the battering of the iron cages, cracking and splintering in places but holding together. The thing we hadn't expected was that the flaming resin would stick to the shields.

And burn. Furiously.

Behind our shield wall, the air was almost too hot to breathe, and we were blinded by the scorching shimmer of the flames. It wouldn't be long before we'd have to ditch the shields. But maybe just long enough . . .

"V!" I shouted. "V formation! Form on me, Achilleans!"

Cai glanced at me, wild-eyed. I think he thought I'd gone battle mad.

But then he cried out, "Form your wings on Fallon! *Move!*"

Again, the girls slid between each other seamlessly, shifting their blazing shields over their heads and fanning out, dropping them down to face forward as we formed a sharp-angled wedge. With me as its lead point.

"Advance! Triple-time!" Cai shouted.

We charged forward at a dead run—a single, solid wedge of fire—roiling, roaring flame that nothing could withstand. Not even a pack of mythical Amazon warriors. We chased them back, cresting the ridge like the gods' own Furies, fiery vengeance, bearing blazing disks of celestial fire. Howls of battle turned to cries of alarm as we charged, rushing forward up a ridge of earth to leap at our foes.

The Amazons dropped their fire chains and scrambled to draw swords and battle-axes as we pressed our attacks. The combined heat from the flames was too much to bear, and our line broke as we split off into individual combat, attacking with blade and flame, and a descent into the chaos of desperate battle.

I saw Hestia battered down to one knee by a long-limbed warrior who wielded a club and danced from side to side to avoid the sputtering fire on Hestia's shield. The gladiatrix looked beaten, but when the Amazon went a handsbreadth too close, she suddenly found herself hamstrung by the wickedly curved sica blade Hestia put to such good use as a thraex fighter in the arena.

She fell writhing in pain, and Hestia was back up and standing in an instant, shaking the smoldering, now-ruined

shield from her arm and stepping over her fallen opponent
to engage another fighter. Elka's shield was gone too, but
that just gave her more freedom of movement to swing the
short spear she'd carried ashore like a scythe, clearing a
circle around her and knocking the blade from the hand of
an Amazon.

I saw bodies on the ground but couldn't identify any as
Achillea girls.

And then I had no more time to look.

Vorya shouted a warning, and I spun on my heel as a
woman with long gray hair in braids swung an oak staff at
my head. I still bore my shield—flames guttering, wooden
slats charred and crumbling at the edges—and I caught the
blow at an angle. The staff scraped across the surface of
my shield, flame and tar sluicing off and clinging to the
Amazon's weapon, effectively turning my fiery advantage
back on me.

The Amazon matriarch was all lean muscle and sun-
dark skin, with eyes like polished black river stones, hard
and cold. She fought with precision, determination, and an
utter lack of visible emotion. And she was winning . . . up
until I saw a fraction of an opening and ducked beneath
a wide swing, lunging up from my crouch to head-butt
her in the face. I felt her nose break. Blood gushed and she
reeled backward, pain-blind, and I sprinted toward where
Arviragus was still sawing at the bonds that held my sister
captive.

"These . . . women . . ." he grunted at me, hacking desperately at a multitude of intricate knots that held Sorcha

bound ". . . have too much time . . . and too much damned *rope* . . . at their disposal!"

"Sorcha!" I skittered to a stop in front of her and grasped her by the shoulders. "Sorcha—look at me . . ."

"You shouldn't have come for me," she said in a parched rasp. "Any of you."

"Staying back at the ludus wasn't exactly an option for us, Sorcha," I said. "And you didn't think I'd let you leave me behind again, did you?"

I expected a dry retort. A raised eyebrow at the least.

But there was nothing. I looked my sister in the face, and it was almost as if a flame had been snuffed out inside of her. She squeezed her eyes shut to avoid my gaze and turned her head away from me. The side of her face, beneath the curtain of her hair, was livid with bruises.

My breath hissed between my teeth when I saw the injuries. "What have they done to you? Are you all right? I saw blood in your room at the ludus—"

"Hers," Sorcha ground out through clenched teeth. "Not mine. In a fair fight, Thalestris never would have gotten the drop on me."

"She had Nyx's help, I'm guessing?"

She nodded, anger and crushing disappointment stark in her face. "I'm a fool, little sister. I misjudged everything so terribly and now all is lost. All of it . . ." Bitter tears escaped through her lashes to spill down her cheeks. "I'm so sorry . . ."

"Sorcha?"

"Everything is gone . . . everything . . ."

Her head lolled to one side, and I felt a swell of fear for her. This . . . *this* was not my warrior sister. She wouldn't just give up like that. What had Thalestris done to her? What had she said?

That was easy to guess. She'd told her about the ludus. And Pontius Aquila. And shattered Sorcha's dream.

A shrill cry of agony split the chaotic discord of battle noise, and I looked up to see another one of the Amazons crumple to the ground. Fallen girls—theirs mostly, it seemed—lay sprawled all over the clearing. Dead or wounded, I had no way of knowing, but it seemed as if years of living in isolation had dulled the edge of the legendary Amazonian prowess. The tide of battle was definitely turning in our favor. The Amazons were holding their own— for the moment—but in spite of facing superior numbers, the Achillea girls were pressing their attacks. If the Amazons dug in and fought to the bitter end . . . they would lose. And it would be a slaughter.

"Fallon . . ." I turned back to see Sorcha surveying the gathering carnage through horrified eyes. "Stop this madness."

"I'm not leaving you—"

"Go!" Sorcha snapped with a hint of her usual spark. "Just . . . *stop* this fighting!"

I glanced over at Arviragus, who managed to shrug as he continued to saw through a knot the size of my fist. "Do as she says," he grunted. "I'll manage this. Eventually . . ."

I hesitated for another moment. Sorcha lifted her face to me, eyes pleading.

"*Please*, Fallon," she said, her voice raw like a wound. "I want no more dead girls on my conscience. No more blood on my hands. No more ruin . . . Make this *end*."

How? How could I do that? I didn't even know that I wanted to. I wanted revenge on Thalestris just as much as she'd wanted it on my sister and . . .

That's it.

The thought brought me up short. I realized then that, in a way, I was locked in the same cycle Thalestris was. And I had been, ever since Sorcha had first disappeared from my life when I was a girl. All I'd wanted was revenge until the moment I'd found her again, alive and whole and mine. But when she'd been taken from me a second time . . . that thirst for vengeance had reawakened. Spilled over into my quest for retribution from Thalestris and her tribe, and I'd dragged my ludus sisters straight into the bloody heart of it.

They were getting hurt. They were hurting others. And it wasn't even their fight, any more than it was the Amazons'. The only problem was that, as much as it might have been *mine*, I was one girl with two swords, and I couldn't stop the fighting with my blades. But maybe . . .

Maybe I could stop it with my words.

XII

I STEPPED AWAY from Sorcha and shouted "Stop!" as loudly as I could.

I had to shout it three more times—twice in mangled Greek—before anyone even started to take notice. Cai and Quint, oddly enough, were the first to put up their swords. Used to taking orders, I supposed.

"Stop!" I shouted one more time, my throat raw. "Gratia, *damn it!*—put that girl down!"

Gratia looked at me like I was mad but, eventually, she lowered the Amazon girl she had lifted off the ground in a rib-crushing bear hug back down to her feet. The girl collapsed to her knees, gulping for breath, her face flushed purple. One by one, the other duels subsided. All except the one raging between Elka and Thalestris. The two of them were locked in a vicious struggle to disarm each other of their spears. With Elka distracted for the barest instant by my shouting, Thalestris managed to thrust her away, and they both backed off into defensive postures.

Like a pair of hungry tigers, they circled each other, waiting for an opening.

"Achilleans!" I shouted one last time. *"Drop your weapons!"*

Well, then they really *did* think I was mad. I could see it in their faces. Disarm? We'd been winning. But then I threw my own swords—both of them—to the ground to show them just how serious I was.

"Elka!" I strode through crowd of combatants. "Do it."

To her credit, my dear friend trusted me enough to do as I said. Elka dropped her spear at her feet. Thalestris went statue-still, her spear still held at the ready. But for the moment, she didn't move. In her mind, I'm sure, my command to disarm was most likely a ruse.

One eye still on her opponent, Elka turned to the two gladiatrices nearest her—Hestia and Kore—and barked, "You heard her. Do it. Blades on the ground!" She turned to the girl on her other side—Antonia—and glanced down at the weapon strapped to her arm. Antonia raised an eyebrow at her.

"You can just put your arm up, maybe," Elka said.

Ajani stepped forward then and gestured to the rest of our girls to drop their weapons too. The moment they did, the Amazons closed in, still bristling with *their* blades, and surrounded us.

Thalestris spun in a circle, howling, "Kill them!" as she brandished her spear over her head and brought it down in a lethal arc—aimed straight at Elka's head—only to have her blow blocked by the staff of the Amazon matriarch whose nose I'd bloodied with my head-butt.

"Hold!" the gray-braided warrior shouted.

"Don't cross me, Areto!" Thalestris snarled, straining against the staff.

"There is no honor in killing an unarmed opponent," the woman named Areto said through gritted teeth.

She heaved like her muscles would crack and threw Thalestris off, holding her at bay with a defensive stance. The other Amazons were frozen, visibly torn by the conflict in their own ranks, but it felt as though Areto's command was a fragile dam holding back a deluge. And if my gamble failed, they would cut me and my now-unarmed friends to pieces.

"There is no honor in this fight at *all*," I said, directing my words to the Amazons in general, but mostly to Areto.

"*You* are the ones who began it," she said.

"No." I pointed at Thalestris with an outstretched arm. "She did."

"Liar," Thalestris snarled at me, teeth bared like a hunting cat. "I seek only to avenge a wrong and appease the goddess that we Amazons may once again thrive. Your Roman-loving sister's lifeblood in exchange for the blood of *my* sister, Orithyia—precious, sacred *Amazon* blood—that watered the sands of the bastard Romans' arena."

"Your sister died in honorable combat," I said, then turned to address Areto again. "*You* profess there is no honor in killing an unarmed opponent. And yet you would

sacrifice my sister to your goddess like some dumb bellow-
ing beast trussed up on an altar? Without even giving her a
chance to defend herself first? *That's* what you deem your
goddess's justly deserved spoils?" I turned back to the others. "What kind of a warrior people are you?"

"We are Amazons!" a ragged few called out. "We are—"

"The Amazons are myths!" I shouted over them. "Relics.
Painted on vases, carved on monuments. The men of Greece
brought you here as slaves. But they're gone. Why do you
continue to live like slaves?"

Thalestris went white with rage. But the others, weapons still at the ready, were listening to me. And I knew that
whatever I said next could mean my death. I stood at the
center of their oppidum, defenseless, and I could feel the
cold iron of every blade trained on me as if they already
pierced my skin.

"What is one death supposed to accomplish?" I continued. "What kind of goddess is this Cybele that you hope
to appease her and regain some measure of bygone greatness by spilling the blood of a woman who—by all rights—
should be your sister?"

"She *killed* my sister!" Thalestris's voice skirled wildly
upward. "Murdered Orithyia in cold blood—"

"You mean defeated her in a fair fight!" I countered. "A
matched duel that they were both forced into, against their
wills, by *men*! And what glory would Orithyia have won
for herself if Sorcha hadn't fought for her life with every
measure of her warrior soul? You said it yourself, Areto.
There's no honor in killing the defenseless. The outcome of

that battle was kill or be killed. And there is no dishonor in your sister's defeat. No stain, no shame . . ."

The warrior women exchanged glances.

"The *only* shame here is what Thalestris has done in the name of base vengeance—"

"Retribution!"

"*Vengeance!*" I took a lurching step toward her, my own fists clenching convulsively. "And to do it, you betrayed our entire ludus to a man—a *man*—who would enslave us once more so that he can force us to kill each other and then feed our souls to *his* black god!"

That hit home. For a moment, at least.

Thalestris's face twisted in an expression that was half fury, half wretched anguish. I almost felt sorry for her. Almost. I turned away before pity had a chance to take hold, and saw the fishergirl who'd attacked us on the path murmuring to some of the younger warriors. They shifted uncomfortably, casting frowning glances at Thalestris. Clearly, what I'd just described was *not* the kind of endeavor they considered worthy of their tribe.

I turned and addressed those women directly, and the fishergirl translated my words into Greek as I spoke. "Thalestris bartered Sorcha's life," I said, "for the lives of the young women warriors that she swore an oath to protect and train. Without a second thought she abandoned us to the cruelties of a man who would feed on our strengths and our souls like a leech. She *did* that. Knowingly." I shook my head sadly. "My sisters are to me as yours are to you," I said. "And I would grieve for the loss of any one of them bitterly. But I ask you this: Is one life—taken unwillingly and at the behest of a *male* oppressor—worth the lives of so many kindred spirits?"

The murmuring among the younger Amazons grew.

The older ones exchanged glances.

"My sister told me what your Queen Penthesilea once said," I continued, remembering clear as day the words Sorcha had recited to me when I'd stood beside her looking at the stone carving of the legendary queen and her warriors, "'Not in strength are we inferior to men' . . ." I took a step forward, pleading my case directly to the younger girls: "'the same our eyes, our limbs the same; one common light we see, one air we breathe. What then denied to us have the gods on man bestowed?'" I looked from face to face. "Help me prove the truth of her words. Help me see that we are not only the equal of men, we are better."

Areto turned then and, in the softest of voices, said, "Lay down your weapons. We will not carry this battle any further today."

It could as well have been a shouted command. The response was instantaneous as every one of the Amazon warriors threw their weapons to the ground. Every one except Thalestris. Areto waited for a moment, and then stepped forward to take the weapon from her clenched fist.

"Enough, child," she said. "Orithyia's honor remains unstained. Yours should too."

"Thalestris." I stepped forward and held out my hand. If I could make peace with her, I would. Even if only for the simple, calculated reason that it would make for a safer path for the rest of us to walk. "Will you let go of this vendetta and help us retake what is ours?"

She was having none of it. The grief and rage she'd carried around inside her had eaten her soul hollow, and there was nothing left there that could reconcile itself with forgiveness. Instead she just glared at me in bleak hatred.

"How?" she ground out between her teeth, ignoring my outstretched hand. "How did you even find me?"

I dropped my hand back down by my side and held my peace. So be it.

After an eternity of nothing but silence from me, she broke eye contact and her focus shifted, gaze roaming over the faces of those at my back. Her glare turned narrow, and I glanced back to see that she had picked Leander the kitchen slave out of our little crowd. With all the cocky guile I'd always known, he grinned apologetically and winked at her. For a moment, I wondered if she wouldn't just lunge for him to wring his neck, but she did nothing. She just turned her back on him—on everyone—and walked toward a cluster of small, thatch-roofed houses on the outskirts of the oppidum. She ducked low through the door of one and, a few moments later, emerged with a small leather traveling satchel slung over her torso, and a fishing spear clutched in her fist.

She ignored the Achillea crowd and addressed her Amazon sisters.

"May the goddess forgive you," she said in her harsh, unmusical voice. "I won't." Then she walked past them all, head high, eyes flashing eternal defiance, and disappeared into the deep shadows beneath the ancient olive trees that cloaked the hillside beyond the oppidum.

Once she was gone, it was like the air itself shivered in relief.

"You will rest here," Areto said. "And then you will leave with the sun's first light."

There was no room for argument in her tone.

"And Thalestris?" I asked.

"She has made her choice, and she will not return. If she does, she knows that she will die for it. It is our way."

It wasn't that I expected my sister to throw sheaves of flowers at my feet and crown me with laurels. But a simple thank-you would have been nice. Instead, I was treated to a bitter remonstration for my reckless endangerment of myself and my Achillea sisterhood.

"You *know* you shouldn't have come for me," she said—again—as Neferet silently tended her wounds in the house that Areto had made available for us.

I blinked at Sorcha when I realized she was still scolding me and sighed.

"You should have left me to my fate, Fallon," she continued. "You should have run far and fast the minute you gained your freedom. You're the daughter of a king. Without the ludus to keep you safe, you should have gone home, where you could have claimed your place in front of the hearth in the great hall in Durovernum and left Rome and Caesar and me to our own devices."

I sat there, silently fuming at people trying to ship me back home without so much as asking my opinion on the matter, but I held my peace. There was something inside Sorcha that had been damaged by her capture. Some core belief had been shaken and cracked almost to the point of no repair, and I had to be careful, or it would shatter her from the inside out. I knew my sister. I knew that she didn't give her trust or her friendship lightly, and she'd given Thalestris both. For years.

Now she was more angry at herself than she was at her former primus pilus, because she blamed herself for having been so blind. Of course, she wouldn't readily admit that, and so she was taking that anger out on the next most convenient target. Me.

"You should have thought about your *own* survival," she continued. "*Not* mine. Did I teach you *nothing*, little sister?"

"You taught me that what we do is more important than who we are or what fire we sit in front of," I said with a shrug, doing my best to keep a leash on my own temper. "You taught me that my fellow gladiatrices—every single one of them, even *you*, Sorcha—deserves the chance to choose their destiny."

"Fallon—"

"Those of us who escaped are infamia and rebels in the eyes of Rome and have no hope of that without the Ludus Achillea," I argued. "The ones who are still Aquila's prisoners? Even less so. I don't want that on my conscience. Do you?"

She frowned, and I knew I'd struck a nerve. "Of course not. But you still didn't need to put yourself at risk for me—"

"And just how, exactly," I interrupted, "would you expect me to retake the ludus without my legendary warrior sister at my side?"

"How many times do I have to tell you?" she snapped angrily. "I'm not what you think I am, Fallon! Not anymore . . ."

I sighed in exasperation. "Morrigan's bloody teeth! You don't seriously think that we could leave our friends, our fellow gladiatrices—our *home*, damn it all—in the hands of that mad bastard Pontius Aquila, do you?"

I could see the spark of that impulse kindle behind her eyes. But I could also see the cold fear, the hurt of Thalestris's betrayal, and the disappointment in herself, threatening to snuff it out. I wasn't about to let that happen.

"He wants to pit *his* god against *our* goddess?" I said emphatically, driving home my point. "His carrion crows against the Great Raven? He'll *lose*."

Sorcha's eyes narrowed as she gazed at me. Her old warrior self was still there, still a faint, flickering ember. It hadn't yet been completely extinguished.

"You have a clever plan, little sister?" she asked.

"I'm working on it," I said, and left it at that. For the time being.

But Sorcha didn't stand a chance against me if she thought she could shy away from this fight. I would fan that warrior spark into a flame. And I would feed that flame until it was a bonfire.

We made camp, our backs to the hill that rose above the oppidum. I tried to curb my impatience at having to stay. But even without bowing to the offered hospitality, such as it was, there was no way we could have made it back down that path to the ship in the darkness. By the time I was done building up a small fire and laying out my bedroll, Antonia had come by to tell me that Neferet and Leander were helping tend to the Amazon injured—after seeing to our own, and administering a sleeping draught to Sorcha, who'd already succumbed to a deep slumber.

"In the morning, she should be well enough to travel, Neferet says," Antonia assured me. "Maybe just a little slowly."

"Good," I said. "All I want is to take my sister home."

Antonia nodded and headed back in the direction of where Neferet still worked, dressing wounds. But before she'd turned, I'd seen the hesitation and the question in her eyes: *"Home where?"*

I sighed. *That* was going to be a little more complicated than I wanted to deal with in that moment. I looked across the fire at where Quint and Cai were setting out their bedrolls by a small, neat, no doubt legion-regulation fire and wondered to myself, *What next?*

Cai saw me watching and came over to crouch beside me. He was still dressed in full kit, and his armor creaked.

I breathed deeply, inhaling the scent of leather and metal, my fingers itching to reach for the buckles that held his breastplate on and undo them . . .

"What will you do now?" he asked me.

"*You*," I thought. *Not "we"* . . .

I shrugged. "I just want to go home," I said.

When he didn't reply, I turned to look at him. A night bird sang somewhere far off, and the firelight danced on Cai's face. On the calluses of his palm, which he rubbed absentmindedly. I found myself staring at his hand, remembering the charcoal-on-vellum drawing of it he'd sent me. It was tucked away in my trunk back in my cell at the ludus.

"Home to the *ludus*, Cai," I said.

He nodded and smiled at me—an uncertain expression that I wanted to stop with a kiss. A gulf of unspoken words seemed to have opened up between us, and I didn't know how to cross it. Because standing on the bridge over that chasm was Aeddan. And right behind him, Kassandra. And behind her . . . shadows. Shapes of those I couldn't make out but knew, somehow, that they'd come between Cai and me.

"We're posting a sentry guard for the night," Cai said, breaking the silence. "Me and Quint."

I frowned. "Areto's shown us hospitality in good faith," I said. "I don't want to do anything that might offend her."

"It's not Areto I'm worried about," Cai said.

I couldn't argue that point. Thalestris was out there somewhere. And Areto might trust that her pride or their code or the goddess Cybele herself would keep her from

returning that night, but Cai was far too much an officer of the legions to place his trust in that alone. I didn't
blame him.

"We don't need to dig a bank and ditch and set a perimeter guard," he said. "I'll settle for a single sentry up there."
He pointed to a place where the stone outcropping provided a natural vantage point. "See? Nice and discreet, and
no offense offered to our gracious hostess. I'm taking first
watch. Quint'll take second."

"I'll take one," I offered.

"You," Cai said, raising an eyebrow at me, "will take
your ease and get a good night's sleep."

"But—"

He put a finger to my lips. "You *deserve* it after that masterful bit of oration, Fallon," he said. "Believe me. Caesar
prides himself on his public speaking skills, and even
he would have crowned you with laurels for that bit of
brilliance . . ."

He seemed to notice then that he was still touching my
lips. His gaze flicked from his finger to my eyes and back,
and he ran his tongue over the edge of his teeth. I lifted a
hand to his and turned his palm over so that I could rest
my cheek against it. Cai made a sound, deep in his chest,
and drew me into an embrace.

"Give yourself permission to rest, for once, Fallon," he
murmured into my hair. "And give others permission to be
strong in your stead. I promise, they won't disappoint you.
I won't."

"I know," I said.

I leaned against him, for as long as he would let me. Until he pushed me gently to arm's length and bent his head to kiss me.

"First watch," he said. "Remember?"

I looked up at him, telling myself that he wasn't taking first watch to avoid finishing our conversation from the beach. "You can always come get me for a turn," I said. "If you can't pry Quint away from Elka."

I nodded over to where, rather to my surprise, Elka had gone to sit by the little fire Quint had built.

"I'll keep that in mind," Cai said and, after kissing me one more time, stood and went to take his watch.

After he'd gone, I turned and saw the young fishergirl Amazon sitting alone, sharpening the blade of a dagger with a stone. She had not gone to join her sisters. I walked over to her and sank down and stretched out my hands toward the warmth of the fire. We sat in silence for a while until she finished sharpening her blade and tucked it back in the sheath at her hip.

"You fought well today," I said, nodding at the weapon.

"Well, maybe." She lifted a shoulder, staring into the flames. "But on the wrong side."

"You didn't know."

"I should have." She shook her head. "I listened to Thalestris with deaf ears. Followed her with blind eyes."

"In many ways, I understand the place where Thalestris is coming from," I said. "I lived there myself for a long time. I used to think that honor was more important than

anything. That righteous vengeance was the only way forward. I was foolish."

"But what you said today was wise—and right." She
turned to me, her eyes gleaming in the firelight. "Those
men who brought our mothers here against their wills are
dead and gone, and yet we live on in isolation, scraping out
a threadbare existence on fish and sand and our own pale
whispers of a someday retribution. For what? From whom?
When Thalestris brought your sister here—a mighty warrior who'd spilled the blood of our own—and bound her
to the altar, I believed what she told us. I thought a sacrifice would make everything all right again. I see now that
it wouldn't have. I think the goddess would have turned
from us forever."

"I learned the hard way—I'm still learning—that every
time I thought *my* goddess had abandoned me, it was in
truth I who had turned away from her." I put a hand on her
arm. "You want a sacrifice? *Make* a sacrifice. Take a chance.
Step outside the boundaries that have been placed around
you, and make your lives your own."

She fell silent then, and I could feel the weight of my
words pressing heavily on her. I didn't want to leave her
with nothing but that burden. "What's your name?" I asked.

She was silent for so long, I didn't think she would tell
me. But when I started to get up to leave, she said, "Kallista.
My name's Kallista."

I sat back down and watched her for a moment as she
went back to sharpening her blade. "Where did you learn

to speak Latin, Kallista?" I asked, striving for a lighter tone. "I thought your tribe hated Rome—and all things Roman."

"We do." She shrugged, smiling a little now, but still staring into the heart of the fire. "I mean, *they* do . . . I've never been as sure. I was taught to hate them, but it's hard to hate all Romans when some Romans are . . . kind."

She reminded me so much of myself in that moment. I'd grown up hating Rome and Romans and one particular Roman most of all. And then that had all changed. Well— not all of it, maybe. I still didn't understand the Roman mind and didn't approve of a great deal of Roman culture, but I'd also met Romans like Cai and his father. Soldiers like Junius. I'd even found much to admire. Even—the Morrigan help me—in Julius Caesar himself.

The great bloody tyrant, who'd been kind to me.

"Who was kind to you?" I asked Kallista.

She turned her face to look at me and said, "My father."

Of course. She must have been the progeny of one of the stolen boys from the other side of the island, and it wasn't beyond believing that he might have been kind toward a daughter. Loving, even. I wondered . . .

"What's his name?" I asked.

"Secundus. His name is Secundus. Was."

Secundus. The second son. The second out of five.

"What happened to him?" I asked, a sudden knot constricting my throat.

"Marsh fever," Kallista said. "Four summers ago it was very bad. It took my mother first. Then him. We were even going to take him over the mountains, back down to the

Roman town to see if they could help him, but he was too weak."

Quint's brother had been alive only four years earlier, I thought.

The cages we'd seen hadn't been used in far longer than that. Maybe Secundus had lived a freer life here among the Amazons than Quint had thought. Maybe even one touched by love. With a daughter he cared for . . . Looking at Kallista then, I could see the close resemblance to Quint and wondered why it hadn't struck me before that moment. Maybe it was because I just hadn't been looking for it, but she had the same tawny coloring, the freckles and gray-blue eyes. Maybe, under different circumstances, she would have even had something of his sense of humor.

I stood abruptly and held out my hand to the girl.

She looked up at me, frowning.

"Come with me," I said. "There's someone you should be properly introduced to."

Quint was, unsurprisingly, still sitting beside Elka. Because, perhaps a bit more surprising, *she* was still sitting beside *him*. The fire he'd built was bright enough to illuminate Quint's face clearly through the shimmering heat and bursts of sparks climbing upward into the night. I opened my mouth to make the proper introduction, but I didn't get the words out of my mouth before I heard a soft gasp. I turned to see Kallista staring at her uncle.

She looked at him—*really* looked at him, without his helmet on his head or a sword at her throat, without the veil of fear that would have fogged her eyes on the path when she'd ambushed us with arrows and fish—and she knew. I heard her murmur the word "Father . . ." under her breath, and the knot that had closed up my throat got tighter.

Quint looked back and forth from me to the girl, a frown of confusion on his face. Inasmuch as he'd come here to assuage his own feelings for never having tried to save his brother, it seemed not to have dawned on Quint that he might find—if not his brother—someone else who shared his blood.

"Quintus, this is Kallista," I said.

"Uh, the fish girl, yeah?" he said.

"Her father was the one who taught her to speak Latin, Quint."

He blinked at me for a moment. "That's nice . . ."

"Your *brother*, Quintus."

"My . . ."

It still took him another long moment. As if what I was telling him was something he quite simply couldn't wrap his mind around. And then, finally, his jaw drifted slowly open, and his gaze shifted to the girl standing at my side.

"You're . . . My brother Secundus is your . . . father?"

"Was." Kallista nodded, her eyes filling with tears. "He always told me you were the idiot brother . . ."

Quint choked on a sudden, strangled laugh. "He always told *me* that too."

She bit her lip—to keep it from trembling, I suspected. "He missed you so much," she said, her voice breaking. "He . . ."

Then Quint was up and hugging her, and Kallista collapsed into that embrace. I looked over to see that Elka was blinking rapidly at the exchange, the gleam of unshed tears rimming her eyes, and my heart clenched in my chest. We'd both caught the look on Quint's face when he'd seen the empty cages in the cave at the head of the path. His hopes—whatever they'd been—had been dashed in that moment. Finding Kallista might just have redeemed the journey for him.

And then some.

Elka and I moved a discreet distance away, back to the other fire, to give uncle and newfound niece a chance to get better acquainted. Elka was silent for a while, poking at the charred wood with a stick, lost in thought.

"Family," she murmured eventually. "It's . . . something, *ja*? An important thing, I mean. Sometimes."

"All times," I said.

"For you, I guess." She nodded her chin at Quint. "For him . . ."

"For you too."

She raised a pale eyebrow at me over the flames.

"What do you think *they* are?" I gestured at the clusters of Achillea girls hunkered down in front of the fires on the other side of the clearing. "What do you think *I* am, you great thickheaded brute?"

"Besides a constant thorn in my shoe?" She grunted a laugh and then subsided back into silence, frowning. When she spoke again, it was with a shrug that I suspect was supposed to be casual but came off as more of a shudder. "I suppose you're right." She sighed. "Well . . . I guess it was nice while it lasted. Belonging to something and all that."

"What are you talking about?"

"You have your sister back, Fallon," she said. "That's what we came here to do. It's over—the quest, the adventure . . . Now? We all go our separate ways."

"What makes you say that?"

"What else is there for us to do? It was bad enough when we were just infamia. Now we're outright rebel fugitives."

"We are not."

"We *are*." She snorted in frustration at my stubbornness. "You can tell yourself another story if you like, little fox, but I'm the pragmatic one, remember?"

I snorted right back at her. "And were your pragmatic ears not listening back in Heron's infirmary when I told you that, once we rescued Sorcha, we'd go back and retake the ludus?"

"Oh no, I was listening," she said. "I just assumed you'd lost your mad little fox mind again."

I shook my head and she tilted hers, regarding me warily.

"You were serious," she said.

"Deadly."

"Retake the ludus."

"Mm-hm."

"With what army?"

I opened my mouth, but found I had no immediate answer. Elka was right. I looked back over at our gladiatrix sisters. While we'd fared far better than our adversaries, we'd still collected an impressive degree of injuries. None of us had escaped without cuts and bruises of varying degrees. Neferet suspected Hestia might have a fractured bone in her wrist, and Anat had suffered an ugly shoulder burn when her shield had shattered during our fiery rush. Then there was Gratia, who kept telling everyone she was perfectly fine—even though it had taken more than a dozen stitches to close a deep gash on her thigh. I suspected the ample mead the Amazons had supplied before Neferet had begun stitching had gone a long way to influencing Gratia's opinions of her own hurts.

Even before the fight, we'd been too few to win in a pitched battle against Nyx and Aquila's contingent of gladiatrices and Dis warriors. The only thing going back to the ludus in our *present* state would achieve would be to land us in chains. And then, inevitably, in one of Pontius Aquila's evil munera fights. I frowned and looked away from Elka, searching the darkness for the answer. My gaze drifted back over to where Kallista still sat with Quint, heads together, and then on past them to where the lights of the Amazon fires flickered through the trees just beyond the oppidum's tumbled walls.

"We don't need an army," I said, responding, at last, to Elka's question. "We need a war band."

"I fail to see the distinction."

I felt myself smiling as a hazy, half-formed plan began to coalesce in my mind. "When I was a little girl," I said, "all I ever wanted was to follow in my sister's footsteps and join my father's royal war band. *Warriors*, Elka. Not soldiers. Not mercenaries. Not Aquila's killers. Not even gladiatrices, fighting alone. No. What we need to be to make this happen is warriors. Few, fearsome, and fighting as a family."

She shook her head. "We're not enough."

"No." My gaze drifted back toward Kallista. "But we will be."

XIII

THE SUN BROKE over the horizon as we were finishing a breakfast of fish and crabmeat wrapped in grape leaves on a bed of soft, roasted grains, washed down with cups of cold spring water. The repast had been left for us, laid out on flat stones at the edge of our encampment, some time before dawn broke. Even if it was grudging, one couldn't fault the Amazons for their hospitality. Which was only surpassed by their enthusiasm to get us started on our way, I thought, as Areto and a small council of the older members of the tribe came to bid us farewell.

Unfortunately for them, I suspected—*hoped*, rather—that there would be a slight delay before we left them to their rugged solitude.

As we made our final preparations to depart, I kept glancing off into the distance, where Cai and Quint had gone, waiting anxiously for them to return. Sorcha noticed my fretfulness and asked me what the matter was.

"Nothing," I murmured. "Nothing . . ."

Then I saw movement beneath the trees, and I turned to grin at her.

"Just . . . here comes my clever plan."

Sorcha turned to look as Kallista and more than a dozen of her sister warriors appeared—girls who, as Kallista had told me the night before, had voiced their own doubts about the rightness of the Amazon way. Together, the group of young women climbed up the steep path from the clusters of huts beneath the pines. They all wore traveling cloaks over their ragged tunics and had packs slung across shoulders and torsos. All of them carried their weapons, and a few had even painted their cheeks and foreheads with symbols, not unlike the war paint my sisters and I had arrived wearing. They strode toward us, walking as tall as they could, as brave and as fearless, in the face of what they were about to do.

I waited.

Kallista stepped up and cleared her throat.

None of the Amazon matrons turned their attention toward her. At first.

"I will go with this gladiatrix on her journey," she said, just a little too loud.

That got their attention.

I wondered if it was the journey itself or the act of announcing her intentions to the Amazon matrons that had put the hint of a quaver in Kallista's voice. Whatever the case, I silently cheered her bravery.

"What's this, young one?" Areto said over her shoulder—but only after a sufficiently intimidating pause.

"I will go and I will help her win back her home," Kallista continued, thrusting her chin forward. "We all will."

Areto regarded her with a stone-hard gaze. "Will you now."

She nodded gravely.

"This is not our war to fight."

"But it is *ours*." Kallista took another step forward. "Because we choose to make it so."

"Kallista—"

"I'm *tired* of hiding on this island, Areto!" She flung her arm out to the girls with her. "We all are! I'm so tired of telling myself every night I am descended from greatness, only to wake every morning to practice my spear throwing at nothing but the fish in the lagoon. The *fish* are tired of it!"

One of the Amazon matrons—the one with the long, puckered scar that ran from her hairline, down the side of her face, and past the collar of her tunic—crossed her arms and pegged Kallista with a pointed stare. "What if we don't wish to let you leave, young ones?"

The other girls standing shoulder to shoulder behind Kallista bristled with silent rebellion, defiance in their eyes, but not one of them opened her mouth in protest. That seemed to settle it for the warrior matron. She sniffed and turned away.

"No," she said. "Return to your houses."

"We don't have houses!" Kallista's voice cracked with protest. "We have huts. Leaky ones. With dirt floors and hard beds."

"You crave leisure?" Areto asked. Her tone was harsh, but for a flashing instant, I thought I saw something in her gaze that might have been approval. Or veiled pride.

"I crave something beyond the stones and trees of this island and talking to myself just to hear something other than birdsong and wind," Kallista pleaded with a desperation I could feel in my soul.

"Ah." The older of the women remained unmoved. "You crave adventure. You know nothing of the world of men. They will make vile sport of you in the moments before they send you to your deaths."

"Only if you've trained us to be weaker than them," Kallista snapped, seemingly no longer caring whether or not she would be punished for speaking out. "Lesser. Is that what you're telling me? That everything you've taught us has only served to render me—to render us—incapable of living and fighting in a world that isn't just other girls with swords?"

The older woman's fists clenched white at her sides, and for a moment I thought she might actually strike Kallista for her impudence. But then Arviragus suddenly stepped forward into the tense space between the Amazons.

It was a brave thing for him to do.

"What if . . ." he began in a conciliatory tone as the Amazon leaders turned their flinty glares on him. "What if I were to suggest a compromise? A means of solution to this impasse? These young ones are the future of this tribe. It is understandable that you do not wish to simply give them over into the keeping of outsiders when you gain nothing in return. What if we were to make a bargain with you, instead? An exchange, as it were."

Sorcha and I shared a confused glance, and I made a grab for his arm. This was *not* part of my plan. "My lord, what—"

He held up a hand to silence me.

"Honored Warrior Mother," he said, directing his words to the scar-faced Amazon, "my name is Arviragus of the Arverni. I was once known in the world of men as Vercingetorix. But even here, in this place, I think you will have heard of me."

She had. They all had. That much was obvious from their expressions—mostly surprise and wary respect—as they watched with unblinking stares while Arviragus reached over his shoulder for the shield he carried on his back and tossed it to the ground in front of Areto's feet. He unbuckled his sword belt and threw it after the shield.

My breath caught in my throat.

"I've only ever done *that* once before," he said.

"Why, then, do you do it now?" Areto asked. "Your side won this time."

Arviragus grinned wanly in response to the jab. "I do it as a sign of respect," he said, "and as a plea for parley on my companions' behalf . . . and refuge on mine."

"Refuge?" the scarred one asked.

"I cannot go back to Rome," he said. "Nor back to the lands that were once mine. And I do not wish to wander the wide world as an outcast for the rest of whatever borrowed life my gods and this brave girl"—he gestured to me without looking—"have granted me."

My heart cracked a little in my chest.

Areto and the scarred woman glanced at each other.

"Rather," Arviragus continued, "I will pledge myself as hostage in exchange for any of your warriors who wish to join Fallon and Sorcha's cause. Among my people, there is no greater nor more honored tradition than that of hostage exchange. We foster our young as guests among the tribes to ensure mutual peace." He nodded to Kallista and the others. "I am not young, but Caesar himself will tell you I make a decent, mostly well-mannered guest. And if one of your girls does not return home, you may take my life as forfeit."

The two women turned inward and walked away from us, conversing in low tones, and Sorcha put a hand on Arviragus's shoulder.

"This is madness," she said.

I stepped up beside her. "She's right, Arviragus—listen to her!" I said. "I'll find another way. *We'll* find another way."

"I don't think there is one, bright little thing," he said, putting a hand on my shoulder.

Sorcha shook her head adamantly. "You've only just escaped one confinement—one death sentence—and you would commit yourself to another?"

"There's a reason I lived through that, Sorcha," he said. "With you and Fallon as my only friends, my only comfort. I do this willingly, and I believe *this* is why the Morrigan let me live as long as she has. You need these girls, and I need somewhere out of the way to live out the rest of my days. Maybe I can help these women see that not all men are to be hated and reviled. Or maybe they can teach me a thing or two. Whatever the outcome, at least the sea air might do me some good, and I can get a bit of exercise fixing a leaky hut roof or two. And the honey mead here is excellent."

"One year."

I turned to see that Areto and the scarred woman had returned.

"One year," the woman repeated. She turned her piercing gaze on Sorcha and me. "If these young ones do not return to us here in one year, he will die. Slowly. Painfully. With fire and steel and—"

"Understood!" I snapped, not wishing to hear a detailed recipe of my dear friend's demise should I fail to keep safe the girls I was about to lead into extreme harm's way.

Arviragus just rolled his eyes and winked at me.

"Then we have a bargain," he said.

He unsheathed his dagger and drew it across his palm. A thin line of blood welled up, and Areto did the same. They clasped hands, and I saw there was a gleam of respect—and maybe the tiniest spark of intrigue—in her gaze. I could hardly blame her. Arviragus was nothing if not intriguing.

My childhood hero. My friend.

I owed him more than I could ever repay, and I would miss him deeply.

Again.

The sun was still behind us as we left the Amazon oppidum and began the trek down the twisting trail back to the bay where—I silently, fervently hoped—Charon and his boat waited. Sorcha was pale from the whole ordeal, and I saw her jaw clench as she stumbled on a stone in the pathway. But when I put a hand out to steady her, she gave me a look that told me—rather pointedly—she would be just fine, thank you, and didn't require her little sister's help. I grinned to myself and felt my heart lifting, beating light and strong and free like the wings of a bird in my chest. For the first time in many days, I felt as if everything would turn out all right.

Behind us, Elka started singing quietly—a song of her Varini tribe we'd all heard her sing back at the ludus whenever she cleaned weapons or pulled duty sweeping in the stables or sometimes even when she practiced in the yard. We all knew the words, even though they weren't ours, and one by one Elka's ludus sisters picked up the tune and began singing with her. Even the Amazon girls were nodding in time with the cantering tune and smiling and chattering with each other in Greek as we threaded our way down through the hills.

We'd reached the lower slopes of the hills where the path cut a channel through a ragged-walled ravine and the trees arched overhead, forming a green tunnel with their canopy. I was still keeping a discreet eye on Sorcha when Leander caught up with us, throwing an arm around both of our shoulders—something he *never* would have dared do back at the ludus—his grin outshining the sun. I'd told Sorcha the night before how it had, in fact, been the kitchen boy who'd been largely responsible for leading us to her in the first place, and so her only reaction was to shake her head at him indulgently.

"I hear I owe you a debt of thanks, Leander," she said.

He nodded at her, dark eyes gleaming with delight.

"Yes, domina!" he said. "But think nothing of it. I knew it would all turn out." He waved his hands airily. "We're heroes, after all, are we not—"

There was a noise—a hiss followed by a wet snapping sound like a green tree branch breaking—and Leander abruptly stopped talking. His body stiffened and jerked, chest thrust forward, and the glistening red tip of a spear blade appeared as if by some evil magic, sticking out of the center of his tunic.

Sorcha cried out, and I grappled at Leander to keep him standing.

He turned to me, his expression one of surprise, rather than pain or horror. But when he opened his mouth to say something, all that came out was a gout of bright blood. Then he pitched forward onto his face on the path, the fishing spear sticking obscenely upright from the middle of his back. Sorcha fell to her knees beside him, and I looked up to see Thalestris standing high above on the cliff's edge, a black silhouette against the pale blue sky.

She stood for a moment, staring back at me.

I screamed her name, sending a startled flock of swallows flapping into the air as she turned, deliberate and unhurried, and vanished back into the wilderness of the Corsican hills.

We buried Leander beneath the gnarled branches of an ancient olive tree with all the rites due a fallen warrior.

I stared down at the trench dug in the earth that would be his resting place, a far cry from the ludus kitchen alcove, and whispered a prayer for the Morrigan to guide his soul's flight. As Cai and Quint lifted the last, largest stone and placed it carefully over Leander's grave, I looked around to see that most of the Achillea girls were red-eyed with weeping. The irony of that—of Leander finally getting all the gladiatrix attention he'd ever craved—wasn't lost on me. I hoped that his shade had lingered long enough to see, and smile.

"Annoying little wretch," Ajani muttered, glaring down at the grave.

"He was fond of you too," I said, wiping at the fugitive tear that had escaped my lashes and slipped down my cheek.

Kallista and the other young Amazons had gone into the hills hunting for Thalestris, only to return with unbloodied weapons. I knew before they went that the search for their murderous sister would prove fruitless. In the same way I knew that Thalestris could just as easily have chosen me or Sorcha as her target with that spear throw.

She'd chosen Leander. A punishment for him, a fulfillment of her promise.

And a message for us. We hadn't seen the last of her.

I could tell from the look on Sorcha's face as we stepped together back out onto the path to continue on our way that she was thinking the same thing.

"I will avenge his death, little sister," she said, at last, without looking at me. "Thalestris will pay in blood for her betrayals. For *all* of her betrayals. And so will Nyx."

I felt a sudden fierce swell of vindication at the sparks of Sorcha's old fire I saw kindling to life. "I was hoping you would say that."

Sorcha glanced at me sideways. "And why is that?" she asked warily.

"Because . . ."

I picked up my pace, like a hound on the hunt that had finally caught the scent of the quarry. The trees opened up before us, and in the distance far below, the sparkling blue bowl of the bay shimmered into view—along with the ship, still anchored there, that would take us all home.

"Don't tell me . . ." Sorcha said. "It's all part of your clever plan."

XIV

OUR SHIP BOUNDED over the waves, the breath of the wind god, Zephyrus, filling our sails and speeding us on our way. There was an air of anticipation among the girls, even if there was a pall of uncertainty too. I could hardly blame them—the closer we sailed to Rome, the more I was beginning to worry that I hadn't really thought my clever plan of retaking the ludus all the way through to its logical conclusion. For one thing, even though her spirit seemed on the mend, to say that Sorcha had been less than convinced of her part in the scheme would be putting it lightly.

When we'd first gathered to discuss our options, I began by telling her what we were up against. When she heard everything that had passed at the ludus since her abduction, Sorcha was aghast. Furious. Disgusted and enraged by Pontius Aquila's machinations.

"Rebellion." Sorcha's lip curled as she said the word. "Within the walls of *my* ludus. What a load of horse manure."

"A lie, and a foul one," Charon agreed. "But it's one that resonates deeply. We all know that, and we all know why."

"Aye. Thanks be to Spartacus the Interminably Unforgotten," Sorcha snorted in disdain.

At which point, Elka had sighed gustily.

"Will someone *please* enlighten me?" she asked. "What does any of this—what do any of *us*—have to do with this Spartacus fellow? His name keeps getting bandied around, and I can't quite figure out why."

Cai turned to her. "It's been only a few years since Spartacus, the legionnaire-turned-slave-turned-gladiator, fomented an uprising that led to a war that *directly* threatened the heartland of Italia," he explained. "Some even thought he and his followers were bent on taking the city of Rome itself. The plebs haven't forgotten, and the patricians haven't forgiven. Talk of gladiators and rebellion in the same sentence makes people . . . excitable."

"Nervous," Quint added.

Charon nodded grimly, his gaze fixed on Sorcha's face.

"And now Aquila has laid the groundwork for the story of a gladiatrix rebellion at the ludus to become the official interpretation," I mused. "We will be branded as criminals and traitors to the Republic. We will be hunted down mercilessly and crucified. Unless we stop him first."

"Stop him how?" Sorcha leaned forward, her eyes narrowing.

"We use the plebs—and their excitability—*against* their Tribune."

"I'm listening . . ."

"We can't retake the ludus by sheer force," I said. "Not without an army—one that Caesar would never give us for the simple fact that Aquila has possession of the written deed to the place, signed over to him by Thalestris. Even if you were to step forward now and reassert your claim, I don't know that it would do any good. It's unlikely to be general knowledge that Aquila has seized the ludus through deceit."

"The legalities are doubtless tricky," Cai said, scratching at the stubble of his chin and thinking over the implications. "It would have to go before the courts, and that could take months if not years to settle."

"And Caesar," I said, "as I've come to understand, is a stickler for legalities."

"He has to be." Quint shrugged. "It's all in the public perception."

"Right," I continued. "So—as I said—we use the public to our advantage, and we call Aquila out."

Cai's eye glinted. "Call him out?"

"Issue a challenge. A very public challenge." I could feel my own fierce excitement brewing over the idea. "Before Aquila has the chance to perpetuate the myth of a rebellion, we meet him head-on and quash that fiction."

"How do we do that?" Elka asked.

"We announce a match," I said. "A *big* one—just like the ones in the Circus Maximus—but to take place in the field outside the Ludus Achillea. Set a date and a time, and let it be known that the main attraction of the day will be a rematch between Victrix of the Triumphs and her nemesis,

Nyx—a gladiatrix contest to end all contests! Throw the promise of a wolf pack of wild Amazons into the mix and they'll be salivating for such a spectacle."

Elka was grinning at me fiercely.

Cai gazed at me with something approaching amazement.

Quint, though, wasn't entirely convinced. "What if she doesn't come out?" he said. "What if Aquila doesn't rise to the bait?"

At that, Elka laughed and slapped him on the back. He sputtered a bit and turned pink, whether from the heat of the slap or of her attention, I couldn't tell.

"You don't know that bitch the way we do," she said. "A chance to even the score with Fallon? She'd reach down Aquila's throat and pull his guts out his mouth if he dared to stand in her way."

Quintus turned to me. "And you think it's a *good* idea to fight this creature. Carry on, then."

"I have some ideas about that too," I said, glancing over at Sorcha.

She cocked her head and regarded me warily, but for the moment, I held my peace. Those ideas—specifically as to what *her* role might very well be in the whole drama— were still not fully formed, and so I kept them to myself. For the moment. My mind flashed back, as it had done for the last few days, to the docks and the last conversation I'd had with Meriel before she'd sacrificed herself for my escape. She was right: I'd never truly beat Nyx in a one-on-one fight. The chariot crash that ended our rivalry during the Triumphs had, in many ways, been the result of team-work. And sheer bloody-minded luck. And so Quint's sardonic concern for my well-being in such a matchup wasn't entirely without merit.

I didn't know that I could beat Nyx in a duel.

But maybe . . . just maybe, *I* didn't have to.

"It's an interesting idea," Cai said, still rubbing his chin as he worked his way through the logistics. "And you're right. It could forestall any rumors of a rebellion. But a challenge match outside the ludus still doesn't win us back the ludus itself."

"No," I agreed. "It doesn't. But while everyone's attention is focused on the field outside the *front* gate of the compound . . ."

I smiled at my friends and shrugged innocently.

"Oh." Quintus blinked, understanding blooming in his expression. "Oh . . . I see."

Sorcha's wariness became downright suspicion. "I don't."

I took a deep breath and reached out to put a hand on her shoulder. "Remember when you were having the marble frieze installed at the ludus, and I told you I thought you should consider fighting again, sister?" I said. "Well, it's time for Penthesilea to lead her Amazons onto the field of battle. And this time . . . she's going to win."

The argument that erupted between us was one for the ages. By the time it was finished—*not* resolved—the deck space all around me and Sorcha had cleared, and everyone else had found something to occupy themselves with that didn't involve coming anywhere near the two of us. When Sorcha finally threw up her hands and went to go brood stormily half a ship away from me, the winds had died to a gentle breeze, and I could just make out the mainland on the horizon.

Never mind Sorcha, I told myself, glancing skyward. *There's time yet to convince her. Time, at least, until Aquila's munera.* I searched the breaks between the clouds stretching across the day-blue sky as if I could see the moon and stars there. A fortnight. We had a fortnight to bring my plan to fruition. And then it would be too late. Aquila would hold his munera instead, and Achillea girls would die.

I would *not* let that happen.

And neither, I knew in my heart, would Sorcha.

I looked toward the bow of the ship and saw that Charon had gone to speak with her. I admired his courage. And, to be perfectly honest, his selflessness. Because what he was trying to convince my sister of, in that moment, carried with it a great risk to himself. To his heart, his honor—and strange as it seemed to me, Charon was *not* without his own particular honor—to his one impossibly slim chance at the kind of happiness he'd craved for years.

I watched him lift a hand as they spoke—not quite touching the side of Sorcha's face that still bore the scars of the chariot accident that had ended her gladiatrix career—and I saw her own hand come up to meet his, to push it away . . .

But she didn't.

Whatever Charon was saying to her, Sorcha was listening—not relenting, maybe, not *yet*—but listening.

They stood there, hands clasped between them, and she did not turn from him. Not immediately. When she finally did let go of his hand and walked away, he stood there for a long moment, his hand still lifted as if he caressed my sister's face. As if she stood there letting him.

Later, I didn't ask Charon what had passed between them, and he didn't seem inclined to tell me. But he carried on as if our scheme was still set in motion, and to that end, there was a great deal to be accomplished before we made landfall. Not the least of which was figuring out how to smuggle not just the Achillea gladiatrices but a band of Amazons—all hardscrabble warrior girls dressed in little more than rags and bad manners—into the city. The first of many hurdles. When Cai expressed that very concern as I sat plotting and planning with Charon outside the captain's tent, the slave master smiled at him benignly.

"Don't fret, decurion," he said. "These girls won't be attracting the attention of the legions or Rome's vigiles."

"They won't?" Cai raised an eyebrow at him. "We're pulling in to a smaller port, then?"

"No." Charon took a deep breath, seeming to sniff at which way the wind was blowing. "I'm going to drop anchor in the same place I always do. The wharf on the west bank of the River Tiber. Inside the very walls of Rome herself."

Cai followed the slave master's gaze to see his men pulling down the sail with its subdued, faded colors and replacing it with a bright-striped one. I recognized the colors from the very first ship I'd sailed on with Charon.

With that, and the shields removed from the side rails and stowed belowdecks, even I had to admit that it looked like an entirely different craft. It looked like one of Charon's fleet of slave galleys.

"I see." Cai nodded. "And . . . then you have a plan to get the Amazons through the city unmolested by Rome's authorities."

"I do." Charon nodded, pushing himself to his feet as the crew hustled about the deck. "But they're not going to like it very much."

He flashed us a jaunty, slightly feral grin and went to confer with his men.

Cai turned to me, and I shrugged apologetically for not having had the chance yet to confer with *him*. But I'd needed to be sure, first, that what I'd had in mind with Charon was possible before I could slot the next piece of the mosaic into place. And the shape of that next piece was up to Cai himself.

"And the rest of you and your Achillea cohorts?" he asked, one eyebrow raised. "I trust there's a plan for that too?"

I nodded and, beaming up at him with the best, brightest smile I could muster, said, "You once told me your father was rather fond of his wine?"

The mainland loomed ever larger on the horizon, and for one brief moment, I found myself alone on the deck, watching the port of Ostia creep closer across the waves. I felt as if I was standing in a field, bathed in sunlight, watching the sky darken as thunderclouds advanced over the horizon. The calm before the storm.

Cai and I had discussed my plan, worked through the potential pitfalls and contingencies, and arrived at the best course of action that either of us could come up with—even though it meant imposing on Cai's father's hospitality in his absence. With the senator away on his trade mission to Brundisium, there was a great empty marble palace right in the middle of the capital available to hide a contingent of rebel gladiatrices. Getting us there was simply a matter of logistics—the kind I'd left up to Charon, who'd grinned his nefarious grin when we told him, along with Quint and Aeddan, my idea.

Quint was onboard from the outset. Aeddan's brow had furrowed, and I could sense him brewing storm clouds, but he'd declined to offer a dissenting opinion in front of the others, and I left him to his brooding. For my part, my only reservations about the plan were that I didn't want to do anything to implicate the senator if we were caught.

"If my father was here, Fallon," Cai had assured me, "I know—in my heart—that he'd be the first to speak up about these nonsense charges of 'rebellion.'"

"Even if it put his career at risk?"

"It wouldn't. But yes, even then." Cai leaned out over the railing, gazing east. Toward his home. "He's my father."

I stood beside Cai and closed my eyes, and memories of *my* home—of Prydain, and Durovernum, and my own father—flooded my mind.

For a moment, as I stood there, my mind wove a daydream.

I had my sister back. We had a ship and freedom, and we could have just as easily traveled west instead of east, round the Iberian Peninsula to sail clear all the way back to the Island of the Mighty. I pictured me and Sorcha, in the company of our very own royal war band of gladiatrices, marching straight up to the gates of Durovernum, right to very doors of our father's great hall. King Virico Lugotorix would welcome his long-lost daughters with tears and open arms and great, foaming vats of good dark Cantii beer, and give us all land and cattle. We would build our own town and marry who we pleased. Charon would give up his slaver's ways, and Sorcha would finally open her heart to him. My father would embrace Cai as a worthy suitor for his daughter's hand, and my sister and I would build a kingdom as co-regents. And no tribe—not the Trinovantes, nor the Catuvellauni, nor the Coritanii—would dare to raid against us.

We would have peace . . .

And the girls left behind at the Ludus Achillea would pay the price.

With their lives.

The Sons of Dis would make them fight and kill, and feast on their brave hearts after they fell. And it would be all my fault. The pleasant, ridiculous fantasy of returning home shattered and fell to pieces all around me. The arena was my home now, I thought. And those girls, my family.

I would fight with every strength in my soul for them. For their freedom. And pray to the Morrigan I would not fail.

"Fallon?" I heard Cai's voice from close behind me. "Are you all right?"

I tried to say I was.

But in that moment, I suddenly felt so lost. I knew what I had to do, and why I had to do it, but I honestly didn't know if I could. I feared, in that moment, that I *would* fail. Fall and be defeated and die a horrible death. And I didn't know if I had the right to lead others to that same fate. In spite of the cloudy-bright sky overhead, I suddenly felt as if I was back in Tartarus, behind a wall of bars, staring into the black eyes of the man who wanted to claim my life and soul. That was the madness that I was willfully returning to face.

I questioned my own sanity.

"Are you afraid of what's to come?" Cai asked me.

I turned to look up into his clear hazel eyes and could not find it within me to lie. "Yes," I said.

He smiled at my answer and said, "Good."

"Doesn't that make me a coward?"

"No. Sweet Juno, Fallon, no." He took me by the shoulders, his face close to mine, and I could see in his eyes that he wasn't just trying to make me feel better. He meant what he said. "It makes you *human*," he continued. "And it keeps you sharp. Caesar once told me—on the eve of a battle—that he did not want men under his command who didn't have the good sense to be afraid to die. He wanted men who wanted to *live*. Only fools or desperate men rush blindly into the fray without giving at least a fleeting thought to what they stand to lose if they don't come out the other side."

"I grew up thinking that to be a warrior meant to have no fear," I said. "To be brave above all else."

He thought about that for a moment. "That's one way to approach it, I suppose," he said. "But I suspect real bravery is knowing fear intimately—I mean feeling it in the very *center* of your bones—and then going ahead and fighting anyway."

I thought of what Pontius Aquila had said to me in my cage. About how he taunted me, saying he would take my courage, my bravery, and make it his own.

Fine, I thought. *He can have it.*

Instead, just as Cai said, I would keep my fear. And I would use *that* to bring Aquila and his vile Sons of Dis, and Nyx, and everyone who thought to cut me down, to their knees.

I reached up and pulled Cai's head down so that I could kiss him.

"You don't think any less of me," I said, "now you know fear is my companion on the battlefield?"

"No." He grinned. "I think you choose your companions very wisely. Well, except for maybe Quint. He's not quite right in the head."

I laughed. "No, he's not. But with his help, we'll send Aquila packing with his toga tucked up between his legs. Him and his wretched Sons of Dis."

A flicker of a frown twitched between Cai's brows. So brief, I thought I'd imagined it. "Right," he said, as his gaze slipped from my face and drifted over my shoulder. "And his Sons of Dis . . ."

"We'll send them screaming back across the River Styx to Hades," I said.

I expected to see an answering spark in Cai's eyes, but his gaze had turned cloudy and distant. I put a hand on his arm, but it was clear that he was suddenly miles away from me.

"Cai?"

He blinked at me, as if just then remembering I was there, and smiled. But when he opened his mouth to speak, we were interrupted by Charon, hailing from the captain's perch. Cai shook his head, as if to dispel an unwelcome thought.

"Be right back," he said, and kissed me on the top of the head.

I watched him stride across the deck, wondering. There were still unspoken things—those shadows on the chasm bridge—hovering between Cai and me.

When all of this is over, I thought, *I will take him to our secret place in the ludus gardens and sit him down and talk those things to death. Then, once they are dead, I will forget they were ever there, and I will kiss Cai in the moonlight until it will seem like they never existed at all.*

I turned to go find Elka and almost bumped into Aeddan, who was suddenly standing right behind me. Dressed still in his black cloak and armor. A shadow on the chasm bridge. I stifled an impatient sigh and moved to one side so that I could slip past him—only to have my way blocked when he mirrored my steps.

"What *is* it, Aeddan?" I asked, woefully unsuccessful at my attempt to conceal the irritation in my voice.

He ignored it or didn't notice. I looked at him and saw that he was staring after Cai and Charon. I crossed my arms and waited, one eyebrow raised, until he looked back at me.

"Don't you find it disconcerting to have placed your complete trust in the hands of the man who stole you from your home and sold you into slavery?" Aeddan asked.

I shrugged. "No more than I find it disconcerting to place *any* trust in you."

He ignored that too. "And the Roman?"

"If you mean Cai, then—"

"He will betray you."

Shadows on the chasm bridge . . .

I shoved away the whisper of thought, glaring at Aeddan and suddenly angry. "You don't know what you're talking about."

"I think I do," he said. "I know what the whore warned him about back in Rome before we left. Do you?"

I felt my temper flaring. "Her name is Kassandra—"

"It's *bad*, Fallon," he snapped. "Very bad."

Shadows . . .

"What is?" My patience would allow him two more words out of his mouth. Maybe three. It turned out that was all Aeddan needed to make me listen. And they weren't what I was expecting. Not at all.

He hesitated for a moment, and then said, "Cai's father."

"Senator Varro?" I frowned. "What of him? Has something happened—"

"He's *one* of them, Fallon!"

I stared at Aeddan, not understanding.

He shook his head in frustration. "One of the Sons of Dis."

I burst out laughing, just like Cai had with Kass in the prison courtyard.

The very idea was laughable. Senator Varro—elegant and eloquent, kind and caring Senator Varro, a decorated hero of the legions and a respected statesman of the Republic—could not conceivably be one of those monsters. Preposterous.

"It's true," Aeddan said.

I stared at him hard, struggling to find the joke. Aeddan's expression remained humorless.

"Senator Varro is a war hero," I said. "An honorable man. He served in the legions under Pompey the Great—"

"And that makes him *honorable*?" Aeddan gaped at me. "The Fallon I used to know would never have said such a thing. Would he have been honorable if he'd served in the legions when they came to conquer *our* land?"

"That's not what I meant—"

"It doesn't matter." He shook his head and turned a withering glare on me. "Here's something I know about the esteemed Senator Varro from the time I spent with Pontius Aquila, Fallon. Since Pompey's death, Varro has been vocal in his support of Caesar, but it's a *lie*, Fallon. He hates Caesar, just like so many of his fellow snakes in the senate do. Hates him and fears him. Varro is secretly on the side of the Optimates—the very faction *of Romans* that Caesar is off fighting now in Hispania."

"So he doesn't agree with Caesar's politics," I argued, growing increasingly uncomfortable with the turn the conversation had taken. "That doesn't mean he's part of that sick, subversive cult."

"That sick, subversive *political* cult, Fallon. Don't be naïve," he scoffed. "The Sons of Dis think the gladiatorial sacrifices grant them power. The kind of power they can channel into bringing down the mighty Julius Caesar. Whether someone like Varro buys into their beliefs or *not*, he still might very well see them as a useful means to an end. Caesar's end. Add to that, the delicious irony that it would be a downfall set in motion by Caesar's own treasured Spirit of Victory. *You*."

I looked down to see that I was clutching my arm where Aquila had carved his mark into my skin. I unclenched my fingers like they'd touched something hot and hid my arm behind my back.

"I followed the girl back to the brothel, Fallon," he said. "That night. She told me everything she knew."

"Liar. She wouldn't tell me—"

"I'm not you. I'm not as polite."

I glared at him, wanting to turn on my heel and walk away from his nonsense, but needing to know what he'd learned in spite of myself. "And what did she tell you, then?" I snapped. "What proof did she have? Is Varro, himself, one of her . . . her patrons?"

"No." Aeddan shook his head. "There is a junior senator named Fabius. A frequent visitor at the brothel. A fool, yes, and usually addled with poppy wine. But according to the wh—" He stopped himself when he saw the look in my eyes and amended what he'd been about to say. "—according to Kassandra, he's never said anything while in his cups that hasn't borne out as truth. That day, he was running off his mouth about secret gatherings, about 'blood sacrifices' and how he was going to be a force to be reckoned with soon . . . How the 'great dark god' would grant his 'sons' the strength to take on a tyrant. How 'his master' would soon be one of the most powerful men in Rome—"

"Listen to yourself!" I shook my head. "You're actually giving credence to the third-hand boasting of a drink-addled brothel hound, Aeddan!"

So that was it, I thought, finally understanding Cai's reluctance to even mention his conversation with Kass and realizing all along that I'd had nothing to worry about. It was ridiculous and embarrassing—nothing more than the delusional proclamations of a drunken degenerate—and I was sure he hadn't wanted to tell me for fear that I might think less of a man I'd come to admire. His father. Senator Varro had been kind to me. Accepted me. *Me.* A gladiatrix, infamia, darling of the unwashed mob and wholly unsuited to even be seen talking with the likes of a senator's son. Kassandra—and Aeddan—had it all wrong. And I couldn't help but question Aeddan's motives, at least.

"Did Kassandra tell you whether this fool, as you yourself call him, ever even mentioned Varro by name?" I asked.

Aeddan's surety faltered. "No," he admitted. "But if this Fabius is a protégé of Senator Varro—"

I put up a hand to forestall any more of his nonsense. "I've heard enough. You can rest assured *I'll* be the first one to sound the war horns if I see even the shadow of one of those twisted bastards, believe me . . . But you're striking at shadows that aren't even there."

"Am I?" He looked at me bleakly. "Tell me something, Fallon. Did you see any of the faces of the men that night in the catacombs of Domus Corvinus?" His eyes burned into me. "Do you think they were commoners? That party was attended by Rome's powerful elite. How do you know Senator Varro wasn't one of them?"

"How do you know he was?"

"I don't. You're right. And I don't want to find myself in a situation where I can be certain. All I'm saying is . . . you'd better be careful. Keep hold of your wits—*and* your heart."

"What could possibly have made you say such a thing?" I asked, growing angry again. How dare he even *pretend* to have a care for my heart. After everything he'd done . . . "Is this some sort of twisted jealousy, Aeddan? Because I know—I *know*—Cai would never betray me. Not for anything—"

"Not even for his *father*, Fallon?" Aeddan shook his head. "Lugh's teeth! And you want to take us into the man's very *house*. It's folly. Dangerous folly."

"Even if I believed you—which I don't—what, *exactly*,

is it that you think Senator Varro can do to us from the other side of the Ionian Sea, Aeddan?"

"He doesn't need to be there to exert a powerful influence on his son, Fallon. Think about it—once we're there, Cai will be surrounded by all the things that will remind him of the man who raised him, provided for him—"

"You're wrong—"

"I *know* the way the Romans think!" he snapped. "Their parents are more like gods to them than family. They *worship* their ancestors! And if—*if*—it comes down to it . . . who do you think your handsome decurion will choose, Fallon?"

I was silent for a moment. Then I said, "Me."

"Over blood?"

He stared at me, and I thought I saw a flicker of compassion in his eyes. It made me even angrier. How dare he pity me? "Stop it, Aeddan. I already know you tried to convice Cai to send me home—"

"For your own good—"

"And I know what he told you—"

"It's *blood*, Fallon!"

"Like the blood you shared with Maelgwyn?" I scoffed. "That didn't stop you from thrusting a knife through his heart!"

The minute the words were out of my mouth, I regretted them. Aeddan's face looked like I had just slapped him with an armored fist. I wished desperately that he would just go. Take what freedom he had and, once the ship docked, leave. Leave me.

"I'm sorry," I said. "I don't know what you expect from me, Aeddan—"

"*Expect* from you, Fallon?" His head snapped toward me, and his gaze burned where it fell on me. "I expect nothing. You've already taken everything from me that I could have ever hoped to offer. I have nothing. I am nothing. I have no tribe, no torc, no house . . . I have no brother—as you've so very graciously reminded me. No family. No honor. Thanks to you, Fallon ferch Virico, I've lost my very soul."

"Then why do you stay? Why subject yourself to me like this?" I spat. "There's a whole wide world out there. *Leave*, Aeddan."

"That's the irony of it." He laughed bitterly. "I can't. I've lost everything, and now, all I can do is make sure I don't lose *you*. The one thing I could never have had in the first place. You can curse me, spit on me, ignore my warnings, and pretend I don't even exist, but I will not leave you. I will do whatever I have to, to keep you safe. Because your safety, your life . . . your . . . *you*—the sum of all my nothings—is the only thing I have left."

I stared at him, speechless and stunned.

"I expect nothing," he murmured again, his gaze drifting from my face, unfocued. "But I'm not leaving."

Silence descended between us, broken only by the snapping of the new sail overhead as it caught the wind and billowed full, and I realized in that moment that something I'd always accepted as truth was, in fact, a lie. Aeddan looked nothing like his brother. Nothing at all. I'd grown up thinking he and Mael were like two tapestries woven from the same threads. There were variations in the patterns, to be sure, but the similarities were far more striking than the differences. At least, that's what I'd always thought. I couldn't have been more wrong.

Aeddan was nothing like his brother.

And, for some reason, that suddenly made it harder to keep on hating him for Mael's death. An accident? No, it hadn't exactly been that. The two of them had fought with every heated intention of ending the other. I knew the feeling—the red rage that descends in the middle of a fight, the blind driving need to kill, to win, at whatever the cost. For Aeddan, the cost had been his own blood.

Like he'd said of Cai and his father. Blood. Betrayal. I knew he was wrong about Varro. And I knew, in my heart, that even if he was right . . . Cai—brave, honest, honorable to a fault Cai—would do the right thing.

Whatever the "right thing" was.

XV

"SO YOU'RE NOT only a slave trader, you're a smuggler as well."

"A successful businessman knows how to diversify."

Quint nodded in open appreciation of Charon's honesty. Or possibly his methods. Predictably, the slave master had been right when he'd said that the Amazons weren't going to like his plan for getting them through the city. Kallista and the others did *not* take particularly kindly to the means by which he would smuggle not only their weapons but the girls themselves north up the Via Clodia, straight to the gates of the Ludus Achillea.

The weapons were easy enough. Upon docking on the west bank of the Tiber, inside the walls of Rome, Charon's men had procured a cage cart, like the one in which Elka and I had been transported through Gaul as slaves. Only this one had a false floor with shallow compartments beneath—just roomy enough to hide a wealth of unsuspected hardware—camouflaged beneath a layer of straw.

The girls, on the other hand, were to travel hidden in plain sight. Riding in the cage cart, iron slave collars around their throats, shackles and chains at their wrists and ankles. It had taken a great deal of convincing on my part to reassure them that they weren't, in fact, being taken to a slave auction for sale. Kallista had extracted blood oaths and promises, and at one point, I think she even cast a looming curse-in-waiting on my head should circumstances ultimately prove I'd been lying.

Growing up in an Amazon tribe must have been rough, I decided.

But when Charon and I had first devised the scheme to infiltrate the Ludus Achillea by way of our new warriors, we'd given them all an even rougher history, in order to account for their delivery to the academy.

"I'll tell Nyx that my suppliers sent word they'd picked up this pack of lovelies from a pirate brothel in Tunisia that burned down a few months back," Charon proposed. "I'll say I offered them for sale to the Lady Achillea and that they're already bought and paid for. I'll even have the bill of sale with Sorcha's seal on it as proof"—he gestured to Sorcha—"of the bargain."

She almost smiled as she cocked an eyebrow at him and reached down the front of her tunic for the seal that hung perpetually from a chain around her neck. I wondered why they hadn't taken it from her when she'd been a captive, but then—according to Pontius Aquila's lie, and so the world—Sorcha was dead. And the seal was of no use to anyone.

"Nyx is hardly going to refuse delivery," Charon continued. "Especially not of a whole new feisty crop of potential munera fodder for her master. In fact, knowing how she operates, she'll probably take credit for the whole deal."

I eyed the Amazons over my shoulder, none of whom remotely resembled the only girl I'd ever known who actually *was* a brothel worker. Every single one of them looked far more likely to cut a man's throat in a bedchamber than anything else.

"Do you really think Nyx will believe all that?" I asked.

Charon shrugged. "I suppose that will depend on whether she's ever been to a Tunisian pirate brothel."

"Fair enough."

It was a risk, but then again . . . so was the whole damned plan.

Sorcha would stay at Charon's house in the city and help him coordinate our two disparate objectives. It was easy enough for her to move through the city in relative anonymity—the fame she'd earned as the vaunted Lady Achillea in her arena days had faded in the eyes, if not the minds, of her many ardent fans. And the elegant patrician figure she cut now bore almost no resemblance to the fierce mythic creature she'd been back in those days.

The same could not be said of her little sister and her companions. *We* had to adopt a different strategy altogether. Which was why, in the port of Ostia, at the mouth of the Tiber where it emptied into the sea, we'd docked briefly for a single purpose: to bring onboard a shipment of empty wine barrels. I wasn't about to risk sneaking myself and the Achillea girls off the ship in twos and threes. I would not risk a repeat of the scenario that had led to the loss of Meriel. But there was only one way I could think of to avoid it, and after mulling over the outlandish idea with Cai and Charon and the others, we'd agreed that it was the best— probably the *only*—hope of success we had.

I'd teased out my idea from a story Antonia had once told after the evening meal at the ludus, about the hero from her land named Odysseus, and how he and his war band had infiltrated a city hidden inside a wooden horse. Not having one of *those* handy, we'd had to make do.

"Whatever was in here previously was a cheap vintage," Ajani muttered, crinkling her nose as she lifted one long leg over and climbed gingerly into the empty barrel. "And musty."

"Don't be a wine snob." Gratia rolled her eyes, stifling a grunt as she attempted to fold her muscled bulk into a small enough ball. "At least you've got room to breathe."

"That's not necessarily a plus," Neferet gasped. "I'll be giddy on fumes by the time we get to where we're going!"

The ship deck was awash with grumbling gladiatrices:

"A slave cage is starting to look like a pleasant way to travel . . ."

"Lucky Amazons . . ."

"There's a rat in my barrel, and I think it's drunk . . ."

"Oh, don't be such a pack of princesses!" Antonia rolled

her eyes as she hopped nimbly into her barrel. "I think it's a brilliant ploy."

"You only think that because Fallon got the idea from your ridiculous Trojan horse story," Vorya said, crouching reluctantly.

"*Ja*," Elka concurred. "And the horse probably smelled better." She waved at Antonia's prosthetic weapon. "At least you can carve your own air holes once you're in there."

Antonia just grinned in response, waving the crescent blade in a little circle.

"It's not a far journey," I said, ignoring the rough wooden splinters digging into my flesh as I climbed into my own barrel.

"Better not be," Elka grumbled as Quint lifted the lid of her barrel.

"It isn't. I promise."

It wasn't. Well . . . not *that* far. Only up a twisting road and through the gates of the sprawling Varro estate, perched high on the Caelian Hill. It really was a desperate gamble, but we'd all agreed that it was the only way we were going to get off Charon's ship without being immediately arrested. Even with Rome's vigiles on the lookout for us, no one would think to stop a shipment of libations being transported through the city at the behest of one of its wealthiest and most powerful senators. That was the hope, at any rate.

I settled myself as comfortably as I could inside the oaken cask as Charon's men hammered the lid on, breathing as slowly and shallowly as I could, trying to ignore the dizzying scent of the long-gone wine and the faint stirrings of panic the cramped confines provoked. It felt as though I had been entombed, like in the stories Neferet had told us about how they buried dead Aegyptian kings, trapped forever in darkness, sealed up in a sarcophagus for all eternity. When finally they carried the barrels up onto the deck, then tipped them over to roll down the gangplank, it took every ounce of self-control I had not to scream or vomit.

Assuming none of the others did either, I thought, and we managed to get through the city without discovery, I was going to owe a whole cellarful of wine-stained gladiatrices an unpayable debt.

The trip through the winding streets of the capital was nerve-wracking. Every time the cart slowed or stopped, I feared it was because we'd been discovered. Every voice I heard calling out was surely the vigiles ordering us to halt for inspection. When, finally, I felt my barrel being lifted down off the cart, I felt a surge of fear strangle my throat. I had no idea if we'd actually reached our final destination. For all I knew, we'd been diverted to the Forum to be arrested and hauled away.

I held my breath as the lid above my head was pried off and the rosy light of the setting sun poured into my wine-soaked casket. It blinded me for a moment, and then Cai's head and shoulders blocked the twilight gleam as he reached down and lifted me out of the barrel and set me down on wobbly legs.

He tried to keep a straight face, I could tell, but it was

no use. The bare whiff of me up close was enough to bring
tears to his eyes. He took a step back and mustered a watery,
breath-holding smile of welcome.

"Welcome, daughter of Bacchus, to Domus Varro," he
said as he tucked a straggling, sticky lock of hair back behind
my ear.

I rolled an eye at him. Bacchus, the Roman god of wine,
was probably gazing down on us from his purple-stained
couch, high on Mount Olympus, and laughing himself silly.

Quint was nowhere near so diplomatic as Cai.

"Whoo!" he exclaimed, waving a hand in front of his
face as he helped Gratia and Elka step from their barrels.
"You lot smell like a legionnaire mess tent after a right good
pillage of a Gaulish vineyard!"

It was entirely true. But it had also worked. We were
safe. I looked around at the vaulting stone arches of Cai's
father's wine cellar, and at my companions, and couldn't
help the grin spreading across my face. For the first time
since our desperate escape from the ludus, I dared to hope
that we had not seen the last of our home *as* our home.

Home . . .

As places to grow up went, Domus Varro must have been
an extraordinary one. The kind of home that I'd never imagined existed in all the years I'd spent scampering through
the forests around Durovernum like a wild deer, leaping
over moss-covered logs and diving into secret springs,
climbing into bed at night to nestle under heaped furs while

the fresh-cut straw crinkled in the mattress beneath me and owls hooted outside my window, perched on the eaves of my cozy little roundhouse.

A world—*worlds*—away from the airy, elegant, marble-and mosaic-clad halls and courtyards of Rome. I still missed Durovernum. Sometimes with an ache so deep it felt like broken bones. And yet, as I sank chin-deep into the warm, lavender-scented waters of the bathhouse's tepidarium pool, I distantly marveled at how easy it had been for me to become accustomed to this kind of life. I wondered: If I were ever to return home again, back to Durovernum, how would I get along with only the cramped copper tub in the corner of my hut for bathing? Would I miss the spacious-ness of Roman homes, the echo of voices down their colon-naded corridors? The wide skies of Italia open to the stars at night, not hemmed in by the lush spreading branches of ancient, mighty oaks? How different would I have been growing up here, I mused, as I floated half-dreaming beneath the fantastical murals that arched overhead.

The other girls had retired after washing off the day's winey residue, but I'd stayed behind, reveling in the peace and stillness after the ordeal of the last few days. When I heard the barest ripple and splash from the corner of the pool, I opened my eyes to see the torches had burned low in their sconces, and the swirling steam rising from the sur-face of the water veiled the room in a sparkling, misty haze.

But even in the dim light, I could still see Cai—head and shoulders of him, anyway—where he rested against the blue-tiled edge of the other side of the pool, staring at me. The flickering torchlight glinted off the water droplets on his shoulders and chest, and sparked fire in the depths of his hazel eyes. I felt a fluttering, like birds startled to flight, in my chest and could hear my pulse surge in my ears as he pushed himself away from the edge and floated toward the center of the pool.

That rare, secret smile played about the corners of his lips, but there was a flicker of uncertainty in his eyes as Cai swam near. I felt it too. My mind flashed back to the day when Cai had told me he loved me—the same day Caesar had declared me his Spirit of Victory. But how well did we *really* know each other, I wondered in that moment. He'd been gone on campaign for most of the time since. And before that . . . when we'd first met, my life had seemed like being caught in the middle of a whirlwind. I'd been stripped of my self and my soul—a princess-turned-slave, taken from my world and thrust into another—and nothing about that time had seemed safe or certain. Nothing except Cai.

Nothing except the soldier who'd worn the armor of my enemy.

"I remember the first time I ever laid eyes on you," I said as Cai drifted close, wreathed in the steam rising from the rippling bath water.

"On the wharf. In Massilia." He nodded ruefully. "I seem to recall . . ."

"All that metal and leather. I could barely see the person beneath."

"There's none of that now," he said, grinning. "You may feast your eyes."

I laughed. But I didn't look away.

"I remember how you looked at me *that* day," he said. "I can still feel the flames on my face."

"Ha." I splashed a handful of water at him. "And I remember how you looked at *me* that day."

"To be fair," he said, "there wasn't very much of you that I could see, either. You were more caked-on road dirt and rags than girl."

"True." I had to agree with him there. "Although I remember Charon telling you we'd all clean up well enough. You didn't believe him."

"I should have."

"I didn't believe him either!" I reached for a bathing sponge in a basket on the side of the pool and handed it to him, turning around and lifting my hair away from my shoulders. "I didn't know at the time that you Romans had such baths. At home, I had a river. And a cramped copper tub for special occasions . . ."

Cai was silent, scrubbing the sponge in slow, gentle circles across my shoulders and back, squeezing the water out over my neck.

"Sometimes I wonder if you—if all the Romans I've met—still think of me as a barbarian," I mused. "If you, even with what you said to Aeddan, don't still sometimes wonder if I wouldn't be happier sleeping under furs beneath the thatched roof of my hut . . ."

His hand on my back went still, the water from the sponge trickling down my spine. "Would you?"

I let my hair fall and spun in a slow circle in the water until I faced him again. "Would *you* be there, under those furs, beneath that roof, beside me?"

"Under thatch . . . under marble and glass . . . under stars in the middle of a desert, Fallon," he said, his voice catching in his throat. "I would lie beside you in a cave on a mountaintop if you wanted me to. And if I ever thought of you as anything other than my equal—and more—then that is to my deep shame."

"As much as it's to mine that you were right—what you said on the beach at Corsica. That I haven't let myself fully trust you. I haven't treated *you* as an equal."

He shook his head. "It's all right. I understand—"

"No." I huffed a little. "It's *not* all right, and you really need to stop being so understanding, Cai. I don't always do the right thing, and as much as, yes, I need you to trust me, I also need you to question me. Challenge me. Keep me from trying to prove myself too strong to need anyone else. Because I *do* need you."

Desperately . . .

He reached up and cupped my face in his hands. There were water droplets on his lips and on his eyelashes. "You have me," he said, holding my gaze with the strength of his.

"Is it madness?" I asked. "Going up against Aquila and his monsters . . . My friends could die if we go through with this, Cai. My sister. Me . . . You."

"You're doing it because you think it's the right thing to do."

"But *is* it?"

He gazed at me then, with those far-sighted eyes that always seemed to look right through me to see my secrets and sorrows and strange, nebulous fears.

"All right." He sighed. "I'd be lying if I said there weren't times I've seriously thought about talking you out of it. Spiriting you away to Cyprus or Bithynia. Or back to your thatched-roof hut in Durovernum." His brow creased in a frown. "But I also listened to what you said to those girls back on Corsica—what you've been saying all along to your sisters at the ludus—and you're right. Together, you are stronger than any legion of men, and you deserve—*they* deserve—a place where you're allowed to flourish in that strength. When I was a boy, my father nearly lost his mind when my mother died. She was the true strength in their union. It took a lot for him to build himself back up, and I think there is still a part of him that is weak. Wounded."

"My father was the same," I said.

"We men think we rule the world." Cai laughed a little. "We're wrong. You *deserve* the Ludus Achillea, Fallon. You and the rest of those mad, marvelous—occasionally quite terrifying—girls. And I'll do anything I can to help you get it back. Even if I am one of those wretched males of the species."

I reached out and brushed the water droplets from his lips, one by one.

"You are anything but wretched, Caius Antonius Varro," I said.

His smile bloomed deeper beneath my fingertips. I put my arms around his neck and he cradled me in his, swimming out to the middle of the pool where the water was deep enough that my toes couldn't touch the pool bottom. And then he kissed me, and I lost myself to the sensation of his skin sliding against mine as he stopped swimming and, together, we sank beneath the surface of the water, breathing only each other's air.

XVI

IN THE DAYS since we'd arrived at Domus Varro, I'd slept less than half of each night, waking each morning well before sunrise with my heart pounding from half-remembered dreams and the near-constant fear that there was some aspect of our grand plan I hadn't yet taken into account. Something I'd failed to consider that would trip us up and shatter to pieces our painstakingly constructed scheme.

The crux of which amounted to this: Pontius Aquila wanted us to fight? Then we'd fight. We would issue a challenge to the Tribune of the Plebs, false master of the Ludus Achillea, and the leader of the Sons of Dis. We would call him out from behind the walls of our—*our*—academy, and we would engage his warriors in the biggest battle since Caesar's Quadruple Triumphs.

Right there in the field beyond the ludus walls.

When I'd initially presented my spark of an idea, Charon was the first to embrace it. Indeed, most of the details that went into how it would come to pass had come from him. Without his multitude of connections to the Roman merchants' and builders' guilds, I don't know that it would have been even remotely feasible.

I was on my way to the scriptorium, a central room in the house we'd commandeered as a kind of hub of operations, where Cai was waiting for me. I'd just rid myself of the scrolls announcing the tournament challenge, an advertisement that would appear in the public spaces all around the city, and the purse full of denarii to pay for them. Cai had written out the details on sheets of vellum as I watched, still mostly baffled by the meaning of the lines and shapes he scribbled across the pages in neat rows, but trusting he knew what he was doing. After, I'd gone in search of Quint, so he could carry the scrolls to the guild head of the city notice-painters and the Forum crier.

I was thinking about Charon's blessedly useful connections—and about what Aeddan had said, warning me not to trust my fate to the kind of man who'd been responsible for my slavery in the first place—as I rounded the corner of a corridor leading through the domus atrium. I wasn't expecting anyone else to be there.

Let alone the master of the house.

I froze.

But Senator Varro had heard my footsteps approaching across the marble floor and turned. He wasn't supposed to be there, I thought frantically. Not for another month at least . . . But he *was* there. Then. And when his dark eyes locked on me, I felt like a deer in a clearing that lifts its head to find itself surrounded by hounds.

"Fallon?"

The breath stifled in my lungs at the sound of his voice.

I couldn't move, couldn't turn and run . . .

I heard Aeddan's voice in my head: *"He will betray you . . ."*

Suddenly, all I could do was remember his admonition about my blind trust in the boy I loved. And his father. I wondered if one of the faces behind those hideous masks on that horrid night at the Domus Corvinus *had* been Cai's father's—

"Fallon!"

The senator strode across the light-filled room, eyes flashing, hands outstretched to grasp me by the shoulders . . .

"My dear girl!" he exclaimed and wrapped me in a fierce, unexpected hug. "You're safe! Thank Jupiter, I was so worried."

I remained stiff and teetering, shocked immobile for a moment, before I could return the embrace. But when I did, all my remaining fears and foreboding washed away like rain running from leaves to disappear into the earth. This was Caius Antonius Varro's father. And I had *nothing* to fear.

When, finally, the senator pushed me to arm's length and peered intently into my face, I could see the genuine concern in his gaze. "I heard rumors, Fallon," he said. "Terrible stories of things that happened at the Ludus Achillea . . ."

Everyone had, it seemed.

"Stories of rebellion," he continued, "and bloodshed. I heard the Lanista had been murdered by her charges and that legion soldiers had encouraged and even aided in the uprising. I heard one of them was Cai."

"It's not—"

"But if you're *here*, then that means that the rumors were wrong. Of course they were wrong! Where is Caius?" His gaze swept the room. "Is my son all right?"

"He's fine, sir. He's in the scriptorium—"

Before I could get another word out—about what had really happened, about my still very much alive sister, or about Pontius Aquila—Senator Varro had turned and was hurrying down the marble hall toward his scriptorium. If the swathes of material that made up his toga would have allowed it, I think he would have broken into a run. I followed close on his heels.

"Caius!" he called out, bursting through the carved oak double doors. "Caius!"

"Father!"

Cai spun around where he stood beside the desk that still held an ink jar and stack of vellum. His gaze flicked back and forth between me and his father, confused and surprised. And—I wondered if I was imagining it—alarmed. Kassandra's warning must have still lingered in his mind.

"I . . . I thought you were on your way to Greece," he stammered. "What . . . what are you doing back here?"

"I wasn't yet at Brundisium when word reached me of what was happening at the Ludus Achillea," the senator explained. "A revolt in the same vein as Spartacus, I was told! With my own *son* a traitor in the service of it."

"I wasn't. And there was no revolt—"

"Of course not."

"How did you even hear such—"

"I have informants, Caius." Senator Varro brushed aside his son's confusion, deeming it more important to convince himself of Cai's actual well-being. "You can tell me what *actually* happened later. In the meantime, I want you to see my personal physician."

"Why? I'm fine."

"Aside from all this ludus nonsense, do you forget you were discharged of your legion duties due to injury?" Varro frowned sternly at his wayward son. "You've subsequently endured long travel, confinement, escape, and the gods know what else, all under—I'm assuming—violent circumstances. You are too thin, and there are shadows under your eyes. You'll see my physician."

"When I have time, perhaps. At the moment, I'm a bit busy—"

"*Now*, Caius." Varro glared balefully at Cai. "I'll send a slave to fetch the man. And you will submit yourself to an examination." He turned to me. "Both of you, I should say. You, dear girl, look to be in almost worse shape than *he* does. And that will never do."

"I'm fine. I just haven't been sleeping too well—"

"Then I'll have my physician prepare you a draught before bed." He put a hand up. "No arguments."

All that being said, the senator turned and strode across the room, the matter clearly decided. As he pulled the oak doors shut behind him, I blinked at Cai in bewilderment. To be fair, he seemed a bit bemused himself, but he shook it off and held out a hand to me.

"Did I mention my father's a bit overprotective?" He smiled ruefully.

I thought of my own father. Of how he'd been willing to marry me off to a boy I hadn't loved just to keep me from becoming a warrior. To save me from myself. I supposed that I couldn't really blame Varro.

I sighed and took Cai's hand. "I know the feeling."

He pulled me close and kissed my forehead.

"I don't really look *that* bad, do I?" I asked when he lifted a hand to smooth my hair back from my face.

Cai laughed. "I think you look perfect," he said. "But then, I'm hardly one to judge. According to my father, I'm halfway across the River Styx myself."

I looked down at the stack of vellum on the scriptorium desk and picked up the stylus Cai had used to write the challenge to Pontius Aquila.

"Do you think your father will try to stop us?" I asked. "When he learns what we're going to do?"

"He can try." Cai shrugged. "But I don't think he will. For all my father is a politician and a businessman, there's one thing I know about him: He's a man who hates injustice.

I have a feeling that once he knows what's really going on, he'll be more than happy to do what he knows, in his heart, is the right thing."

It was reassuring to hear his sentiment echo mine about Cai himself.

Kass and Aeddan could believe what they wanted.

I would believe in the good of the people I knew to be good. I felt a weight I hadn't really realized I'd been carrying lift from my shoulders. There were still others heaped there, but that one, at least, was gone.

"Is what we're planning here folly?" I asked, wondering—not for the first time—how in the wide world we were going to pull off such an audacious scheme and take back the ludus.

"Folly? Maybe." Cai tilted my chin up so that I was looking into his eyes as he smiled at me. "Or maybe it's just what you do. You *fight*, Fallon. And I'll fight alongside you. We all will."

"Of course we will." I looked over to see Quintus poking his head through the doors the senator had just left through. "Was that the good Senator Varro I just saw storming off in the direction of the stables?" he asked.

"Aye." Cai nodded. "Apparently, word of the ludus 'rebellion' traveled faster than winged Mercury and forestalled his journey to Greece."

"That's not going to become an impediment to our plans, is it?" Quintus frowned worriedly.

Cai shook his head. "I don't think so. My father has a less than elevated opinion of the Tribune of the Plebs. As

I told Fallon, I suspect that he'll rather cheer us on in this endeavor."

Something occurred to me then. "Cai . . ."

He turned to me.

"Don't tell your father Sorcha still lives," I said. "She's our secret weapon. She needs to *stay* secret. None of this will work without her. And none of it will work if anyone even suspects that she still lives. If so much as a hint on the breeze drifts over the walls of the ludus and reaches Aquila's ears, we'll fail."

Cai frowned, clearly at odds with the idea of deceiving his father—even if only through the act of omission—but I think he also knew I was right. We hadn't even told Cai's freedman servant, a boy named Actaeon, who delivered messages to and from when we sent him running to Charon's. Where Sorcha remained, hidden away and safe, and—I imagined—restless and cranky.

"I understand," Cai said. "I won't say a word about your sister."

The rest of the details of our plan—and the challenge—we were more than happy to share with Senator Varro. In fact, it was to our advantage to do so. For the past year, ever since the Quadruple Triumphs had ended and Caesar had left the city on campaign, there had been an increasingly clamorous demand for games. Distractions. The mob was easily bored, particularily in the wake of the Triumphs—an entire month of gruesome spectacle that had whetted their appetites for excitement and bloodshed.

Of course, the mob didn't know about the Sons of Dis.
They only knew what they'd been told.

About me and my friends . . . about our so-called
rebellion.

What *we* had to do was get them excited enough—
without actually stirring them to fear or panic—so that we
could use them as shield and surety against our arrest the
second we stepped foot out in public again. So we'd cir-
culated rumors that the renegade Victrix would present
herself and her war band for judgment—in trial by combat—to the Tribune of the Plebs and his noble fighters. And
there, in front of everyone, decide the matter as to just how
guilty we were.

Then we had the announcements sent out.

Excitement in the city, or so I was told, was instantaneous. And fevered.

The senator, for his part, was instrumental in convincing other key members of the senate that this was a
better—a safer—way of dealing with a rebel uprising than
what had happened before with Spartacus. *And* it had the
added benefit of distracting the mob from the current political situation. With the tacit agreement, then, of the men
in power, spectator stands went up in the fields outside
the ludus where, we'd been informed, Pontius Aquila had
taken up residence. And we would be allowed to travel
there in peace on the day of the challenge tournament. It
set my teeth on edge to think of that despicable man living in the Lanista's quarters, but I comforted myself with
thoughts of all the frantic hammering and sawing of the

carpenters building the makeshift arena just outside the wall. I sincerely hoped that it was keeping the gracious Tribune awake long into the night.

Finally, it was the day. Everything that could be done had been. All that was left was for us to show up. And fight. And win. I felt as though my nerves were threads of lightning sparking and flashing beneath my skin. My heart, full of thunder like a storm cloud. That evening, we would take back our home.

Or die trying.

Cai and Quint were at the stables with the gladiatrices, and Aeddan and I were on our way to meet them there. We strode down a long, light-filled corridor in a wing of the house I was less familiar with, Aeddan three paces ahead of me and as prickly and silent as ever. I knew we should make haste, but for reasons that escaped me, I found myself slowing as we approached a richly carved door made of ebony wood and silver. I'd never seen it open, but that day it was a handsbreadth ajar, and there was a flickering illumination spilling out from within. I couldn't say why, but I was drawn to that light. I stopped in front of the door and, after a moment's hesitation, pushed it slowly open.

"Fallon?" Aeddan said, stopping to turn back, an irritated frown on his face. "What are you doing?"

Satisfying my curiosity, I supposed, was the easiest answer.

Listening to the whispers of the Morrigan was probably more truthful.

The room beyond the door was windowless and unfurnished, with high, wide double doors set into the opposite wall that must have led out to the main courtyard, if I remembered the layout of the house correctly. I'd certainly never seen them open, though. In fact, it felt as if this room had been kept shut up and locked tight for a long time. The air was oppressive, and it had the stuffy, close feeling of a vault.

Or a shrine . . .

As I stepped inside I saw that, all along one wall, there were rows of sculpted alabaster faces resting in metal sconces. I'd heard of the Roman practice of creating funerary masks of the dead, and I supposed that was what this was. The faces had been placed in front of lit lamps, and the delicate, translucent stone transformed the lamp flames into the soft, eerie glow that lit the room.

"They worship their ancestors," I remembered Aeddan saying to me on the ship. When he'd tried to warn me about Senator Varro. About Cai . . .

On the opposite wall, there was a breathtaking display of ceremonial armor and weaponry. Polished to gleaming, the breastplate and helmet reflected the light as if the armor itself was made of molten gold. It must have belonged to Senator Varro, I thought. Of course it had. He'd been a celebrated general in his soldiering days, and this room must have been a sacred place to him. A place where he could pray to his gods. Thank them for his victories.

Pledge to them his sacrifices . . .

Suddenly, my blood ran cold.

In a recessed alcove at the far end of the room, there was another lamp. A single, wavering flame that illuminated what seemed to be an altar stone. And on top of the stone, there stood a set of scales. In one of the scale dishes, there lay a single feather, wrought in gleaming silver.

The scar on my arm tingled, and I heard Aeddan's sharp intake of breath as my own voice strangled in my throat. He knew, just as well as I did, what we'd found. Senator Decimus Fulvius Varro—Cai's beloved father—was one of the Sons of Dis. Kassandra had been right all along. And no one had believed her. Almost no one.

"Go," I managed in a croaked whisper. "Aeddan . . . find Cai. Bring him here—*hurry*—he needs to see this . . ."

"Fallon—"

I turned on him. "You were *right*," I snarled. "Is that what you want to hear, Aeddan? That you were right about Varro? You were. I was blind. I was foolish. And now we are in great danger. So go! Find Cai and bring him here! Before it's too late . . ."

Aeddan hesitated for an instant. Then he spun on his heel and stalked from the room without another word. I turned back, moving toward the altar as if drawn to it by some unseen force. The scar on my arm burned with a sharp, searing sensation as I reached out my hand and touched the empty dish of the scale. It bobbed gently up and down, and even in the uncertain light, I could see the stains of old blood that marred its polished surface.

The sight of such a thing, the unassailable proof that Kassandra had been right all along—that his father was one

of the Sons of Dis—would break Cai's heart. But I needed
him to believe me beyond any doubt. Because, without the
evidence of the scales right in front of me, I don't know that
I would have believed it myself.

"Now, Fallon," Varro's voice interrupted my horrified
thoughts. "It isn't polite to enter rooms you aren't invited
into."

I closed my eyes and swallowed thickly, fear churning
suddenly in my stomach. When I turned around, I almost
didn't recognize the man who stood before me. In the
dimly lit room, his face was as stark and carved as one of
the masks that hung on the wall. His eyes, always so keen,
so kind, were black.

"It's all been a lie," I said, my voice a grating rasp. "All
of it, from the beginning, hasn't it? You were never on your
way to Brundisium. There was no trade delegation. You
knew about the attack Pontius Aquila had planned on the
ludus. You are one of the Sons of Dis."

"Well, yes." Varro spread his hands wide, smiling mod-
estly. "Their leader, actually. Pontius Aquila will tell you *he*
is, but Aquila is really nothing more than a useful, tractable
puppet. He believes fiercely in his dark gods, and I find it
very convenient to let him. He thinks *you* are some kind
of divine instrument." He chuckled. "I simply happen to
think you are a marvelous weapon. One that I intend to
use most effectively against that would-be dictator Caesar,
thanks—in part—to the audaciousness of you and your
friends. And my own dear son."

"I don't understand."

"Oh, come now. This challenge tournament you've all so industriously conjured into existence?" He shut the door behind him and walked toward me. "Brilliant. I had thought only to capture Caesar's prized ludus while his back was turned. It was to be a mostly private injury to him. Now, because of you, dear Fallon, I can add very public insult to it. And no one will ever be able to say that it was me."

"I will."

"Oh, dear child." He shook his head, smiling indulgently. "You won't live long enough to do any such thing." His gaze drifted toward the wall of faces, and his expression became thoughtful. "But you can rest easy in your afterlife knowing that you were instrumental in crushing the spirit of the monster who would defile the Republic with his whore Aegyptian queen. The Republic my ancestors fought and died for."

"I think you vastly overestimate my importance, Senator." I took a step away from the altar. "I'm just a lowly gladiatrix."

"You're Caesar's lowly gladiatrix," Varro said. "That's the difference. For all the man is a monster, he's one with a mighty heart. It's made him strong. But it's also his greatest weakness. You see, Caesar cares deeply for those people he considers 'his.' And you, by a clever trick of the Fates, are one of those. I had a long conversation with him after the Triumphs, in fact, about how he sees the spirit of his dear dead daughter in you. You, his Victrix, the glorious symbol of his Triumphs."

When he reached the altar, he plucked up the feather from the scales and held it carefully between two fingers, turning it so it could catch the lamplight.

"You're a remarkable young woman, Fallon," he continued, as if we were having a pleasant discussion about something as meaningless as the weather. "And Caesar is not the only one you've beguiled with your—admittedly barbaric—charms." He put a hand to his heart. "I too feel such kinship with you. Affection, even. Perhaps not in the same realm as the hopeless yearning my son bears for you, but I almost feel you are the daughter of *my* heart, Fallon. Not Caesar's. Perhaps, when you are dead, I will honor your passing with a mask in this very room."

He gestured with the silver feather to the wall of ghostly faces, and a shudder of revulsion ran through my entire body. Then he turned and held the feather out, pointed at me, as if it were a dagger. He took another step toward me when, suddenly, the ebony door swung open, and I almost gasped with relief as Cai stepped into the shrine room. Quint and Antonia were with him. Antonia was wearing her crescent blade strapped to her arm.

"Step away, Father," Cai said. *"Please . . ."*

"Caius—"

"Now!"

The rasp of scabbards as Cai drew his double blades was enough to make the senator close his mouth and take a single step backward, away from me. But a dangerous anger flared in his eyes as he glared at his decurion son.

"Fallon," Cai said, "come to me."

I walked backward in the direction of Cai's voice, not taking my eyes off his father. I was almost there when the double doors leading to the courtyard burst open and a wash of blinding daylight flooded the room, accompanied by seven men in the armor and regalia of the city vigiles.

With Aeddan at their head.

"Your carriage driver is waiting, my lord Varro," he said to Cai's father, with a deferential bow.

"Ever the snake," I said, glaring at Aeddan as if I could set him on fire with my eyes.

He met my gaze unflinchingly and shrugged. "At least I'm consistent."

"Thank you, Aeddan," Varro said. "You are a loyal Son of Dis, and you will be rewarded."

Cai took a step forward. "Father—"

"No, Caius!" Varro silenced him with a slash of his hand through the air. "I will brook no further opposition from you. This isn't a game, boy, and you have no idea what's at stake. You don't understand—I know that—but one day soon you will come to realize I'm doing this for the Republic. For *you*, my son."

"I'm not your son," Cai said, his face twisted with conflicting emotions—grief, disappointment, betrayal . . . love. "Not anymore. You've forfeited the right to address me as such."

Varro's mouth disappeared into a hard line, and the planes of his handsome face twisted into a bitter grimace. "The girl is not to be harmed," he said to Aeddan and the vigiles. "My *son* . . . is not to be killed. The others, I do not care what happens to them."

Aeddan nodded and unsheathed the sword that hung at his hip. His mouth turned up in a smile, but his eyes remained cold. "And the ludus challenge?" he asked.

"Must go on as planned." Varro was adamant. "See to it that you get her there and in costume and ready to perform."

"I won't lose," I said.

"Yes, my dear, you will." He gazed at me with an expression of bleak satisfaction. "I'm sure you think your abilities are at their peak, but it's amazing the subtle, barely discernible diminishing in one's muscle strength that occurs when one has consumed small amounts of hemlock in wine over the course of several nights. I think that, when the time comes and the cornua horn sounds to start the fight, you'll find that your strength is not what it was. Your reflexes, just that fraction of a second slower. Your eyesight, just a touch blurry . . . Oh yes, you *will* lose. And with that defeat, so go all of Caesar's victories. That stain will stick to him like tar. And it will spread. And the mob will turn on him."

Aeddan's face remained impassive as his eyes locked with mine.

"I'll leave your tainted heart for Pontius Aquila to feast upon." Senator Varro smiled at me, an expression of pure malice. "Perhaps, if I'm very lucky, the spirit of the hemlock will rid me of him as well."

Then the leader of the Sons of Dis cast one last, bleak look back at his son before he turned and stalked through the double doors, the folds of his purple-striped robes billowing in his wake. Aeddan closed the doors behind him, plunging the room back into a sepulchral gloom, and the vigiles Varro had left behind—all hard-bitten men by the looks of them, probably veterans of the legion—fanned out in a loose circle around us.

Wordlessly, Cai handed me one of his swords, and stepped up to flank me. Quint stepped up on the other side. Antonia started to hum a little under her breath in anticipation of the coming fight and turned to guard my back, her crescent-blade weapon reflecting fire all along its edge.

But we were outnumbered two to one. At least, I thought so.

The sound of hoofbeats and the creak of Varro's carriage wheels in the courtyard grew faint, disappearing into the distance. Aeddan stood by the doors, listening, and then turned his attention back to the room. I tightened my grip on the hilt of my sword as he strode across the marble-tiled floor . . . *through* the circle of vigiles . . . to take up a defensive stance between me and Quint. I saw him share a glance with Cai.

"He's gone," Aeddan said.

"Good," Cai answered, the rasp of iron in his tone. "Then let's get this over with so we can be on our way as well."

One of the vigiles—the most scarred, battle-worn one— snarled in Aeddan's direction. "You treacherous scum," he said. "The Sons of Dis will have your heart out for this."

"I doubt it," Aeddan said. "And they wouldn't find it palatable if they did."

Then there was no more time for talk.

The vigile's snarl turned to a grunt of exertion as he launched himself into an attack, aiming for Aeddan's shoulder. Aeddan ducked, and I darted in with a slash of my blade that drew an arc of blood from the fleshy part of the attacker's sword arm. But I wasn't fast enough to evade the punch he aimed at my head without even pausing to acknowledge the wound I'd dealt him. His knuckles caught me a glancing blow to my chin, and I reeled back, off balance and cursing.

When he came at me again with a second punch, I didn't bother to duck. I just blocked the blow with my sword. He didn't have time to scream in pain before I circled my blade through the air and lunged forward, burying the point in his chest. He fell back, and I yanked my sword from between his ribs, kicking away his slumping corpse.

As I regrouped for another attacker, I saw Antonia put her crescent blade to good use. The man she used it on didn't even know that his throat had been opened up before he was on the floor, staring empty-eyed up at the ceiling. Quint saw it happen too, and offered a grunt of approval. Then he turned and dispatched his own attacker. The remaining vigiles fought grimly, but they proved no real match for two trained legionnaires and three angry gladiators.

Soon, the room was quiet. Still.

Red.

The blood pooled beneath our feet, seeping from the mortal wounds of the seven dead vigiles. I stood there, catching my wind, when Cai turned to Antonia.

"Find Neferet," he said. "Hurry—and tell her to bring her satchel!"

I blinked at him. None of us was injured.

"I don't think it'll do them any good," I said, gesturing at the bodies of the vigiles on the floor.

"It's not for them. It's for you," Cai said, grabbing me by the shoulders and making me look at him. "Perhaps we're not too late . . ."

"Too late for what?"

"The hemlock."

"Cai—"

"Aeddan, find something she can sit down on."

Aeddan heaved at the marble altar, tipping it over on its side. It fell heavily, and the scales and feather hit the floor with a crash.

"Cai! Aeddan—stop!" I shrugged out of Cai's grip as he tried to make me sit. "Antonia, stay here!"

They froze, all of them staring at me as if I might shatter.

"I'm fine," I said.

Antonia frowned. "But the hemlock—"

"I didn't drink any hemlock." I snorted. "The senator's physician sent a cup of wine to my room every night to help me sleep. But I had such terrible dreams the first night, I just kept pouring the stuff out the window."

Cai looked at me. "You didn't drink the wine."

I shrugged. "I didn't want to seem rude."

He laughed and hugged me fiercely.

"I've decided I'll stick to good old Prydain beer," I said, my voice muffled by his chest. "You Romans put too many strange things in your drink."

Cai let go of me, grinning. "All right," he said. "We'll celebrate with a great foaming vat of the stuff when this is all over, but now it's past time we left this place."

He moved swiftly to the single door that led back out into the house and cracked it open, checking to see if there were any of the domus slaves about. It seemed the way was clear.

"Wipe the blood from your sandals on that one's cloak," he said, pointing to one of the dead vigiles. "Let's go."

Before we left the room, I put a hand on his arm. "Cai? I'm sorry about your father," I said.

"No." He shook his head, but I could see the anger—and the heartbreak—in his gaze. "*I'm* the one who should be sorry, Fallon. I should have believed Kass. And I damned well should have told you of her suspicions. Instead, I let my love for my father blind me, and I led us all into danger. Aeddan was right."

I glanced at Aeddan, who looked back at me, a grim vindication in his eyes.

"You knew he knew?"

"He came to me when we first arrived here. I didn't want to listen at first. But he was right." Cai nodded at him. "And loyal. He sent for me first before going to get those thug Sons of Dis just now." He looked back at the dead men on the floor. "I'm just glad I was with Antonia when he found me—she's a walking weapon."

Antonia threw him a casual salute with her nonweaponized hand as she finished cleaning the blood from her crescent blade.

"At any rate," he continued, "so long as my father thinks Aeddan is still loyal to *their* order, then that's an advantage we have. He might be able to get close to Aquila, and that might prove useful."

The thought of getting anywhere near Pontius Aquila sent a chill through me, but he was right. And I owed Aeddan an apology when everything was said and done. Several, perhaps.

Cai slipped out through the ebony door into the corridor beyond and we followed him as he ran, heading in the direction of the stables, where the rest of my fellow gladiatrices waited with horses saddled and a gilded war chariot hitched up and at the ready. Elka grinned as she held out a full kit of armor that was an exact duplicate of the ceremonial Victrix gear I'd worn during Caesar's Triumphs.

"Charon's doing?" I asked.

She nodded. "The man has definite connections in the artisans' guilds."

Then she and Gratia helped me armor up. There would be no mistaking who I was as we rode through the city and north on the Via Clodia. All the way to the gates of the Ludus Achillea. Our destination, and our destiny.

As we rode, we fanned out in a V formation: Victrix in her chariot, followed by two wild-geese wings of fellow warriors, mounted on noble steeds, helmet crests tossing, cloaks flowing out behind us, weapons and armor gleaming. We presented a magnificent spectacle, worthy of the marble frieze that graced the main gates of the ludus, as we rode through the crowds that had lined the city streets, expecting us.

They parted before our horses like long grass before a storm gale.

And they were cheering.

Cai had the reins of my chariot and he drove, bareheaded and standing tall, his face set in a stern expression. I rode bareheaded too, standing behind him with my feet braced wide. I carried my helmet in the crook of my arm and left my hair unbound to stream behind me. The crowd recognized me instantly from my victories and threw laurel sheafs beneath the hooves of my chariot ponies. Some of them recognized Cai as the handsome young decurion who'd leaped the barrier to sweep me off my feet in a passionate kiss after my Triumphal win. If they'd thought before that the Achillea gladiatrices were rebels after the fashion of Spartacus—an unruly band to be feared and hated—that impression vanished in that instant. I could feel it.

We weren't rebels or renegades.

We were defiant heroes, on our way to reclaim what was ours.

And once we got there, we'd give them a show they'd never forget. As we traveled up the Via Clodia, the crowd followed, swelling with each mile, a festival parade. When we arrived, the mob that had gathered in the fields and in the stands, beneath the striped awnings and banners snapping in the evening breeze, roared mad approval. The closer we got to the arena, the more I could feel the bloodlust that fogged the air, thicker than I'd ever tasted it. Even during the Triumphs. It pressed against my skin and made me feel, for a moment, like I was suffocating. The mob was the only reason we'd been able to engineer this challenge, but they were not why I was fighting. Not who I was fighting for. I was fighting for the girls I rode with. I was fighting *with* them.

This fight was for no one but us.

Another wave of shouts and cheers went up, echoing off the distant hills and shaking the very walls of the Ludus Achillea in front of us. Pontius Aquila would have no choice but to send out most, if not all, of his gladiators—male and female. If he and his fighters stayed hemmed in behind those walls, I had little doubt the mob would storm the ludus in outrage at being denied their bloody spectacle. At the very least, he and Nyx and his whole Amazona contingent would become little more than a laughingstock. There would be no more munera for the Sons of Dis—not from Aquila at any rate—and he would lose any influence he wielded in the political circles of the Republic. I smiled to myself grimly. The mob didn't know it, but they were our most powerful weapon in rendering the Sons of Dis powerless. They might very well achieve their desired bloodshed this night, but I swore to the Morrigan, it would not be in the way they expected.

They could choke on the blood we would spill for all I cared.

As the sun began, finally, to sink over the far distant hills, painting the arena purple with dusk, hundreds of torches flared to life. The roars of the crowd were like the gales of a summer storm, thundering in waves across the fields to slam into the walls of the ludus and roll back again over the makeshift stands. The sloping hills that cradled the lake on either side gathered the noise and echoed with the roars of "Victrix! Victrix!" making it seem as though the crowds of spectators were even larger than when I'd fought during the Triumphs in the Circus Maximus.

Their cries shook my bones.

Even as my sister walked out onto that field of combat in my place.

Dressed in *my* Victrix armor.

XVII

I LAY IN the bottom of a boat, drifting across the silent water of Lake Sabatinus, half a mile away from the Ludus Achillea, listening to the faint dull roar of the crowds. I reached over, searching for Cai's hand. His fingers, long and strong and calloused, tightened on mine, and he flicked a glance toward me, his clear hazel eyes glinting in the starlit darkness. The sun had long set, but there were so many torches burning in the makeshift arena in front of the ludus that the sky in the southwest seemed lit on fire.

Still, I was grateful that it was the night before the new moon. The overarching darkness would make it easier for Sorcha, wearing my Victory helmet, to pass as me. And with any luck, it would also serve to help us infiltrate the Ludus Achillea from the lakeward side.

It has been Arviragus's strategy—one that he'd suggested to me when I'd told him back on Corsica about my idea to retake the ludus. Something learned from his time

battling Julius Caesar in the forests of Gaul: Never commit all your forces to only one front of attack. As strategies
went, it certainly wasn't groundbreaking in its innovation. But then again, Pontius Aquila was no soldier, and I
could only hope that he didn't have the necessary strategic
instincts to become one. With the massive spectacle we'd
orchestrated in front of the ludus, I was counting—hoping,
praying—on him having committed all, or at least most, of
his defensive elements to dealing with the roaring tigers
clawing at his front gate.

Leaving the back door open to the silent, sneaky rats.

It had gone according to plan, so far.

Once our contingent of gladiatrices had arrived at the
field arena, we'd made our way through the excited throng,
straight to the pavilion tent Charon had commissioned to
have built for us at the south end of the makeshift arena—a
waiting place where the combatants could prepare for the
coming spectacle, away from the raucous crowds. Sorcha
had been waiting inside the tent since before dawn, and
she and I had gone about our business swiftly and with
minimal chatter. I shrugged out of my armored breastplate
and battle kilt, my greaves and bracers and helmet, and
handed over my signature weaponry—my dimachaerus
swords.

Sorcha was only a little taller than me, and with the
crested Victrix helmet on her head obscuring most of her
face beneath the decorated visor, no one would be able to
tell the difference. Even I almost felt as if I was looking into
a mirror once she settled the helmet on her head.

As for me, I pulled my hair back into a quick, clumsy braid, hiding it under a tatty felt cap, and wrapped a shapeless servant's cloak around me. Seated on folding campstools all around us, the other Achillea gladiatrices looked magnificent in the armor and weapons Charon's abundant wealth had provided for them. They would accompany my sister onto the field as if she were me. All of them, Ajani and Elka included, though the latter had protested bitterly. But even she had to admit that it would look strange, indeed, if the Victrix's "frost maiden"—as, apparently, Elka had become known among the plebs—wasn't at her side for the battle.

And so, while my sister gladiatrices fought honorably at "my" side, in reality, Cai and Quint and I would be carrying on the dirtier business of double-dealing.

"This feels so awkward," Sorcha muttered, shifting my two swords on her hips so that they sat comfortably. As comfortably as possible for one who wasn't used to wearing them.

"Just let her disarm you on one side as soon as you can without making it look intentional," I said. "And then you'll have all the advantage you need in the fight."

"I might not have to *let* her disarm me," she said, drawing a blade with her left hand and spinning it in her palm— just a tiny bit clumsily. "I might just drop the damned thing trying to hold it!"

I hid an indulgent grin, only because I could tell that Sorcha was actually—and this was something I hadn't expected—nervous. What I was counting on was that once she was in the ring, my legendary warrior sister would remember who—and what—she was, and all would be right. Our entire strategy hinged on the deception. Nyx knew me. She knew how to fight me. She knew how to beat me.

She was expecting it to *be* me out there in that arena.

And that was why she would lose.

Once Sorcha began to fight *her* way—the way she'd retrained herself to fight after the injury in the arena that had ended her career—she would destroy Nyx. In a way that I could never hope to do. And while she did, I would be busy retaking the ludus. Just like I'd promised. To that end, it was time to put the second phase of the plan into motion. I nodded to Cai, who put a hand on Quint's shoulder. They stood and hefted legion packs onto their backs that made heavy, dull clanking sounds as they settled the straps on their shoulders.

"Time to go," he said.

Quint saluted Sorcha and the girls, but before he had a chance to leave the tent, Elka stood up and stepped in front of him.

"Behave yourself around that pack of she-wolf Amazon cubs," she said.

"I will." Quint nodded without thinking. And then froze, blinking dumbly, when he realized Elka had actually spoken to him. "I . . . what?"

"I like my men with their virtue unsullied," she said, grinning wolfishly herself as she reached out to grab him by the chin.

"Un . . . sullied . . ."

"By anyone but me," she continued.

Then she leaned in and kissed him, full on his open, astonished mouth.

I bit my cheek to keep from dissolving into gales of laughter as she sat back down, leaving the poor boy standing there, looking for all the world as if he'd been shot, not with Cupid the love god's arrow but Diana the Huntress's. A whole quiverful of them.

Before the others could tear him to further pieces with mockery, Quint ducked his head and pushed his way out of the tent. Cai followed. I waited for as long as I could stand it, then hugged my sister, hefted an empty basket up onto my shoulder to help hide my face, and ducked out of the tent myself. No one looked at me twice as I shouldered my way through the crowds, following the crests of Cai's and Quint's helmets. No one was looking for Victrix in the body of a lowly serving slave. Once we reached the outer perimeter of the crowd, I ditched the basket and the three of us broke into a run, heading in the direction of a road that circled off to the east, leading to the opulent villas on the other side of Lake Sabatinus.

When we arrived at the gates of one particularly sprawling estate, the bulky-muscled eunuch who'd been called to deal with us had been aghast at granting me an audience with Cleopatra. I was fortunate that Sorcha's name carried far more weight than mine. I told him what our situation was—as succinctly as possible—and the Aegyptian queen's chief bodyguard grunted and grumbled but finally led us to a triclinium, where we were to wait for her Royal Highness.

As the skies began to grow dark I started to fret that my plan would unravel if we didn't see her soon. And then the far gilded doors flew open and Cleopatra came striding across the marble floor, golden-beaded sandals slapping a war tattoo as she came. Cleopatra, it seemed, was itching for a healthy dose of vengeance in Sorcha's name.

"Dead, they told me!" she exclaimed angrily. "When I sent my maids calling at the ludus for your sister to come visit me. Dead in an uprising and at *your* hand, little one."

"But you didn't believe them?" Cai asked deferentially.

She laughed and threw herself down upon a gilded couch, motioning for us all to sit. "Take it from one who has—and on more than one occasion—*actually* tried to murder her sister. Not for a second." She turned to me. "There is nothing of that in you. I know how much you love Sorcha. I'm almost as fond myself. And therefore, anything you ask of me, on her behalf, you may have."

"A boat, Your Highness," I said, perching anxiously on the edge of a carved ebony chair. "That's all. Just a boat to get us across the lake unnoticed."

"A stealthy attack?" the queen said, leaning forward on her couch and swinging her sandaled feet back down to the floor. "But there are only three of you."

"There are more of us, inside the ludus." I told her of the gladiatix sisters I'd left behind. And of the Amazons that Charon had "sold" to the ludus. "All we have to do is get to them and set them free."

"That sounds exciting!" Cleopatra's wide dark eyes glittered dangerously. "Of course you can have the use of my boats. Take my barge if you'd like. And my men—there aren't many of them, and they're mostly fat and lazy like Sennefer here." She waved a hand at her eunuch body-guard. "But I approve in Caesar's name of this adventure."

"Well . . . less an adventure, perhaps, than a dangerous folly," I allowed.

"Perhaps I shall come with you—"

"Absolutely not!" the eunuch erupted in argument, his face going purple.

Cleopatra rolled her eyes. "Sennefer has no sense of adventure."

Perhaps not, I thought, but I was glad of it. While I suspected—from what I'd heard from several sources, including Caesar himself—that Cleopatra was likely more than capable of killing an enemy with poison or an unex-pected knife in the back at a dinner party, I had no relish of the prospect of utilizing her lethal charms that night. What was to come would be chaotic and dangerous . . . and dirty. Quite frankly, if I could have killed Nyx without hav-ing to look her in the eyes first, I would take that opportu-nity, because I knew that, under the same circumstances, she certainly wouldn't do me the courtesy of a tap on the shoulder first.

But that was my business. Not the queen's.

At any rate, Cleopatra relented almost immediately with a shrug.

"He does, however," she continued, "have a point. I am the daughter of the gods and, as such, should probably leave such robust bloodshed to you who are trained in those arts."

I bowed low and stood, so that we could be on our way swiftly.

"Wait." Cleopatra stopped me before I could leave. "You're not planning on going out dressed like that, are you?"

"Uh . . ." I looked down at the plain linen tunic and sandals I wore. "I gave my armor to Sorcha so she could fight in my place."

"Well." The queen wrinkled her nose. "That will never do. Sennefer, fetch."

Sennefer rolled his eyes, but seemed to know what his mistress was talking of, even if I didn't. He left the room by a side door painted with scenes of a royal hunting party. The wooden trunk with which he returned, when he opened it at my feet, was full of a sight to make my warrior's heart soar with longing and delight.

Armor. *Glorious* armor. Fit for a queen. Or a Cantii princess.

"I have, on occasion, bestowed gifts on your sister," Cleopatra said, clearly delighted by my reaction. "But this time, I have something for you, Fallon ferch Virico. It was to be a gift—for your first arena fight under the Nova Ludus Achillea banner. Which, I suppose, technically this is. Or will be—if you win. So please do. I hate wasting presents."

As Cai and Quint helped buckle me into the new gear, Cleopatra had one more gift for me.

"Truly, I am sorry that you and my dear Sorcha have found yourselves entangled in the webs woven to ensare Caesar," she said, as she rose and walked over to a coffer-like jewelry box resting on a table in a corner of the room. It was almost as big as the trunk in my cell at the ludus— the one that held everything I owned of value. "And I know," she continued, "that were he here, my lord would be both proud and grateful to you, Fallon. Since he is *not* here, allow me to act in his stead." She rummaged for a moment, and emerged with a silver and faience pendant— the elegant head of a lioness. "This," she said, smiling, "is Sekhemet. One of my goddesses, and much like—if I understand what your sister has told me—your own goddess, the Morrigan."

The queen fastened the necklace around my neck, and I could feel the cool silver warming almost instantly against my skin as I tucked it beneath my new armor.

"She was an adversary to Anubis, who is akin to Dis," she continued. "She is wise and loving and tender . . . and merciless."

I looked into Cleopatra's eyes and saw a dark, implacable glint in her gaze.

"Now," she said with a terrifying smile, "go get the bastards."

• • •

Sennefer escorted us down to the lake dock.

"You cannot have her barge," he said.

"I don't need the barge," I agreed.

"And you cannot have her soldiers."

"I don't want her soldiers."

"Good." He stopped abruptly and looked at me, his expression grave. "The queen has not thought of it this way," he said, "but she is in danger as grave as any you face. And from the same men. They hide in shadows, pray to dark gods for power, whisper and scheme in the halls of the politicians, and use the mob's thirst for the gladiators against their masters . . . and all of it for a single purpose. To throw down Caesar. This you already know. But if they succeed, if the great general topples from that lofty height, then Cleopatra will have no friend here in the land of the Romans. They hate women. They hate powerful women. They hate her, most of all."

I thought about that for a moment and knew it to be true. The Optimates saw Cleopatra as a vile foreign seductress. A barbarian whore who prayed to false gods and tempted Caesar to think of himself as one of those gods. At least, that's the way they would frame the picture if it ever came time to act against her.

"Take care of her, Sennefer," I said. "As much as she will let you."

He sighed. "I always do, lady. May Osiris bar the doors of his underworld kingdom to you. For as long as he can."

He turned and clasped wrists with Cai and Quint, and

then left us to ourselves at the edge of the water. On a far dock, I saw the boat we'd used during our naumachia for the queen, with its chopped-off mast still sticking up midship like the trunk of a felled tree. It seemed like only the morning past we'd performed the whole silly spectacle, but it wasn't. It was a lifetime in the past. Leander's lifetime. Meriel's. Probably Tanis and Lydia were gone too. Maybe others from the handful of girls who hadn't made it out of the ludus that night.

We chose a boat that was small and sleek, low to the water, and painted dark blue. Cai and Quint loaded their legion packs into the boat, and I climbed in, crouching as low as I could. Then we pushed off, Cai rowing as silently as he could. The oars were well oiled in the locks, and there was barely a creak and splash as we glided over the black water of the Sabatinus. As we approached the shore where the ludus walls loomed above us, the noise of the gathered crowds in the arena field beyond was like the roar of surf on the ocean. The dark skies were bright with the multitudes of flaming torches that illuminated the spectacle about to begin. I felt my heart beating like a war drum in my chest as the shallow keel of the boat grated, slithering up the sandy beach, and we dropped over the sides.

Down the strand, I saw the second boat from our naumachia moored where there was a narrow wharf that jutted out into the water. It occurred to me then that whoever owned it—one of the obscenely rich patricians who kept a villa near Cleopatra's—must have been a close friend of

Pontius Aquila's. And more than likely, one of the Sons of Dis. I wondered how deep beneath Rome their thorny roots really did grow.

"Where now?" Cai asked in a whisper.

I gestured for them to follow me, and set off down the beach. There was only one gate built into the high, smooth wall topped with jagged stone. But that wasn't the only way in. As irritating as he'd been endearing, when it came to locked doors, Leander had proved his usefulness. For Nyx, and now for me. She'd used him to break out of the Achillea townhouse in Rome. I would use him now, gratefully, to break into the ludus itself.

"There," I whispered to Cai and Quint. "A service gate cut into the rock that leads down to cold-storage cellars linked by a tunnel to the kitchens. Leander described it to me on Corsica."

It was the gate through which Thalestris had stolen away—along with my captive sister—on that terrible night. I doubted even Nyx knew about it. I prayed to the Morrigan that she didn't. Or if she did, that she hadn't thought to suggest that Aquila station a guard there. Not that it mattered. It was our only way in and, guard or no, that's where we would go, because I not only had Leander's knowledge of the door, I had his key. I'd taken it from a leather thong he'd worn tied around his neck, before we'd buried him.

I whispered a silent thanks to his spirit and hoped that whatever afterlife he'd gone over to was a pleasant one full of laughter and love—or at the very least, abundant flirting. The thought of Leander's shade charming his way through a bevy of admiring female spirits brought a fleeting smile to my face.

It faded the minute I stepped through the unlocked door, into a dark, rough-hewn stone tunnel that reminded me entirely too much of the catacombs beneath the Domus Corvinus. Sennefer had given us a few small traveling lanterns—lamps with dark glass shades that cast just enough of an eerie glow for us to be able to make our way through the passage without breaking our necks tripping on the uneven floor. After what seemed like hours, we came out the other side to a deserted kitchen. Hopefully, the rest of the compound would be just as empty, with all the occupants up on the wall or out in the arena field.

Charon's ruse had worked well enough, we already knew, and the Amazon girls he'd "sold" to Pontius Aquila were still being kept at the ludus. Nyx had apparently been quite pleased at the propect of a whole new crew of girls for her to bully and beat into submission. I reasoned that she would have most likely locked them away somewhere they could be kept watch on but also isolated from each other. That is, if she'd learned anything at all from having locked all the Achillea gladiatrices together in the infirmary, before we'd made good our escape.

My hunch turned out to be right—unfortunately for the guard they'd stationed at the main entrance to the gladiatrix barracks.

Once inside, we discovered that there were newly installed slide-bar locks on the outside of every cell door in the wing that had been our home. On every door except one, that is. When I reached it, I pushed my own door slowly open with a fingertip. The tiny room was empty, and just the way I'd left it . . . except for one thing. My oath lamp. It had been sitting in the middle of my cot as a message for Nyx. Clearly, that message had been received. And understood. There was nothing left of the delicate, colored-glass thing but shards scattered across the floor. In spite of the destruction of one of my most prized possessions, I felt myself smiling grimly. I pulled the door quietly shut and turned to Cai and Quint.

"Open the doors," I said in a low whisper. "Set them free."

One by one we slid the bars aside to open the cell doors, and the Achillea girls and Charon's smuggled Amazons stepped out into the hall. Kallista, my headstrong young fishergirl, did a quick head count of her friends and breathed a sigh of relief. I did a quick count of mine and discovered girls were missing, Lydia and Tanis among them. But when the last door opened, and Damya lumbered through into the hallway, I almost cheered at the sight of her. She looked gaunt and pale—as if they'd been starving her—but her eyes were clear, and her gaze sharpened like honed iron when she saw me.

She was down the length of the corridor and mauling me in a crushing bear hug before I had the chance to say anything. "I knew!" she said in a fierce whisper. "I knew you'd come back."

"Damya—"

"That stupid goose Tanis. She was wrong, and I knew it!"

"Where is she?" I asked, squirming loose of the dire embrace. "Tanis?"

I was afraid she was about to tell me Tanis was dead.

"She's with *them*." Damya's mouth twisted and she spat on the floor. "With her—Nyx. Sold herself cheap as surely as if she'd still been a slave."

"What about Lydia?"

Damya's plain, open face turned stony. "Lydia is still in the infirmary. Heron calls her 'unresponsive,' but I don't think even he knows what's really wrong with her. She just lies there."

I winced, remembering how Nyx's whip had opened up the side of the poor girl's face. Maybe it had flayed her spirit too. I looked around at the other girls from the ludus.

"Two others—Persis and Marcella—are dead," Damya said.

I felt my heart clench. "What happened?"

"Nyx got bored waiting for Aquila to start killing us. So she threw those two into the ring one night with one of the Dis gladiators." Damya shook her head, wincing. "He was near on three times their size, and you could tell he didn't want to fight any more than they did. But he also didn't want to die."

I closed my eyes against the anger and sadness I felt.

"The girls did the Lady Achillea proud," she continued. "That gladiator will have to learn how to hold a sword without a thumb. And he won't be called on to entertain rich Roman matrons in their bedchambers anymore."

"Good for them," I said, choking on a laugh that was half sob.

"Aye." She nodded. "*That* was the last thrust of Marcella's blade, but one worthy of an Achillea gladiatrix. He cut her down before her next breath. They dragged away their bodies for burial, and that was the last I saw of them."

For burial. I prayed to the Morrigan that their ends had been so. As wicked as Nyx was, I could hardly imagine her participating in the kind of grotesque sacrificial rites the Sons of Dis perpetrated. I shuddered. And then I ignited.

A coal of anger suddenly burst to life in my heart. This. *This* was the fate Aquila would consign my sisters to, I thought. *This* was why we were going to stop him. End him. And men like him . . .

Men like Cai's father.

I glanced away from Damya to see that Cai's gaze was locked on my face, his bright hazel eyes full of storm clouds. I could tell that he'd read my thoughts, and my heart ached for him. I wondered if he would ever be able to forgive me for what we were about to do. But as he looked at me, I saw his mouth harden into an implacable line. He nodded curtly, once, and then gestured me to lead on.

I only wished his father hadn't been able to read my thoughts as well as his son did. But the moment we stepped out into the lesser courtyard, that's exactly what it seemed had happened. For all our stealth and subterfuge . . . for all the distraction of the spectacle going on outside the ludus walls, it seemed that Senator Varro had been expecting us, regardless. Because there he stood, dressed in black leather armor with a sword in his hand. And a detachment of Dis gladiators at his back.

XVIII

"I KNEW SOMETHING was amiss." A self-satisfied grin stretched across Senator Varro's face. "You see, *you*, Fallon . . . you never fought like you were playing for time."

He'd known. His soldier's keen eye had told him that it wasn't me out there fighting in the armor of Victrix.

"Keep them here," he said to his guards. "Or kill them." His glance flicked over to Cai and then away again.

He turned and strode off, and his men wasted no time in idle parley but went straight to the attack. Cai parried and threw the first man aside and snapped a quick "Go!" over his shoulder. Then he and the others moved to clear a path for me.

I swore, stomping the Dis fighter I'd knocked to the ground in the face with my heel. He went limp, and I leaped over him, running after the senator. If he managed to make it to Aquila, then all was lost. Everything.

I sprinted headlong through the causeway, out into

the small stable yard—and took the length of a pitchfork shaft in the stomach. I dropped to the ground, wheezing, and my swords fell from my hands. He'd ambushed me, lured me there away from the others, and hidden behind the wall, waiting.

He bent down and picked me up. By my neck.

Varro's fingers tightened around my throat, squeezing. Scorching-hot tears splashed down my cheeks as I struggled, clawing at his muscle-corded wrists, my feet kicking helplessly as he lifted me off the ground. The blood roared in my ears as I tried to breathe, to no avail.

"I fought against Spartacus and his cursed rebels, girl," Varro hissed. "My legions cut them down like wheat in the fields. You are nothing against the might of Rome—"

"*Father!*" I heard Cai shout, his voice ragged. "*Let go of her!*"

But Varro was far too intent on wringing the life out of me to hear his son's cry. He seemed to notice we weren't alone in the stable yard only when Cai slammed into him shoulder first, knocking the senator off balance. With a snarl of rage at the interruption, Varro turned and threw me through the air. I glanced off Cai's armored chest and landed in a gasping heap on the ground. It felt as though my head had been torn half off. The air I sucked into my lungs seared my raw throat, and I lurched up onto my hands and knees, retching hot saliva that pooled on the ground in front of me. The edges of my vision were tinged reddish gray.

I tried to speak Cai's name, but the only sound I could produce was a rasping growl. When I lifted my head, I saw through my tears that he was standing in front of me, legs braced wide, a sword held in either fist.

"You even fight like one of them," Varro sneered. "Like a filthy gladiator. A real legion officer would be ashamed."

"If you're what's considered a real legion officer, then I'd be ashamed to bear that title," Cai said, his face twisting with bitter disappointment and grief. I watched whatever love he still bore his father die in his eyes in that moment.

"You disappoint me, Caius. Your loyalty to that would-be emperor and his gladiatrix whores has twisted your mind."

"You were the one who pleaded with Caesar for my place as decurion!"

"So you could see for yourself firsthand what kind of monster he is."

"Caesar doesn't eat the hearts of his warriors!"

"No, he just turns them into useless lumps of quivering, fearful flesh." Varro drew the sword that hung from his belt and took a step forward. "Get out of my way, Caius."

"You know I won't."

"Then you'll die."

Cai's father was a head taller than his son, and even though he'd been retired from legion duty for almost as long as Cai had been alive, he'd clearly lost none of his strength or prowess with a blade. But he'd also clearly never fought a gladiator before. Cai had. With two swords, as dimachaerus, all so that he could spar with me.

What I'd learned on the boat, and on Corsica, was that a legionnaire was drilled in such a way that attacks and defensive moves came automatically, without thought. Denizens of the arena were drilled to think on their feet. To improvise and innovate. Varro might have thought it was weakness to fight with such a lack of discipline. I knew, in certain situations, it was strength. Cai knew it too. He knew it so well that his father never even anticipated that, while one of Cai's blades parried his hard-struck blow, the other was on its way to finding the side gap in his breastplate.

I watched in horror as, without the slightest hesitation, Cai thrust the blade between his father's ribs. Right to the hilt. Varro's eyes went wide and his mouth fell open in a silent gasp. The sword dropped from his hand and he reached for his son's face.

"My son . . ." he murmured, his eyes clouding.

"You have no son," Cai said, teeth clenched in a frightful grimace. "I renounce you, and your name, and your blood. I will not perform the rites for you, old man. I will not put coins for the Ferryman on your eyes. You go to Hades with no issue, no legacy, and no hope to ever walk the fields of Elysium beside my mother's shade."

Varro uttered a wordless, strangled sound of protest as Cai pushed him away and then stood, the sword in his left hand dripping red, to watch impassively as his father's body slumped in a heap on the ground. When Cai turned to me, there was no sadness in his eyes. No more remorse or grief. Only a slow-fading fury.

"Fallon . . ."

He strode toward me, dropping to his knees, to take me by the shoulders.

"Fallon, can you speak? Are you all right?"

I nodded, still retching and gasping for breath. The dark umbra at the edges of my vision made it seem like I was looking up at him through a portal, and I still wasn't able to talk. But I could stand. And I could fight.

"Give . . . give me my swords, Cai," I managed finally in an ugly rasp as I staggered to my feet with his help. I could still feel his father's hands around my throat, crushing the life out of me. "I'm going to finish this."

"We'll finish this together," he said.

He pulled me close and bent his head to mine, kissing me hard on the lips. Then, without a second glance at the body on the ground, he retrieved my swords from where I'd dropped them when Varro had winded me with the pitchfork. He handed them to me, and together, we advanced toward the main gates of the ludus.

Leaving his father, and his father's hate, far behind.

We headed back to where Quint and Kallista waited with the others.

"What happened to Varro's men?" I asked.

Quint snorted. "Seems these girls really *were* spoiling for a fight," he said. "All of them."

Damya grinned. "I like them," she said. "Where'd you find them?"

"I'll tell you all about it when we're done," I said. "Let's go."

Swiftly, silently, we made our way to the main yard of the compound. There, we prepared for what I hoped would be the final act in the drama. The sounds of clashing weapons drifted back over the walls, but the ludus was almost entirely deserted. Pontius Aquila had turned out all his fighters, and he himself sat beneath a torchlit awning, high on a constructed platform that extended out from the guardwalk that topped the ludus walls. The platform was decorated in such a way that you could be forgiven for thinking it was Caesar himself who sat there. Even from that distance, I could see Aquila was surrounded by a crowd of fatuous, fawning men dressed in voluminous togas, and flanked by armed guards dressed head to toe in black. Their collective attention was wholly focused on the fighting that took place down below. I squinted past the fading spots that still clouded my vision and saw Aeddan was up there too, standing off to one side and dressed in the black garb of the Dis warriors. Clearly Aquila still trusted him. I wondered how Aeddan could stand being that close to the man.

I wondered even more how Tanis could.

She stood there, bow in her hand and a quiver on her back, dressed in black armor, and a wave of bitter disappointment swept over me. She truly was lost to us, and her betrayal of the ludus was my fault. I'd failed her.

I would not fail the others.

I glanced over my shoulder and saw that Damya and the Achillea girls had formed up behind Cai; the Amazons, behind Quint. In front of us, the main courtyard lay open to sky, with nothing and no one to come between us and the gates, which stood wide that night, a testament to Aquila's arrogance. Then again, how much arrogance was it, really, when his forces clearly outnumbered ours?

Or so he thought.

I was also fairly certain Aquila expected that the moment "Victrix" succumbed to the perilous combination of Nyx's vicious onslaught and the hemlock Varro had supposedly been dosing me with, the Achillea warriors would lose all heart and either flee the field or be cut down like wheat before the scythe.

But he was about to be disappointed.

And it was Nyx who would falter. *That*, I swore to the Morrigan.

I signaled to Cai and Quint, and, together, we all moved out. Keeping to the cover of the shadows beneath the walls, I led my gang of stealthy warriors to the open, beckoning gates. Signaling them to wait, I peered around, spying through the crack between the great oak doors and their enormous bronze hinges.

Nyx's back was to the ludus. The timing couldn't have been better.

I stepped into the empty archway.

The warriors at my back followed.

Sorcha saw us standing there, framed by the yawning maw of the gates, like the Morrigan's own war band, loosed from our bonds in the Lands of the Blessed Dead and sent forth to exact the goddess's vengeance on the unworthy. Sorcha raised her sword in that moment and backed off. I suspected that Nyx was already furious and frustrated at not having been able to kill "me" yet, and that must have only added to her confusion. She wasn't alone.

The crowd expressed their confusion and displeasure right along with her.

"Come on, damn you!" Nyx howled over the hectoring voices.

And then Sorcha reached up and snapped open the buckle on the side of her helmet. She lifted it from her head, and Nyx staggered back as if she'd seen a ghost. She probably thought she had. As far as *she* was concerned, Thalestris had already ended Sorcha's life, days earlier, beneath the light of a full moon and surrounded by her tribe of warrior women.

The mob in the stands knew none of that.

But still there were gasps and cries of outrage when the crowd realized that it hadn't been me under that helmet after all. A confused silence followed, and then a gathering murmur that raced through the stands like wildfire when they realized who it *had* been. Many of them—*most* of them, from the sounds of it—still remembered the Lady Achillea from her arena days. The crowd was ecstatic. Their cheers, deafening.

But something inside Nyx broke in that moment.

I watched as she retreated from Sorcha, shaking her head.

"No!" she cried. "*No!* This isn't how it's supposed to be . . ."

"You disappoint me, Nyx," Sorcha called out, her voice carrying across the arena and silencing the cheering crowd, who held their breath in anticipation of what was to come. "But then, you always have."

"I won't fight *you*!" Nyx's face twisted in rage and anguish. "I won't—"

The spear that came out of nowhere sang as it flew. Sorcha heard it just in time to dive for Nyx and tackle her out of the way as the spear thrower—dressed all in black, like the rest of Aquila's fighters—stalked forward.

Thalestris.

Sorcha rolled away from Nyx, who lay gasping and winded—but alive—beneath her, and leaped to her feet.

"If you're too weak to finish this fight, gladiolus," Thalestris called out to Nyx in her raven's-croak voice, "I assure you, I am not."

Cai nudged my shoulder. "You said she'd be back. You were right."

"I hate it when I'm right."

What I hated even more was that whereas Nyx didn't know how to beat Sorcha in a fight, Thalestris—my sister's primus pilus, the woman who'd helped her develop her unique style—most certainly did. My hate was mitigated by the fact that I'd been half expecting the disgraced Amazon to put in an appearance that night. And to *that* end, I had prepared a welcome for her.

I would fight fire with fire.

A lot of fire.

"Ajani!" I shouted. But my voice, hoarse from the ravages of Varro's choking, was lost in the din of the mob. Quint put a hand on my shoulder and, instead, blew a deafening blast on his whistle. I waved my hands over my head and cried, "*Now!*"

Out in the field arena and waiting for my signal, Ajani drew her bow and arched her back, aiming at the stars overhead. Then she loosed and shot a flaming arrow arcing up into the sky. It hung there at the top of its arc, like a blazing star itself . . . before sailing down to slam into the ground right between my feet. The missile stuck there, still aflame, and my Amazon contingent ran forward—each of them now equipped with one of the fire chains Cai and Quint had carried with them in their legion packs.

Kallista and her sisters gathered around Ajani's arrow and set their cage balls alight. Then they poured through the ludus gate and out onto the field of battle, swinging their flaming weapons in great roaring circles above their heads. The appearance of fire-wielding Amazons sent the crowd in the stands into a rapture of bloodlust as the girls from the ludus that was named after Amazons now had to turn and face *real* Amazons.

At the sight of us, the Achillea gladiatrices who'd accompanied me to Corsica sent up a Cantii war cry and surged back into the fray with renewed vigor. Bloodied, battered, but on their feet. Every single one of them, and a glimpse of Elka—right in the thick of it—hewing a circle with her spear did my heart as much good, I'm sure, as it did Quint's. He and Cai wasted no time wading into the fight, and I left them to it, turning my attention to the rest.

The makeshift arena had erupted into fresh chaos with our arrival.

I saw Thalassa and Kore fighting back-to-back like they were partners in a dance. Hestia cut a swath through a clot of Dis guards with her sica blade, and Gratia faced down an Amazona gladiatrix who was actually bigger than she was. Ajani laid down arrow-fire cover for those who needed it, and Antonia brandished with devastating grace the crescent blade that had become almost a part of her. Everywhere the crowd looked there was something for them to slake their thirst for excitment. At the center of the ring of clashing combatants, there was a wide, empty space—an arena within the arena where Sorcha and Thalestris battled grimly.

I rushed to join my sister so that, together, we could put an end to all the madness that Nyx and Thalestris had wrought.

"You're weak, Sorcha," I heard Thalestris taunting in a voice like spitting venom. "Lame and old and half-blind . . ."

"My only weakness was trusting you, Thalestris," Sorcha answered. "My blindness was in thinking you were worthy."

The Amazon snarled. "You were never the warrior they said you were."

Sorcha circled to her left, guarding against attack on that side.

"You're right," she said. "I was never Achillea. I was Sorcha of the Cantii. And it's high time I reclaimed that name. And that mantle."

My heart swelled to hear those words, but it wasn't going to be easy for her. Sorcha was holding her own, but she wasn't gaining any ground. They were too evenly matched.

It was my intention to disrupt that delicate balance.

I circled around to Thalestris's flank, but she wouldn't be drawn away from her focus on Sorcha. Instead, she kicked up a discarded retiarius net that lay on the ground and kept me at bay with it while she still wielded her spear one-handed like it was an extension of her arm. I darted and feinted, probing for any gap in her defenses, but Thalestris had none. The crowd jeered and shouted, urging us to spill blood, but I was nothing more than a nuisance to her. A buzzing fly. Barely a distraction.

So I made myself a target instead.

The next time she whipped around with her net, I let her catch my blades—both of them—in the knotted ropes. A fatal mistake of a young fighter. A gladiolus . . . Thalestris was used to that, and she pounced on my vulnerability, teeth bared in a triumphant grimace as she yanked the net forward. I let her pull me off balance. Into the circle of her striking distance. The makeshift stands thundered and shook as the crowd roared madly and stomped their feet.

I prayed to the Morrigan that my sister could see what I'd done . . .

That she would be fast enough . . .

She was my brilliant warrior sister. And she didn't disappoint.

I'd left myself wide open to the strike. But in the scintilla of a moment when Thalestris reared back with her spear, she left a space. It was on her defensive side—an opening most fighters wouldn't have been able to exploit—but in her drive to end me, she forgot for that instant who her other opponent was.

The Lady Achillea. Sorcha of the Cantii.

She sprang forward, with her off-kilter style, and dropped to one knee. Sorcha brought her blade up and around . . . and thrust into the space beneath Thalestris's arm as she tore my swords out of my grasp. Thalestris's body bent like Ajani's bow, arcing away from the blow.

All at once, the crowd fell silent.

Every other fighter in the field froze.

"When you greet your sister in the afterlife," Sorcha said through bared teeth, "you can tell her I beat you too. Me, and *my* sister."

Thalestris was dead before she hit the ground.

When I'd killed the Fury in my very first fight, her gaze had softened and her lips smiled, and a lifetime's worth of rage had emptied out of her. She'd found serenity with her last breath. Thalestris went to her death grappling her anger and hatred to her soul. Defiant to the last, she would not relinquish her vengeance, not even as she passed from the world. Her face remained frozen—like one of Varro's death masks—in a rictus of malevolence. A countenance she would wear for all eternity in the Lands beyond Death. I could not even pray for her peace.

But it was over, finally. For Sorcha. I thought it was for me too.

She bent to retrieve my blades, and I reached up and dragged the helmet from my head, and the crowd cheered wildly. A cheer that turned to a horrified gasp as a ball of flame slammed into the ground right beside me. I dove out of the way instinctively as a comet of heat and smoke roared past my head. My shoulder slammed into the ground and I rolled, springing back up to my feet to see Nyx standing before me, one of the Amazons' smoldering fire chains dangling from her fist. I'd somehow managed to forget one of the most important lessons Sorcha had taught me as a child.

Never let down your guard until you're off the field of battle.

And I was most definitely still on the field.

My sister tossed me my swords, and I nodded at her to step back.

This was going to have to be my fight and mine alone. The crowd would have it no other way. Nyx was clearly fine with that. She might not have been willing to fight Sorcha, but unsurprisingly, she seemed to have no such qualms about me. I felt my stomach twist with apprehension. The things Nyx was capable of doing with a whip had been my downfall every single time I'd fought with her. Seeing her now, with what amounted to a war god's version of the same weapon—a whip, only made of metal *and on fire*—was almost enough to make me turn and run.

And then I remembered something.

Just like Sorcha, I didn't have to fight Nyx the way I'd always fought her.

There were no rules here. No referees. Nothing confining me to one weapon or another. Nothing but my own choices. The rest of the arena had gone silent; all of the other fights had dwindled to stillness. Nyx and I were the absolute focus of every pair of eyes there. High up on the ludus walls, beneath his fringed awning, Pontius Aquila's face was white and stark. His hands gripped the rail in front of him as he leaned forward, his eyes pools of shadow that threatened to grow large enough to swallow me whole.

I could almost sense his anticipation of my death.

Not tonight, Tribune, I thought. *Not ever for you.*

I saluted Nyx and the crowd with both my swords . . .

Then I sheathed the blade I held in my left hand.

Nyx sneered at me as I stooped to pick up a shield that lay on the ground. Nyx had never seen me use one in single combat before. Which also meant she had no idea what to expect from me.

"Come on, then," I said, sinking into a ready stance. "Let's finish this."

The flaming cage of Nyx's fire chain slammed into my shield, and a bloom of flame licked out around the edges. I felt the heat, but no hurt, as she swung the thing back and attacked again. And again. All I had to do was anticipate which angle she was coming at me from and move to block. If it hadn't been for all those hours of practice on the ship, I don't know that I could have done it. But I remembered

Cai's shouted instructions to the girls as Quint blew his whistle commands. I kept my feet moving. My shoulders tucked and angled. My head down . . .

The fire cage put a drag on the end of the chain that Nyx wasn't used to. Her whip had been a supple weapon, the tip of it like a darting serpent's tongue. The fire chain handled more like a bludgeon. When I saw her winding up for one of her signature attacks, I made my move. The fire cage dragged for a moment as it hit the ground, longer than Nyx was used to. I dove for it and slammed my shield down, driving the cage into the earth. The flame extinguished, and the chain went taut between us. With a great cry, I hacked downward through the metal links with my sword. They parted in a shower of jagged shrapnel.

And the blade of my oath sword shattered with them.

I uttered a cry of denial that was echoed through the crowd.

With my shield edge lodged in the earth, Nyx snarled in triumph and reared back with the truncated length of chain, aiming to smash it down on my defenseless skull. In her enthusiasm to spill my brains, it seemed she'd forgotten that I had a second sword. And she'd left herself wide open.

Hidden behind the shield, my second blade slid free of its sheath . . .

She lunged at me, and I buried it between her ribs.

Just like she'd once buried her knife between mine.

"Count yourself lucky, Nyx," I said quietly as she slowly sank to the ground in front of me, a look of disbelief on her face. "I'll see you get the burial you deserve. But I won't let your dark master eat your heart."

The roar of the crowd was deafening.

It filled my head and made the ground shudder up through my feet.

It masked the whine of the arrow.

The shaft hit me squarely on the left side of my chest, above my heart, and knocked me off my feet. I looked up through a haze of pain to see Tanis, the archer, draw another arrow from her quiver and nock it to her bow. If I had been wearing my usual armor, I would be dead. But the breastplate Cleopatra had given me was—unsurprisingly—heavily decorated with scrolling metalwork and made of the finest, thickest bull's hide. It dented on impact, and I felt like I'd been hit by a catapult stone, but I was alive.

Unpunctured, maybe, but unable to move.

I looked up, helpless as Tanis sighted down the length of the arrow shaft. I closed my eyes. Prayed to the Morrigan she would take my soul in flight . . . Waited for impact. For death.

But nothing came. I opened my eyes to see her still standing there, frozen in hesitation. The crowd held its breath, but Pontius Aquila's patience was at an end. He stood and lunged for Tanis, wrenching the arrow and bow from her grip, shoving her aside. Then he turned and, competently enough to tell me he had some archery skills at least, nocked the arrow and sighted.

This time I didn't close my eyes.

And so I saw when Aeddan leaped in front of Aquila, taking the second arrow that was meant for me square in his chest.

"Aeddan!" I cried and staggered to my feet, clutching a hand to my wounded shoulder.

He spun around in a grotesque dance, balanced on the edge of the rampart. Then slowly, gracefully, he toppled off the wall and hit the ground below. I ran, stumbling toward him, and dropped to my knees at his side.

He was breathing still, shallowly, and with each breath a fresh wash of blood spilled from his mouth.

"Fallon . . ." He lifted a hand to my face.

"Rest," I shushed him, taking his hand in mine and holding it as tightly as I could.

"I'm . . . sorry . . ."

"Rest now . . ."

He nodded weakly and his mouth moved, forming a single word. A name. "Mael . . ."

"Greet your beloved brother for me, Aeddan," I said, choking on the sob that clutched at my throat. "Tell Mael . . . tell him I miss him . . ."

My tears spilled onto his cheeks, mingling with his blood.

He managed another nod, and his hand clenched convulsively on mine.

"I'll miss you too." I leaned forward and kissed him on the forehead. "And I will see you both one day again, in the Lands of the Blessed Dead. And we shall all be friends there."

And then he was gone.

The crowd had gone utterly silent, soaking in my grief.

I stood, slowly, and turned my attention to Pontius Aquila. He had dropped the bow, sensing the mood of the crowd turning ugly against him. They were on our side now. And there was nothing he could do about it.

Someone from the stands lobbed a torch at his platform as my sister stepped up beside me. "Give me back my ludus, Pontius Aquila!" she shouted up at him, her words ringing through the air. "It belongs to me, and it belongs to these girls. They are not rebels, they are not renegades. They are heroes. And you are not welcome in our home."

"Achillea! Achillea!" the crowd began to chant. And "Victrix! Victrix!"

Even if the mob did not fully comprehend the subtleties of what they'd witnessed there that night, they knew they'd had a roaring good time. And with me and Sorcha and our fellow fighters ensconced back at the academy, they were likely assured of many more like it.

The shouting grew to a roaring.

Aquila went even paler, and I saw him step back away from the edge of the rampart. Another torch flew tumbling toward the platform. And another. I was thankful the walls of the ludus were high and made of stone, else the crowd that had just cheered our winning back the place might well have burnt it to the ground.

Aquila's guards had already hurried down the ladders to the ground, and I saw them rush to close the gates, while the Tribune and his vile Dis cronies scrambled to follow. Tanis fled with them. Some of the crowd from the arena stands charged the gates, pounding on them and demanding justice, but I just watched him go. They would scurry down to the beach, I knew, and take to their galley. I smiled to myself, thinking just what kind of reception they might find, once they got to Cleopatra's side of the lake.

"I don't think he will return," Sorcha said quietly. "Here, or anywhere in the Republic where someone might recognize his face. We've won, little sister. You did it."

With only one good arm, I wrapped Sorcha in the tightest embrace I could muster. "*We* did it." I said. "Together. All of us."

"AH-CHILLEA!" The shouting grew to a roaring. "AH-CHILLEA!"

Sorcha turned and, out of view of the crowd, rolled her eyes. I grinned at her, and together, we held hands and turned to face the crowd. When my glorious sister punched her fist into the air, the world erupted around us.

Wine and beer barrels appeared as if by magic, along with flutes and drums and lyres. There was singing and dancing and laughter, and I had a feeling that this was a party that would last until dawn. For the crowd at least.

My shoulder throbbed painfully, and I saw Neferet pushing through the crowd to get to me, her physician's satchel slung across her torso. I turned and surveyed the field arena, strewn with a few scattered bodies. I didn't yet know if any of them were ours. Or the Amazons'. But our adversaries had thrown their weapons to the ground in defeat, and as my friends came slowly forward, shoulders hunched in exhaustion but heads held high in victory,

I realized that we really had won. We'd won the right to fight another day. On our own terms.

The walls of my home rose up at my back.

The Roman mob celebrated all around me.

My friends were there to keep me from falling to my knees.

And Cai, with his beautiful eyes full of love, and strength. Sadness too. But no regret. I took his hand and my warrior sisters crowded all around us, and I'd never felt more like I belonged. Elka was weeping openly, one arm wrapped around Ajani, the other around Quint. And he had an arm wrapped around Kallista, who grinned from ear to ear at having finally done something truly exciting. Charon had come down from the stands and stood at my sister's side—not *quite* touching her, in the same way as she was not *quite* touching him. Night and stars and fire and song spun all around my head in a glad and glorious chaos of celebration. We were the eye of a whirlwind.

Tomorrow, we would bury the dead. We would throw open the Ludus Achillea gates. And we would carry on.

Defiant, triumphant, together.

Acknowledgments

CONTINUING FALLON'S ADVENTURES in *The Defiant* has been a great joy for me as an author—possibly more fun than one person should be allowed to have (especially what with all the mentally carving up friends and foes alike with very sharp weapons . . .).

But, like Fallon at the Ludus Achillea, I most certainly didn't do it all on my own. In fact, I had my very own war band to accompany on the journey.

As always, the indomitable Jessica Regel, my agent and very own primus pilus—and she's probably getting tired of me saying this but—she remains a constant source of encouragement, inspiration and enlightenment. Thanks also, once again, to the wonderful crew at Foundry Literary + Media.

Next up, the other two Jessicas in my J-Crew—Jessica Harriton and Jessica Almon. Your editorial excellence, unflagging support, and creative drive amaze me. I am so grateful for you guys, and for Ben Schrank and the rest of the incredible Razorbill crew, for continuing to believe in me and my pack of wild gladiatrices. That same shout-out goes north of the border to Suzanne Sutherland and Jennifer Lambert and all the amazing folks at HarperCollins Canada, who always take such good care of me. Much appreciation also goes out to Elyse Marshall and Maeve O'Regan, my fantastic publicists, for going out into the world and championing this book in so many wonderful ways. And

I'm still in deep margarita-debt to Tiffany Liao and Hadley Dyer both, for getting so very behind this series in the first place.

Also, a special thanks goes out this time to Casey Hudecki for helping me brainstorm some of the weapons sequences. This is a woman you want on your side in a gladiatorial smackdown. Trust me.

Love and gratitude, always, to my family, especially my mom and brother.

All the battle hugs I can give to my readers and fans. In person and online, you guys are so ferociously cool, you never cease to amaze me.

And finally, most of all, to John. You told me to set things on fire and you weren't wrong. You never are.